MUNA SHEHADI

THE
Paris
AFFAIR

REVIEW

First published in 2024 by Headline Review
An imprint of Headline Publishing Group Limited

This paperback edition published in 2025

1

Cataloguing in Publication Data is available from the British Library

Paperback ISBN 978 1 0354 0778 1

Typeset in Sabon by CC Book Production

Printed and bound in Great Britain by
Clays Ltd, Elcograf S.p.A.

Headline's policy is to use papers that are natural, renewable and recyclable
products and made from wood grown in well-managed forests and other
controlled sources. The logging and manufacturing processes are expected
to conform to the environmental regulations of the country of origin.

HEADLINE PUBLISHING GROUP LIMITED
An Hachette UK Company
Carmelite House
50 Victoria Embankment
London EC4Y 0DZ

The authorised representative in the EEA is Hachette Ireland,
8 Castlecourt Centre, Dublin 15, D15 XTP3, Ireland
(email: info@hbgi.ie)

www.headline.co.uk
www.hachette.co.uk

Muna Shehadi's lifelong love of reading inspired her to become a writer. Muna grew up in Princeton, New Jersey, and lives on the beautiful coast of Maine, which she couldn't resist featuring in her Fortune's Daughters trilogy. *The Paris Affair* is the first title in her Women of Consequence trilogy.

For more information, visit her website: **munashehadi.com**

By Muna Shehadi

Fortune's Daughters trilogy

The Summer Sister (*previously published as* Private Lies)
The Winter Sister (*previously published as* Hidden Truths)
The Spring Sister (*previously published as* Honest Secrets)

Standalone

The First Wife

Women of Consequence trilogy

The Paris Affair

This book is dedicated to Bryan and Carolyn Welch, for the peace, health and goodness they add to the world, even in the face of its sometimes cruelty.

Author's Note

During World War I, in an attempt to revitalize the French doll and fashion industries, the sculptor Albert Marque was hired by the couture fashion house Margaine-Lacroix to design a doll. The result was a figure nearly two feet high, head and body made of bisque, an unglazed porcelain. One hundred copies were made of this lifelike child, numbered and signed by the sculptor. Each was exquisitely and uniquely dressed by seamstresses at the Margaine-Lacroix house as various characters, including members of the Ballet Russe and French royalty, and in French regional styles. The dolls were displayed and available for purchase in 1915. Most have gone missing; those that remain today are considered the Holy Grails of the antique doll world and fetch hundreds of thousands of dollars at auction. As far as I know, the Sarah Bernhardt doll in this story exists only in my imagination.

THE
Paris
AFFAIR

✂ Prologue ✂

Cornwall, 1915

Thomas Haynes pulls up to Bryony Manor, the family's country home for generations, which as eldest son he inherited along with his father's shipping business. It's the house to which he brought his wife, Deborah, in 1897, and where she gave birth to their daughter. It's where Deborah succumbed to pneumonia, leaving Thomas and fifteen-year-old Penelope bereft. Over a year later, her absence still makes coming home more bitter than sweet.

Johnston, balding and regal in his uniform, meets the Rolls-Royce Silver Ghost and greets Thomas somberly as always. He enquires after his master's trip, this time to Paris, to hammer out agreements with French merchant shipping companies over wartime demands. Exhausting, Thomas says, and means it. Not only the business and travel, but the feeling he should be doing more, *would* be doing more for his country if his lameness hadn't prevented him. Yet deep down, guiltily, he is grateful Penelope won't risk losing both parents in such a short time. Even the thought makes him burn with panic.

Johnston reaches into the Rolls's back seat for Thomas's trunk and a large wrapped box. Thomas gestures to his long-time servant for the package. He will take the extravagant Christmas gift in to Penelope himself.

His daughter is in the sitting room in front of the fire. In Thomas's absence, his staff have decorated the house for Christmas. The mantel is festooned with pine and holly, golden Swedish angel chimes glow by lamplight, and the colorful crèche his parents brought back from Italy occupies its usual central place of honor. A tree decorated with candles, white paper chains and red ribbon stands in the corner in front of the heavy damask drapes. The air smells faintly of smoke and cinnamon.

Penelope's face is rosy from the fire. She sits on the chair her mother favored, shoes cast onto the carpet, knees drawn up under her chin, navy skirt cascading. Her life should be full of parties and dancing, flirting with boys, dreaming of a someday marriage. Not grieving, not feeling the terrible weight of war and its pains and losses.

Dad! She jumps from the chair, expression bright, the girl he used to know, and races toward him, arms outstretched. He has to put down the box to hug her; her body is warm and sweet – has she grown even in the month he's been gone? He feels her relax her grip, start to pull away, and resists the urge to press her closer and cling. She's too old for that now. I missed you, he says.

Her face clouds. You were gone nearly forever.

Thomas picks up the box again, two feet high, wrapped in shiny black paper that shows the stress of its journey in tiny white webs and creases. He holds it at arm's length. I brought you a present.

Thank you. She glances at the package, eyebrows raised, the spark of joy at his arrival already extinguished, shadows under her blue eyes, so like her mother's. You can put it under the tree.

He tells her she can open it now if she'd like, aware that his eagerness is more childlike than hers.

She shakes her head. It should wait for Christmas proper.

Thomas watches her carefully place the box under the decorated tree, the pain in his heart almost too sharp to bear. He's been a fool. The exorbitant gift is not what his daughter wants or needs. Neither his money nor his power can provide her with that.

Cornwall, 1921

Penelope stands by Bryony Manor's library window, holding the present her father gave her the year before he died. The doll is unchanged, having been in storage for the past four years, since Thomas Haynes was fatally thrown from his horse. She is still magnificent, sad but sweet-faced and lifelike, a representation of the French actress Sarah Bernhardt. She wears an elaborately embroidered emerald gown, a fur cape and a jeweled necklace and brooch. In her hair, a sparkling circlet. The doll is lovely, but to Penelope she is also a reminder of the grief at losing both her parents, and of her lonely life of privilege. At twenty-one, she is leaving England and its heavy, foggy burdens, sailing for the United States to begin again in the freedom and anonymity of New York, eager for the city to infuse her with its young, bold energy.

Sarah will not be making the trip. Penelope will give her to the daughter of one of her housemaids, a girl she has come to love and admire. At fourteen, Jeanette already plans to break free of her parents' and grandparents' lives of service to become a great actress on both stage and screen. Penelope wouldn't bet against her. The child has tremendous self-possession, confidence that would approach arrogance in a disposition less generous.

Jeanette enters the room and stands waiting, preternaturally poised, not classically beautiful but with a presence that commands and holds attention. You sent for me, miss?

Penelope hands her the doll without explaining its origins, ignorant herself of its true significance. This is for you, Jeanette. She's meant to be Sarah Bernhardt, so of course you should have her.

Jeanette's eyes widen, she shakes her head. The gift is too much for a girl of her station. But her mistress insists until Jeanette relents and cradles her prize, thanking Penelope over and over. Sarah Bernhardt is her idol, she says; the doll will inspire her to the heights she aims to reach. She touches the jewels, the fur, then lifts her head, questioning. *Real?*

Penelope shakes her head, of course not. She's wondered the same thing but doesn't know, and doesn't want Jeanette to wonder either. There should be no pressure to sell, no worry about maintaining value. She should enjoy the doll as a normal girl would.

Jeanette's features relax; her smile returns. You won't regret giving her to me, miss. I'll take care of her and do her proud.

Penelope embraces the child, says truthfully that she believes her with all her heart.

Not long after, Penelope journeys to the United States with an abundance of fair weather and anticipation. She settles on Manhattan's Upper East Side and finds the city exactly as she'd hoped: thriving, blunt and astonishingly diverse. Two years after her arrival, she marries a handsome Harvard graduate from Connecticut. She never returns to England, though she follows the acting career of Jeanette Alcott and thinks fondly and often of the Bernhardt doll inspiring and bearing witness to that success.

London, 1931

At a party in the Ritz Hotel ballroom celebrating the opening of Jeanette Alcott's latest film, she meets a French widower from an aristocratic Parisian family. Pierre Laurent tells her he fell in love with her first on stage, then on screen, and that it would be a great honor if she would accompany him to dinner the next night at the Savoy.

Despite the age gap – Jeanette is twenty-four and Pierre is nearing fifty – she is attracted to his kind, gentle eyes and impeccable manners, as well as the security his wealth promises. She knows her star turn won't last forever.

Their dinner the next night is the first of many, with Pierre crossing the Channel often to court his *chère actrice*. In 1933, they are married, quietly but in great style, and honeymoon abroad. On their return, they settle in Pierre's elegant apartment on the rue Lyautey in Paris's exclusive 16th arrondissement, a home that has been in his family for generations.

The Bernhardt doll moves with them and resides on a stand in Jeanette's bedroom, protected under a glass dome. Sarah has been her constant companion from the day she received her. Jeanette considers her a good-luck charm, and enjoys half believing that Bernhardt's magic came to her through the likeness.

In 1945, aged thirty-eight, Jeanette dies of complications from childbirth. Pierre mourns the dead infant and his *chère actrice* until his death from heart disease at eighty-six. Natalie Laurent, Pierre's daughter from a previous marriage, inherits the Paris apartment. She visits her country and ancestral home during summer breaks from her professorship at the University of Kansas.

Sarah Bernhardt stands patiently on the stand in Jeanette's old bedroom, safe from dust and wear under her glass dome. No one who has seen or held her since Thomas Haynes, early in the century, is aware of her value, and not even he could predict how rare and precious she would become.

⁓ **Chapter 1** ⁓

Ah! It's a perfect night for sleeping
The stars shine like fire in the stream
And the sky hasn't a single cloud
One could say it's only for Love
That such a lovely night replaced the day.
Marceline Desbordes-Valmore, 'L'adieu du soir'

Sunday, May 25, 1975

Helen pulled impatiently at her ball of yarn, finished the row, then held up her work. Hmph. After knitting forever, what would someday be a sweater for her boyfriend Kevin still looked like a scarf for a toy poodle.

She'd been back in Indiana, her hometown of Zionsville, for four days, six since the University of Kansas's 103rd commencement, at which Robert F. Bennett, governor of Kansas, had urged them all to go forth and do great things for their families and countries.

Did knitting count? As pleasant as it was to be sitting on the roomy front porch of the house her grandfather built, on this warm sunny day, with smells of Mom's Sunday roast wafting through open windows, restlessness had already settled in.

Fledged from college, she'd been primed, along with her fellow graduates, to soar into life. Instead she'd been plopped back into her parents' nest after they shot down the idea of her sharing an apartment in Indianapolis with her college roommate, Stefanie. *Not so fast, young lady.* Helen should stay home and save for her future, then see what kind of life she could afford. Parent code for *Stay where we can keep an eye on you until Kevin proposes and we can hand you off safely.*

The youngest of her three younger brothers, Buddy – christened Alfred, but call him that and risk violence – sat on the porch swing, one arm around his girlfriend, Bridget, a sweet and mostly silent Cindy Brady lookalike whom Buddy had been dating since ninth grade. He was smirking. 'Hey, Hellenback. Think you'll finish that sweater in time to bury Kevin in it?'

'Nice, Buddy.' She picked a bit of wool off her cotton dress, noticing how its color had faded, wishing she could buy a new one. Maybe after a few paychecks. 'If you're that worried, why don't you learn how to knit and help me?'

He scoffed. 'Girl stuff!'

'Not at all.' She started the next row, keeping her expression placid. 'A lot of guys at KU were knitters. Football players in particular. It was part of their training.'

'No way.' Buddy sounded just doubtful enough. 'Really?'

'Oh yeah.' Helen nodded earnestly. 'They donated what they made to local charities. Sweaters and hats and scarves, bra and panty sets they liked to try on each other while dancing the—'

'Hey!' Buddy's voice cracked with outrage.

'Oh my gaw!' Sweet Bridget burst out laughing. 'I totally believed you!'

Helen grinned. 'It could happen . . .'

'Hellooo!' Rosy, their down-the-street neighbor on her daily amble up Valley View Drive, hands clasped behind her back, plastic twist-tie protruding from her mouth – her comfort item after giving up smoking. Following dutifully, fast as he could waddle, her overweight Scottie, unimaginatively named Scotty.

'Uh-oh.' Buddy brightened into smug glee. 'You're in for it now, Hell. Nosy Rosy, ready to find out everything you've been up to since spring break.'

'Hi, Mrs Cooper,' Helen called.

'Helen, welcome home!' Rosy moseyed up the Kenyons' front walk, removing the twist-tie to speak. 'Congratulations, graduate. You must be proud of your sister, Buddy. Maybe she'll inspire you to go to college too.'

'Not me.' He jerked his head of frizzy red hair toward Helen. 'She's the brains of the family.'

'Aw, don't say that.' Bridget play-punched his arm. 'You're totally smart, Buddy. You got almost straight A's. Well, a few anyway. At least this past semester.'

'Come to think of it . . .' He puffed out his skinny chest. 'I'm brilliant.'

Rosy dismissed him with a gesture. 'What are your plans, Helen? Are you and Kevin engaged yet?'

'Not yet.' Helen spoke cheerfully over a burn of annoyance. Some people . . .

'Don't you worry, it's only a matter of time. Such a nice boy.' Her eyes gleamed with curiosity behind thick glasses. 'What will you do in the meantime?'

'I'm working at Henkel's again this summer.' Three months scooping ice cream, no hope of parole. Toward the end of senior-year craziness, taking the same old summer job had seemed like the easiest way to make Mom and Dad stop asking what she was planning. 'Then I'll see what's next.'

'She doesn't need to worry. High-paying jobs will fall into her lap. Her and every other French major.' Buddy guffawed.

'Four years and thousands of dollars to study some dead medieval poet.'

'Nineteenth-century, not medieval. *La belle* Marceline Desbordes-Valmore.' Helen sang the name in her most overdone French accent. 'I'd be happy to quote you some or all of her poem "L'adieu du—"'

'*No.*' Buddy covered his ears.

'Your sister will have the same job as your mom – a wife and mother. Plenty good career for any woman, despite what those feminists say.' Rosy pointed her twist-tie at Helen. 'Mark my words, Kevin will ask you. I saw how he looked at you last Christmas.'

Helen smiled politely, glad to be able to keep her eyes on the wool, nerves fluttering as they invariably did when she thought about Kevin proposing, a combination of excitement and a darker emotion she put down to normal jitters. Something was certainly up with him lately. He'd been harried and mysterious during their last weeks of school, and when she'd called last Wednesday to tell him she and her parents had arrived safely back in Indiana, he'd still sounded keyed up, and vague about when she'd see him again. She knew better than to press. He'd tell her in his own time. They loved and trusted each other absolutely.

'Mmm.' Rosy sniffed the air. 'Sunday dinner sure smells good. Your mom's the best cook on the street.'

Helen heard a muffled groan from her brother and saw Bridget elbow him to be quiet. Rosy had a talent for getting herself invited to meals. Maggie Kenyon was a total softie when it came to the aging widow.

Helen was not. 'I'll pass along the compliment. She'll appreciate it.'

'Children?' On cue, Maggie, aka Mom, appeared at the

screen door of the house, slender and lovely in a floral sleeveless sheath, fancier than her usual Sunday wear, pearls at her throat, rust-orange hair up in a bun. 'Dinner will be ready in fifteen minutes, give or take. Hi, Rosalie, good to see you.'

'I was just telling Helen the smells out here are spectacular.'

'Thank you.' Mom stepped onto the porch, spreading aromas of roast pork and Eau de Rochas, her favorite perfume. She was flushed, eyes sparkling.

'Mom, look at *you*!' Buddy whistled between his teeth. 'What is *up*?'

'Do I need a reason to dress nicely? It's lovely having Helen . . .' Maggie did a double-take at her son and put her hands on her hips. '*What* is on your feet?'

Everyone looked. Buddy had made an effort to dress for Sunday dinner as Mom always insisted, wearing a collared shirt and clean khakis, but his sneakers were untied and filthy.

'I couldn't find my good shoes.'

'They're in your closet. March right upstairs and put them on.'

Buddy left, grumbling. Sweet Bridget looked blank, caught between pleasing her probably future mother-in-law and supporting her beloved.

Helen hid a snort of laughter. Her brother thought himself the family rebel, but he'd fallen close enough to the tree to be tangled in its branches. Likewise, Dustin and Conroy had followed their father's path into the army after high school, and would probably settle back here in a few years to run the Kenyon Hardware stores with Buddy and Dad.

Like Rosy, Helen was sure Kevin would propose, and equally sure he wouldn't want to live in Zionsville. Not being engaged yet, they'd discussed the future only in general terms, careful not to take forever for granted until they legally could, but she

11

could tell his heart wasn't here in Indiana. Aside from a few years served in Vietnam after high school, he'd lived his whole life in Lawrence, Kansas, home of their alma mater. He'd want to move somewhere new, as she did; maybe California or Texas or Vermont. Helen was dying to explore more of the country. Heck, she was dying to explore the world, though Kevin had no interest in leaving the US. Once he proposed they could talk about their plans more openly.

In any case, there'd be no Kenyon Hardware in her future.

'You'll excuse us, Rosalie.' Mom put her arm around Helen. 'Family celebration today.'

'Well. I was just leaving.' Rosy turned stiffly and started back down the sidewalk, Scotty waddling behind her.

'See you soon!' Mom waited until Rosy was out of earshot, rubbing her daughter's shoulder affectionately. 'I love dogs, but that mutt is a disgrace. Not his fault, but really.'

Bridget giggled. 'He can't hardly move!'

Helen shoved her needle tips into the ball of blue wool and put the barely started project into a quilted bag her grandmother had used for her needlework. Mom had passed it down the previous year, along with Grandma's full set of needles and other doodads – counters and crochet hooks and tiny rings that must be used for something. Helen secretly loved the old-fashioned idea of sitting in a rocking chair, pregnant with Kevin's child, knitting baby things in their home.

'I suppose it's some comfort to her to spoil the creature.' Mom gave Helen one last squeeze, still staring at the spot where Rosalie last stood. 'I can't say I know how I'd act if I was left on earth without your father. I'd probably lose my marbles.'

'Too.' Helen finished what her mother was too polite to say.

Behind them the phone gave half a ring. Maggie started, then lunged for the front door.

Inside, Buddy shouted, 'I'll get it.' His feet thundered down the stairs.

Mom stayed at the door, rigid and alert, while Helen and Bridget exchanged glances and shrugged.

'Your father will be down in a few minutes.' Mom turned back, apparently satisfied that nothing urgent had happened. 'We'll sit down when the—'

'Hellenback, it's for you!'

'Ooh!' Helen jumped to her feet. 'Maybe it's Kevin.'

She ran eagerly to the den, where Buddy stood covering the handset mouthpiece. 'Some lady with a weird accent. "Ma-*damn* Low-run" or something.'

'Madame Laurent, my French professor.' Helen held out her hand for the phone, dying of curiosity. 'And in every other country and most of this one, you have a weird accent too.'

'Ma-damn Lawkkkkkhhh.' Buddy put a hand to his throat, fake-choking on a French r.

Helen yanked the phone away and turned her back, gesturing Buddy to leave the room. Natalie Laurent was her favorite teacher and her adviser. She'd been adamant about wanting Helen's phone number so they could stay in touch after graduation, mentioning something about an opportunity she hadn't yet been able to discuss. Maybe this was the time! '*Bonjour,* Madame Laurent, *comment allez-vous?*'

'*Très bien, merci.* I'm sorry I wasn't around to congratulate you on your graduation. An excellent student and a joy to teach.'

'That's okay, and thank you. I loved all the classes I took with you. And I was so grateful for your help with my final project.'

'*Ce n'était rien.* It was a pleasure. Marceline Desbordes-Valmore deserves much more than the anonymity society forced her into. You did a marvelous job.'

'Thank you.' Helen's heart sank a little. Was that the only reason she'd called?

'*Alors!* So! I am calling to let you know that I'm retiring this year.'

'Oh no! Or . . . congratulations.' How did people feel about retiring? 'Your students will miss you. Definitely the university's loss.'

'Thank you, my dear. It is time, and I'm happy about it. But also you may remember I spoke of an opportunity.'

'Yes.' Helen's heart rose again, fingers lacing through the curlicue phone cord, as if she were still in high school on calls dependably long enough to annoy her parents.

'I had to wait until I notified the university of my retirement, but I can tell you all about it now. I'll be going back to Paris in a few weeks. I own an apartment on rue Lyautey in the 16th arrondissement, which has belonged to my family since the nineteenth century. It's too large for one person, so I'm going to move to a smaller place, and my nephew and his family will move in sometime next year. The apartment has generations of belongings still in it, which is more than I want to cope with alone. You mentioned how much you wanted to visit Paris, so I am inviting you to come help me. There are many things in the home that will interest you, and of course there is the city and all it has to offer.'

Helen hardly dared breathe. A lifelong dream suddenly within reach. It was hard to comprehend.

'You can be as independent as you want, maybe work with me in the mornings and explore in the afternoons. I will provide room and board and a small salary for whatever you'd like to do. Also, my friend Cybèle has a flower shop near the Jardin du Luxembourg, and would be happy to hire you a few hours a week if you'd like a little more cash. Your only expense would be the plane to get there and back. You may stay as long as you wish, starting in September. Three months, six months, living like a real Parisienne. What do you say?'

Helen became aware that her eyes were open about as wide as they could get, and that she was clutching the cord to her chest, fingers tangled in the grubby rubber.

Paris!

'Oh my gosh, Madame Laurent, that sounds like everything I've ever dreamed of.'

The Frenchwoman snorted. 'You need bigger dreams.'

Helen laughed. Natalie Laurent was a sharp-tongued but deeply kind person. Halfway through Helen's junior year, overwhelmed and near tears over three papers due on the same day, she'd bumped into her professor on the way to the library. Madame Laurent had taken immediate charge, brought Helen to her house, made tea and offered home-made shortbread. While Helen sat gratefully sipping, trying not to eat all the cookies, Madame Laurent gave her a pep talk about her own struggles as a young woman in a foreign country, determined to become a college professor at a time when women simply weren't. She'd ended with a flourish and a Molière quote: *Plus grand est l'obstacle, et plus grande est la gloire de le surmonter.* The greater the obstacle, the more glory in overcoming it.

Renewed in body and spirit, Helen had gone back to the library and finished wrestling the papers into submission.

'So what do you think?'

She wanted so much to sound like an independent *oh là là* woman of the world, in charge of her own life and decisions. Unfortunately, she wasn't. 'I'll need to—'

'Of course, you will want to discuss with your parents.'

'Yes. But thank you so much for thinking of me, Madame Laurent. It sounds absolutely fantastic.'

More than fantastic. It sounded perfect. But she'd need to talk it over not only with her parents, but also with Kevin, since they'd been more and more serious lately about planning a future together, fulfilling Kevin's dream of owning a farm.

'Take your time. I'll be spending the summer on the coast of Brittany with a friend, so you wouldn't be traveling until September at the earliest. I'll give you my number here in Kansas. You can let me know what you decide before I leave in a few weeks.'

Hand shaky with excitement, Helen jotted Madame Laurent's number on the message pad by the telephone, and thanked her teacher about a million times, only half of what she wanted to. After she hung up, she stood pressing her hand to her hot fore-head, trying to calm down enough to think rationally.

Paris!

Really, was there anything else to consider?

Of course there was. She and Kevin hadn't been apart for longer than a few weeks since they started dating two years earlier, though she had complete faith that their relationship would outlast whatever life threw at it, and equal faith that if she decided to go, Kevin wouldn't object. He'd heard more of her travel fantasies than anyone. And he'd shared his, which were brief and to the point: none. Unless dramatic changes took place, Helen would be exploring the world on her own.

A loud honk out front made her jump.

'Helen?' Her mother's pleasant voice from the kitchen. 'Can you go see who that is? I'm busy in here.'

Frowning, Helen turned toward the window. Since when did Mom think honking instead of ringing the doorbell was anything but ignorably rude?

One step later, she got a view of the car parked out front

and let out a squeal, almost tripping over a chair in her race for the front door.

Kevin! She burst out of the house and practically knocked him over backwards leaping into his arms. 'What are you doing here?'

'Trying not to get killed.' He chuckled, swung her around and kissed her, then gazed into her face with deserved smugness. 'Surprised?'

'Completely! I'm so happy to see you! Come in, come in. How long have you been on the road? I think dinner's just ready. Mom?'

Mom was already outside, followed closely by Helen's tall, handsome father, wearing a jacket and tie. They were both beaming.

'Welcome, Kevin.' Her mother hugged him, Dad waited to shake his hand and thump him on the shoulder.

Helen danced toward the house. 'I'll put another plate on the—'

'Already done.'

'What?' She spun around incredulously. 'How did you know?'

Her mother tapped her head. 'ESP.'

Helen lifted her arms and let them drop. Now she got it. The fancy dress, the coat and tie, the jump for the phone . . . 'Apparently I'm the last to know.'

'Kevin, can John help with your suitcase?' Mom asked.

'I'll get it later, thanks.' Kevin strode up to Helen and took her hand. She squeezed it, grabbing hold of his upper arm as they walked toward the house, his biceps thrillingly hard under a beige jacket she hadn't seen before. He was even better-looking than usual, a flush on his cheeks, blue eyes snapping. Spring sun had brought gold to his pale skin, and his straw-colored hair, grown shaggy at school, was neatly cut, shorter than she was used to. It emphasized the fine shape of his head and revealed the scar behind his ear where, miraculously, a Vietnamese bullet had only grazed him.

'Why all the secrecy?'

'Just wanted to surprise you.' He turned and kissed her again – briefly, in front of her parents – then dropped his voice as he ushered her inside. 'You look totally edible, by the way.'

'Why thank you, Mr Foster,' she whispered back. 'Think I'd taste as good as Mom's roast?'

His eyes warmed. 'I'm pretty sure you would.'

'Okay, you lovebirds.' Dad followed them inside. 'Wash up and come eat. I'm starved.'

Lovebirds? Helen grimaced surreptitiously at Kevin. 'Are we on *Father Knows Best*?'

Kevin chuckled and let his hand slide along her hip as he passed toward the guest bathroom.

She watched him go, bubbling with happiness. He seemed more like his wonderful relaxed self today, no more of that edgy impatience. Her excitement over the call with Madame Laurent was already receding. Kevin hadn't been here five minutes and she wanted to cling like a barnacle. A long separation would be agony.

But Paris . . .

The family gathered around the dining table, Kevin in the place of honor at her mother's right, Helen at her father's, Buddy and Bridget taking the other two chairs. Dad carved and served the fragrant pork with its garnish of roasted vegetables while Mom passed rolls and butter. When everyone was served, they joined hands and bowed their heads, waiting for one of Dad's typically rambling blessings.

'Lord, thank you for this food, thank you for bringing so much of our family together on this beautiful day, and thank

18

you for those who aren't here. Keep our sons Dustin and Conroy safe so they can be among us again soon. We are so grateful to have Helen back home, and are thankful for Kevin's visit. And we welcome Bridget this afternoon, who is also practically family. And then also, thank you for this wonderful food we are about to eat, and for the wonderful, beautiful woman who made it. Amen.'

'Amen,' agreed the rest of them.

'Let the eating begin.' Buddy already had a potato halfway to his mouth.

There was a manic air during dinner – laughter louder than usual, conversation more boisterous, eating accelerated. Mom and Dad were used to having Kevin and Bridget around, so that wouldn't be nervous-making. Helen caught Buddy frowning speculatively at Mom, then Dad, so it wasn't just her imagination.

In the pause before dessert, Kevin caught her eye during a lull in the conversation, smiling mischievously. 'I have an announcement.'

Electric silence, both of Helen's parents frozen in anticipation, smiles and eyes wide. Whatever Kevin was about to say, they already knew.

Helen stiffened in horror. He wasn't going to ask her to marry him *now*, was he? In front of the whole family? He couldn't. She wasn't ready. It was completely the wrong—

'I bought a farm.'

Helen blinked.

'How wonderful!' Mom clapped her hands together, doing a credible imitation of a surprised person. 'This is such exciting news.'

'Dude bought the farm!' Buddy laughed at his joke. So, of course, did Sweet Bridget.

A farm? He bought a farm? *Their* farm? *Already?*

'Congratulations. We're thrilled for you, son.' John Kenyon nodded his sandy head, peering over the black half-glasses he needed only to read and constantly forgot he was wearing. 'Well done.'

'Isn't it great, Helen?' Her mother's voice had an edge to it, Mom code for *What's the matter? Why aren't you reacting?*

'It's great, yes!' Pressure increased in Helen's chest. 'Where?'

'In Lawrence.' Kevin looked at her curiously. She tried to smile, but had a feeling she looked ill. 'Five hundred acres with a house, barn and paddock.'

In Lawrence. Helen was appalled to find herself dismayed. He'd bought a house in the place he'd spent ninety per cent of his life, the place she'd just said goodbye to, not expecting to return except maybe for reunions. She'd always imagined the two of them, newly engaged, with a map of the US spread in front of them, deciding together where to live, what kind of farm they wanted to start or take on, what kind of farmhouse, how many bedrooms for how many children. 'How did you afford that?'

Mom cleared her throat.

'Helen,' Dad said gently. 'That's his business.'

'No, no.' Kevin held up his hand, still watching Helen carefully. 'It's her business too. A combination of savings and a VA loan. With luck, I should be able to pay it off in twenty years.'

'We are so happy for you.' Maggie Kenyon's smile pivoted to include her daughter. '*All* of us.'

'It's wonderful, Kevin.' Helen managed more spirit that time. 'Your dream come true. You deserve it.'

'We deserve it.' His eyes were loving across the table. 'I bought it for us, Helen.'

'Yes.' She reached for her water glass, aware of all eyes on her. She was miserable to have spoiled his moment, especially in front of her whole family, but she couldn't control the flood of emotions. 'I'm thrilled.'

No one believed her.

Kevin's left eyebrow rose.

'I, for one, can't wait to see it,' Maggie said warmly. 'I'm sure it's lovely.'

'I can't wait for all of you to see it.' Kevin nodded too many times. The silence stretched.

'What'd your Frenchy professor want, Hell?' Buddy came to Helen's rescue, though he might have traded one can of worms for another.

'Your teacher called here?' Her father's thick brows knitted. 'Is there a problem?'

'No, there's no problem.' Helen scrunched her napkin in her lap, deciding it would be worse to try and pretend the call was unimportant, which wouldn't fool anyone. 'She's offering me the chance to go to Paris.'

'Paris! Good heavens.' Mom looked alarmed. 'We can't afford that.'

'She needs help going through family things before she moves out of her apartment. I'd be staying with her and—'

Dad's face darkened. 'You'd stay in this woman's apartment?'

Dad code for *She must be a predatory lesbian.*

'Yes, I would stay with her, rent-free. The apartment's been in the family for generations. It's in the 16th arron—' She laughed awkwardly, searching how to make sense of the term for her homebound family. 'It's in a wealthy, fashionable part of Paris, near the Arc de Triomphe. I'd get to explore the city, see all the things I've been studying. Madame Laurent can even get me a part-time job working in a flower shop.'

'What about your job at Henkel's?' Mom broke the silence. 'They're counting on you.'

'Mom, c'mon!' Buddy held out his palms to symbolize scales. 'Paris? Henkel's?'

'I wouldn't go until September.'

'Why isn't she teaching in September?'

'She's retiring, Dad. She's moving back to France.' Helen looked around the table, bewildered by the lack of even a fraction of the interest and enthusiasm Kevin's news had sparked.

'How long would you be gone?' Kevin spoke in a quiet monotone. He had his soldier face on, impossible to decipher.

'I don't know. It would depend on how long she needed me and how long I wanted to stay. She suggested six months.'

Her parents gasped.

Buddy's mouth dropped; Bridget's eyes widened in alarm.

'Six months.' Kevin looked stunned.

'I told her I'd have to think about it. And that I'd talk it over with you, and with Mom and Dad.' Helen hated how defensive she sounded. It was a trip to Paris, not a fatal disease. 'It's a fantastic opportunity. Something I've dreamed about for so long but never imagined would come true this soon.'

Kevin looked down at his dessert fork.

More uncomfortable silence.

'Well. This is all very exciting. Great opportunities for both of you. I know you'll work it out.' Dad folded his napkin and got up to clear plates. 'Speaking of great opportunities, dessert is spectacular. Just wait till you see. I think Maggie spent the last three days making this one.'

'No, no, nothing like that.' Mom pushed back her chair, smile a show of teeth. 'You sit, darling. Helen will help me clear.'

Mom code for *We are going to get to the bottom of this.*

The kitchen door hadn't even swung closed when she started in, arms folded across her chest. Helen resigned herself to being lectured.

'Sweetie, I know you didn't mean to spoil Kevin's news, but he's worked like a dog the past few weeks to put together financing to buy this place and get himself here to surprise you with what amounts to a marriage proposal. And all you can say is that you want to get as far away from him as possible? For *six months*?'

Helen decided it wasn't the time to point out that there were many places farther away from Kansas than Paris. 'Buddy asked me what the call was about. You think I should have lied?'

'No, of course not.' Her mother's face softened. 'But it came right after you reacted to his news about the farm like someone had socked you.'

Helen also wouldn't point out that being handed the rest of your life when you thought it was yours to help choose felt very much like that. 'It was a lot to take in.'

'He's offering you everything, his whole life.'

She gave her mother a sad smile. 'Everything except Paris.'

Maggie sighed, shaking her head. 'You've always been a dreamer, Helen. No matter how hard your father and I tried to keep you tethered to reality. You wanted to go to college and study French, okay, we supported you in that. But your school days are over. Your adult life is starting. And your place in that life is helping Kevin in the enormous and difficult task he's set for himself, not gallivanting off to some foreign country while he works himself half to death. You want to go to Paris? Go with Kevin someday, with your husband, when your life together settles down.'

Helen felt her temper rising, a particularly hot resentment that ballooned when she knew she was in the right but being logically outmaneuvered. 'Kevin has no interest in going abroad. Ever. This could be my only chance.'

'I know it feels that way right now. You don't realize yet how young you are and how much of your life is ahead of you. But there is plenty of time. Kevin loves you, but you saw his face. He wants you with him.'

'He would not be selfish enough to stop me from going.'

'Probably not.' Her mother took her forearm, squeezing gently. 'But I want you to consider that you're being selfish wanting to go.'

Helen pinched her mouth shut, resisting the impulse to run to her room, slam the door and throw herself on her bed for a good cry, which would only add fuel to her mother's point. 'Okay. Thank you. I'm going back into the dining room.'

'Take these with you?' Her mother laid cake plates and a silver cake server in her hands, not letting go of them until she had her daughter's attention. 'I've said my piece. You and Kevin are adults. You'll work this out.'

She let go. Helen strode into the dining room, where she barely resisted plunking the pile of plates at her father's place like a challenger throwing down a gauntlet. Maggie glided in soon after, holding a perfect chocolate-frosted cake decorated with pink dianthus blooms, purple pansies and sugar pearls, to a chorus of rapturous oohs and aahs, her consummate-hostess smile in place as if she'd just been discussing the weather.

Helen had no idea how she could box her emotions like that. Mom could be run over by a car and still say, *Oh, it's fine! I love the tire track look!*

During dessert, she sat trying not to scowl while Mom and Dad chatted with Kevin, asking questions about what animals he planned to raise, and what crops. Kevin glanced at Helen now and then, his answers long and detailed, indicating the depth of his planning and research.

Helen had always shared everything with Kevin. Too much, probably. But he must have been working on this plan during the entire four years of his agronomy major at KU, if not before.

And not one word to her beyond the generalities of wanting to own a farm someday.

Whereas Helen had been considering a trip to Paris for all of an hour, and shared the possibility at the very first opportunity, so they could decide together. Ahem.

When servings of the cake had been eaten – picked at by Helen – and lavishly complimented, Mom shooed her and Kevin out of the kitchen to take a walk, 'Because it's such a beautiful day.'

Mom code for *Apologize and make this right before it's too late.*

In the soft, sunny May afternoon, the two of them fell into step, heading by silent consent to 6th Street, where they crossed and turned left toward Eagle Elementary. The school abutted large forested grounds through which they often strolled on pretty days like this. Usually they went there to make out, since Helen's parents insisted on separate bedrooms and had a habit of knocking with some pretext if Helen and Kevin were together in either one for more than five minutes. Today, making out was not going to happen.

Trees were leafing, tenderly still, dogwoods and star magnolias blooming white in various yards alongside lilacs, peonies and rhododendrons. Chickadees flitted, blue jays squawked. Cars were few. So were words. The topic hovered over and between them like a personal dark cloud.

Helen decided she'd do her mother a favor and start. 'I'm sorry I didn't react the way you wanted about the farm, Kevin. Or the way anyone wanted.'

'I shouldn't have surprised you with something that big in front of your family. I've been so excited about it for so long, and your parents were excited too when I told them. It never occurred to me you'd feel differently.'

Guilt came skulking. She'd dealt him quite a blow. 'Honestly, it would never have occurred to me either.'

'So?' He looked at her expectantly. 'Maybe you can explain.'

She wasn't sure how to find the right words. 'Panicked,' 'dismayed' and 'betrayed' wouldn't come across so well. 'I guess it was the surprise mostly.'

'We've talked about our future before.'

'Yes, we have. Yes. You're right.' She hated walking on eggshells around him. They'd always been so relaxed together, communicated so effortlessly. 'I just hadn't realized how . . . far along you were in planning it.'

'I have to be, Helen. I'm out of school now.' His voice was light, easy, he was looking around, seeming to enjoy the pink blooms of a crabapple. 'This is when the future starts. Our future.'

'Yes. I know, I know. I just . . .' She had to force herself to go on. If they were going to be together for life, she couldn't hold back. 'I guess I thought I'd have some say in the timing, and in where we lived.'

Kevin turned questioningly. 'You never said where you wanted to live. Besides Paris, which is pretty tough to farm in.'

Helen made herself laugh, wishing she could melt the blocks of tension in her chest and stomach. 'I thought we'd have plenty of time to talk about the specifics after we were engaged. I don't know. Just . . . all the possibilities would have been fun to consider together. Don't you think?'

He shoved his hands in his pockets; his long stride slowed and shortened. 'You think you'll be unhappy in Kansas?'

'Oh, no. I really don't.' That much was true. Lawrence was a lovely, lively town, and the surrounding countryside was beautiful. It was just . . . what? No surprises? Any place would be empty of surprises once you got to know it. 'It's probably that

I went from anything-could-happen to knowing exactly what would happen in one second. I'll adjust, I'm sure.'

'Okay.' Kevin dropped his eyes to the ground. 'You have to close doors as you go through life. You can't keep them all open, Helen.'

'No, of course not. Of course not.' She felt stupid now, and frustrated. He was being patient, trying hard to understand. She wasn't communicating well. Usually he understood her completely, sometimes before she did.

'I think . . . maybe I was enjoying that uncertainty? We haven't been out of school a week yet. It's exciting when anything's possible.'

'Sure.' He grinned at her, took her chilly hand in his warm, solid one. 'But you can't live in uncertainty. I want to provide for and take care of you, and someday our kids. I need to make decisions now.'

'Yes. I know.' He was making nothing but mature, rational sense. But for whatever reason, Helen couldn't shake the feelings of unease. Maybe still the dreamer, as Mom called her, holding onto her fantasies for dear life. Maybe also selfish, when Kevin had sacrificed so much toward their future. She didn't know.

They walked on in miserable silence toward the looming woods, Helen struggling to find a way to smooth this over. They had always thought the same things, wanted the same things; it was almost eerie how good they were together. This was new territory.

'How about you tell me more about the Paris thing.'

She told him again what little she knew about Madame Laurent's offer.

His silence was unnerving.

'I really haven't decided yet, Kevin. I mean, she just called. It sounds amazing, thrilling really. I have money Grandma gave me for graduation that would go a long way toward paying for the plane fare, so it wouldn't cost—'

'It's not the money. It's the time.'

'Yes.' Helen's mind raced, trying to assemble words that would accurately and carefully describe her feelings. She didn't know why France had always called to her so strongly, beginning with often-read copies of *Madeline* and *The Red Balloon* in grade school, blossoming from there. In her imagination, the US was a broad-shouldered cowboy, full of bullish enthusiasm, ever ready to spit, fight and shoot. France was an elegant, wise and weary soul who'd experienced enough over the centuries to know that a glass of wine with excellent cheese was preferable to rushing off at every provocation.

Being in Paris would give her the chance to inhabit that world, maybe become a little more sophisticated herself. Like putting on a costume. Maybe the new look would bring hidden parts of her to life. Maybe it would just be fun playing dress-up. Either way, she wanted the chance to try on something other than plain old Midwestern Helen.

'I think it's that I was a child, then a student and your girlfriend. Now, if I go from Mom and Dad's house to yours, from daughter to wife and eventually mother, I'll never get to be just me.'

'I would never ask you to be anything but yourself.'

'No. You wouldn't. I know that.' He didn't understand. 'You said you want to take care of me, and that's lovely and generous and wonderful. But this could be my only chance to prove I can take care of myself.'

'You could get an apartment in Lawrence. We don't have to move in together until we're married, if you didn't want to.'

'An apartment in Lawrence.' She stopped walking. 'Kevin, she's offering me the 16th arrondissement.'

'Six months, Helen.' He swung to face her, impatience peeking through. 'You'd be making me start our life together all alone.'

Heat rose in her cheeks. That wasn't fair. 'You planned our life together all alone. We should have done that together.'

'I was doing what I knew we both wanted, doing that for *us*.' He gestured harshly. 'Going to Paris is not something I want. It's only for *you*.'

Helen lowered her eyes. He was right. She couldn't deny it. He was repeating what her mother had said, what they all thought. She felt like a butterfly trying to knock over a statue.

'Having said that . . .' He closed the distance between them, lifted her chin so she'd look at him. His blue eyes were serious but clear and earnest. 'I would never stand in the way of something you really wanted. If you want to go to Paris, you should go, for as long as you want, and do whatever you want. It's your decision.'

She was unable to feel any kind of relief or joy. Just more guilt.

But along with that guilt and her need to be the get-along girl, Helen was tasting some new flavors of determination. Mom always told people she had been an easy-going baby, unless she discovered something she wanted. Then watch out.

Helen wanted to marry Kevin. She wanted to live with him for the rest of her life – maybe not in Lawrence, but if that was done, it was done, and she'd adjust. She wanted to be a good, helpful and supportive farmer's wife. She wanted to share the good and bad, richer and poorer, sickness and health, and raise their children to be respectful and well-educated, productive and polite.

But the restlessness she'd been feeling on her parents' porch; the trapped feeling looking ahead to a same-ol' same-ol' summer; the fear when she thought Kevin was about to propose; the panic hearing about the farm as a *fait accompli* . . . all of it now made sense.

She wanted to try living outside of anyone else's guiding or restraining arm, she wanted to face challenges somewhere she'd have no one else to rely on to get her through them. She wanted to try and fail and try and succeed on her own merits, find out who she was and what she was made of. To immerse herself in that elegant, wise and weary aura, soak some of it into her skin.

And come back transformed, even just a little.

✎ Chapter 2 ✎

Present day

Teresa reached to the top shelf of the highest cabinet, where the forbidden foods had been consigned to a hermit's existence since she'd started dating Joe, who wouldn't touch anything processed. Somewhere, months ago, with her last vestiges of sanity, she'd stowed a box of Cap'n Crunch cereal.

'Come to me, my precious.' She coaxed the box toward her with her fingertips, one of the few times she was happy for her nearly six-foot height. Katie and Addie, her college friends from the University of Arizona and long-time apartment-mates, had to drag a footstool around the kitchen to reach anything.

Bowl next, a large one. Spoon. Only skim milk in the refrigerator, but there was a carton of half-and-half she could mix in for fatty fun. Misery deserved only the best.

The cereal made a satisfying gravelly clatter against the porcelain. Teresa glugged in the improvised whole milk and took her most excellent breakfast outside to their fenced-in backyard – dirt and gravel between the sparse plants and trees, because growing grass in Arizona was a waste of water.

The metal chair, painted yellow in one of Katie's decorating fits, grated over concrete as she dragged it into a shadier spot. The air was already heating toward the nineties. Even having grown up here, she found the Phoenix climate dehydrating and difficult, especially these days, when it got so hot so early. Way back in her ancestral line must lurk a Canadian.

She sat and started eating, resting her feet on the edge of the clay planter holding Katie's beloved fig tree, letting the crunch reverberate through her head, trying not to think about last night or she'd start crying again.

Katie's electric car, a Chevy Bolt named Usain that she treasured almost as much as her ginormous engagement ring, purred into the driveway. Katie had spent the night at her fiancé's place due to some wedding-y appointment early that morning. Hard to keep track of all the parts that needed to be decided, paid for and worried over. Teresa's ideal wedding was eloping to a deserted beach or mountaintop, if she ever got to that point. At twenty-seven, she'd only had one relationship longer than six months. It was getting hard not to think there was something wrong with her.

Usain's door slammed. Teresa kept crunching, waiting for Katie to find her.

'Hey, I'm back. Got some big news for . . .' Katie broke off, staring at Teresa's bowl. 'What is that?'

'Arrr, this be the Cap'n, matey!'

'What happened to no processed foods? Wait, have you been crying?'

'No Processed Foods broke up with me last night.'

'Oh *no*!' Katie's elfin face crumpled. 'Right before your road trip next week, the bastard.'

'No more Vegas.' Teresa tried to sound cheerful. She and Joe had only dated for three months, so she wasn't allowed deep sadness. Mostly she was grieving another freaking rejection, and battling the fear that no matter how cheerful, devoted and obliging she was, men would always get tired of her.

Maybe next time she should try being a selfish bitch.

'Crap, I'm sorry.'

Teresa shrugged and shoveled in her next mouthful. 'It's not like' – *crunch crunch* – 'I thought we'd get married, but' – *crunch crunch* – 'we were having fun together. I don't know what's wrong with that.'

'You *were* having fun. You *are* fun. What is his problem?'

Teresa swallowed, already loading up another spoonful. 'I don't know, me?'

'Definitely not you.' Katie sat in the chair opposite. She was expert by now at listening and clucking until Teresa recovered from her I-stink funks. 'He was a royal dickhead.'

'I'm expert at finding them.' Teresa kept her voice light. 'So what's the news?'

'Oh God. Yeah.' Katie stole a Cap'n crunch pellet and tossed it into her mouth. 'Timing sucks now.'

'Why?'

Katie cringed. 'Addie and Carter got engaged last night. She wanted me to tell you because . . . Carter.'

Ouch.

'Oh, pfft. That was years ago.' Teresa's one long-term. Carter had been yang to her yin, getting her up and out to go running, hiking, biking, dancing, to concerts and weekend getaways, all experiences that without him she'd have missed in favor of a book in bed. She'd taken on his energy and become the kind of don't-waste-a-second person she usually envied. Like Addie, born with the same vibrant spark he'd had to drag out of Teresa. Even though he and Addie hadn't started dating until a year after he dumped Teresa, it had taken her months not to want to bawl whenever she saw them together. 'They are a perfect match. She didn't need to worry about me.'

To prove it, she texted Addie an enthusiastic, emoji-laden congratulations message, not trusting her voice to sound convincingly thrilled on the phone.

'You are a goddess, Teresa.' Katie gave her a loud puckered smack on the cheek. 'Ross and I are going to see a movie tonight, want to come?'

Teresa made a disappointed face, relieved she wouldn't have to play pitied third wheel. 'I can't, it's Sunday. Dinner with Mom.'

'Oh, right.' Katie wrinkled her nose, looking adorable. It was effortless to be Katie Brougham. She flattered every outfit; her straight blond hair fell just right without fuss; she didn't grow stray eyebrow hairs or have to wax all summer long; she got along with everyone, always had a boyfriend – now a fiancé – came from a close loving family, had a well-paying job she adored . . .

It was not effortless to be Teresa Clark. Gangly and too tall, with wavy hair that did whatever it wanted and a too-loud laugh, a father who'd ditched his wife and kids for new ones, a crap love life and a job fundraising for South Mountain Community College that was a fine way to earn a paycheck but not her calling. Whatever that was.

'How's Chernobyl Granny?' Katie opened her enormous pink purse and started rummaging in it. 'I meant to ask yesterday before I left.'

'Still in the hospital. It was a bad break. Mom's working on moving her into a retirement home where she'll be safer, but there's the issue of clearing out her house before they can sell it. Mom's brother refuses to help, Mom can't go because of her bad back, hiring a professional will cost a ton, and . . .' Teresa took a melodramatic breath. 'You know, a mess.'

'Ugh, I'm sorry.' Katie shook her purse to redistribute its contents, and continued exploring. 'When is this all supposed to happen? With the house?'

'Asap.'

'Why don't *you* go to Kansas?' She made a sound of frustration and peered into the bag's impressive depths.

'Me?' Teresa was so surprised at the offhand comment, she stopped eating her Cap'n Crunch, risking sog. 'Why would I go?'

'Why not? You're in a funk and you have two weeks off for a vacation that's not going to happen anymore. I mean, it's not a wild road trip with Mr Dickhead and friends, but given how he turned out, it might be more fun.'

'Huh.' Teresa had no idea what to say to that. Totally not on her radar.

'Something to think about. Aha! Here's the little bastard. Now you must admire.' Katie held up the card she'd finally located. On it were little rectangles of color. 'Ta-daaaa.'

Teresa stared, searching for something to be excited over, and came up empty. 'What am I looking at?'

'Our wedding colors! We chose them this morning. Blush, Fern, Wine, Sea and Linen. Aren't they gorgeous?' Katie smiled lovingly at the cardboard. 'I was tempted by another palette, which had like Juniper and Dusty Rose and Whisper Pink. But then I got worried about too much pink.'

'They're beautiful.' Teresa examined the colors with the kind of care she'd want Katie to put into examining hers someday, except she couldn't imagine herself worrying about colors. 'It's going to be a gorgeous wedding!'

'I know.' Katie gazed at the stripes with a blissful sigh. 'Promise you'll tell me if I turn into Bridezilla.'

'You couldn't.' Though in the coming months when Katie and

Addie both got going, Teresa might want to invest in a pair of noise-cancelling headphones. 'It's your day.'

'I know! I'm going to be a bride! I still can't believe it.' She put the card back into her purse, where it would probably take an hour to relocate. 'So? What are you doing this afternoon?'

'Feeling sorry for myself. You?'

'Taking you to bridal shops to look at wedding dresses, and maid-of-honor stuff now that we have our colors. I want to go to the best stores in town and pretend we have that kind of money, just to see what they've got. You in?'

Teresa's stomach turned sour. Kate would have a blast playing little rich girl in front of snooty sales ladies, while Teresa would be an anxious, guilty mess that they weren't planning to buy anything.

No fear.

'As long as I'm back in time to get ready to go to Mom's.'

'God, yes, I don't want to take all day. Put on something that looks expensive and let's go.'

By the time they got back from the embarrassing and exhausting rounds of faux-shopping – it had come close to taking all day, the rest of it anyway – Teresa had just enough time to change back into shorts and a tank top and jump into her car for the half-hour drive from their place in Old Town Scottsdale to Coronado, where Mom, Teresa and her twin brothers had been forced to relocate after Dad ran away with his hygienist and all the money.

Thanks, Dad.

Only ten minutes late, in spite of traffic, she emerged from the car into the cooling oven of the evening, still tasting the metallic heat. The neighborhood was mixed, flawlessly rebuilt tear-downs next to shabby ranches with junk cars in the yard next to houses that were somewhere in between. Mom's tiny house was one of the in-betweens, a brown ranch with a brown tile roof on a brown-pebbled yard, the brown relieved only by a scarred palm and an ironwood tree that provided shade for the pebbles.

Teresa let herself into the silent house – her brothers, twins Michael and Isaac, nicknamed Mike and Ike, must not be there yet. She headed for the kitchen, empty and blank-smelling. Dinner was usually ready to go on the dot of six.

Her mother's muted voice came from her bedroom. She must be on a call. A long one if dinner hadn't even been started.

Teresa got herself a glass of water from the sink and drank, lifting her hair off her sweaty neck, annoyed at herself for not grabbing an elastic before she left home. To save money, Mom hardly ran her air-conditioning, so the house was as stuffy as it was still.

'Hi, sugar.' Cheryl Foster – she'd taken back her maiden name after Dad bolted – emerged wearing a pastel top over white capris, stretched from recent weight gain. She looked Teresa up and down, overplucked eyebrows making her look perpetually surprised, and a new shade of foundation giving her a ruddy complexion, as if she'd been tanning or drinking heavily.

Teresa felt a stab of protective tenderness, wanting to drag her mother to a salon and transform her to the way she used to look before she'd started feeling she wasn't okay as she was.

'Where's dinner?' Cheryl asked.

'What do you . . .' Teresa clapped a hand to her forehead. 'Oh crap, I forgot. I'm so sorry, Mom.'

'You forgot.' Quick sigh. 'Okay. I'll come up with something.'

'No, no, I'll take care of it, I'm so sorry.' Teresa hunched her shoulders. How could she have forgotten? 'I'll order out for something. Are Mike and Ike coming?'

'They have tickets to some concert tonight. I can hardly get them to come over anymore.' Cheryl bent to open her freezer. 'You'll have to make do with Lean Cuisine.'

'That's fine.' Teresa groaned inside. The whole point of her offer the previous week was to give her exhausted mom a break. 'I'm sorry. I owe you.'

'Just don't forget next Sunday.' Cheryl pulled out a couple of frozen boxes and examined the pictures. 'I was on the phone with your grandmother when you came in.'

'How's she doing? Katie was asking about her.'

'Confused. The dementia's much worse. Horribly worse. She thought we hadn't spoken in a week, when we've been in touch practically every day since she fell.' Cheryl kicked the freezer door shut. 'I've been telling James for years that she needs to make arrangements to go into a retirement home. "She's fine," he says. Fine? How is losing your balance in the middle of your kitchen fine? How is being in the hospital fine? Chicken Parmesan or four-cheese pizza?'

'Either one.'

The eyebrows lifted. 'Decision?'

'Um . . .' Mom wouldn't want the chicken. 'I'll have the chicken.'

Her mother glanced wistfully at the box. 'You got it.'

Wrong guess. 'I'm fine with pizza if that's what—'

'Nah. You chose. It's dinner, not life or death.' Mom grabbed the glasses dangling from a chain around her neck, perched them on her nose and peered at the instructions.

'I'll set the table.' Teresa hurried over and opened one of the chipped pressboard cabinets.

'You know, my worst nightmare is that Helen will deteriorate to the point where I'll have to fight James to have her declared incompetent, and take over the estate myself. I definitely do not need that mess.'

'Is that likely?'

Her mother nodded, looking grave. 'Dementia does not get better. Accidents like hers can accelerate the deterioration. It's happening already.'

Teresa felt Mom's burden as if it were her own. 'When will she get out of the hospital?'

'A few more days, then rehab in the same building. Breaking your hip is a big deal at her age, even without dementia.' Cheryl sighed heavily and tore open the pizza box. 'I don't know what James is thinking. Kevinjay might agree with me, but fat lot of good that does me when he might as well be on Mars over there with his foreign wife.'

'Hmm.' Kevinjay was Mom's younger brother, Kevin Jr, who'd moved to Hawaii to study biodynamic farming, married a Japanese woman and settled there. James, the youngest, had dutifully stayed in Kansas, but resented both his siblings for leaving him with the job of taking care of their mother.

'A seventy-two-year-old alcoholic with severe dementia running a ranch all by herself? It's crazy.' Cheryl banged the microwave door shut. 'I knew something like this was coming, and that no one else would do anything about it, so I put her on a waiting list at a retirement home a year ago. It's a very nice place. Most importantly, she'll be safe there.'

Teresa set plates opposite each other on the small kitchen table, wishing Mike and Ike were there to distract Mom with their boisterous humor and charm – 'Chernobyl Granny' was one of theirs, because Helen was such a disaster. As the three siblings grew older, the truth about Cheryl's childhood had emerged in stories of Grandma Helen's drinking, cruelty and serial infidelity. Teresa had been horrified to learn of all their mother had suffered – as if Dad leaving her for another woman wasn't enough.

39

'I called the home right after she fell. Enough is enough.' The microwave beeped a tune as Mom poked the appropriate numbers. 'They'll have an apartment for her in a few weeks, after she gets out of rehab.'

Teresa picked out flatware from the squeaky drawer next to the sink. 'Is she okay with the idea of moving?'

'She's not in any shape to make that decision. Going home would be dangerous, possibly fatal.' Cheryl folded her arms, shaking her head. 'We can't take the risk.'

'And your brothers?'

'Kevinjay will be fine. He trusts me. James'll be angry at first. But he needs to face that his mother is old and declining. He pushes things away. It's how he still gets along with her, I guess. I've tried, but I can't forgive her. She destroyed Dad with her boozing and cheating. He was tough as they come. A real man's man.

'Helen would take vacations every year, with "friends". The minute she left, your Grandpa Kevin would go into deep depression. Nothing I could do to cheer him up. I remember hearing him sobbing his eyes out in his room and having no idea what was wrong, but not daring to ask. I was too afraid of the answer, and I also knew he'd hate that I heard him at such a weak moment.' The microwave beeped completion. Cheryl drifted toward it. 'That sound isn't something you forget.'

'It must have been terrible.' Teresa should know. She and her brothers had heard Mom doing the same plenty of times after Dad left.

'Cheaters are poison in human form. My mother. Your father.' Cheryl's voice rose, shaking. 'Special place in hell for them all. Helen broke Dad's heart so badly it stopped. She might as well have taken a knife to him. And you know the worst.'

Teresa stopped setting the table. Even after hearing the story many times, she found her mother's anger and pain close to unbearable. She wished Mom would see a therapist, work through this so she could leave it behind. She deserved some peace. 'I know. I'm sorry.'

'After all that, all she did to him, he left her everything. The farm, the house . . .' Cheryl's voice broke. 'Daddy loved that place so much. He put his whole self into making it the success it was. And what does she do? Sells off most of the acreage, our inheritance, and changes what's left, like she couldn't erase him and his accomplishments fast enough.'

Teresa made herself put forks down beside the plates, wishing she had the superpower of being able to change the past. 'It sucks. It really does.'

'Thanks, sugar. I know I go on about it.' Cheryl plunked the chicken entrée onto Teresa's plate. 'Anyway, we have to be practical. The land that's left and the house are worth good money, and there are things inside that are worth something too, things Helen won't need in the new place. Some of the older furniture, my father's woodworking shop, my grandparents' silver, Helen's doll collection . . . You used to play with that, remember? All of it needs going through as soon as possible so we can sell the place quickly.'

'I do remember the dolls.' Teresa opened the frozen pizza box and handed the meal to her mother, Katie's words in the back of her head. *Why don't you go?*

Before the dual bombs fifteen years earlier of Dad's desertion and Mom's discovery that while she was growing up, Helen had been unfaithful to Grandpa Kevin, Teresa's still-intact family had gone to Kansas a few times a year to see Grandma, Uncle James, Aunt Alicia and Cousin Jim. Teresa still missed the five of them boisterously cramming themselves into a present-loaded car, Dad cracking jokes about making sure they didn't eat too much Christmas turkey or they wouldn't fit on the way home, Mom rolling her eyes and worrying about traffic and snow on the roads, the extended family gathering around Helen's table, laughing, teasing and overeating. Back then, Teresa's life had felt . . . whole.

After Dad left and Mom all but severed her relationship with Grandma Helen, Teresa and her brothers' relationship with family dwindled to awkward birthday and holiday phone calls with their grandmother. Teresa could remember only vague images of Helen as a tall, capable woman with seemingly boundless energy. Whatever demons possessed her had either been exorcized or kept hidden.

Grandpa Kevin, however, even though he'd died the year before Teresa was born, remained vividly alive in her imagination through Cheryl's countless stories. Handsome, strong, courageous, hard-working, a little stubborn, a lot old-fashioned, but honest, long-suffering and loyal to a fault. A real American man, Mom said. Teresa wished she'd known him.

'It'll take weeks to clear out the place. I can't do it with my bad back, not to mention my job.' Cheryl played another atonal song on the microwave keys and set it humming. 'I never imagined I'd have to work full-time to survive. As a receptionist, my God, dealing all day with other people's stupid little tasks, as if they can't handle them perfectly well themselves. But your father gave me practically nothing when he left. He could afford a shark lawyer, and I was too devastated to fight. You need to make sure you're independent, Teresa. You can't count on men.'

'I will be.' The advice always made Theresa feel as if she weren't doing enough, making enough. Rent plus expenses plus student loans made it hard to do more than sock away a little every month. Then every time she'd accumulated the beginnings of a nest egg, another emergency would pop up to smash it. Car repair or dental work . . . something.

'The only reason I didn't cut Helen totally out of my life was because of you and the twins. I don't have much to leave you, but your Grandpa Kevin made a good living on the farm and saved carefully all his life. You deserve your share of that money, if Helen hasn't spent it all on booze and lovers. And frankly, I deserve to live better than *this*.' Cheryl gestured disparagingly to the small, shabby kitchen. 'Maybe it's shallow, but I felt like somebody when we lived in Paradise Valley with your father in that beautiful house. All those bedrooms, the pool . . . do you remember? It was a dream life. Here I feel like a big nothing.'

'You are *not* nothing.' Teresa put her hands on her hips, regarding her mother sternly, angry all over again at her cheater-pants father, who'd ditched the family without a backward glance. Only much later had he deigned to contact Teresa and her brothers – as if he could erase the devastating years of his absence with emails. Teresa had deleted them all. 'You are a remarkable woman who's had to deal with a lot of unfairness.'

Her mother hugged her, making Teresa feel like she'd won a prize. 'You're sweet as sugar, sugar. I guess I do all right with what was dealt me. Though at this rate, I'll never get to retire.'

Behind them, the microwave announced its completion. Bolstered by Cheryl's rare show of affection, Teresa rushed to ask what she'd been wondering for a while. 'Have you ever tried dating, Mom?'

'Date? Me? Oh, that's funny.' Cheryl brushed back a lock of Teresa's hair, tugging gently before stepping back and flinging out her arms. 'Who's gonna look at this? I'm fat. I'm old, I'm—'

'You're forty-eight!'

Mom went over to the microwave. 'Men don't want middle-aged divorcees with no money.'

'Aw, c'mon. That's not true. I bet you could find someone wonderful.'

'Yeah?' Cheryl plunked the plastic tray of pizza on her plate. 'If it's so easy, why haven't you?'

Teresa absorbed the blow she probably deserved. 'At least I'm trying.'

'What about whatsisname? How's that going?'

'Dumped me.'

'Oh no, *again*? What are you doing to these guys?' Her mother's forehead wrinkled in dismay as she sat down. 'I'm sorry, sugar. It's not your fault. Men leave. Always bolting for something better. It's what they do. Dinner's ready, such as it is. Glasses?'

'Sorry.' Teresa retrieved the one she'd used earlier and a clean one, filled them with water, then pulled out her chair and sat opposite. 'And sorry I forgot to bring dinner.'

'Next week.' Her mother picked up a slice of pizza. 'Dig in.'

Teresa tried to eat, watching Mom alternate talking with mouthfuls of food. She'd seen pictures of Cheryl as a young woman, a girl really, back in Kansas, a couple of years before she eloped with Richard Clark – Kevin approved, Helen pitched a drunken fit. Mom had been fresh-faced, joyous, pretty, with her father's wholesome features. In Teresa's favorite photo, framed in Mom's bedroom, Cheryl, about sixteen, was nestled against Grandpa Kevin, her arms around his waist, his around her shoulders, double grins in front of a knee-high field of corn.

At what point had she looked in the mirror and started wanting to change the woman looking back? It made Teresa ache with compassion.

'. . . so there's no way around it, I'm going to have to hire someone to clear out Helen's house. Or, more accurately, my father's house. It'll cost an arm and a leg, but it has to be done.'

Teresa tried to picture the ranch. She remembered air that was sweet and heavy, loaded with plant, earth and animal smells – had she been there in spring the last time? Lots growing, green everywhere, grass and trees instead of cactuses and rocks. Cooler summers. Days of rain. *Snow* in winter – had they gone there for Christmas? She could remember a decorated tree. And a yellow bird in a cage who could whistle Beethoven.

Her brow furrowed. That must have been a dream. There'd been many Kansas dreams over the years, fantastical, cozy, nightmarish. Teresa was admittedly curious to see the ranch again, confirm which memories were fantasy, which reality.

Her heart beat faster. Hadn't the house been on the side of a hill? Single-story? No, there'd been a lower level with a playroom, Helen's doll collection and Grandpa Kevin's wood shop. Teresa and her dad had spent lots of time among the saws and drills, as they had at their old house in Phoenix, designing, building and mending. It had been the one thing she felt she had real talent for, something she'd felt special sharing with her father.

'. . . even if I can afford to hire someone, there's no telling what they'll do in that house. Probably steal anything worth more than a dime. They have you by the balls when they know you have no other choice.'

Teresa stopped eating. *There was another choice.*

Katie had been right that she was in a rut. Maybe she could use a break. From Phoenix. From her job. From feeling rejected and stuck, and now, with both roommates engaged and looking forward to their own households, left behind.

'What's wrong? Chicken bad?'

'I was just . . .' Teresa swallowed convulsively and reached for her water, wishing Mom had something stronger in the house, 'thinking.'

'Thinking?' The too-thin brows lifted. 'About what?'

'I was thinking that . . . I could go.'

'Where?'

'To Grandma's. To take care of the house.'

'*You?*' Cheryl put down the pizza slice she'd been about to bite into. 'Well. That's sweet of you, Teresa, but . . . I mean, organization isn't exactly your strong suit. And last time we were there you were afraid of all the animals. Even the cats.'

'I was twelve.' Teresa took a sip of water to moisten her dry throat. Animals still made her nervous, but she was able to control her fear better now. 'Who's taking care of the place while Grandma Helen's in the hospital?'

'James and his son, your cousin Jim, the one who became a vet.'

'So I wouldn't have to deal with the cows and . . . whatever. Sheep? I don't remember.'

'Hmm.' Her mother's expression changed from frowning to thoughtful while inside Teresa the idea grew like an inflating life vest. Change of scene. New challenges. A chance to play grown-up and make Mom's tough life easier. And two weeks much more productively spent than sitting home thinking about how she wasn't in Vegas, and imagining the flawless woman Mr Dickhead had found to take with him instead.

But also a huge responsibility. Teresa would have to navigate an unknown town and make quick decisions about a house full of a lifetime of someone else's possessions. Mom was right – not her strength. She might also have to navigate her uncle's objections, though that would be on Mom to sort out with him.

Despite the worry, her adrenaline was on full buzz. It must mean something that she was excited. Maybe going was the right thing to do?

She pushed chicken around the tray, telling herself to open her mouth and say it.

No fear.

'How's Katie coming with all the wedding—'

'I was serious, Mom. It's a serious offer.' Her ears heard the words before her brain had consciously decided to let them out.

'Really?' Her mom looked astonished. 'Just like that? You'd pick up and go? What about your job?'

'I have vacation time scheduled.' She was still talking like she meant it. 'Two weeks. I can go.'

'Good Lord.' Her mother stared over her pizza as if she'd never seen Teresa before. Then her eyes crinkled into a rare smile. 'You won't get halfway there and want to turn around, like you did when I sent you to ballet class?'

Teresa shrugged, smiling back. 'If that happens, you'll be no worse off than you are now.'

'True.' Cheryl finished her slice, then scanned the table, holding up grease-slicked fingers. 'Napkins, Teresa?'

Oops. Teresa jumped up to grab two from the holder on the counter and handed one over. 'Sorry.'

'Thanks.' Cheryl wiped her fingers. 'You'd be doing me a huge favor, sugar bear, if you really can manage this. Huge. I'd be so grateful. You can't imagine how much sleep I've lost wondering how to get it all done from here, how to afford it even . . .'

'I can manage it.' With her mother's gratitude warming her, Teresa even believed she could.

'Well. Okay then. I'll get you the dimensions of the new apartment at the home. You'll only need to save enough furniture for that. Bed, table, chairs, lamps, maybe a desk. We'll sell whatever she doesn't need. Be sure and put aside anything that might be worth something.' Cheryl looked animated for the first time since Teresa walked in. 'Then when she passes, or God forbid we have to declare her incompetent, we'll sell the property. She won't need that money where she's going. I'll finally be able to get out of here. Your Grandpa Kevin would be so happy. He'd want that for me.'

Anxiety slithered around the edges of Teresa's excitement, looking for a way to take charge again. 'Shouldn't I ask Grandma before selling her stuff?'

'Oh no, trust me. She won't be able to make rational decisions. Besides, Daddy paid for ninety-nine percent of what's in that house. Maybe more. Don't ask James, either. He's too sentimental. He'll want to keep everything. Just do your best. You can always call if you run into problems.'

Fear's tentacles advanced further. Uncle James had stayed on good terms with Helen after Cheryl broke the Chernobyl Granny cheating scandal. 'You'll tell him I'm coming, right? And why? And Helen too?'

'I'll give you a day to make sure you want to do this, then yes, I'll call them. Though you'll probably have to tell Helen over and over before she'll remember. She might never understand.'

'Will James be . . . upset?'

'He'll have to admit the house needs decluttering. He has no time to do it. I have no time to do it. Now Helen won't ever be able to do it.' Her mother's gaze held Teresa's in an unmistakable *don't back out* challenge. The same look she'd used to prod Teresa out of her fear when she was younger. Fear of ballet lessons, fear of school dances, fear of class presentations, fear of dates . . . all those mini triumphs had added up to the power older Teresa needed to maneuver through the anxiety on her own. 'Eventually James'll realize moving her now is the right thing to do. If she goes back to the house, she'll just fall again. Plus it'll be much easier for her to go straight to the new place from hospital rehab than from home later on. She's already away and disoriented. But that's all on me, you won't need to discuss any of this with your uncle.'

Teresa nodded, calming some. 'Okay.'

'I'll call him tomorrow. Or the next day . . . ?'

'No.' Teresa shook her head, gripping the edge of the table. She didn't want any more time to think it over, any more time for anxiety to get another shot at her decision. 'I'll take care of this for you, Mom. You can call him right now.'

~ Chapter 3 ~

What is it that troubles me, what am I waiting for?
I'm sad in the city and bored in the village
The pleasures of my age can't save me from the
    passing of time.
        Marceline Desbordes-Valmore, 'L'inquiétude'

My darling Helen,
You've barely been gone and the pain is constant. I don't know how I will survive six months without you! I think about you all day long, your gorgeous smile, your beautiful body and your lovely laugh. You brighten every day I'm around you. I want you to do this trip for you, and I also wish you'd never left me. Only your daily letters keep me sane. I'm so grateful we promised those to each other.

It's good that you're enjoying yourself, sweetheart, but I admit it's hard to understand what's so exciting about a shop that sells cheese. There are shops selling cheese right here in Kansas! I'm also a little worried about how often you mention drinking. Even at lunch? That's not like you. I do like my beers in the evening, sometimes a little rum and Coke, but you haven't ever been into it. Be careful, my sweet girl.
    Adoringly,
    Kevin

Monday, September 29, 1975

'Okay, that's enough for this morning.' Madame Laurent – she'd begged Helen to call her Natalie, but it was so hard to change – tossed the letter she'd been reading on top of the 'throw away' pile in her father's old bedroom, which she was using as a study. 'If we keep on with these, we will want to hang ourselves.'

They'd started the job of clearing out Natalie's magnificent apartment with her father's business correspondence, 'the boring bits', as she called them. Her family had made its money centuries earlier as landowners in rural France, then hung onto that wealth through the generations, various branches involved in the silk, dairy and wine industries, though Madame Laurent – *Natalie* – had mumbled something about nobility and court relationships with 'the Louis', as she called France's kings. In the mid nineteenth century, her grandfather moved the family to Paris and joined the Ministry for Foreign Affairs. Her father, Pierre Laurent, followed him into the ministry, working for the French embassy in London. He must have saved a draft copy of all the letters he ever wrote, and kept all he ever got. None had proved to be the least bit interesting – until they uncovered a trove of love letters from his second wife, Jeanette, which had prompted Natalie to make the inimitable Parisian sound of disgust and dump them into the trash.

Either she wasn't a romantic, or she hadn't been a fan of her stepmother.

'Come.' Natalie rose from the embroidered chair she'd been sitting on – everything in the apartment seemed so precious and remarkable, it had taken Helen days to stop wanting to wash before touching anything. 'I'll show you something before lunch, as a reward for this dull morning.'

'Oh, fun, thank you.' Helen followed her out of the high-ceilinged bedroom, down the hall, past the ornate room Helen was staying in, which had been Natalie's mother's, past Natalie's equally ornate room, past the gold and marble bathroom, toward a door at the end of the hall that had been closed in the two weeks Helen had been there.

'I'll show you my stepmother's room.' Natalie's heels tip-tapped down the polished parquet flooring. 'Her name was Jeanette Alcott, an English actress, moderately successful, and quite a character. My father met her at a party in London. She was barely ten years older than me. I'm afraid I was awful to her, poor thing. You see, I adored my mother.' Natalie paused outside the closed door. 'She died when I was eleven. After that, it was Papa and me, alone in our grief and mutual support, then alone in our companionship. When he met Jeanette, she became everything to him. Not coincidentally, after they married, I decided to attend Smith College in the US.'

She opened the door, stood back and gestured Helen inside.

Helen peered around the jamb. 'Good Lord.'

'You see that she and I were nothing alike.'

Deep pink. Or maybe reddish mauve. Or dark salmon. Whatever color, Jeanette must have loved it. The walls were papered – on closer inspection, not paper, but cloth – in that color with vertical stripes of white flowers. The same fabric upholstered the matching chairs and draped the four-poster bed in elaborate swoops and swooshes. A floral rug completed the vertigo-inducing color scheme. As in most of the apartment's rooms, a crystal chandelier hung from the center of the ceiling, decorative plaster molding around its base and the ceiling's edge. Also as in most rooms, a fireplace, this one in pink marble that came remarkably close to matching the pink/mauve/salmon color. The dresser and desk – as beautifully designed and gilded as the rest in the apartment – had been touched with pink, floral and cream elements. Hanging around the room, black-framed photographs of a young dark-haired woman in various costumes. Jeanette, on stage.

'What do you think?'

'It's certainly . . . eye-catching.' More like eye-numbing.

Natalie laughed and lifted her head with its cloud of dyed auburn hair to gaze at one of the framed Jeanettes. 'She was eye-catching herself. *Très jolie*. She was always very kind to me. I didn't deserve it. I was too full of resentment for her stealing my Papa.'

'It must have been hard when you'd been so close to him.' Helen couldn't imagine living in that room. In spite of its generous size, the repeated color and pattern made it claustro-phobic, like stepping into a big open mouth. She moved around the bed, and a small table came into view on which stood a large doll, two feet high, protected under a glass dome. 'My goodness. Who is this?'

'Jeanette called her Sarah. She was quite fond of her. Said she was her good-luck charm. I was curious to know more, but being a sullen brat at the time, I wasn't going to give her the satisfaction of appearing interested.'

'So you never asked where she got her?'

'I never did. Jeanette died young, in childbirth. The baby – my half-brother – also died. Very tragic. My father was devastated. He closed the door to her room and it's stayed closed for all this time.' Natalie paused to calculate, pushing up her silver-framed glasses. '*Mon Dieu*, exactly thirty years. She died in 1945. The room has only been touched by cleaners since then. Her clothes are here, her jewelry, everything. We'll go through it all later.'

Helen nodded, staring at the doll, an utterly captivating crea-ture with mournful brown glass eyes and meticulously painted brows and lashes. Her nose turned up slightly, mouth a pink Cupid's bow, cheeks baby-plump, chin fetchingly round. Her hair was a wavy mass of natural-looking dark curls contained by a circlet of rhinestones. In contrast to her child's face, the dark emerald dress – gown, really – was worthy of a prince's ball, embroidered and ruffled, accessorized by a rhinestone necklace. Over it all, a fur cape with a jeweled brooch.

Helen couldn't wait to go through the rest of this room. She wanted to know more, where Jeanette had gotten the doll, why she thought it brought her good luck, and why it occupied such a place of honor. Why the doll's maker had given such a richly clothed girl such a lonely expression. She reminded Helen of the heroine of one of her favorite childhood books, *A Little Princess*, about a girl who'd come from, lost, and regained a life of luxury.

She bent closer to examine the sad eyes, the perfectly painted individual lashes. Had any little girl ever enjoyed this gorgeous toy, or had she always been carefully isolated from her purpose? Helen wanted to lift the glass cover and touch her. 'She looks so . . . wistful.'

'Perhaps she misses her mistress. Would you like to hold her? I can take off her space helmet.' Natalie carefully lifted off the glass dome. 'It will do her good to get some fresh air, don't you think?'

Helen waited eagerly.

'Go on, go on.' Natalie gestured impatiently. 'Pick her up.'

'Thank you.' Helen cradled the doll, awed by her size and the careful details in her clothes and her lifelike face. Her expression was heartbreakingly sweet, making Helen want to take care of her, or do something silly to cheer her up. 'She's exquisite.'

'I admit I never had much use for dolls. Did you play with them?'

'Oh yes. Barbies, of course, and others I'd been given or saved to buy. I'd make little outfits for them and set up their houses with my stuffed animals for pets. I couldn't get enough.'

'Where are they now?'

'Back home in boxes, waiting to move with me when Kevin and I get married. But I have nothing like this . . .' She stared and admired until she worried she was overdoing it, and put Sarah back on the support stand, making sure she didn't tip over. 'Thanks for letting me see her. She's wonderful.'

'Come.' Natalie replaced the dome and beckoned Helen out. 'Lucas will have lunch ready for us, and then you can tell me what you plan to see this afternoon.'

Helen left the enchanting doll reluctantly, but was relieved to be out of the aggressive color scheme and back into the muted tones of the rest of the apartment – not that she felt at home there either. 'I've been doing so much church and museum sightseeing since I've been here, I thought I'd explore the Jardin du Luxembourg today.'

'Excellent idea. You will love *Les Jardins*. When I was a girl, my mother used to take me to ride the *carrousel*. I'd try to catch the brass rings. When I was older, I would sail the little wooden boats on the pond. It's all still there. You'll see. Some of the delights of Paris don't change.'

After another delicious lunch, poached fish in a basil cream sauce with peas and boiled potatoes, followed by slices of apple-brandy tart – Helen was still adjusting to having the equivalent of Sunday dinner every day – she headed to the Métro, where she did her usual triple-checking to make sure she was on the right track, then nervously counted stops, repeating when she had to switch lines. At the Notre-Dame des Champs station, she followed other passengers out onto Boulevard Raspail, trying to look nonchalant while hoping she was walking in the right direction. On the way, she drank in the smells, sights and sounds among the cream stone buildings with bluish slate roofs and wrought-iron balconies so characteristic of the city. These afternoons of exploration were what she'd come for. None had yet disappointed.

Working at Henkel's had been even more boring and predictable than usual with college behind her and Paris in the offing. Kevin had been busy with the farm, and had only driven out to Zionsville twice for rather tense reunions. Over them both hung the late-spring disagreement and its consequences. In the end, they'd decided Helen would be in France for five months so she'd be back in time for a Valentine's Day proposal, but Kevin was clearly uneasy with her leaving, and her parents were tight-lipped. A summer of ice cream and guilt, dished out in equal measures.

The saving grace had been the last two weeks before she left. Helen had scheduled her flight for mid September and quit Henkel's at the end of August so she'd have time to spend with Kevin at their future home. From the first moment she stepped out of Kevin's car – greeted with enthusiasm by Valmore, a miniature American shepherd Kevin had generously named after Helen's French poet – and saw the pale yellow house on a rise overlooking the land, she was in love. The property glowed in late-summer sunlight. The house wasn't the big white farmhouse with wraparound porch of her imagination, but it was spacious and practical and designed in a way that took beautiful advantage of the views and landscape.

She'd followed Kevin everywhere for the two weeks they had together, learning as much as she could about the animals – chickens, a horse, cats for the mouse problem, and the dog – and the machinery he'd need, about the processes for readying the fields for the soy and corn they'd plant in the spring, and the miraculous new world of fertilizers and pesticides that would increase the harvest exponentially. Together they'd talked paint colors and renovations; she'd gone with him to pick out a kitchen table and some lamps. They'd stood, dreaming, in the doorway of what would someday be their children's rooms, and over morning coffee and evening beer they imagined endlessly what the place could be, what it would be with hard work and determination and love.

The last night of her stay, Kevin had invited over childhood friends of his and college friends of both of theirs, and they'd grilled burgers and sat out on the back deck, watching the sun set and the stars collect, listening to the gentle sounds of the insects and animals and feeling the breeze's touch while inhaling the scent of smoke, green earth and life itself. Helen had felt a profound sense of peace and joy, a deep connection to the land, to the animals and children they'd raise and protect, to the friends they'd keep and make, and most of all, to the man who'd had this vision and included her in it.

After that stay, leaving Kevin and her country had been wrenching in a way Helen couldn't have imagined, given her excitement. And yet, when she'd first emerged onto the streets of Paris, bleary-eyed with fatigue after being unable to sleep on the plane, she'd been enthralled. The city existed so unselfconsciously, all its Parisian elements so quietly in place. She'd felt that every brick and tile should be trumpeting, *Look at me, I am glorious!* Every bakery shop window, every market stall, every fish shop and cheese shop, flower stall and butcher's display case was a work of art; food, beverages and wares arranged as if they were gracing the cover of *Gourmet.* Yet people passed in throngs with only occasional glances, as if none of it was miraculous.

Helen gawked at everything, wanting to shake the arm of the woman next to her: Can you believe those little fruit tarts, how perfectly aligned they are, and how fantastic the color contrast with the glistening chocolate eclairs in exact parallel next to them? Look at that remarkable pyramid of flawless strawberries! Who took the trouble to arrange fish filets alternating skin-side up and down on such a smooth bed of crushed ice? Who cared enough to curl each shrimp into the exact same direction and arc?

Streets were lined with men wielding twig brooms, sweeping clean the gutters of discarded cigarette butts and Métro tickets. Shopkeepers spray-washed the sidewalks in front of their establishments. Inside the stores, those same shopkeepers were unfailingly polite, *bonjour, mademoiselle, bonsoir, mademoiselle*, as if they were welcoming her into their homes. Parisians were famed for their rudeness, but Helen hadn't encountered any, at least not yet, all of which fueled her years-long fantasy of the city and delighted her. Even the ubiquitous motorbikes zooming through the streets – mosquitoes, Natalie sneered – cluttering the sidewalks by parking on them, and the near-constant *bee-baw, bee-baw* bleat of the police vans charmed her.

Her daily letters to Kevin were filled with the details, trying to bring the sights and experiences alive for him, hoping to communicate well enough so that he might be curious about joining her, or at least entertain the idea of the two of them crossing the ocean together one day. It was so hard to experience all this beauty and wonder without him there to share and explore it with her – the only flaw of the trip.

She turned on to rue de Fleurus, double-checking her Michelin guidebook map, and saw with relief in the distance one of the distinctive black-painted iron fences with the gold spear tops that surrounded Parisian parks. Through the gate, she entered a typical tree-lined dusty expanse, devoid of grass except in specific areas that were generally not open to foot traffic. She passed tennis courts on the left, following the map straight to the magnificent Palais du Luxembourg and its famous fountain centered in an enormous shallow pool. Kids were playing with the same wooden sailboats Natalie had played with, originals – except for the sails – from 1927, the year an enterprising young man had the idea of renting them to children. The boats glided across the pool, pushed by the wind and, when they got too close to the fountain's edge, by children wielding wooden sticks, until they again caught the breeze and sailed onward.

Helen joined clusters of parents, students and tourists chatting and watching, standing or sitting on metal chairs grouped around the perimeter. She stood for a while absorbing the scene, imagining fifty years ago, and fifty years into the future, when the same boats would probably still be making the same voyages.

After a time, she headed for the merry-go-round Natalie had mentioned. Gleeful children still rode the colorfully painted wooden horses around and around, still waved to their parents. Some held sticks with which they tried to dislodge brass rings as their mounts circled by, exactly as Natalie had done probably sixty years earlier. The age of this city, its continuity through such a long history, astounded her. Helen had been walking streets that had been walked on for multiple centuries. It wasn't uncommon to turn a corner and happen on a church or memorial built in the twelfth, thirteenth or fourteenth century, grand and patient among thronging pedestrians, noisy traffic and bustling shops.

In comparison, Indiana and Kansas felt so new, so untried and untested. In her next letter to Kevin, she'd try again to capture some of this feeling, not to persuade him if he really didn't want to come, but to help him understand what she valued so much about this opportunity. When she was seeing buildings commissioned by Napoleon, and contemplating a trip to see Marceline Desbordes-Valmore's grave, it was hard to get excited about his search for used farming equipment.

Helen chided herself. The equipment was vital to their new life together. When she was back on US soil, her perspective would return to normal. Though that seemed a shame, like being transported to a captivating world in a book that you were always aware would have to end or be put down.

She strolled on until she found an empty bench under parallel rows of shade trees. Her feet could use a break from the miles of daily walking. She sat and started to leaf through Michelin. Four pages in, the sound of American English distracted her. Glancing up, she saw two women walking along the wide pathway, one tall, wearing a navy pantsuit, blond hair in a bun, carrying a briefcase, all clean, sharp lines, tailored and professional. The other, short and dark, flowed and billowed in a full maxi skirt, sandals and a peasant blouse, hair in a sloppy braid halfway down her back.

The pair sat one bench down on the opposite side. Helen couldn't help peeking now and then, registering more details. They were about her age, probably a little older. Their chatter made her retroactively lonely, as much as she loved her one-woman forays into the city. The evenings were particularly hard, since Natalie disappeared after dinner. Having new friends here would help her feel more enmeshed in the city, less torn between the two continents. She was tempted to go over and say hello.

Four more pages, more glances, more shy indecision, then a shadow fell over her book. '*Bonjour, mademoiselle.*'

She looked up into the face of a young man with nice features, a pleasant, smiling expression and eyes that gave her the creeps.

She mumbled *bonjour* and went back to her reading.

'American?'

Helen wanted to growl. No matter how good she thought her French sounded, they could always tell. She didn't lift her head. 'Yes.'

'New York?'

As much as it amused her that everyone seemed to think the US was either New York or California, she didn't smile. 'No.'

'I can sit?' He pointed next to her.

Helen shook her head. 'No thank you. I'm reading.'

'I'm not bothering you.' He sat very close.

'Please go away. *Va-t'en. S'il vous plaît.*'

'We can be friends, I think.' He touched her thigh.

'No.' Helen jumped up and faced him, hands on her hips, aware of a jingling sound behind her. 'I want to be alone. *Je veux être seul.*'

'*Mais non*, a woman so beautiful must not be alone.' His creepy eyes went past her; his smile turned wary. 'Ah. *Bonjour, mesdemoi—*'

'She said she wanted to be alone. Which means you need to leave.'

Helen spun around. The tall, suited woman had spoken, her voice a quiet monotone, eyes hard with warning. Helen was impressed. She would not want to be on the receiving end of that stare.

The man lifted his hands in surrender. '*Non, non*, I was not trouble.'

'For her you were, and she was pretty clear about it.' The short woman pointed down the path with a stern flourish. '*Va-t'en!* Get outta Dodge, pardner.'

'Okay, okay.' The guy got up and walked off, muttering something under his breath.

Helen turned to her rescuers with a wide smile. 'Thank you. That was nice of you.'

'*Ce n'est rien, mademoiselle.*' The shorter woman spoke French easily, but with a strong American accent. *Suh nay ree-yeng* . . . 'The thing about guys is that unless you're saying "Please go kill yourself", all they hear is "I want to have sex with you."'

Helen thought of Kevin. 'Not the guys I know.'

'Hmm.' The short, colorful one looked her up and down. 'I'm thinking . . . Midwest?'

She was dismayed. 'Is it that obvious?'

'Connie, for heaven's sakes,' Blue-suit said.

'Aw, it was a lucky guess. I'm Connie Pappas.' She moved forward for the French cheek-kissing ritual, catching Helen off guard. Kiss-kiss, one on each cheek. So bizarre between strangers. 'This is my adored friend and roommate, Lilianne Maxwell.'

'Helen Kenyon.' Helen braced herself for more kissing, relieved when Lilianne stuck with a handshake. 'Nice to meet you both.'

Really nice. Helen enjoyed using her French, but it was a relief to be able to speak her native tongue with someone outside Natalie's apartment.

'What brings you to Paris, Helen?' Lilianne asked. When she wasn't threatening men, her voice was husky and musical, without a discernible regional accent. 'Student? Tourist? Expat?'

'A little of everything. I'm here until mid February, staying with my French professor from college, helping her clear out a family place in exchange for the chance to live in Paris. What about you?'

'Ooh, lucky girl.' Connie's smile displayed dimples in both cheeks, on her chin a shallow cleft. From her ears hung silver wire earrings interspersed with black and yellow feathers, and bells sewn somewhere on her clothing jingled like one of Santa's

reindeer when she moved. Her eyes were dark brown and mag-
netic. Everything about her seemed as warm and welcoming as
Lilianne seemed cool and aloof. 'I'm here because it's Paris, and
I was bored with the States. I'm on a spiritual quest, to experience everything beautiful life has to offer. You dig?'

Lilianne snorted.

'Sort . . . of.' Not really. Helen had grown up with conservative parents who had strong opinions on hippies and were not
shy about sharing them. Helen would like to think she was
kinder than that, but a life spent experiencing beauty didn't
seem like something that would sustain a person – or contribute
much to society. 'What about you, Lilianne?'

'I work for a bank.'

Helen waited for her to go on. She didn't. 'Doing what?'

'She hates talking about her work. It's her dad's bank; she
plays with numbers all day.' Connie gestured back toward their
bench. 'Come sit with us and we can talk. Or even better, let's
go grab *un café* together.'

'Connie loves hoovering people up,' Lilianne said gently. 'If
you'd rather stay here and keep reading, that's—'

'No, no, she *can't* stay and read. We've just adopted her.
Where should we take her, Lilianne? Le Tournon is closest.
Totally groovy bar where black writers and artists like Richard
Wright and James Baldwin hung out in the fifties and bitched
about American racism. Or there's Les Deux Magots, which I
was really bummed out to learn doesn't mean "the two mag-
gots". You've heard of it, right? Where Sartre and Camus and
Simone de Beauvoir and all those brilliant depraved people used
to go. Café de Flore is right near . . . oh, Picasso too, I forgot
Picasso. And I'm sure there were more. I mean, these cafés were
founded in like eighteen-something, so who knows how many
other brilliant people hung out there too but never got famous.'

Helen gaped at her, feeling a little bludgeoned.

'Connie is an enthusiastic speaker.' Lilianne watched her friend with affectionate amusement. Her eyes were a deep shade of blue, remarkably deep, and she nearly perfectly matched Helen's height. Her linen suit was impeccably tailored to her slender figure, the blouse underneath was snow white and wrinkle-free. The kind of woman who made Helen feel like a frump no matter what she was wearing. 'Le Tournon is closest, but the others aren't that far and it's a beautiful day for a walk. Any of them appeal?'

'Oh gosh, yes.' Helen heard herself say 'gosh' and wished she hadn't. 'Les Deux Magots would be great to see. I was a French major. I've studied all those people.'

'Ooh, a college girl. I did one year at U Vermont, but it was not my groove. Life is my teacher. Life and love and beauty. Let's go.' Connie tucked her arm under Helen's and started them off. 'Lilianne graduated from Wesleyan. She's a total brain. Speaks fluent French, plus Arabic.'

'Why Arabic?'

'My mother is Egyptian. She emigrated as a teenager. My grandparents still live in Egypt.' Lilianne shrugged. 'So I was interested.'

Helen was pretty sure that by the time she went back to rue Lyautey, she'd know a whole lot more about Connie than about Lilianne.

As if to prove her point, to a soundtrack of Connie's chatter, they exited the park onto city streets, Helen craning to see the names and commit them to a mental map. Rue de Vaugirard, rue de Bonaparte, past what Connie said was the 6th arrondissement's city hall, Boulevard Saint-Germain, one of Paris's major thoroughfares, past the Catholic University of Paris, and then the green awnings printed with *Les Deux Magots*, and matching green umbrellas over tables and chairs spilling onto the sidewalk.

'Table alert, table alert, I'll get it.' Connie made a jingling beeline and plunked herself down at one of the tiny round tables as if daring anyone else to claim it, then patted the chair next to her. 'For you, Helen. Isn't this great? Touristy but fun.'

'Touristy is fine for me.' Helen settled herself next to Connie, thrilled to finally be in a café and not feel obviously alone, though plenty of Parisians seemed not to mind being singletons. 'I've been doing nothing but touristing since I've been here. I decided to get that over with, the big stuff I mean, Notre-Dame, the Eiffel Tower, Sacré-Coeur, et cetera, then really experience the city – as much as anyone can in five months.'

'Why don't you stay longer?' Connie asked.

'Oh.' Helen pursed her lips. 'I'll want to get back to real life.'

'That's bogus. Reality should always be postponed.'

Lilianne put a warning hand on Connie's forearm. 'What is your real life, Helen?'

'My boyfriend, Kevin, bought a farm for us a few months before I left. In Kansas. So I'll be going back there. I know it doesn't sound as thrilling as Paris, but to us it is.' She was annoyed to hear herself sounding apologetic.

'Well.' Connie folded her arms across her ample chest, looking perturbed. Then she brightened. 'Farms are dead in the winter. Is he coming to join you later?'

Helen kept a calm smile going. 'Kevin isn't interested in travel.'

'*What?*' Connie gave a dramatic gasp. 'What's wrong with him?'

Lilianne rolled her eyes. 'Not everyone is you, Connie.'

'Well they should be.' She beamed around the table. 'Imagine a world where everyone was me.'

'Noisy.' Lilianne watched pedestrians stroll past. 'Very colorful. And economically disastrous.'

'*Bonjour, mesdemoiselles.*' Their waiter approached, all in black with a long white apron that looked like a skirt. '*Qu'est-ce que vous prenez cet après-midi?*'

'*Trois cafés.*' Connie looked at Helen questioningly. '*Au lait?* Black? *Noir pour moi, s'il vous plaît.*'

'*Noir ici, merci.*' Lilianne's French was flawless.

Helen tried not to be self-conscious. '*Noir aussi. Merci, monsieur.*'

'Your accent is *très bon.*' Connie nodded approvingly at Helen, who was trying not to wince at Connie's pronunciation: *tray bone.* 'Sorry if I was rude about Kevin. You can always go places without him. In fact you can come see us! We'll be around, won't we, Lilianne?'

'Barring a fatal accident, yes.'

Connie patted Lilianne's shoulder. 'That's my sunny, funny friend for you.'

Helen grinned, wondering if she could leave Kevin to travel once they were married, or if it would feel like desertion. Once they had kids, she'd certainly have to stay put. But given how much she was enjoying Paris, it seemed impossible that this would be her only overseas trip. She and Kevin would have to work something out.

'I am dying to hang out in Spain. Supposed to be mellow to the max. And Crete, where my grandparents came from. Italy would be totally righteous, Morocco I'd love to see too. Then there's Jerusalem, Beirut, Damascus, Istanbul, the Far East . . .' Connie paused for a breath. 'The world is my oyster.'

'Can I ask a nosy question?' Helen said.

'No such thing.' Connie detangled some hair caught in her feathery earring. 'I'm an open book.'

'How do you afford all that?'

'That's easy. I find jobs wherever I am. Here, I babysit for one American family and do some cleaning for another. But I've picked grapes, scrubbed floors, shoveled chicken shit ... whatever is needed wherever I am. Then I spend whatever I've earned. I'm taking a cooking course at La Varenne right now. Fantastic.'

Helen felt a mixture of admiration and horror. 'I couldn't live like that. I need stability.'

'Most people do.' Lilianne glanced at a couple sitting at the table next to them. 'Or at least more than Connie does.'

'I'm free, sister. Don't fence me in. You know that Cole Porter song?' Connie sang the title in a husky alto, even though Lilianne and Helen had nodded yes. 'Well you're here now, Helen, and we have months to work on you until you fall so in love with Paris that you call Kevin and tell him you won't be home until spring, if ever. I mean, you *gotta* see Paris in the spring.'

'Connie, leave her alone.'

'Me?' She put a hand to her chest, blinking innocently. 'What did I do?

Helen turned to Lilianne, curious about her background. 'Where are you from, Lilianne?'

'Connecticut.'

'*Rich* Connecticut. I think her family owns most of Long Island Sound. *Long Guy-land*, as a New Yorker would say it.'

'Ha ... ha.' Lilianne's body was relaxed against the back of her seat, but she seemed to be interested in everyone around them. 'I grew up in Southport. Pretty harbor town on the Sound. Dad's a banker. Mom is a professional Southport volunteer: library, garden club, church. I had a pretty typical silver-spoon childhood. Tennis, golf, country club, et cetera.'

'I'm from the total sticks in Vermont. Tiny town you've never heard of.' Connie held up her thumb and forefinger a quarter-inch apart. 'Hills, cows and trees. Left as soon as I turned eighteen. I hated being in one place and I hated everyone knowing everything about me and judging, judging, judging, like there's something wrong with the way I choose to be human.'

'Don't you miss your families?'

'Nope.' Lilianne raised an eyebrow toward her friend. 'Connie?'

'Nope.'

'Wow.' Helen found this unutterably sad, and wondered if it explained Lilianne's reticence and Connie's wanderlust. Her own family was the bedrock of her existence. She couldn't imagine feeling safe launching herself into the world without home and parents as emergency refuges. 'I miss mine, and it's only been a couple of weeks.'

'*Voilà, trois cafés.*'

The coffee – espresso really – came in small cups, dark, strong and bitter, a far cry from the stuff Helen's mom made or what Helen had gotten used to in the college dining hall. She wasn't sure she loved it, but doing as the Parisians did was enjoyment itself.

'Have you met people yet? Made friends here? It must be a little . . . quiet at home if your hostess is older.' Lilianne's smile was a rare jewel next to Connie's near-constant grins. 'Though I've known some pretty active senior ladies.'

'Madame Laurent – Natalie – is amazing, but she does get up early and turns in early.' Helen put down her cup. 'You're the first people I've spoken to except to ask directions.'

'You totally lucked out. We are fantastic. I'm sure we're going to be great friends. In fact . . .' Connie leaned forward on her elbows, 'our roommate, Christine, is leaving to go back home to Providence. You can move in with us!'

'Connie.' Lilianne gave her a look of amused tolerance. 'We should probably get to know each other a little better first.'

'If you say so. But I'm telling you, the three of us are still going to be soulmates when we're old ladies. I feel the vibes of permanence.' Connie took in a deep breath with closed eyes, as if their lifelong friendship was smelling really great. 'Soak up this moment where it all begins, sisters. It's unreal.'

'That would be Connie talk for she thinks you seem like a nice person.' Lilianne had a hand beside her mouth as if speaking in confidence, but didn't lower her volume. 'Poor thing never made it out of the sixties.'

Connie's dark eyes popped open. 'The sixties were about love, acceptance, peace and more love. Who'd want to leave that?'

Lilianne finished her coffee and set the cup gently down in its saucer. 'Point taken.'

'So, Helen, our new love. Here is our schedule for today and every day if we can manage it. When afternoon coffee time is over, wine time begins. You must come to our apartment and share a bottle. Or two bottles. We can pick up food for dinner and celebrate meeting each other and starting the rest of our lives as best friends.'

Helen hesitated. Her parents – and Kevin – had warned her to stay in public when first meeting people. They seemed convinced everyone outside of the US would be looking for ways to kill her. She knew they were just feeling vulnerable because she was too far away for them to protect, but she had promised to be careful.

'Great idea, Connie. We'll get some champagne, make an evening out of it.' The couple at the table next to Lilianne got up to leave; Lilianne bent to pull her briefcase into her lap. 'That is, if you're free, Helen. Otherwise we can have a glass of wine here, or say *au revoir* right now. No offense taken.'

'Are you kidding me? I'd be horribly offended.' Connie winked across the table. 'Of course you do what you want. I know I can be sorta bossy.'

'I wouldn't call you sorta bossy,' Lilianne said sweetly. 'I'd call you extremely bossy.'

Helen laughed. Ninety-nine to one they were harmless. Opening up to strangers was exactly the sort of risk she'd come here to take. Otherwise, she'd go home the same. She wanted Paris to leave its mark, especially if she never got to come back. 'I'd love to, thank you.'

'Outta sight!' Connie smacked a hand on the table. 'Lilianne, pay the man.'

Lilianne had already signaled their waiter, who weaved his way over to their table. '*L'addition, s'il vous plaît.*'

Helen reached into her purse, preparing to fumble with the still-confusing franc coins.

'No, no.' Lilianne put a hand on hers. 'This is my treat.'

She considered fighting, then decided there'd be more important battles coming up. 'Thank you, that's very nice. I'll contribute toward dinner.'

Connie waved that thought away. 'Lilianne's loaded. She can't even tell when money leaves her wallet. In fact, it's my considered opinion that it grows back immediately every time she spends it.'

Lilianne gave Connie a look. 'Where are you staying, Helen?'

'In the 16th, near the Passy Métro stop.'

'*Oh là là.*' Lilianne shook her hand as if it were dripping wealth.

'*Mon Dieu!*' Connie whistled. 'Your hostess must have *beaucoup* bucks.'

'It's a nice neighborhood. Quiet. A little staid.' Helen collected her Michelin and stood. 'Natalie comes from an old French family, going back forever. I'm guessing they were nobility from the beginning. Highbrow anyway.'

'My family has always been distinctly lowbrow,' Connie announced proudly. 'My grandparents, Stavros and Lydia Pappas, came over from Greece with practically nothing. Went through the whole Ellis Island thing. Are we ready?'

'We are ready.' Lilianne stood too, brushing something invisible off her suit jacket.

'Where do you live?' Helen pushed her chair back under the metal-rimmed table.

'Right here in the 6th.' Lilianne pointed in the direction of the Luxembourg Gardens. 'Rue Pierre Nicole. It's a long walk if you don't mind, or we can find a taxi.'

'Walking in Paris?' Helen smirked. 'I'll try to bear it.'

'Oh goody.' Connie took her free arm. 'We'll go by Saint-Sulpice. It's a humongous church, not like Notre-Dame, but close. Have you seen it yet? We'll have to take you one Sunday to the service so you can hear the organ. Holy *mère de Dieu*, it's incredible.'

The walk was a delight, filled with laughter and effortless conversation, and the beginnings of certainty that the companionship Helen had been hungry for had just landed in her lap. Maybe Connie was right and they would end up friends for life.

They made a few stops to pick up champagne, bread, pâté and a few cheeses, plus charcuterie salads of grated carrot and celery root, and little tomatoey tarts with criss-crossed anchovies on top. Lilianne and Connie chose effortlessly, while Helen drank it all in, looking forward to when she could do the same instead of being halted by anxiety, indecision and drooling awe.

On rue Pierre Nicole, Connie stopped outside one of the stone apartment buildings typical of the city, this one with a black fence separating the sidewalk from the set-back entrance.

'This is our building. Ain't it swanky?' She gestured grandly at the ornately carved stone doorway arching around a wrought-iron and glass door, beyond which was a dimly visible marble hallway lit with sconces. 'Only the best for us.'

'Uh-huh.' Lilianne headed past her toward a plain metal door. 'This is our entrance. We live on the top floor, the old servants' quarters.'

They entered through a dingy tiled tunnel into a courtyard where voices and footsteps echoed upwards, and trooped across its uneven cracked surface to an ancient creaky elevator, the type with metal scissor gates that opened and closed manually. The three women crowded in.

Connie jabbed the button for the fifth floor, making the elevator jerk and clank upwards. 'Don't you feel like you're at the Ritz?'

'It's a decent apartment,' Lilianne said. 'Great neighborhood, good amount of room for the three of us, and because you have to come in this way, which no one with an ounce of pride would tolerate, it's cheap. For Paris.'

'Cheap for me and Christine, she means. We are generously subsidized.' Connie nudged Helen. 'And you will be too, since you're moving in soon.'

The ticking and clanking stopped, Lilianne slid back the elevator gate and they stepped onto a balcony passage strewn with potted flowering plants that led to the apartment's door. Inside, a small kitchen with a square metal and green Formica table and four yellow plastic chairs. A stove, a few cabinets – beige with black handles – and a refrigerator only slightly bigger than the tiny one Mom and Dad kept in the basement for grocery overflow.

'Welcome.' Lilianne dropped her briefcase next to the door. 'The butler will be out shortly to take your coat.'

Helen couldn't help herself. She gestured to the fridge. 'How do you fit a week of food in that thing?'

'*Ah, mais non.*' Connie jingled over and gave the appliance a loving hug. 'You do like zee French do and shop every day.'

Helen was aghast. 'Every day?'

'But of course every day, *ma chérie*! One store for each ingredient, like we did today. The baker certainly, first thing in the morning. French bread only lasts one day, so you have to get it fresh unless you toast it or want to build up your jaw muscles chewing. Then zere is zee butcher, zee charcuterie, grocer, fishmonger, cheese shop, et cetera, et cetera. You can spend half of every day shopping for food.'

'Considering how the French eat, it's hard to complain.' Lilianne bent to put the salads they'd bought in the tiny refrigerator. 'There are supermarkets, but they're not nearly as fun.'

'Oh, we'll have to take you to the rue Mouffetard market.' Connie rubbed her hands together. 'It will blow your mind. Dozens of shops put out their produce – cheeses, meats, fish, pretty much everything, all of it beautiful and crazy fresh.'

'We'll eat in the living room tonight.' Lilianne crossed to the cabinet and grabbed three glasses. 'There's nowhere comfortable to sit in the whole joint, but that room beats the kitchen for ambience.'

'Be there in a sec,' Connie said. 'I gotta see a man about a horse.'

The kitchen led into a hallway, off which branched the living room on the left and bedrooms and a bathroom on the right. After the over-the-top wealth of Natalie's apartment, the place seemed very real, in spite of its sparse and frankly cheap furnishing. Helen perched on the edge of the bilious-orange sofa draped with an olive-green blanket, feeling much more at home than on the probably priceless Louis-the-something settees in Natalie's living room.

'The place came furnished. Nothing is to our taste, but the price was right.'

'How did you and Connie meet?'

Lilianne twisted the wire cage off the champagne bottle. 'You will not be surprised to learn that Connie found me not long after I arrived in Paris, and suggested we live together about ten minutes later. She and Christine had discovered this apartment and needed a third.'

'How soon before you agreed?'

'I made her wait a couple of weeks.' She turned the bottle and the cork came out with a soft pop. 'Connie is much more trusting than I am.'

Helen wanted to ask why, but Lilianne didn't invite personal questions. 'It's a good and bad trait, I suppose. Trusting easily.'

'Like every human characteristic, given the right or wrong situation. Too much affection can be smothering, too much honesty can be hurtful, too much trust can get you in terrible trouble.'

'I like that idea.' Helen gave up trying to get comfortable on the orange couch, and focused on the topic. 'And if you look at "bad" traits, lying could save your life, indecision could keep you from making stupid choices too quickly, and a little laziness could keep you from being Type A and dying young of a heart attack.'

'Exactly.' Lilianne gave her an admiring glance and poured three wine glasses half full of the bubbly liquid. She handed one to Helen and sat on the other end of the couch, raising hers. 'This is a Blanc de Blancs, only Chardonnay grapes. I hope you like it.'

'I won't be able to notice anything except that it has bubbles and is fun to drink.'

'What more do you need?' Connie flowed and jingled into the room, took her own glass from the coffee table and raised it in a toast. 'Cheers, Helen! We are so happy to meet you.'

They took their first sips of the cold, clear and to Helen's taste slightly sour wine. Maybe she wasn't such a Blanc de Blancs fan after all. She tried to imagine announcing that to Kevin and made herself smile picturing his face.

Moments like those she missed him most.

'Now.' Connie collapsed all over an overstuffed brown chair. 'Tell us more about you. How did you meet this Kevin?'

'I met him sophomore year of college, in a history class. We've been dating since then. He's older than I am. I'm twenty-three, he's twenty-nine.'

'I'm twenty-five.' Connie pointed at Lilianne. 'She's the old lady at thirty.'

'Go on, Helen.'

'He joined the army after high school, then worked for his dad's flooring company while he was in the reserves. So he started college late.'

'He served in Vietnam?' Lilianne asked.

Helen nodded.

'Ugh, what a clusterf—' Connie slapped a hand across her mouth. 'I shouldn't say that.'

'It's okay. I'm proud of him but . . . conflicted about the war. About any war.' Helen rarely admitted as much. Her family wouldn't agree, so there was no point, and once she met Kevin, saying so would have felt disloyal. 'It's such a misuse of human potential.'

'It is,' Lilianne said. 'But you'd have to get everyone on the planet to agree to change before we could do away with it.'

'Even then, there are always going to be Attila the Huns who make it necessary.' Connie drank deeply of her champagne. 'You know, the jerks who keep popping up throughout history, and ruining everyone's peaceful groove.'

'Yes, I know.' Helen curled a leg under her to see if she could defeat the couch. 'I'm being an idealist.'

'We need idealists.' Lilianne put down her glass to take off her heels, which she lined up perpendicular to the couch. 'So, Kevin bought a farm. In Kansas.'

'He's wanted to be a farmer since forever.'

'Following his dream.' Connie nodded approvingly.

Lilianne picked up her glass again, eyes on Helen in that way that made Helen want to fidget. 'What's *your* dream, Helen?'

'I've always wanted to live in Paris, so I'm getting to do that now. And . . .' Helen braced herself for a reaction, 'I know it's old-fashioned, but I've always wanted to get married and have children. So that's next.'

'If being a mom ever goes out of style, we'll die out,' Lilianne said comfortingly. 'It's human nature, not old-fashioned.'

'Wait, with Kevin? You're engaged?' Connie blinked in surprise. 'I thought you said he was your boyfriend.'

Helen looked down into her champagne. 'I asked him to wait to propose until I get back.'

Lilianne seemed to snap to attention. 'Why did you want him to wait?'

'Because . . .' Helen laughed nervously. 'This will sound weird, but I wanted to feel like I was really here.'

Lilianne's eyebrow arched. 'You wanted to feel free of him.'

'A free woman in Paris . . .' Connie hummed a few bars of the Joni Mitchell song. 'We can totally help you sow those wild oats. I myself am something of an expert.'

'No, no, that's not what I meant.' Helen felt herself flushing.

'Why not? What better time to go a little wild?' Connie got up to refill her glass. 'Mom and Dad aren't here, boyfriend isn't here. When the cats are away . . .'

'Not other men.' Helen's face was hot by then. 'I wanted Paris to be a clean dividing line. Me single on one side, Kevin and me married on the other. Plus I didn't want to say yes I'll marry you and then leave the country. That would be weird.'

Lilianne smiled faintly. Connie looked skeptical.

Helen wasn't surprised. Nerves had made her voice high and forced. 'What about you two? Are either of you seeing anyone?'

'I am. And then I'm not. Whoever happens by, you dig?' Connie waved her glass one way then the other, nearly spilling her drink. 'Sometimes he hangs around for a year or more, sometimes only a couple of hours. I celebrate all kinds of love.'

Helen hid a cringe. 'Do you think you'll ever marry?'

'Nope, not for me.' Connie gave Lilianne a sly look. 'Though *somebody* thinks one of these days I'm going to meet someone, be a total goner and renounce everything I think I believe now. But I say, hey, *somebody*, if that happens it happens. That's life, right? I accept it as it comes.'

'What about you, Lilianne?'

'No one at the moment.' She shrugged out of her jacket and hung it carefully over the arm of the sofa.

'Lilianne is married to her work.'

'Hardly.' She settled back into the corner of the couch and stretched her arm along its back toward Helen. 'There always seem to be more interesting things to do.'

Helen had no idea how to respond to that. Anything interesting was ten times better done with someone you loved. 'You haven't met the right man yet.'

Lilianne looked at her with something like pity. 'Maybe that's it.'

'But you don't think so?'

A lazy smile spread her mouth. 'No, I don't.'

'Lilianne is extremely mysterious,' Connie announced. 'And I am extremely hungry. Nothing in me right now but coffee and delicious alcohol.'

'Oh gosh.' Helen jumped up guiltily. 'I need to call Madame Laurent and let her know I won't be home for dinner.'

'Oh gosh indeed!' Connie dimpled a smile and pointed. 'Phone is in the hall on the dresser.'

After a panic during which she couldn't find Natalie's number, Helen located it on a tiny slip of paper between two ten-franc bills in her wallet and made the call.

Natalie wanted to know all about her afternoon, and was delighted to hear that she'd met Connie and Lilianne. Helen was welcome to come home any time of night, and was not to worry about waking Natalie or having to get up early to work. 'Stay, stay! You're young. Have a good time.'

While they chatted, Helen was aware of the two women going back and forth carrying dishes and furniture. By the time she hung up, the kitchen table and chairs had found their way into the living room, table loaded with the food they'd bought.

'One final touch.' Connie fiddled with the stereo and found a jazz station. 'There. Good wine, good food, good music, good people.'

The food was delicious, the conversation effortless, the wine free-flowing. By the time she left, several hours later, Helen agreed with Connie's assessment of their friendship potential. She took the subway home, trying not to look as tipsy and nervous as she felt. Kevin would have a fit if he knew she was alone on the train at night. But there were other single women riders, looking calm, and in one case, half asleep, which was reassuring.

Back at Natalie's elegance, missing the casual fun of the girls' apartment, Helen brushed her teeth in the gold and cream bathroom, then tiptoed into her bedroom and stopped short.

Natalie had moved the doll, table and all, minus the glass dome, into her room. A note read: *It's been a long time since Sarah had company. Enjoy.*

How fun. Sarah would make a wonderful companion, looking even more beautifully melancholy now that she was no longer overwhelmed by the chaotic pink of Jeanette's room. Helen picked up the doll, more relaxed around her without Natalie standing guard. Such a beautiful dress, so expertly made. Peeking out from under it, tiny green matching shoes that she hadn't noticed before. She turned Sarah prone to examine them. On the sole of each, stamped into the leather, a miniature figure, too small to identify as male or female. On impulse, Helen slipped off one of the shoes to see the doll's foot. Written on Sarah's sole in neat script was *Bernhardt #47*.

Of course! The famous French actress Sarah Bernhardt, Jeanette's inspiration. No wonder she'd kept the doll so close during her life. How many other Sarahs were scattered across Paris or wherever she came from if this was number 47? What fun if she got to meet one of her sisters someday.

Still smiling, Helen slid into bed, whispered goodnight to Sarah and gathered the covers around her shoulders. She let herself relax, dreamily going over the day. Kevin would have enjoyed the afternoon and evening with Connie and Lilianne, wouldn't he? The meal at least? He couldn't hate *everything* about Paris.

Her eyes flew open. Kevin. She hadn't written to him tonight. He'd asked her to write every day.

Ugh. The bed was so warm; the night had turned chilly, a promise of fall in the air. Maybe Helen could get up early and write before the mailman came. She yawned again, alcohol dragging her down toward sleep. Or take it to the post office herself, or . . .

He'd survive. She'd written every day so far. He couldn't expect her to keep up that pace for the whole five months. Helen would write tomorrow, double length. Lots to tell him.

She drifted off, looking forward to seeing her new friends again, feeling as if the life she'd always hoped to live in Paris had finally begun.

✄ Chapter 4 ✄

Teresa turned left at the Lawrence Country Club onto West 4th Street and followed the remaining GPS instructions to the brick rectangle of Lawrence Memorial Hospital, where Grandma Helen was recovering. She parked the rental car in the lot, turned off the engine and sat for a moment, gearing up for their first meeting since she was twelve, when she'd had no inkling of the pain and havoc Helen had inflicted on her children and on Grandpa Kevin. Everything had happened fast after Teresa told her mother she could make the trip to Kansas, exactly a week earlier, but Teresa had put a lot of thought into how she'd handle first meetings with her estranged relatives.

She wasn't the cause or any part of the current tensions or long-held grudges and judgments. She was here to help her grandmother move on to the next phase of her life, something Mom said Helen had finally agreed to in a recent call. If there were problems, it would be up to Cheryl and Uncle James to figure out the hard stuff.

One more deep breath and she pushed out of the car and stretched, gratefully inhaling the sweet May air. The temperature was perfect, in the mid seventies, moderate humidity – though anything other than dry-as-desert felt life-giving to her.

Following her plan, Teresa had come straight to the hospital from the airport, detouring only to grab a quick lunch at a nearby sub shop. It had been tempting to go to the house first, take a nap to refresh, but she knew herself too well. Once there, she'd take any excuse to hang onto the safe, familiar and calm. From there, the visit to Grandma Helen would seem like a hurdle instead of a logical next step.

She locked the car and moved confidently toward the front entrance, taut with nerves. Nine times out of ten, whatever she worried about either didn't materialize or didn't turn out nearly as badly as she'd imagined. Unfortunately her anxious self never seemed to learn from its mistakes.

No fear.

The hospital lobby was a sparklingly clean cream and black space decked out with giant columns that seemed unnecessary in such a low-ceilinged space. Teresa registered as a visitor and got a green 'Sunday' sticker from the cheerful woman behind the desk.

'Rehabilitation, fourth floor.'

She found the elevator and joined a scrubs-wearing woman about her age – and two thirds of her height – carrying a cup of coffee that reminded Teresa she'd been up at four to catch a six a.m. flight, and hadn't remembered caffeine after lunch. Adrenaline would have to carry her through.

The doors opened onto the fourth floor, bringing closer what her anxiety felt was a life-changing moment, but which would only be a brief and, at worst, uncomfortable chat with her Chernobyl Granny. Helen had made a lot of people's lives hell, but she could do nothing to Teresa's.

She strode out onto the highly polished floor, gray, brown and cream reflecting cold neon from the ceiling lights, creating a chilly, impersonal vibe. Farther down the hall, a small area with a couch, table and chairs and a fireplace – at least they were trying. But warmer colors and softer lighting would go a long way toward making the place feel more homey.

At the nurses' station, Teresa asked for Helen Foster's room.

'Four-seventeen.' A plump arm pointed to a doorway down the hall while the rest of her continued chatting with a colleague.

'Thank you.'

One foot in front of the other, jitters increasing as the distance lessened.

A gentle knock, though the door was ajar. 'Grandma Helen?'

'Come in.' The words were low, wavery, tired, so different from the cheerful voice Teresa had heard on the phone over the last decade and a half.

She pushed into what turned out to be a private room. Her grandmother was lying in a blue hospital gown on a bed whose head tipped up at a forty-five-degree angle.

'Hi, Grandma.' She closed the door gently behind her. 'It's Teresa. I just arrived from Phoenix.'

Helen blinked, owl-like, through glasses that made her blue eyes look enormous. 'I'm sorry. Who are you?'

Teresa tried not to look startled. It was a shock to be confronted with how much older Helen looked, and – in spite of all the awful things Teresa had learned about her – how warmly familiar, as if there were two grandmothers, the callous degenerate of Mom's stories, and the one Teresa had adored as a child. 'I'm your granddaughter, Teresa. Cheryl's daughter.'

Helen frowned. 'Cheryl's daughter is younger than you. Much younger.'

Teresa hunched her shoulders. She'd prepared for this, but it was still hard. Mom had said the years of drinking had probably contributed to Helen's mental decline. Such a waste. 'I was twelve last time I saw you, a long time ago. I'm twenty-seven now.'

'Let me put on my glasses.' Helen turned toward the table by her bed.

'Um . . . you're wearing them, Grandma.'

'Oh.' She felt around the frames with shaky fingers. 'So I am. I was napping. I usually take them off to sleep. I guess I didn't this time.'

'I guess not.' Teresa shifted her weight. 'Well ... it's good to see you.'

'Now, now.' Helen opened her arms. 'If you're my grand-daughter, you can do better than that. Gently, though. I seem to be breakable.'

Teresa approached reluctantly and hugged her grandmother's thin frame as carefully as she could.

'Teresa, you said.' Helen searched Teresa's face, laid a hand on her cheek. 'I thought you were a redhead.'

'Mom is a redhead. My mother is Cheryl. Your daughter Cheryl.'

'Cheryl. Yes, of course. I'm sorry. I get so confused.' She pointed despondently to her head, her long blond hair chin-length now and lightened by gray. 'I'm terribly afraid that when they operated, they took out my brains by mistake.'

Teresa recoiled. 'I'm ... pretty sure they wouldn't do that.'

'Oh my.' Helen wheezed weak laughter. 'Don't look so fright-ened. I was joking.'

Teresa melted in relief. 'I didn't realize. Sorry.'

'Come sit.' Helen patted the bed. Teresa perched awkwardly on the mattress. Much easier to judge and find guilty someone who wasn't vulnerable and human right in front of you. 'So you came to visit your old grandma. Are you staying with James?'

'No, at the ranch. At your house.'

'All alone? Why not with James?'

Teresa's mind whirled. How much to say? She decided to risk the truth. 'I'm helping you get ready for the move.'

'Move?' Helen's straggly gray brows flew up. 'I'm going home soon? I thought they said not for another few—'

'No, no.' Teresa colored. Five minutes and she'd screwed this up already. 'Your move to the new place.'

Helen frowned. 'They said I was going home from here.'

'Okay.' Teresa's discomfort grew. Helen had already forgotten what she'd agreed to on the phone with Mom. 'I'm here to help organize your things at the ranch.'

'My things . . .' Helen cocked her head, taking in Teresa's face with a furrowed brow. Then her expression lit. 'I remember you liked the dolls. And you spent a lot of time with your father in Kevin's workshop. And you were afraid of the animals. I remember now. Adorable little girl. I was so taken with you.'

'That was me.' A rush of tenderness Teresa shouldn't be feeling. This woman had destroyed lives.

'The dolls are still there. When I get home, I'll show them to you.' Helen patted Teresa's forearm. 'Are you taking me there now? I thought they said I need to stay longer.'

'You do, yes.' Teresa swallowed the lump in her throat. 'They're not finished with you here.'

'No.' Helen blinked slowly. 'They have me doing things all day long to get me moving again. They're surprised how strong I am. Life on the ranch keeps me strong. How are my animals?'

'I came straight from the airport. I haven't seen them yet.'

'James is taking care of them until I get back. And his boy Jim. Do you know them?'

'Yes. My uncle and my cousin.'

'Of course, of course. I'm sorry. I get so confused.' She gave Teresa a slow, wicked smile. 'You know, I think when they did the surgery they took out my brains.'

Teresa laughed dutifully, shoulders tight from tension. 'Did they really?'

'Terrible having an empty skull. All those thoughts rattling around up there with no place to put them.' Helen shook her head mournfully.

Teresa forced another laugh. 'Maybe they'll grow back?'

'That would be lovely.' Helen yawned and gave a slow blink. 'Thank you for spending the afternoon with me today, Teresa. It must be an awfully long drive home to where you live with your mother. I'm worried it will get dark.'

'I'm staying here in Lawrence, Grandma.' Teresa spoke gently; she'd been there five minutes, tops. 'At your house.'

'Yes, yes, of course. At my house. You told me. Give it a hug for me.' Helen's eyelids drooped, lifted, drooped again. 'I know it misses me. And the animals. They'll all be missing me. Tell them not to worry. I'll be back soon.'

Teresa got up and moved toward the door, shaken by the conflict between tenderness for her grandmother and the righteous anger she should be feeling.

As for the move to the retirement community, she'd counted on her mother's assertion that Grandma Helen was okay with it. Teresa would have to decide if it was better not to mention it again, or to keep reminding her grandmother until the idea stuck, so the transition would be easier on everyone. 'It was nice to see you, Grandma.'

'Delightful. Thank you.' Helen's lashes fluttered down again. 'I need a little nap before they come get me for more exercises. I have to do them all day long, you know.'

'Yes, you told me.'

'Did I?'

'It's okay.' Teresa's voice thickened. 'I don't mind.'

'You'll come back tomorrow, won't you? I won't be so sleepy then.' Helen opened her eyes when Teresa hesitated. 'Won't you?'

She couldn't say no. 'Yes. Sure. I'll come.'

'Good.' The drooping lids closed again. 'Drive safely. It's

such a long way. Say hello to your mother. I haven't spoken to her in weeks.'

'Bye, Grandma.' Fighting tears, Teresa left the room, made her way down the hall past an older woman on a walker and a younger man in a wheelchair with bandages around his head.

Back on the first floor, she crossed the shiny black-and-white-checked lobby and pushed out into the soft May air with relief. The resurgence of loving feelings for her grandmother had been unexpected. It was not going to be easy to stay neutral. At least she'd be better prepared tomorrow.

After forgetting both where she'd parked the rental and what it looked like, she found it, loaded the ranch's address into the GPS, then searched for the nearest grocery store. Only one more nervous moment today – the first meeting with either her uncle or cousin. Mom said one or the other came to check on the animals twice a day. She could only hope their reaction to her would be as kind and welcoming as Helen's, and that she could stay better composed.

In the meantime, she'd buy groceries, get to the house, collapse into the nap of a lifetime, then dive into a vat of coffee.

An hour later, she drove up the long gravel and dust driveway to her grandparents' home, southwest of the city of Lawrence, off the picturesquely named North 175th Road, nap thoughts chased away by twin surges of adrenaline and affection. She parked close to the pale yellow house, its front awash in blooming pink and white peonies. Until this moment she'd barely been able to summon a mental picture of the place; now every detail was instantly familiar.

Pushing eagerly out of the car into the breezy afternoon, her peripheral vision caught the approach of an enormous animal. She whirled toward it, braced for retreat, then remembered her grandmother's Great Pyrenees – though this couldn't be one from her childhood. The breed was huge, like golden Labs on steroids: bigger, wider, longer hair, more white than golden, but a similar muzzle shape and benign expression. She remembered they were excellent guard dogs, instinctively taking on a protector role for the animals and property, and, most importantly, very gentle with humans.

The dog moved slowly and greeted her with a calm sniff. Teresa could deal with calm dogs. She even patted its enormous head. Gingerly. 'Hi, dog.'

There. All good. They were friends.

With her new escort, she walked around the side of the house to get a view of the land. The fifty acres was still the same oasis of unmowed prairie, bushes and trees where she and her brothers had played with Cousin Jim when they were shooed outside, and wide stretches of grazing pasture amid the unchanging sameness of corn and soy fields surrounding it. So much green! Enough to make Phoenix seem sere and lifeless.

Grandpa Kevin's original farm had been five hundred acres, ten times the size of Helen's lot. But this little patch had always seemed magically enormous to the young Teresa. Not so enormous now – the house was also smaller than she remembered – and it was less magical being here alone.

In Phoenix, she was surrounded by the energizing buzz of city life and plenty of people who'd hear her if she had to scream. She couldn't imagine living here in such silent isolation with only creatures for company – a mule, a few bulls, sheep, goats, a couple of donkeys, chickens, and a herd of cows. The same species she remembered from her childhood, though probably none of the same individuals. Most would have died or been eaten by now. Helen had long ago explained the purpose of the ranch in simple, matter-of-fact terms, 'And this is how all of nature works.' Little Teresa had been appalled.

She inhaled the familiar grassy aroma, tinged pleasantly with warm animal, relishing the lost memories. Without warning, a streak of black and white shot from below the house and came racing up the hill. Before Teresa could react, it leapt up and slammed into her solar plexus with both paws. She gasped and bent forward, struggling for breath, then took off for the house, shrieking when the paws landed on her lower back, making her stumble and nearly fall.

At the front door, she fumbled frantically for the key under the mat where James had said it would be. The dog circled away, then came to a halt, looking back at her as if bemused – or amused – by what it had done.

The key turned easily. Teresa darted inside and slammed the door behind her.

This was not the symbolic slow step over the threshold into her mother's turbulent childhood home that she had planned. Instead of standing still, drinking in the familiar smells and the bittersweet atmosphere with a faraway look in her eye, perhaps a glistening tear or two, Teresa was trembling and breathless, brushing dirty footprints off her shirt, muttering curses because she'd have to go back out again, at least twice, to unload the car of her suitcase and three bags of groceries.

She peeked through the front door. The first Pyrenees had been joined by a second one, not quite as big – female? The crazed black and white dog was not around. Teresa had prepared herself for several scenarios that might arise during this complicated, fraught trip, but even her worrywart brain hadn't anticipated being held hostage by a deranged mutt.

C'mon, Teresa. Think this one through.

Point one, the first Pyrenees didn't blink at the other dog's appearance. Ergo, the attack dog was familiar. Point two, Grandma Helen wouldn't have a aggressive dog on the premises.

Maybe it was being affectionate? The majority of Teresa's experience with dogs had consisted of avoiding them, but it was hard to see knocking someone over as a love language for any species. More likely the monster thought she was an intruder.

Either way, she didn't want to spend any more time on the receiving end of dog impact.

She opened the door. The Pyrenees milled happily around. Still no sign of the jumpy one. As quietly as possible, Teresa stepped outside, senses on high alert. She made it to the car, yanked out her suitcase and one of the grocery bags and speed-walked back inside without being slammed again.

Success!

One more trip.

Out the door, four steps down the driveway, the black and white dog appeared again, ears high, tongue out, tail wagging. Teresa told her legs to keep moving.

'Hey, how's it going, sweet puppy?' She spoke in a high-pitched croon, retrieving the other two grocery bags. 'Who's a good boy? Or girl? Or non-binary canine? You're so beautiful. And so calm. I'm just going back into— *Crap.*'

The dog flew at her. She flew toward the house.

It was a tie.

Inside, she dumped the bags on the kitchen counter and dusted off a second set of footprints on her hip, still not sure how she'd managed to hang onto the groceries.

At least she was safe and didn't have to go back out until the next day, when she'd bring a defense with her. A pillow, or a bucket of freezing water. Boiling oil? That worked in medieval times. Maybe she'd ask James for advice.

She put away cold things in the refrigerator and shoved canned and non-perishables in the already crowded cabinets. Then she pulled her suitcase into the room she used to stay in with her brothers, at the other end of the house, the room Uncles James and Kevinjay had shared growing up. She needed to feel settled in first, then she'd have a look around.

The room had hardly changed. Boy posters still lined the walls, the Chiefs and the Royals, Star Wars and Dungeons and Dragons. Games lined the bookshelves, Monopoly, Risk and Stratego. The only change she could detect was that the twin bunks with sports-themed bedding had been replaced by a full-size bed under a royal blue comforter.

She unpacked her case into the half-emptied dresser, changed out of her airplane-smelling clothes into sweats and sneakers, washed her face, brushed her too-big teeth, then her toffee-colored hair, patiently blown straight that morning as Mom taught her when she was little, to keep away the ugly frizzies.

Much better.

For the next half-hour she explored, unexpectedly moved by how much she remembered, and how much she'd forgotten and now treasured remembering again. The dining room's focal point was a row of large windows embracing the ranch – the land for the mule and the bulls on the left, the barn and chicken coop, kitchen garden, pen for the sheep, goats and donkeys in the center, then the cow pastures sprawling out to the right.

Inside, at the big wooden dining table, Helen had tried her best to teach Teresa how to knit. The craft had stubbornly remained a mystery to her clumsy fingers, and Mom had finally suggested Helen give up, that Teresa would never learn. She'd been right, but it was sweet of Helen to keep at it so patiently when the outcome was always going to be a disaster.

Such a remarkable disconnect between her memories of Helen and her mother's stories. The mother Cheryl knew had been short-tempered, sharp-tongued, controlling, quick to blame and criticize, a mean drunk most evenings until Kevin died and shocked her sober. It was still hard to imagine the painful and thoughtless things Helen had done, given the sweetly confused woman she was now. But Teresa supposed it was too much to ask that awful people wear signs designating them as such.

Sure would save a lot of trouble.

Next to the dining room, the kitchen – where Teresa and her brothers made annual messes decorating Christmas cookies – had the same row of big windows with the same big view. Helen always had one eye out for the animals, noticing the slightest change in their behavior. 'The bulls are staring at something.' 'The chickens are upset.' 'That goat doesn't seem right.'

Next to the kitchen, the living room still had large comfortable sofas and, in one corner, the birdcage containing Helen's yellow cockatiel, Cheddar – probably the same bird, since they lived for decades – which started a shrill squawk when Teresa came into the room, alarm or greeting, Teresa couldn't tell. She eyed it warily. Helen used to let it out to flap around or ride perched on her shoulder or head. If the bird needed exercise, James or Jim could deal with it. For now, Teresa thought the creature looked perfectly happy in the cage. The dogs stayed outside all the time, she remembered that. There would be cats, too. Helen had said they were essential, or mice would drip from the rafters, an image that had kept little Teresa from ever going near the barn. She wasn't a big fan of cats, but she *really* wasn't a fan of mice, so cats would work. Outdoor cats.

The last room on that side of the house was Helen's bedroom. Teresa stopped at the threshold with a shiver, feeling as if she were trespassing. This room also matched her memories – faded bluebirds flying across curtains that livened up the cream-colored walls. An oval rag rug on the floor in shades of blue, gray and beige. On the dresser, Grandma Helen's silver-handled brush and comb, her small lacquered jewelry box and a nearly full bottle of Chanel No. 5. Also still there, pictures of Helen and Kevin's three kids as babies, joined by baby pictures of Teresa, Mike and Ike, and another little baldie who must be Cousin Jim. On a table next to the old-fashioned sleigh bed, a large smiling picture of a young, handsome Grandpa Kevin.

An attractive, silent room that made Teresa ache with sadness.

She turned away, dreading the job ahead of her. One thing to go through boxes in storage, or a kid's room not lived in for years, but pawing through her grandmother's things, possibly uncovering ugly evidence of her addiction or affairs, while Helen lay helpless in a hospital bed seemed an unthinkable invasion of privacy.

Trying to shake off the unease, she retraced her steps down the hall toward the bedroom she'd saved for last, on the opposite side of the house. Mom's room, which Teresa barely remembered. Eager for a glimpse of her mother's preserved youth through now-adult eyes, she pushed open the door and gasped.

All traces of Cheryl Foster, girl or adult, had been eradicated. The room was neat, anonymous, bed, chair, desk, dresser, a hotel room for guests. Helen had simply erased her daughter, like Teresa's father had erased Teresa and her brothers.

Hundreds of thousands of years of human progress, yet people still couldn't behave in a civilized fashion, take responsibility for the pain they'd inflicted, seek forgiveness and move on. Teresa wasn't so sure man had evolved at all, at least in ways that counted.

She closed the door, praying Mom wouldn't ask questions about her old room and childhood possessions. What a cruel blow to have to deliver. It would be that much harder to keep her promise to visit Helen the next day.

With heavy steps, Teresa headed for the staircase leading to the house's lower level, remembering ping-pong and pool tables and a toy kitchen and playhouse. Lining the walls had been old chests and steamer trunks containing various toys for inside and outside play, and shelves of books and games.

She paused at the bottom step, looking around. Not surprisingly, much had changed. The gaming tables and playhouse were gone, the bookshelves no longer held children's titles or games. A chest freezer stood in place of the toy kitchen. The trunks had been replaced by a few plastic bins marked *Mom and Dad* in thick black marker. Helen's parents? They must have died sometime during the last twelve years. Teresa's mom had never mentioned their passing. Did Helen ever tell her only daughter that her grandparents were gone?

Blowing out a discouraged breath, Teresa turned to the door of the old doll room. She'd only been allowed in with supervision by either her mother or Helen, which had annoyed her. Very hard to let your imagination run wild when a grown-up stood patiently – or in the case of Teresa's mother, impatiently – waiting for you to finish. Helen at least had known how to introduce Teresa to the dolls, telling her who sent them to her, or which relative she'd inherited them from, or what flea market she'd found them in. Teresa hoped her grandmother still remembered those stories, at least some of them. They should be passed down to the new owners.

She tried the door, relieved to find it unlocked, and pushed it open, fingers figuratively crossed. A grin broke out on her face. The dolls were still there, instantly and intimately familiar, like seeing old friends after a long absence.

Helen had taken great pains arranging them, sometimes by country, sometimes by height – similarly sized dolls would be grouped around a painted rocking chair that fit them, for example. Slender kimono-wearing dolls from Japan with jet-black hair and tiny parasols were arranged on heavy paper sprinkled with Japanese calligraphy; those from Spain – flouncy flamenco dancers and a caped bullfighter – in front of an open black fan decorated with deep crimson roses. Red-cheeked blond Dutch dolls dwarfed by absurdly large yellow clogs were surrounded by tiny bouquets of bright tulips in miniature pots. Mexican dolls in front of small cactuses. Swiss in front of the Alps, Russian Cossacks, Argentinian gauchos, Belgian lace-makers, Native American corncob dolls, and others whose origins Teresa had forgotten. Today the display seemed a little cringily stereotyped, but back then the room had been exotic and magical.

On the top shelf, the *pièce de résistance*, a doll that had belonged to Helen's grandmother, gift from a rich aunt who'd bought her on a visit to Germany. She was about a foot and a half tall, with beautiful porcelain skin, a wig of blond hair, a satin gown, and a tiny purse over one arm. Her glass eyes were blue and cheerful, her lips parted over tiny white teeth. Her name was Bertie, for reasons no one had remembered, and she towered over the others in the collection, tirelessly standing in front of a large poster of Neuschwanstein Castle in Bavaria.

Teresa lingered, touching and remembering, until fatigue and hunger's calls became impossible to ignore and she went back upstairs, cheered by the dolls and more optimistic that this job would not be impossible to manage. There was much less clutter than she'd envisioned in a house lived in for so many decades.

Halfway to the kitchen, the front door opened abruptly behind her. She whirled around, hand clapped to her heart.

'Hi, Teresa.' Uncle James, unsmiling, bringing fresh outdoor and earth smells with him. He was a big Kansas farm guy, with a beard he'd had since before beards were a thing, and a new small hoop earring in one ear. He was still handsome, a little weathered by the years, but young and robust and very much Helen's child, with a lighter, more intense version of her blue eyes and a copy of her wide, thin mouth and sharp nose. The biggest, most startling change was that he was now a few inches shorter than Teresa. 'Sorry to scare you.'

'It's okay. Hi, Uncle James.' She started forward for a hug, then stopped abruptly when he made no move toward her in return, leaving her floundering. 'I just got here. I mean, a while ago.'

'I saw your car outside.'

'Yes. Right.' She laughed stupidly. 'It's a rental. I flew in today.'

'Uh-huh.' He shoved his hands into his jeans pockets. From the living room, Cheddar chirped a greeting, or at least it was different from the noises he'd made when Teresa walked in. James glanced toward the sound. 'So. You're here to do some clearing.'

'Mostly organizing. I had a break, a vacation anyway. It's a big job, but I won't get rid of anything without—'

'You been to see Mom yet?'

Ah. Uncle James was not being polite. 'Yes, I went to see her from the airport.'

'How did she seem to you?'

Teresa wasn't sure how receptive he'd be to the truth. 'She'd just woken up. She was pretty tired.'

'She's not quite back to herself yet.' He was looking at her steadily, blue eyes testing, Teresa wasn't sure for what. 'A little out of it.'

'You mean the . . . confusion?' She was not touching the D word.

'Yes. It'll improve.'

'Ah.' She nodded politely, stomach muscles clenching.

Mom had been right about James's denial. No one's dementia improved. 'It was good to see her. It's been a really long time.'

His eyes narrowed. 'That was your mother's choice.'

Teresa pressed her lips together against her instinct to babble defenses, excuses and justifications for Mom's decision to distance herself. That had nothing to do with Teresa's relationship with James. 'Are you still teaching at the KU? Econ, right?'

'Still there.' He released her from his vice-grip gaze. 'I need to go check on the animals, secure the chickens for the night. Your cousin will be by tomorrow morning.'

'It'll be good to see him.' She could only hope Jim would be friendlier than his father. 'I can help too, at least with the bird, if you'll show me what to do. The other animals . . . I don't know. I already got attacked by one of the dogs.'

James looked dumbfounded. 'One of the dogs *attacked* you?'

'The black and white one. He jumped at me, full speed. Tried to knock me down.'

She got an immediate lesson in what Uncle James looked like when he was skeptical.

'I've known Zig since he was a puppy. He wouldn't hurt a fly. Maybe he was saying hello? He does that when he's excited.'

'No, it wasn't that. Full speed run from a good distance, big leap, bam.' She bent over, miming the impact and pointed at her solar plexus and hip, where the footprints no longer showed. 'He did it twice.'

'He was playing.'

'It didn't feel that way.'

'You're still nervous around animals?'

Hmph. Gaslighter. 'Yes, but—'

'We can work to change that while you're here, if you're game. Zig shouldn't have jumped on you. He might need to meet you with a family member around.' James jerked a thumb toward the door, apparently ignoring that Teresa *was* a family member. 'We can try that now, if you want.'

'You know . . .' her voice came out too high, 'I think I'll stay in for now. But thanks.'

'Sure.' He looked amused. 'Maybe next time.'

'Yeah, next time.' Teresa was already dreading it. She could imagine Zig behaving perfectly around James and then slamming her again after he'd gone. 'What do I need to do with Cheddar?'

'He'll need out of his cage for exercise.'

Of course he would. 'Mm-hm.'

'He'll either get to like you and perch on your shoulder or he won't and will ignore you. Either way, he should be out as often as you can watch him. I'll show you how to feed him and where his toys and treats are.'

'All the other animals stay outside?' She hoped.

'Monarch, the orange tabby, always came in to sleep with Mom. You can keep your bedroom door closed if you don't want him checking you out.'

'Okay.' Teresa smiled bravely. She decidedly did not want anything slinking around the house at night, checking her out or otherwise. 'Anything else?'

He looked amused again. Maybe her smile wasn't as brave as she thought. 'C'mon, I'll show you about the cockatiel.'

The lesson went fine. James brought a chattering Cheddar out of his cage and showed Teresa how to feed and water him, and what toys and treats he liked. Teresa managed not to duck or flinch every time the yellow feather-powered jet came nearby, sometimes perching on James's shoulder and pecking at his earring.

By the time they'd finished, Teresa was nearing stupid-exhaustion, starving for the frozen pizza and local Boulevard wheat beer she'd bought earlier.

'I'll give you my cell number and Jim's. Call or text anytime.'

'Thanks. I will.' She entered the information into her phone, determined not to bug either of them except for emergencies.

There better not be any emergencies.

'You'll do fine.' James took three steps toward the front door and turned back warily. 'Uh . . . you remember about the coyotes, right?'

Oh. Crap. She did now. Horrible haunted-house noises in the middle of the night that had terrified her as a girl. How could she have forgotten? 'Yes.'

'It's the neighborhood gang ritual. They show up, the dogs keep them away. It's noisy, that's all. Don't worry, you'll get so you can sleep through it.'

She doubted that very much. 'Sure.'

James smiled. How kind of him to enjoy her fear this much. 'You'll be okay. Jim will be by in the morning. Early.'

Early? Ick. Teresa didn't do early. At home, Katie and Addie would be up, exercised and self-righteously perky by the time Teresa dragged herself out of bed, struggling just to stay upright. At least the time change from Mountain to Central was in her favor. 'Okay.'

He opened the door, then turned back one more time, looking serious.

Teresa's dread-adrenaline flooded back.

'Look. I'm not wild about what your mother is trying to do here. But it's good to see you. I hope we can . . . talk about some of this, and learn to trust each other.'

Teresa froze. Words and emotions rushed up and jammed her brain and vocal cords. Bottom line, she'd like to trust James, but sometimes 'talk about some of this' meant 'try to change the situation to the way I want it'. She'd have to be strong enough not to get caught between him and Mom. 'Yes. Okay. Good.'

'See you tomorrow.' The door closed behind him.

Teresa waited for him to come back in. *Oh, one more thing. I forgot to tell you about the lions and tornadoes and how the house explodes first thing every morning.*

She wouldn't be able to relax completely until he did his thing outside with the beasts and went away, but at least she could pop open a beer and preheat the oven.

By the time her dinner was ready, James was long gone. After two pieces of pizza washed down with the beer, Teresa was so tired she could barely stumble over to the sink to wash up. She'd just put her clean plate in the dish drainer, eyes half closed, when something landed on her head.

She shrieked. Cheddar shrieked louder and flew off.

Teresa let her head drop. She'd forgotten about the bird – and to ask how to get the thing back in its cage.

Ick. She wasn't going to call James now; he'd been gone all of half an hour.

Luckily, Google was happy to offer several suggestions. Number one was that she remain calm.

Thank you, Google. Same to you.

Feeling optimistic, she tried out the next three, which taught her that cockatiels hiss right before they bite, and that their bites feel like being pinched by a staple remover.

The fifth idea, however, she loved: *Leave the bird alone. It will go into its cage when it gets hungry or sleepy.*

Sold!

Ten minutes later, she'd locked the house, pulled on her favorite pink striped pajamas and dived into bed, where she pulled the covers over her shoulders and punched the pillows to try to get the right height and feel.

Now. To relax.

Relaxation wasn't happening. Noises were different. Creaks

and cracks in the house, crickets and other wildlife sounds she had no names for. No comforting swish of traffic, no reassuring voices or thumps of neighbors underneath and overhead who could rush to her aid if she needed them.

Then there was the worry over James's attitude, and Jim's, and over the next day's visit with Helen . . .

Finally, in spite of it all, exhaustion started winning, and Teresa felt the delicious slide into—

A yowling cat.

Monarch, reminding his absent mistress that he'd been forgotten. Teresa said a few not-at-all-dainty words and staggered out into the hall. She'd have to let the beast in through the dining room door.

Opposite the living room, Teresa stopped and groaned. Not quite dark yet. Cheddar was still out of his cage. Cat + loose cockatiel = bad.

Where was the damn bird?

Shuffling into the kitchen, she found the damn bird hanging out on a fancy perch by the window. 'Okay, bird, Cheddar, whatever. I'm tired, and you're a pain in the ass. We are doing this.'

She put out her finger. Cheddar calmly hopped onto it. Teresa was so surprised, she stood staring while he checked her out with shiny black eyes, head cocked adorably, yellow all over except for two orange circles on his cheeks, an elegant crest on his head. Warm feet clung to her finger as she walked slowly back into the living room, cooing what she hoped was beguiling bird-talk, reminding herself that Google had suggested she put the bird into its cage backwards, so it didn't see imprisonment looming.

Miraculously, it worked. Just like in the video, Cheddar hopped onto his perch and settled with what Teresa would take as a thank-you-so-much chirp.

One quick flip of the latch and . . . she'd done it!

Meow.

'Coming.' Flushed with victory, Teresa let Monarch in, tensing for the feel of claws in the back of her leg while she locked the door after him. Never came. In fact, the cat had disappeared, probably into Helen's room, where he usually slept.

Perfect. She strode back down the hall, where she could hear her warm bed's desperate call. Smiling, she went in, closed the door, turned around, and jumped a mile.

Monarch. On her bed.

'Oh no. Just . . . no.' Teresa whipped around and stomped into Helen's room, where she called the kitty as seductively as possible.

Nope.

Head heavy with unfinished sleep, stomach churning with frustration, pleading that cat curiosity would come through, she called again. Waited.

Getting chilly. Getting cranky. Getting sick of this.

Back in her room, she discovered Monarch curled up in the warm spot she'd left, blinking lazily. Little bastard.

'No.' Teresa stalked forward. She didn't want to pick it up. Cats scratched. They hissed, a lot louder than birds, and they had lots of teeth. But . . .

She was not sleeping with this cat.

A half-hour later, she'd learned something new. If you close a cat out of a room, it will object. At top volume. Without stopping.

Eventually she reached breaking point and lay down, rigid, furious, trying not to cry, while next to her Monarch rejoiced in Teresa's defeat with a loud, rumbling purr.

Tomorrow she would figure out a way to trap the stupid animal in the basement and invest in earplugs. Tonight she was too worn out, physically and emotionally, to fight, too worn out even to care if it tried to kill her, wishing she'd never agreed to do this stupid job for her mother, and that she was back in Phoenix in the heat, alone and dumped yet again, with two engaged roommates who had nothing but love and joy to look forward to until the day they died.

Tears spilled over her cheeks and landed in her ears, cold, wet and horrible, making her cry harder.

Monarch stopped purring, got up and lunged toward her. Before she could clap a protective hand over her jugular, he rubbed one side of his head against her jaw, then turned to give the other side equal time, purring serenely. His fur was thick and soft, and he didn't smell animal-y at all. When he'd finished, he sat on his haunches, gazing down at her in the growing darkness.

She gave a sniff, swallowed convulsively. Monarch reached out a sheathed paw and laid it against her cheek, the gesture so shockingly human that Teresa let out an inadvertent *Oh!* of wonder.

Then he turned around, snuggled into the curve of her waist and put his head down to sleep.

Teresa gave a grudging sigh. Okay. This round was his.

She turned her back and pulled the blankets up over them both. If Monarch tried to slash her in her sleep, so be it. She was too tired and miserable to object. With any luck he'd asphyxiate.

To her surprise, after several long, anxious minutes during which the cat didn't move, she found herself relaxing and drifting off again . . .

Until she was jerked awake by an explosion of dogs barking – deep, menacing booms into the silence, followed by the shrill screams and yips of coyotes, the most terrifying, unholy sound Teresa could imagine, especially in pitch blackness. No moon, no street lights.

She lay rigid, heart pounding, eyes wide to their limit, registering nothing but dark. The sounds changed, grew closer. Snarling and more barking. A yelp. Another yelp. Of pain? Were they hurting each other?

Oh God.

The cat emerged from the covers. 'Monarch, what's happening? Make them stop.'

He yawned, stretched and found a new place to curl up. He was used to this. She wasn't.

Twice more that night the coyote–dog duet woke her, then finally, at next-to-nothing a.m., barely light out, the slamming of a truck door, and cheerful whistling. Cousin Jim. Teresa was unshowered, puffy-eyed, nauseated from panic and exhaustion and on the verge of running back to Phoenix. She was not going out there before coffee, into unfamiliar, animal-infested territory possibly littered with bloody dog and coyote parts, and pretending she was delighted to see him again.

She collapsed back onto the pillow. She couldn't handle what this job required, not isolation, not intrusive cats, not stubborn birds or attack dogs, not hostile uncles or cheery dawn-loving cousins or cruel demented grandmothers, and especially not having to make big important decisions about other people's lives.

Mom had been right. She was too anxious, and too disorganized, and she was also a quitter. Which meant getting through the next two weeks was going to take more courage and determination than Teresa had needed in a long while. Possibly more than she had.

✎ Chapter 5 ✎

My God! It's so late! What a surprise!
Time flew like lightning
Twelve times the hour has struck against the sky, and
I am still sitting near you.
Yet far from thinking it's time for sleep, I believe I
see one more ray of sunshine!
Marceline Desbordes-Valmore, 'L'adieu du soir'

Dearest Helen,

I haven't heard from you in a few days. I wanted you to have fun, to indulge your need to be independent, but not so independent that you don't need me anymore! Please keep writing. It means a lot to me to hear from you every day and know you're still thinking about me. You are never far from my mind.

The stuff in Madam Laurent's house sounds cool, but yeah, fussy. I'd feel like I was trespassing. Seems like if her father's books and stuff are that old and no one's reading them, then toss 'em. Glad you got to see the grave of your poetess and spent all that time at the Louvre. I like looking at art, but I don't see what you see, what other artsy types see. Give me a field, though, and I see things none of your foreign aristocrats would see in a hundred years. There's rarefied talent on all levels of human endeavor. We should be careful about valuing only a certain type.

Here in Kansas our farm news is getting more and more exciting. I'm following our guru, Earl Butz (Secretary of Agriculture if you didn't know), when he says, 'Get big or get out.' We're going to pull every bit of corn and soy we can out of this magical soil, my darling. It's going to be a beautiful life. I think we should name it Kellen Farm after both of our names. If you'd rather name it Heaven, that sounds good too! And very appropriate.

Yesterday I bought us a tractor, John Deere 4030, a 75-horsepower diesel. I decided to buy new. Other things we can get away with used, but you want your tractor to last forever. Boy did I want to splurge though. Deere has come out with the first of its Generation II models, the 8430. That baby is four-wheel drive with plenty of power. Too much for us, but what a machine! Then we need to buy grain trucks. I'm looking at Fords, probably will buy used, but the F600 is a pretty hunk of metal.

Tomorrow I'm going to look at another cutting-edge machine that just came out. Also too much for our needs, but I'm really tempted. New Holland TR70 Axial Flow Combine. Doesn't that sound impressive? It cuts stalks, husks the ears, chops up the waste and pours out the corn kernels in one pass. Can you believe it? It's a beautiful yellow, too.

You're going to live on a state-of-the-art farm, Helen, wave-of-the-future stuff. We'll go into big debt to start out, but crop prices are rising, and there are fantastic opportunities for export abroad. Productivity per acre is up and still climbing, weed and insect control means fewer losses per acre. It's going to be great for us.

Write to me write to me write to me. The house is so lonely without you. I guess it's too much to ask you to come home early, but I want to ask that. I worry you'll fall in love with the place and not want to come back, or God forbid fall for some Frenchie who doesn't deserve you like I do.

You are my all, my only love,

Kevin

Saturday, October 18, 1975

When Helen pulled out the last of Jeanette's dresses from her pink flowery closet, she and Natalie made the same ecstatic noise at the same time, a drawn-out *ohhhh* of envy and admiration.

The dress must have been made in the twenties, a sleeveless knee-length flapper style of black velvet, heavy with tiny beads following each other in iridescent pink spirals and bouquets of flowers, with silver stems and glittering rhinestone centers. Around the hem, kick pleats with green and blue patterns that evoked peacock feathers.

'What a dress!' Helen held it up to the light, watching the beads glint and perform. 'Did you ever see her wear it?'

Natalie shook her head. 'It would have been out of style by the time she married Papa. Perhaps she wore it to a costume party? Try it on. This one will fit you.'

'You think so?' Helen looked it over doubtfully. The rest of Jeanette's dresses had been too obviously narrow in the shoulders and tight in the waist. The actress must have been petite. But this one had no sleeves, nor was it fitted. She was dying to see if she could get into it.

'Yes, yes!' Natalie waved, urging her on. 'Try it.'

107

Helen laughed delightedly. She and Natalie had been having a wonderful morning in the overdone diva boudoir. They'd finally finished with her father's room and were fed up with masculinity. They'd read and tossed boxes of dull correspondence, keeping only travel journals and documents relating to the Laurent family history going back to the House of Bourbon in the seventeenth century. They'd thrown out his cigar collection, but kept the antique swords for wall decoration, and packed up suits, hats and shoes dating back to the thirties and forties to donate to anyone who'd take them. 'Theater companies perhaps?' Natalie had said. 'The old ones would make fine costumes.'

In contrast, Jeanette's room had been a girl's delight.

While Natalie tactfully busied herself, Helen took off her shirt and jeans, then slipped the cool velvet over her shoulders. A small panicked moment when the dress stuck and she was desperately afraid she'd tear it . . . then it slid gracefully onto her body, helped along by its considerable weight.

'How do I look?'

'Ah, *oui*.' Natalie clapped her hand together. '*Vraiment*, it was made for you. You look lovely.'

'Thank you.' Helen turned to the mirror hanging on the back of Jeanette's closet door and flushed with pleasure. She looked like a different person, a diva herself. The wide neckline flattered her high collarbone and long neck, and the fall of the dress was perfect for her boyish figure. Finally a dress that didn't make her long for bigger and better curves. She wished Kevin could see her in it.

'So. It is settled. The dress is yours.'

'Oh no. My goodness, no, I couldn't take it.' In fact, she could, but it wouldn't be right. 'Where would I wear it? My life isn't that glamorous.'

'Nonsense. A dress like this is always in style because it's part of history, a work of art. No matter where you go, people will enjoy it. I'm too old for fancy dresses, I have no children, and I want you to have it. Settled.'

'But—'

'*Non!*' Natalie raised an imperious hand. '*Pas un mot.*'

'You are sweet.' Helen impulsively went over to hug her employer, teacher and friend. 'Thank you. I love it.'

'Your face lit up when you saw yourself. *Alors!*' Natalie surveyed the room, stacked with clothes and papers in various piles to be kept, sold or disposed of. 'We made good progress today. What are your plans this afternoon? More fun with your new *copines*?'

'Yes. I'm working at the flower shop this afternoon then going over to their apartment for dinner.' Helen pulled off the dress, relieved when it didn't resist, and stepped back into her jeans, butterflies circling her stomach. Connie and Lilianne had officially offered her their third bedroom when Christine left. The rent they quoted had been so low – Connie must have been serious about Lilianne subsidizing – even Helen could afford it. But she dreaded bringing up the subject. 'I hate to ask you this after you've been so kind to me . . .'

'No, no. No keeping score. That's not how I work.' Natalie stood from the poufy chair she'd been sitting in. 'What did you want to say?'

Helen pulled on her striped sweater top. 'If you promise to give me an honest reaction.'

'Of course.'

'Connie and Lilianne's roommate is leaving next week. They asked if I would move in with them.' When Natalie's face remained impassive, Helen rushed on. 'If you don't want me to, it's fine. I love living here with—'

'Nonsense, *ma fille*.' Natalie clasped her hands, standing straight and calm, her aristocracy on full display. 'I have lived alone all my life because I prefer it. You must go be with your friends.'

'Are you sure?'

One of Natalie's thin eyebrows rose. 'Have I ever bullshitted you?'

The word was so unexpected out of that elegant mouth that Helen giggled. 'No! No, you haven't.'

'I am Natalie Laurent.' She swept her scarf over her shoulder, comically thickening her accent. 'And I do not do zee *bool-sheet*.'

'Oh my gosh.' Helen badly suppressed more giggles. 'Thank you. I will still see you for work every morning, of course, and stay through lunch. Not much will change.'

'No! Nothing will change except you will be able to enjoy your friends in the evenings without a long Métro trip back here. I'm very happy they asked you. Now you will live like a real Parisienne, which is what I'd hoped.' Natalie held up a finger. 'I've decided something else. When you leave, you must take Sarah with you. You discovered her identity. She's now yours.'

Helen's delight faded. 'No, no, no.'

'Yes, yes, yes. She does no one any good here.'

'But she belongs to your family. She might have some value.'

'Jeanette was not my family. She was my father's second wife, and value means nothing to me. I have no children to leave her to, and my nephew has only sons, with no interest in dolls. Yet she's been around long enough that I don't want to sell her to strangers. You are the perfect solution. You can teach your daughters to love her. That's what dolls are for. Not sitting untouched on a pedestal in a mausoleum.' She raised her teacher hand again as Helen started to speak. 'No argument. I am like a tsarina in this. I speak and you obey.'

Helen relented, making sure her smile had love in it. 'Thank you, Natalie. I will take good care of Sarah. And I'll think of you every time I see her or hold her.'

Natalie's cheeks turned pink. She cleared her throat. 'Bon. *C'est fait*. Now we have lunch.'

Lunch was veal cutlets with a tarragon cream sauce, salad, a cheese course, then snipped bunches of grapes served on china plates. So delicious, but as Helen's mom would say, 'too much of a muchness', especially in the middle of the day. It would be equal parts comedown and a relief to go back to easier, more casual food at the girls' apartment. Helen missed the peanut butter sandwiches she and Kevin loved, Helen's with strawberry jam, Kevin's with sliced banana. Neither would work with a tarragon cream sauce.

She and Natalie chatted easily, as they always seemed to, about whatever was on their minds that day, French history, art and literature, stories from their lives, current events, or sometimes just the weather. Helen had more and more admiration for the fight Natalie had waged in her youth, not only being admitted to a PhD program as a foreign woman in the US, but being hired by a university at a time when women were ridiculously underrepresented in academia for reasons that never made sense.

After a stiff espresso to combat the rich food – Helen still couldn't bring herself to drink more than half a glass of wine in the middle of the day – she double-kissed Natalie's cheeks, gathered up her coat and umbrella and headed out into the rain-soaked city, navigating the commute without having to think about it, feeling as she always did the thrill of being able to make her way around with confidence.

The rain was coming down harder when she exited the Métro at the Port-Royal stop and headed for Fleurs du Coeur – Flowers of the Heart – so pleased with the coincidence of Natalie's friend's shop being next to the Luxembourg Gardens, within walking distance of what would become Helen's home for the rest of her stay in France. Peering into the bakery she went into nearly every day on her way to the shop, she waved at Madame Noël, who urgently beckoned her inside.

'*Viens ici! J'ai quelque chose pour toi.*'

'*Ah oui?*' Helen went in with a big smile. Madame Noël had guessed at her love for baked goods, which might have had something to do with the fact that Helen swooned biting into whatever she bought. Midwestern bakeries didn't even come close to the quality that was second nature here. Paris had raised the bar on so much in her life.

Some things about going back home would be . . . a readjustment.

'*Voilà.*' Madame Noël brandished a tissue-wrapped broken Florentine, a blissful mixture of honey, orange peel, nuts and cherries, wafer-thin and dipped in chocolate.

'*Ah, merci, madame. Vous êtes si gentille.*' Helen bit into the crunchy cookie and let the flavors travel over her tongue. '*Mmm, je suis au paradis.*'

'*Mais bien sûr, tu es un ange.*'

Helen laughed. She was no angel, but the cookie *was* heavenly. '*Merci bien, Madame Noël! À bientôt!*'

A bounce in her step in spite of the rain, she finished the cookie practically skipping down the sidewalk toward the bright masses of cut flowers arranged in buckets under Fleurs du Coeur's beige awning, which welcomed visitors with the words *Bienvenue dans notre magasin*. In contrast to the gray weather, the flowers shone even brighter, all shades of tulips, roses and the tightly packed petals of ranunculus and peonies, alongside pots of camellias, cyclamen and dahlias. Inside were masses of orchids, pansies and ferns – Parisians loved their flowers. Shops bloomed everywhere one walked, giving the streets fantastic surprise bursts of color and fragrance.

Helen entered the shop with her dripping umbrella, inhaling deeply the glorious floral scents, even more vivid in the humid air. '*Bonjour*, Cybèle.'

Plump and pink-cheeked, Cybèle Guet had been Natalie's schoolmate; the two women had known each other since early girlhood.

'Hello, Helen.' Cybèle smiled broadly, hair up in a tight bun, wearing a belted silky striped dress and pearls, minus her usual white apron. Unlike most of the Parisians Helen had met, Cybèle loved to show off her English. 'I must go out this afternoon. Can you take over the shop?'

'Yes, of course.' Helen smiled calmly, heartbeat accelerating, and took down her apron from its peg in the back room. The few times she'd been asked to take over, she'd felt this same way, terrified and excited. Terrified of screwing up – she hadn't yet – and excited because she loved pretending she was a Parisian shopkeeper. It was a magical role, one Julie Andrews would play, singing songs and handing out daisies to children dancing on the sidewalks.

'Thank you. I expect a quiet afternoon.' Cybèle was putting on her raincoat and black gloves, tying a scarf around her head. 'I'll be back in an hour if my appointment is not late.'

Over the first half-hour, Helen was moderately busy. She made up two bouquets for women looking to spruce up their apartments, each of whom knew exactly what she wanted, and sold a potted pink cyclamen to an adorably polite dark-haired boy looking for a birthday present for his *maman*.

In the lull following, she did some of her usual duties – dusting, sweeping, replenishing stock. As she was ungracefully scrabbling to pick up a fallen pencil that had rolled under a shelf, she heard footsteps entering the shop.

'*Bonjour.*' She straightened and turned with a welcoming smile on her face, red from her efforts.

A man stood in front of her, also smiling, but as if she amused him. He was fairly tall and broad-shouldered for a Frenchman, typically dark in coloring. And literally breathtakingly handsome, with dark eyes and long lashes that made her entire body fizzy.

Good Lord.

'May I help you?' To her horror, she realized she'd spoken in English. '*Pardon, monsieur, qu'est-ce que—*'

'Yes. You may help me, thank you.' His English was accented but fluid, more British than American. He took a step closer; Helen had to look away. She'd seen many beautiful Frenchmen since she'd arrived, but none had turned her into this much of an idiot.

'What can I get you?'

'I need an apology flower.'

Hah! No point getting herself all worked up. He'd probably cheated on his girlfriend and thought giving her a ten-franc bouquet would fix everything.

'You have several options, *monsieur*. If this is a romantic apology, then—'

'No, no. Nothing like that.' He grinned mischievously. 'I hit a woman with a football in the park. She ran in front of me as I passed to a friend.'

Helen couldn't help smiling, wondering what he'd say if he knew what she'd unfairly decided about him. 'I see.'

'What were you thinking?'

He made the question sound way too sexy, the way you'd ask if you were in bed with someone who'd gone silent. Helen blushed violently and had to pretend to look around the shop for the appropriate flower. 'I have no idea.'

'I apologized to her, but she said she'd only forgive me if I bought her a flower.'

'Ah.' Helen tried not to roll her eyes, sympathies shifting. That kind of manipulative flirtation gave women a bad name. *No forgiveness until you buy me something.* She tried to remember what Cybèle had taught her about the language of flowers. 'I'd recommend roses in any color but red, or white tulips.'

'Hmm.' He was looking at her instead of the flowers, and she was very proud that she kept her cool and didn't blush again. 'I'll have a white tulip, please. And a red rose.'

'One of each.' Helen moved past him toward the buckets on the floor, curious about the selection. Apology first, seduction after? She chose the flowers and took them back behind the counter, where he stopped her from wrapping them together. 'Just the tulip. No need to wrap the rose.'

'Of course, *monsieur.*' Seduction first, apology after? She wrote up the charge, told him the amount and watched him scrabble in his pockets and count out change in his large palm.

'There.' He put the coins into her hand. She was annoyed at how minutely she noticed the contact with his fingers.

'*Merci, monsieur, bonne journée.*'

He took the flowers and tucked the white one in the crook of his arm, then, with a sexy wink and a flourish, presented the red rose to her. '*Merci à vous, mademoiselle.*'

Helen felt color spreading over her face again. 'I'm . . . I can't . . .'

'It's just a flower.' He put it down on the counter, gave her one more devastating smile and walked out of the shop.

Helen nearly collapsed after he was safely outside. The blush stayed on her face, refusing to respect her need to feel unaffected. She could only hope he didn't come back in or bother her again.

Luckily, the rest of the afternoon passed without a sign of him, though she couldn't make herself relax completely. Cybèle returned, and Helen left at her usual time, six o'clock, with the gift flower temporarily hidden under her coat, to avoid questions. She'd been on the verge of putting it back in its bucket, but . . . A handsome Parisian man had given her a rose, then disappeared. Why shouldn't she keep it? Even Kevin couldn't be threatened by an innocent compliment. She and he had forged total trust from the very beginning. They'd met in class, Kevin had asked her out, they'd had a wonderful time, he'd asked her out again, and they'd settled effortlessly into an ever-deepening passionate and honest relationship. The real thing.

Hoping the fresh air and rain would cool her cheeks so the girls wouldn't ask questions – Lilianne in particular noticed everything – Helen strolled along the sidewalks, occasionally smelling the flower, thinking about Kevin, feeling guilty for not having written as often as she'd promised. She was out with the girls several times a week now, at movies, having dinner, listening to music, or simply sitting in a bar or café enjoying each other's company. It was the perfect way to be in Paris, living far from the well-trodden tourist route, and was everything she'd hoped for.

But arriving back late at rue Lyautey, she was often too tired to write a letter. In the mornings, she was up to work with Natalie, and after lunch to the shop, or off on another exploration. Churches, museums or a long wander through a new neighborhood.

She was slowly but surely falling in love with the city, as she'd suspected she would. Such a beautiful place. As much as she was looking forward to her life with Kevin, it made her feel a little desperate to think she might never get back here.

Arriving at the girls' building – soon to be hers too! – on rue Pierre Nicole, she took one more deep inhale of the rose's sweet scent, then waited to be buzzed through the now-familiar metal door to the service entrance. Upstairs, she knocked on the apartment door, just to be polite, and poked her head into the kitchen, which smelled heavenly, like some sort of rosemary-scented stew. 'Anyone home?'

'Yes, we both are. Come on in.'

Helen took off her coat on the way to the living room, considered hiding the rose, then decided that dishing about it with the girls was too good to pass up. She rounded the corner and found Connie sprawled on the orange couch. Lilianne was on the green vinyl chair, putting a file folder back into her briefcase. Her hair was down, a thick, straight mane of expertly cut blond that Helen envied.

'Guess . . .' Helen had been about to announce the news that she'd been Natalie-approved to move in next week, but two things stopped her. One was the ice pack she noticed Connie was holding to her shin. The other was sitting on the coffee table along with bowls of peanuts and olives: a single white tulip in a vase.

'What? Why are you looking that way?' Connie glanced over at Lilianne, who shrugged and picked up a magazine.

'That.' Helen pointed to the tulip.

'Ah, you will never, ever, *ever* guess how I got that.' Connie waggled her finger on each word. 'I was walking . . .'

'. . . through the Jardin and got hit with a soccer ball by some amazing French hunk who bought you a flower to make it up to you.'

Connie's jaw dropped.

Lilianne lowered her magazine. 'Oh my God, she has ESP.'

Helen brandished her rose and plunked it into the vase next to the tulip, proud of her sangfroid. 'Apparently flowers are his thing.'

'No way. No *way*.' Connie burst out laughing. 'That is spectacular. Of course he went to your florist. Never occurred to me that Fleurs du Coeur was closest to us, or that you might be there. I think he'd scrambled my brains.'

'I can see why.' Helen kicked off her shoes and moved Connie's legs out of the way so she could sit next to her. 'He was something else, huh?'

'Un-be-lie-va-ble.'

'Should be an interesting dinner.'

Helen turned to Lilianne. 'Interesting how?'

'He's coming over. Gilles Aubert.' Connie was grinning hugely. 'I invited him. He'll be here any minute.'

'*Here?*' Helen's calm fled. 'He's coming here? For dinner? Tonight?'

'My, my.' Lilianne was looking annoyingly amused. 'So many questions.'

'Yes indeed. How *in*-teresting.' Connie cocked her head, studying Helen intently. 'You seem quite excited, or upset, I can't tell which. What happened? Did he make passionate *amour* to you with his midnight eyes?'

'No, no.' Helen blew out a breath, appalled at her response. Even more appalled that she hadn't been able to control it. 'I'm overreacting.'

Lilianne peeked over her magazine. 'Somebody is blushing *pret*-ty hard.'

'Hmm.' Connie leaned back, looking fascinated. 'I think we're going to have to fight over him.'

'*No!* Of course not.' Helen paused to force her voice down from hysteria. 'I'm already in love. As good as *engaged*.'

'But you're not yet.' Lilianne turned a page. 'I distinctly remember someone didn't want to be engaged while she was in Paris.'

Helen swallowed an angry denial that would only fuel Lilianne's point. Kevin was always telling her to back away from her feelings, to let logic take over.

'Aw, don't be upset. What happened? Did he do something? Try something?' Connie clenched her fists. 'I'll kick 'im where it counts . . .'

'No, nothing.' Helen forced herself to smile. 'Like I said, I overreacted.'

'I don't know about that. I bet there are women seeing psychiatrists all over Paris because they sat opposite him on the Métro.' Connie patted Helen's shoulder. 'Give yourself a break. We're all animals. We can't escape our nature, so there's no point trying. We found this guy whose karma is tied to ours, or whose electrical signals are on the same frequency, or who smells good, I don't know how it works. But it doesn't mean anything unless we assign it meaning.'

'She's right,' Lilianne said. 'It's not your fault the guy is gorgeous.'

'He is beyond gorgeous, Lilianne,' Connie said. 'I mean, the stuff of legend.'

'Fine, he's the stuff of legend. The point is, Helen, you don't have to do anything but be your beautiful and wonderful self over dinner. We're here to rescue you if you get the vapors.'

Helen giggled at that. 'You're right, of course you're right. He took me aback, is all, buying me the rose and . . . I'm being silly. Thanks for understanding.'

'What are friends for?' Connie settled back on the couch,

arms folded. 'So he comes over, maybe he's into you, or me, or both of us, or – ooh, maybe all *three* of us. I've never done—'

'Drawing the line there, honey.' Lilianne put down the magazine and got to her feet. 'I mean, I love you ladies, but . . .'

'I know, I know. The point is, we'll have a great time and be friends, it's all mellow, all cool.'

'I'm getting us a drink.' Lilianne strode on her long legs over to the small cluster of bottles they kept among the books on the rickety shelf in the corner. She pulled the cork stopper from a bottle of Jack Daniel's and brought over a small shot. 'You first, Helen. Medicinal purposes. Bottoms up.'

'Thank you.' The warm liquid heated a path down Helen's throat. Within seconds, she felt it lighting her veins. She'd have to be careful of this stuff. 'Mmm, that's good. I'm already . . . Oh gosh, I forgot my big announcement!'

'Oh *gosh*, say it isn't so!' Connie reached for the shot Lilianne poured her. 'Tell us, tell us.'

Helen stuck out her tongue at her friend's teasing. 'Madame Laurent is thumbs-up on me moving in next week.'

The women cheered, Lilianne poured Helen another shot, glasses were hoisted to clink in the center of the trio and downed, though Helen only sipped hers. Then hugs all around and excited chatter.

The front door buzzer sounded.

Immediate silence, followed almost as immediately by snorts of laughter.

'I'll let the poor guy up. When he sees Tulip White and Rose Red standing here, he won't know what hit him.' Lilianne strode out into the hall, where the intercom hung on the wall. '*Oui? Ah, bienvenue, Gilles. Prend l'ascenseur aux cinquième. Oui, à bientôt.*'

They stood waiting in the kitchen, Lilianne silent and cool,

Helen and Connie giggling nervously. Five floors down, the elevator door rattled open and grated closed. Ticking, clanking noises traveled upward until the car stopped.

So did Helen's giggles. Her head started buzzing. She conjured Kevin's adored face in her head.

The gate grated open.

Kevin's lean and muscled body. His love for her . . .

Footsteps.

'Count of three,' Connie whispered. 'We rush him and tear off his clothes. One . . .'

'Stop that.' Lilianne elbowed Connie in the ribs and craned to watch the door. 'I can't wait to see the look on his face.'

'We should have our flowers!' Connie dashed away.

'No, no,' Helen whispered. 'It's too flirty.'

But Connie was already back. She shoved the red rose at Helen and clasped her white tulip demurely just as Gilles's silhouette came into view through the curtained front door window.

A knock.

Helen's heart was thumping. The rose made her feel as if she were offering herself to this total stranger. He might take it the wrong way.

She should have done that second shot.

'Here we go.' Lilianne crept forward, flung open the door and leapt back.

'*Bonsoir*, Gilles,' Connie crowed.

And then they all got front-row seats to what surprise, embarrassment then amusement looked like on an amazing hunk. Even Helen found herself laughing at the fun of it.

'*Mon Dieu! Ce n'est pas possible.*' He pointed between Helen and Connie. 'You are friends?'

'Roommates. Soon, anyway.' Connie went forward, shook

his hand and craned up to get her cheek kisses. 'This is Helen Kenyon, whom you already know intimately.'

Helen could only meet his eyes for a second as she stepped forward. His hand was warm, as were his lips on her cheeks, one, then two.

'And this,' Connie drew back and gestured to Lilianne, 'is Lilianne Maxwell, a goddess equal to either of us. Lilianne, I give you Gilles, who must owe you a flower.'

'*Ah oui.*' He grinned and shook-kissed with Lilianne. 'Nice to meet you, Lilianne.'

'Likewise.' She was her usual pale, cool self. Was she made of ice? 'Glad you could join us.'

'I brought a gift.' Gilles hoisted a paper bag with words on the side that Helen couldn't decipher.

'Far *out*.' Connie clapped her hands. 'Is that from Lenôtre?'

'A friend lives near the rue Courcelles shop. I was visiting, so I got some dessert.' He put the bag on the kitchen table. 'Strawberry tarts and *éclairs au chocolat*.'

'May God rain blessings upon you.' Connie took his arm. 'Come into the living room. We were drinking Jack Daniel's.'

'Very good. I like Jack.' His eyes locked on Helen's; she wheeled around to go into the living room, hoping he was here to put the moves on Connie.

'How is your leg, Connie?' He took a glass of Jack from Lilianne.

'I'm expected to live.' She pulled up her black and scarlet peasant skirt to show the red welt on her shin. 'Looks worse than it feels.'

He cringed. 'It looks awful. So sorry.'

'It was fate bringing us together.' She sat on the sofa and patted the lumpy orange cushion next to her, accepting a third drink from Lilianne. 'Now you must tell us all about yourself, because we are dying to know. Leave nothing out.'

Helen found her previously abandoned whiskey, which she planned to nurse until dinner. She was plenty buzzed already, and there would be wine with the food. She chose a chair that wouldn't put her directly across from Gilles and prepared to settle in and notice every flaw so she could get over this.

'Let me see . . . I was born in a suburb of Paris. I attended the Sorbonne, where I studied philosophy and photography on the side. I work for Agence France-Presse as a photojournalist.'

'The height of cool!' Connie gazed in rapturous admiration. 'And you play soccer.'

'The game is called football, *mademoiselle*. It is the very best sport. And apparently a good way to meet women.' He grinned at Connie. 'Now tell me about you.'

'I am a traveler of the world, currently an avid student of Paris and Parisians.' She sent him a look that was so melting, Helen felt they shouldn't be watching. 'I work when I run out of money, otherwise I devote myself solely to beauty, food, wine, and love of all kinds.'

'*Ah, bon*. These are worthy pursuits.' He turned the grin on Helen, who started, then hoped to God he didn't notice the tiny movement. She could swear she heard a snort from Lilianne. 'Helen Kenyon, what about you?'

'I'm not very exciting.' She was still having trouble meeting those dark eyes. 'I grew up in the Midwest, went to college there. I majored in French literature. After graduation, my professor invited me to visit her in Paris for a few months to do some work for her. So here I am until February.'

Then I'll be going back home to my serious boyfriend.

She didn't say the words, struck by the certainty that they'd sound pointed, and that she might as well announce she was attracted to him.

'Excellent. Lilianne?' Her name pronounced in his deep-voiced French was transformed from spun sugar into rich dark caramel – yet Lilianne hardly seemed to notice.

'I'm the most boring of all.' She tossed her heavy hair back over one shoulder, unconsciously seductive. Helen just managed to stop herself peeking at Gilles to see if he'd been affected. 'I grew up in the US, in Connecticut, and work for my father's bank. I'm in Paris looking into a French company for potential partnership, all way too dull to discuss. But I'm interested that you chose philosophy. My uncle teaches philosophy.'

'Did you take classes?'

'I did. The basics, ethics, logic, some on the ancients. Not enough, though. I was a history person. What about you two?' She glanced at Connie and Helen.

'Not even close.' Connie shrugged. 'College and I separated ways before it got that serious.'

Gilles looked to Helen. 'And you?'

Helen grimaced. 'Just a survey course. I enjoyed the ancients. But by the time I got to Descartes, it lost me. The idea of wondering if what I know to be true is true or whether the world around me exists or not made me tired. Seeing a fork and believing it's a fork has never failed me. Not once.'

She sat back in triumph. There. Whole sentences. Decently intelligent. Much better than the blush-and-mumble she'd managed so far. She was so pleased with herself she tossed back the second shot, which went down much more easily than she'd expected.

Gilles chuckled. 'There were times I felt philosophic theory was invented to justify the philosophers' neuroses. Kierkegaard got cold feet before his marriage and decided anything not done in service to God was wrong. Wedding cancelled.'

'Oh, that was convenient.' Connie finished her whiskey and got up for more. 'What a dork. If he wanted out, he should have said so.'

'He did love her.'

'Then he's just exasperating. What's the point of denying yourself what you want and need? What every human wants and needs? There is no nobility in suffering.' Connie offered the whiskey around. 'Suffering is a total downer.'

'I did a paper my senior year on a French poet.' Helen allowed Connie to pour her a finger. 'Marceline Desbordes-Valmore.'

'Never heard of her.' Connie recorked the Jack and headed back to the couch.

Gilles leaned toward her confidentially. 'I haven't either, and I'm French.'

'When she was a young innocent, an older female friend she trusted conspired with a man to "ruin" her, as they called it then.' Helen made a face. 'Nice friend.'

'*Ah oui*,' Gilles said. 'Like the French novel *Liaisons Dangereuses*.'

'Yes, like that.' Helen glanced at him, then away. His focus was now on her, and she wanted to stay coherent. 'She wrote beautiful, heartbreaking poems about the experience. Not only that, but in the course of writing them, she devised new variations on the standard poetic meter that eventually became the norm. Except of course she was never acknowledged for her genius because she was female.'

'Oh, there's a big surprise,' Lilianne said. 'So what do we think? Do you have to suffer to create great art?'

'Ah, that is a question.' Connie held up her glass and contemplated it seriously. 'I say absolutely not. It's a choice. As an artist, do you define yourself by your suffering? Or by the beauty of what you create and by the love and happiness around you? Everyone has access to both.'

Gilles took a sip of his whiskey in the silence that followed. 'My pictures aren't great art, but I certainly suffer over them. The ones I miss, the ones that are almost-but-not-quite perfect.'

'That's what might have been,' Connie said. 'Also useless to suffer over.'

'Yes, but it's human nature to strive for perfection. You've told us tonight that you also chase it in your way.'

'Ooh, int-er-est-ing.' Connie cocked her head, blinking up at him, dimples adorably deep in her cheeks. 'I hadn't thought about it like that.'

'I've wondered if artists really do suffer more, or if they're just more communicative.' Helen gestured with her glass, feeling in her element, the type of conversation she hadn't been able to have since graduating college. 'Like an accountant might be just as heartbroken by loss or tragedy, but since he doesn't have a vehicle to express those feelings publicly, at least not in a way anyone would want to hear, we assume creative types suffer disproportionately more.'

'Ah.' Gilles's dark eyes were warm with admiration. 'That is a really interesting theory.'

'It is,' Connie said cheerfully. 'But I just realized that if I have any more whiskey, I'm going to take a dive into the olive bowl.'

Lilianne stood. 'Dinner is ready anytime. We can eat out here, or jam ourselves into the kitchen.'

'Let's jam.' Connie was already on her feet. 'It's that kinda evening.'

They crowded around the kitchen table and ate the lamb and vegetable stew, fragrant with herbs, along with baguette slices and wine Lilianne had bought for the occasion. Conversation flowed easily, and the more wine Helen had, the bolder she felt, and the less Gilles's gaze seemed to control her. He was well read without being pretentious, and seemed to know everything that was going on in the city – part of his job probably. Connie flirted outrageously, but with who-cares charm that kept it from being obnoxious.

After the stew, they downed the gorgeous pastries Gilles had brought – strawberry tarts, crusts crumbly with butter and fruit at the peak of sweetness, and crisp eclairs filled with thick *crème pâtissière* and topped by a rich chocolate glaze.

Dishes done, Gilles brought his camera into the living room, along with the unfinished wine. 'Will you let me do your portraits? If they turn out well, I'll send them to you.'

'Oh, what fun.' Connie struck an absurdly exaggerated sensual pose, draping herself over the couch. 'How's this?'

'Weird,' Lilianne said. 'I'll pass on the portrait, but thanks.'

'Oh come on, Lilianne. Don't be such a stick-in-the-mud.' Connie pulled her sweater down to expose one shoulder and pouted at Gilles. 'This?'

'Even weirder.'

'Let me take the three of you.' Gilles motioned to the orange couch, peering through the lens as they assembled themselves. He adjusted the lighting in the room, took another look, adjusted it again. 'Okay. Be natural there. No, no, you all look posed. Relax.'

'Someone tell a good fart joke,' Connie said.

Click. Gilles captured their laughter and teasing, the reaching of arms around each other and hilarity at the resulting tangle. *Click.* Again and again. And once more.

'That's it for me.' Lilianne stood. 'It's been great meeting you, Gilles. Unfortunately I still have work to do tonight. I hope to see you again soon.'

'Yes, thank you. Dinner was delicious.' They went through the double-kiss routine, then Lilianne left the room.

Gilles turned back to Connie and Helen. 'Now portraits of you two. Individual.'

Helen decided to jump on her cue. 'I should go too. It's late, and I still have to take the train back.'

'Ah no, I'll drive you.' He aimed the camera at her. 'I must take your portrait.'

He must not. For one thing, Helen hated having her picture taken by anybody. Having it taken by Gilles would feel too personal. And speaking of personal, she was desperate to avoid the intimacy of thigh-touching distance in his inevitably tiny French car. She'd had too much to drink and wasn't entirely sure of her ability to act appropriately.

Unfortunately, she didn't see an easy way to refuse.

That wasn't true. She could come up with a very easy way to refuse. *Sorry, but I have to go home and write a letter to my almost-fiancé, who still writes to me every day but hasn't heard from me since last week, and besides all my flimsy excuses about being busy, I don't know what's really stopping me writing back to him, and it's worrying me.*

About time she admitted it to herself. Her feelings for Kevin certainly hadn't changed. Maybe it was the daily-assignment nature of the letters that robbed them of their joy. She'd much rather write to him when she was in the mood. She'd suggest as much in her next letter.

'I'll go first, then you, Helen.' Connie bounced around the couch until she felt suitably settled. 'It'll be fun.'

Helen stood helplessly – at least telling herself she was helpless – watching as Gilles lowered the lighting further and Connie went through one outrageously seductive pose after another, Gilles following her with his camera. *Click. Click. Click.*

By the third click, Helen had figured out what he was doing. Capturing Connie not at the peak of her theatrical excesses, but between, when she was off guard, mouth not as perfectly pouted, body not as rigidly posed, eyes not as deliberately smoldering.

It was brilliantly timed, fascinating to watch.

And then it was over, and Helen's turn to be his camera's victim.

She sat where Connie had been, feeling absurdly vulnerable, trying to look relaxed, legs crossed, arm extended along the back of the sofa, her best smile in place.

No click.

Gilles emerged from behind the lens. 'You're stiff. Not natural. Relax. Lean back. Maybe hold a glass of wine if it makes you feel more at ease.'

Connie was quick to hand over her glass. 'Here, use mine. Just be sure to give it back. Necessary medication.'

Helen accepted the wine and faced Gilles again, trying not to look like she was posing.

Still no click.

'Close your eyes and imagine yourself in the place you love best,' he said.

She hesitated, tempted to call a halt, then gave in and rested her head against the back of the couch, closing her eyes. What place did she love best? She'd never had to decide. She loved Paris, certainly, she'd loved the farm Kevin had bought, she loved her family's summer vacation rental on Lake Wawasee, but she knew none of those places well enough to name one best.

A mental image appeared of the paperbark maple in their backyard in Zionsville. To escape her brothers, she used to take a blanket and her dolls or books out to its generous shade and read or play alone for hours, feeling as if she were in the tree's protective embrace.

Click.

She opened her eyes to find Gilles had moved closer, nearly to her knees. God, he was gorgeous. *Click.*

'Yes, good.' He pulled the camera away long enough to smile at her, a smile that would have had her jittering all over the place earlier in the evening, but which felt natural and right in this light, in this room, on this night.

She smiled back.

Click.

Neither of them moved, Helen with the smile undying on her lips, Gilles with his camera fixed on her face.

'Wow.' Connie inserted herself into their frame. 'Those are going to be fantastic. I wish we could get Lilianne to pose. We'll want these pictures of our time together in this apartment for the rest of our lives. I know it. I feel it.'

'Yes. I'm sure.' Helen forced herself off the couch as Gilles stepped back. 'Thank you, Gilles. I should go.'

'I'll take you home.'

'No, you don't have to.' She headed into the hall and grabbed her jacket, then gestured to Connie. 'Stay and have another drink. I'm used to the trip at night. It's probably out of your way anyway.'

His dark eyes didn't waver. 'I insist.'

What was she supposed to do if a man insisted? She couldn't remember the last time anyone but Kevin gave her a ride home. Probably in high school, after the prom, when Larry Ricca's dad had driven them, insisting that his son not get behind the wheel after the post-prom party. They'd spent the trip pretending they weren't making out in the back seat.

'Thank you. It's very nice of you.' She went to hug Connie, once again forgetting about the stupid kissy thing. 'I'll be in touch about a move-in date. Bye, Lilianne!'

130

Lilianne appeared in the hallway and put her arms around her for an American hug, taking the opportunity to whisper, 'Be yourself. Not who you think you should be.'

That made no sense to Helen's nervous and tipsy brain, but she returned the embrace and smiled gratefully. 'See you soon.'

'Yes.' Lilianne stepped back and gave a saucy wave. 'Have fun!'

Helen wished she hadn't put it that way. It was just a ride home. 'Thanks.'

She followed Gilles out of the apartment into the oppressive silence of the balcony passage to the tiny elevator, in which she said the first thing that came into her head. 'Where did you learn to speak such good English?'

'I've spent time in London. I dated an Englishwoman for a year or so after university.'

The news that he'd dated someone was no surprise, meant nothing to Helen, and therefore should not have caused a jealous heart-stab. 'I've always wanted to go to London.'

He raised his brows at her. 'Then go.'

She laughed. 'It's not that easy, but thanks.'

'It's very easy. One ferry ride across the Channel. I'd love to show you London. When would you like to go?'

Now.

She didn't look at him. No backing down this time. 'I don't think my boyfriend would appreciate that.'

'Why? He doesn't let you have friends?' The elevator landed. Gilles pulled back the gate and motioned her through.

'Of course he does. But . . .'

'I'm teasing. I understand.' They walked across the courtyard in silence, footsteps echoing on the grubby tile, Helen feeling as if more needed to be said, but unsure what that could be.

They pushed through the service door. Gilles pointed to one

of the tinny-looking motorbikes parked all over sidewalks in the city. 'Here we are.'

Helen stared in horror. She was supposed to ride on one of those through crowded streets? At night? Kevin would have a fit. So would her parents.

'You've never been on one?'

She shook her head. 'I don't think . . .'

'Yes you do.' Grinning, he tossed her his helmet, which she had to catch or risk it being damaged. 'You're going to love it.'

She loved it. She loved every minute except the first one, when she realized the only thing she had to hold onto was Gilles, and that the only thing protecting her from the speeding tons of metal around her was nothing.

But the fresh Parisian night air in her face, and the careful skill with which Gilles drove past the fantastic sights of the city of her dreams gradually took over her fears, and by the time they pulled up in front of Natalie's apartment, Helen was glowing with exhilaration.

'You're right. I loved it.' She handed him back the helmet. 'Thank you.'

'There will be more rides.' He turned off the engine. 'I very much like your friends.'

'They are great. I was so lucky to bump into them.'

'What does your boyfriend do?'

'He's a farmer. In the Midwest. In Kansas.' Helen nodded repeatedly, as if giving Kevin approval she wasn't sure Gilles would.

'Is it serious?' His expression was impassive except for a slight groove between his brows, betrayed by shadows from the street light. 'Are you serious with him?'

She was horrified to feel her throat tightening. 'Yes.'

He studied her face. She forced herself to stare back, daring him to find anything worth noticing as a weakness. 'And this is the life you want? With your intellect? On a farm?'

'Yes.' This time her voice cracked and she had to say the word again, too muddled to come up with indignation over his assumption that farming was anti-intellectual.

He nodded, then reached to touch her cheek. 'Then I look forward to being your friend while you're here, Helen.'

Helen swallowed audibly. She'd been honest, true to Kevin and their future. No mistakes, no ugly consequences. And none of the fun Lilianne wanted her to have. 'Me too.'

They said goodnight, dutifully double-kissing. Helen let herself into the building, waited for the door to close behind her, then paused to listen as Gilles started up his bike and drove away, the motor fading into the night.

She couldn't wait to see him again.

∽ **Chapter 6** ∾

Teresa finished her last bite of cinnamon raisin toast and put her dishes into the sink. May morning sunshine gilded the pastures and enriched the ruddy brown coats of the cattle, making it much harder to feel as if her grandmother's ranch had been designed specifically to torment her. During her dawn despair after the hellish night, while Jim was doing whatever he did for the animals, she'd tiptoed down the hall, ejected Monarch from the house as silently as possible, then crept back into bed for her best sleep of the night. A shower and a good breakfast had nearly restored her to normal.

At least tonight she'd be expecting the misery.

She picked up her coffee cup, added another inch from the pot and headed for the stairs, having decided to start the day in the basement, where most of the house's storage—

Ack! She ducked, managing not to scream. Cheddar had chosen that moment to whiz past her head, making her spill hot coffee on her bare foot. 'Ouch, dude, warn me next time.'

The cockatiel responded with a few charming chirps, bobbing his crested head from his landing spot on the stair's newel post. Teresa frowned at him. 'I'm going downstairs, past you. No more sneak attacks.'

Chirp chirp chirp.

She'd fed him that morning, seeds, pellets and small bits of lettuce and apple, and spent a long time watching him crack and ingest the seeds, using his tongue to manipulate the larger ones with amazing speed and efficiency. It was very possible she'd get to tolerate this bird. Possibly – no promises – she'd even get to like it.

Him. Get to like him.

She started down the stairs, talking and getting politely chirped answers. When her head drew even with his feet, Cheddar gave a fluttery hop and landed on her shoulder. Teresa flinched, but screwed up her courage to let him stay. 'I'll give you a ride down, but you can't sit there all day. And don't poop on me. I like this shirt.'

Chirp.

Step, step, step, bird balancing, coffee perilously sloshing, until she reached the bottom and gave her shoulder a shrug and a shake. 'This is your stop. You're adorable, but you're triggering me.'

Cheddar flew off and landed on the chest freezer.

'Good.' Teresa put her coffee on one of the built-in book-shelves and started taking stock. Besides the doll room, there were four other doors, which she opened in turn. One, the bathroom, two a laundry/furnace room, three ... Grandpa Kevin's workshop. She went in, beset by memories and images of working there with her father.

Richard Clark had been one of those people who could build or fix anything. Teresa had been captivated by both talents, following him around their big house, learning and trying, while her brothers showed no interest whatsoever. Dad had also been into model trains, and the two of them had built an entire miniature village around his track setup. Houses, city hall, a church, a post office ...

So much fun. Teresa ran her hands over Grandpa Kevin's

well-used saw table, annoyed at how those memories made her miss her father. All the tools and materials back in Phoenix had disappeared with Dad to his new home and family. How many of his new little ones had he taught the same things he'd taught her? Were any of them girls who replaced her?

Ouch. Every time Teresa thought she'd dug out and discarded the last painful consequence of Dad's desertion, another poisonous tendril would appear, rooted in yet another spot.

She turned and strode briskly back to the main room, where Cheddar welcomed her with a garbled stream of various noises.

'You're right. No point brooding over things you can't change.' Teresa pulled open the fourth door with more force than necessary.

Aha. This would be the bulk of her work for a day or two. Boxes, about a dozen, all neatly labeled. Contrary to what Mom seemed to think, the house was not cluttered with unused crap. Teresa could easily manage all this in her two-week allotted time.

The box nearest her was labeled *Christmas* in black marker. Teresa opened it and poked inside. Helen would want this one. Standard stuff: boxes of ornaments, lights, a string of plastic bells and . . .

Chirp chirp. Squawk. Cheddar paced restlessly back and forth on his box, crest raising and lowering.

'What?' She didn't speak cockatiel yet.

Squawk. Chirp. Gargle.

'Bored?' She took the bells over and laid them next to him. Cheddar gave them a look, then used his beak to move the strand from one place to another. *Jingle jingle* here. *Jingle jingle* there. And back. And forth. Yes, he was cute.

She took out a few more ornaments that seemed bird-safe, then closed that box and put it aside to keep. Helen could decorate her new apartment, though since this was the lone Christmas box as far as she could see, Teresa guessed the holiday was usually spent with James.

The next several boxes were labeled *Records*, dating from 1976 to 1996. Given that Kevin died in 1996, she'd bet these were farm records. Teresa texted James, asking for permission to chuck them, barring any interesting finds, and was gratified to receive an immediate *Absolutely*.

She dragged the boxes over to a corner of the room and spent the next few hours separating recyclable from not, making piles of clips and folders that could be reused or donated and trashing everything else. Occasionally, when he seemed restless, she'd switch out Cheddar's toys for other items from the Christmas box.

He was undoubtedly having more fun than she was.

The next four boxes in the storage room were all labeled *Taxes*, which promised even more excitement. After checking with James, who instructed her to toss anything older than seven years, she was back to the same drill, this time accumulating piles for the shredder as well.

At one o'clock, Cheddar came upstairs with her for a quick lunch and more coffee, then, refreshed and grudgingly ready for more drudgery, Teresa gingerly put out her finger to the bird, and grinned like a fool when he hopped right on. Screwing up her courage to mimic a move James had demonstrated, she gingerly moved her hand near her shoulder. Cheddar immediately stepped on. It was kind of a thrill to interact with a wild-ish creature, even in this little way.

Teresa Clark, bird whisperer.

Downstairs, Cheddar back happily manipulating his toys, she sifted through two more boxes of boredom, then went back for a third, picking her way through the by now impressive mess on the floor. Behind the next box, she found something much more interesting – a small battered steamer trunk with cracked leather handles and locks and latches of dulled brass.

Promising. She pulled it into one of the few clear spaces left in the playroom. The latches gave easily, the opened top revealed twin lift-out compartments with hinged lids.

Old trunks were so cool.

Teresa removed the left compartment, a sturdy box a few inches high, stiff cardboard covered in beige paper sprinkled with faded green fleurs-de-lys that matched the trunk's interior. She paused before opening it, to relish the fantasy that she was on the brink of a monumental discovery – priceless treasure or a portal to a parallel universe. Why not? It happened regularly in the books she used to escape to after her family splintered.

Instead, a pile of postcards and letters, old photo envelopes stuffed with pictures, a wild-looking scrapbook of pictures and drawings and various other keepsakes: matchbooks, menus, museum maps . . . all from Paris, decades old.

Paris! When had Helen and Kevin gone abroad? Teresa's imagination had them firmly fixed at this address. Had they honeymooned in the City of Light, in those early joyous and hopeful years of their marriage, before Helen's alcoholism and affairs torpedoed it into bitterness and dysfunction?

She picked up the bundle of postcards and letters and rifled through them. All seemed postmarked 1975, some from Helen's parents in Zionsville to her in Paris, but most from Kevin with a return address here on the farm. Another stack proved to be letters from Helen sent to Kevin. Not their honeymoon, then. Helen must have gone with someone else. Were they married yet? Mom had never mentioned this trip.

Cheddar chirped out fascinating conversation while Teresa took the carton over by the sliding doors, where there was more light. She chose a couple from the huge pile of Kevin's letters and opened one eagerly, drawn to hear the voice she'd been deprived of by her grandfather's early death.

His letters were short and very plainly written, filled with details of his progress getting the farm set up for the life he obviously couldn't wait to share with Helen. So they weren't married yet. Maybe engaged? Teresa read a few more, and found that while Kevin was undoubtedly a good man, and clearly madly in love with Helen, his letters were pretty dull, and he complained quite often that Helen wasn't writing enough and wasn't there to take care of him. Granted, this was the 1970s, but . . . His gripes didn't age well. A little disappointing.

Teresa picked out some letters from the smaller stack, those Helen sent to Kevin. Within a few sentences, she was struck by how fluidly her grandmother wrote, and how vividly she brought Paris alive.

A memory resurfaced, of sitting snuggled against Grandma Helen in the living room upstairs, being read to. Used to the halting monotone of her parents, Teresa had been entranced by the energy and musicality of Helen's voice, and the changes she made in timbre and accent for each character. Teresa could no longer remember the story, but she remembered the dawning fascination with what a book could be. Back home in Phoenix, she'd made regular trips to the school library, determined to access those magical worlds again. In recent years, reading for pleasure had been replaced by college homework, then by television, by phones, friends and nights out. How had she let herself be drawn away so easily from an activity she loved so much?

After finishing Helen's letter, she went on to another, and another, all filled with lively descriptions of neighborhoods and parks, churches and palaces; even graveyards sounded thrilling in her words. Her stories about the people she spent time with,

Connie and Lilianne in particular, were spirited and often hilarious. Clearly she was having the time of her life.

And yet . . . she also expressed her excitement about joining Kevin on the farm after her stay. She apologized for not writing more often, and explained lovingly that while corresponding every day was a romantic idea, it wasn't always practical. But that he should know she was with him every minute, in her heart and in her mind.

Teresa frowned, and put the letters back in their stack under the cracked, grubby grip of an ancient rubber band, struck by her grandparents' old-fashioned power dynamic. Male demanding, female apologizing. When did that change? Was it alcohol that had brought out the cruel, dominating part of Helen's personality? Or was she paying lip service on paper to appease Kevin while gallivanting all over Paris?

She replaced the letters and slid a batch of photos from a drugstore envelope. As far as she could tell, they were all taken in Paris, and most were of the same two women, one tall, blond and stylish, one short, curvy and bohemian. Connie and Lilianne?

She picked up a larger manila envelope, which contained pictures of the same two women, but now also a third, a pretty blonde with straight shoulder-length hair and girl-next-door features. Teresa studied her for about five seconds, then gasped. *Helen*. As Teresa had never imagined her. So young, so beautiful, so full of sensual energy.

These photos were very different from the previous set of casual snapshots, which Helen must have taken, since she wasn't in any of them. These were beautifully lit, artistically composed. Instead of I'm-having-my-picture-taken smiles, the women looked both natural and posed.

Teresa looked carefully through, gradually getting a sense

of the three subjects, each so different. The stylish blonde appeared less often, only occasionally smiling, photographed lean and long in lights and shadows, mostly black and white shots that emphasized her stunning features and flawless skin. Only in one, when she was looking over her shoulder, did she seem to drop the cool mask, eyes wide and startled, hinting at a haunted soul.

The dark curly-haired woman, on the other hand, splayed herself out in every possible way in every possible color, loving the camera, which loved her in return. Teresa found herself smiling, wondering if Helen had kept in touch with her, what she was doing now, whether she was still inspiring smiles wherever she went, even from total strangers.

The next photo faded Teresa's smile into uneasy awe. Helen, relaxed on a bright orange couch, glass of red wine in her hand, looking into the lens as if it had just caught her eye. Her lips were parted, hair cascading down the back of the sofa to form a curtain around her face. A sensual but not purposeful smolder, an alluring but not kittenish pose, almost as if she couldn't help herself. A remarkable combination of sex and innocence, virtue and sin. It was hard not to imagine it as Helen symbolically teetering between the two. What had happened to push her over? Or had the restless sexuality been in her all along? How had devastating her husband and damaging the lives of her children been worth those annual weeks of stolen pleasure in the years to come?

And the wine . . . a foreshadowing of Helen's devastating addiction?

Her phone's ringtone brought Teresa back to the present. She glanced at the time. Nearly four. She'd promised to go to the hospital again today. Ick. The letters, pictures and memories had further confused her feelings about her grandmother.

'Hi, Mom. Can you hang on a second?' She approached Cheddar, who was poking an ornament across the freezer, then waddling after it to repeat. To Teresa's delight, he again hopped onto her extended finger, then onto her shoulder. 'Just getting the bird to go upstairs.'

Like she did it all the time.

'You're not scared of him?'

She picked her way through the clutter toward the stairs. 'He startled me a couple of times at first, but he's sweet. He keeps me company.'

'You sound okay. Did you sleep well?'

'Nope.' She headed up. 'Coyotes.'

'Oh God, those awful beasts. Sometimes they'd get in fights with the dogs and there'd be blood all over in the morning. Sometimes the chickens would peck one another to death. Vicious place. Have you seen James yet?' Cheryl sounded anxious. 'Did he give you any trouble?'

'I saw him yesterday. And no, not a bit.' Teresa was determined to keep Mom out of tense situations. 'Jim was by this morning, but it was beyond me to get out of bed at that hour.'

'Did you see your grandmother?' Again that worry in her tone, too fast and high.

Teresa rushed to soothe her. 'Yes, she's okay, Mom. You were right about the confusion. It was pretty extreme.'

Her mother gave a long sigh. 'If it ever happens to me, I'm going to kill myself way before I stop making sense.'

'Well that's cheerful.' Teresa managed to get Cheddar back into his cage with a bite of apple, and closed the door. She was getting the hang of the bird thing.

'I don't want to be a burden to you kids. I don't want you and your brothers to go through what we're going through with Helen.'

'Thanks, Mom.' Teresa bit her lip, hating that she was the cause of any more worry. 'We'll be okay.'

'I hope so. Oh, I was remembering – I think one of my dad's parents' friends gave him and Helen an antique liquor box for their wedding. Very fancy, with crystal glasses and decanters inside. You might want to keep an eye out for that. It's probably worth a good bit. And if you want to send me pictures of the dolls, I can do some research on their value and help you out a little.'

'Sure.' Teresa walked to the window in the living room. The sunshine had become intermittent between big puffs of clouds. Chickens were doing their jerky chicken walk, pecking and scratching, pushing off with their back feet as if they were attempting the moonwalk.

In the goat pen, an explosion of movement, a couple of the smaller animals leaping convulsively, jumping as if they were being stung. Teresa felt panicky. What was she supposed to do? 'Uh-oh.'

'What? What is it? What's happened?'

'The baby goats are twisting and hopping around. Is that normal?'

Her mother laughed. 'You are such a city girl. They're called kids, and yes, normal. They get totally hyper. They smell horrible too. The whole place smells horrible. Chicken shit is the worst.'

'Huh.' Teresa didn't find the smell horrible, but then she'd been safely inside most of the time, and was in no hurry to explore the coop.

Muffled laughter broke into the call, and what sounded like an electronic announcement. 'I'm at work, so I can't talk, but I wanted to check on you.'

'At work? It sounds like you're at the mall.'

'Ha! I wish. Someone's on a video conference with the door open. I'll have to shut it. You take care, sweet sugar. And remember, if it gets too much, you come right back here. If it's too tense, if James gives you trouble, you tell him to screw himself and come home. I'll find some way of making the house thing work.'

'It'll be fine, Mom.' Hearing she *could* wimp out made her more determined than ever not to.

'You call me whenever you need me, okay? Middle of the night, whatever. I'm here. I know this is hard for you.'

'Thanks, Mom.' Teresa watched the goats doing their goat thing. Gamboling? Whatever it was called, it looked both hilarious and joyous, like tiny wild broncos trying to unseat non-existent riders. 'I'll be okay.'

'Hmm. I'll check on you again soon, okay? Bye.'

'Love you, Mom. Bye.'

Back in her room, resigned to another hospital trip, Teresa washed her hands of the old-document dust and changed into a dress and leggings with a light spring sweater and flat-heeled ankle boots that wouldn't add inches to her height. Katie and Addie were champs on stilettos and platform shoes, but they looked so uncomfortable that Teresa jumped at the excuse not to wear them.

Speaking of, she should call Katie tonight, see what was up with her. Something to look forward to.

Dressed and reluctantly ready, telling herself it would be a quick check-in visit, Teresa double-checked to make sure she had everything so she wouldn't have to come back inside, in case that dog – Zig, James had called him – was on the hunt. Glasses, purse, phone and . . . In a light-bulb moment, she ran downstairs to retrieve the manila envelope of portraits from the trunk. The pictures of Helen and her friends would give them something to talk about.

Shutting the door as quietly as possible behind her, she did a careful front-yard scan, then tiptoed to the car, jumped in and slammed the door. The second she started the engine, Zig bolted over from the side of the house, stopping in confusion when he realized he'd missed his chance. Ha! Teresa gave him a regal wave and drove off, cackling victory.

The route to the hospital was pleasant on such a gorgeous day, GPS guiding her, windows cracked enough to let in the breeze but spare her the ugly frizzies, oldies station blasting. The parking lot was fuller than it had been the previous day, but she found a spot, accepted her Monday sticker from lobby registration and headed up to the fourth floor with some of the pictures tucked under her arm.

Grandma Helen was in her room, but in contrast to the day before, she was on her feet, hands on a walker. A nurse – or physical therapist? – stood beside her.

'Look who's here.' Helen smiled, and Teresa instantly saw the woman she remembered and adored from her childhood, and an echo of the young beauty in the pictures, endangering her determination to remain aloof. 'Betsy, this is my granddaughter, Teresa.'

'How nice.' Betsy beamed. 'We'll get you back in bed now, Helen, then I'll leave you two to chat.'

'I've been walking. Up the hall and down the hall and up the hall – what an adventure!' Helen winked at Teresa. What a change in one day.

Betsy put a hand on Helen's walker. 'You remember how to do this?'

'I do, yes.' Helen backed up to the bed, extended her right leg and sat, leaning back at an angle. 'I'm not supposed to bend anything too far.'

'That's right. Look at those abs work. You are so strong.'

'Comes from wrestling animals for the past thirty years.' Helen pushed herself farther back on the mattress, then maneuvered her legs up and around bit by bit, until she could relax against the raised head of the bed. 'There. Done. Every day it gets easier.'

'Perfect.' Betsy laid a pillow between Helen's legs before she pulled up the sheet. 'You are all set. Great session. I'll see you tomorrow.'

'Yes, please. The harder I work, the sooner I get out of here. Thank you, Betsy.'

'You're welcome.' Betsy patted Teresa's shoulder as she passed. 'You enjoy your visit.'

'Thanks.' Teresa faced her grandmother, astounded at what she was seeing. Helen was nothing like the broken, confused weakling of the day before. 'You look good today, Grandma Helen. Very strong.'

'So they tell me.'

'I guess they must have put back some of the brains they took out.'

Helen looked startled. 'What?'

'Oh.' Teresa colored. 'You said yesterday that you thought the surgeons had taken out your brains.'

'I said that?' Helen shook her head. 'I was loopy on the drugs they give me. They lowered the dose last night, thank God. I feel much more alive today. I do seem to get confused sometimes, though. I think it's this place. I can't wait to go home.'

Teresa hid a wince. 'Did they say when that might happen?'

'Another week or so. I need to be able to take care of myself a little better. Someone will have to stay with me in the house at first. James said he was looking into hiring someone. Or maybe you can stay with me?' She looked so hopeful, Teresa didn't have the heart to tell her – again – what the plan was for her future.

'We'll see.' She brandished the envelope, exactly the conversation changer she'd hoped it would be. 'I found this in your basement.'

'Oh?' Helen tipped her head back to focus through her glasses. 'What is that?'

'Pictures of you when you were young. You and some friends. In Paris.'

'Where did you find those?' Her voice sharpened slightly. 'Why were you going through my things?'

'I'm here to help.' Teresa pushed back her alarm, kept her tone gentle, thinking about the letters she'd read, trying not to look as guilty as she felt. 'Remember? I'm organizing, clearing out stuff you don't need, like old income tax forms and farm records from decades ago, that kind of thing. To save you having to do it when you . . . move out.'

'Oh. Yes. I remember now.' Again that sharp edge. 'Your mother decided all that. Without consulting me.'

Teresa bristled at the hostility toward her mother, the only one of Helen's children brave enough to do the hard stuff. Mom *had* consulted Helen about moving, and Helen had agreed. She just couldn't remember.

Helen fumbled for the bed controls and brought the head up higher so she could see. 'Where did you find that envelope?'

'In the basement.' Teresa took out the photos before Helen could start asking again what she was doing down there.

Helen took the pictures, gazed at each for a long time before turning to the next, all her sharp edges softening. 'My goodness. I'd forgotten how good he was behind a camera. I haven't looked at these in such a long time.'

'Who took them?'

'Our friend. Gilles Aubert.' She held up the one of herself relaxed on the sofa. 'Look at that. He captured parts of me I

147

don't even remember having. A photographer down to his toes, a photojournalist, more specifically. That girl there, in the one you're holding, that's Lilianne Maxwell. They got married, her and Gilles. And the brunette hamming it up all over is Connie Pappas.'

This was much better. If Teresa could keep the questions coming, she might avoid more of the famous Helen temper. 'Were they friends from college?'

'No, no.' Her grandmother put the photo of herself face-down on top of the others. 'I met them over there.'

'Who did you go with? What were you doing in Paris?'

'I went alone.' She let her head relax back and clasped her hands against her chest. 'To work for one of my professors, Madame Laurent. Natalie. Such a generous woman. Descended from French nobility. She died . . . I get confused when I think about the years. But it was a long time ago. We stayed in touch after I left France.'

'Are you still in touch with the others?'

'No.' She deflated with a sigh. 'Connie died a year or two after these pictures were taken. I'm not in touch with Lilianne and Gilles.'

Teresa watched grief take over her grandmother's features, and felt a stab of reluctant compassion. 'You look like you're having so much fun together.'

'We were. We truly were. Some of the best times of my life. We were young. We had no responsibilities. It couldn't last, of course, but everyone should have a time like that.' Helen lifted her chin to peer at Teresa. 'Have you had yours yet?'

'I . . . Not really.' Teresa thought of Vegas, which didn't happen, wasn't sure that would have counted anyway. She'd started working at sixteen, and never stopped. Mom had no money for vacations.

'You should go to Paris. Or we can go together someday!' Helen's expression turned sunnier. 'I would love that. I haven't been in so long. An enchanting place. It gets into your blood.'

'Did you and Kevin ever go together?'

'Kevin? Oh no. No, he refused. He didn't want to go anywhere, not even Canada. Not a traveler at all. He loved his farm, and he loved his family, and that was enough for him.' She didn't sound hostile or condescending, just wistful, which left Teresa with nothing to defend her grandfather against. 'Kevin and I were all but engaged when I left for France, you know, but I wanted one last chance to be something other than daughter and wife. I thought then that he and the farm would be my life forever after.'

'I see.' Of course it hadn't turned out that way. Helen had left the farm and Kevin quite frequently.

'I couldn't have known, of course, that he'd die so young.'

Of a broken heart. 'How long were you in Paris?'

'Five months, wonderful months, and then . . .' Helen's voice lowered. 'Then it was time to come home.'

The silence lingered. Teresa waited for more, curious in spite of herself.

'There were many times in the years after that I regretted not staying longer. But life is a series of choices. That was mine. Then I found that after making a hard decision, another one rears up. You can live with regret for the road not taken, or you can kick that devil out and find ways to be content. I did the latter. Or tried to.'

Teresa looked down at the sheet covering her grandmother's legs, trying to control her sudden bitterness. There might not be any point in continuing to punish this woman for past sins as harshly as Mom did, but it was hard not to feel anger at someone blithely calling cheating an attempt to be content.

Helen gathered up the pictures and slid them back into the envelope, performing the simple action slowly, as if it caused her pain. 'You know what I've found, Cheryl?'

'Teresa.'

'Hmm? Oh, yes, of course. Teresa, I'm sorry. After I left Paris . . .' Her blue eyes went vague again. 'Now what was I saying?'

'You were talking about making hard decisions.'

'Was I?' She looked troubled, stroking the manila envelope as if it were Monarch curled up in her lap.

'You were going to tell me what you found after you decided to leave Paris instead of staying.'

'Oh, yes.' Helen handed the envelope to Teresa, eyes back in focus but her face gray and drawn. 'I found that the hardest part is learning how to separate healthy, instinctive caution from fear brought on by self-doubt. Before you can choose wisely, you must know yourself well. I'm not sure I did.'

Teresa nodded somberly, not entirely sure what her grandmother was talking about.

'Well.' Helen picked up the bed control and lowered herself back to level. 'I was a different person then. And now I'm very tired, and my hip is hurting, so I'm going to kick you out, my dear.'

'Sure, of course.' A relief. This visit had gone deeper than Teresa had anticipated.

'Do come back. If you're still here after today.'

Teresa pressed her lips together, not wanting to commit. 'It will take me a while to go through the house.'

'Oh. Yes.' Helen stared blankly at the ceiling. 'Your mother's plan to stash me away in an old-people prison.'

'She worries about you, Grandma.'

'I doubt that very much.' Helen's eyes closed. 'Your mother

is like her father, like Kevin. Both of them worried only about themselves.'

Teresa's indignation spiked. She left the room instead of blurting out what she was thinking, that Mom was working like mad to keep Helen safe and cared for, and that Helen should be damn grateful.

In the shiny hallway, she encountered Betsy, who fell into step beside her. 'Nice visit?'

'Short. She's tired.'

'We keep 'em busy here. She's doing great with her therapies, though. One of our stars.'

'She seemed more lucid today.'

'Everything will keep improving from here out.' Betsy stopped at a branch in the hallway. 'More strength, less pain, and the confusion will lessen, probably gone in a few more days, though some can hang on for longer.'

Teresa tried to take in what Betsy had just said. 'Are you saying the surgery caused her confusion? What about the dementia?'

'I wasn't aware she had any.' Betsy took a step away down the hall, impatient to move on to her next case. 'We only meet the patients after their surgeries. You'd need to discuss that with her doctor. But yes, if that's the case, that won't improve.'

'Thank you.' Teresa continued toward the elevator, feeling lighter, the conflict with James in better perspective. Even though he was in denial about Helen's long-term dementia, he was right to say its current level would improve. They could agree about that.

Outside, in her car, she sat with the windows down, not in the mood to go back to the lonely house with its attack dog just yet. Impulsively she pulled out her phone and called Katie, who answered eager to hear the latest. They chatted for a while about the ranch and Chernobyl Granny, and for much longer about what font Katie should use on her invitations, and when the new round of engagement photos would be ready to use on the wedding website, and whether Katie should ask the bridesmaids to buy slippers they could dye to match their gowns.

Teresa had met Katie freshman year in college when she was wallflowering at a party, about to give up and leave. Katie had sidled up next to her, produced a flask and a wink, and surreptitiously sloshed some kind of alcohol into Teresa's cup of boring punch. Flattered that this woman, who was clearly from a higher social stratum, would pick her out for rescue, Teresa had allowed her shy self to be led around the party and introduced. After that, Katie would often materialize in her room and tease Teresa away from studying for some wild adventure outside her comfort zone that she never would have come up with herself. Yes, Katie could be bossy and self-centered, but she was also a boatload of fun, and being around her made Teresa feel more like the so-cool babe she wished she were.

Slightly deadened from her bestie's chatter on top of the difficult visit with Helen, Teresa decided after they hung up that she needed a burger and fries to revive her. Her phone recommended the Burger Stand, which wasn't too far and sounded perfect, except that she hated eating by herself in public.

One lonely and self-conscious hour later, full and somewhat more relaxed, she drove back to the house, girded for the looming battles, whether cockatiel, cat, coyote or cousin. She was also thinking, Zig permitting, that it might be nice to cut some of the peonies blooming out front and arrange them in pink and white bouquets in the dining room and living room.

As she approached the house, she saw a pickup in the driveway, smaller than the one James drove. Probably Jim's. Teresa was still embarrassed at having avoided him that morning, so she'd ditch the peonies for now and go find him.

Zig was nowhere to be seen when she pulled up, so she hurried into the house, deciding to greet Jim from the back deck in case she needed a hasty retreat.

Cheddar chirped as she stepped in, and they had a brief conversation during which she told him he could come out of his cage after she talked to Jim. She wouldn't forget, she promised.

Halfway to the sliding door in the dining room, a thought struck her. She backtracked to the kitchen and grabbed a couple of cold beers, hoping a friendly overture would be welcome, and that Jim would want to stay as neutral as she did. An ally – besides her mom and new heartthrob Cheddar – would be wonderful.

Jim was inside the pen with the sheep, goats and donkeys. He caught sight of her as soon as she stepped out.

'Hey, cousin!'

'Hi, cousin!' Teresa grinned and hoisted the beers. 'Thought you might need one when you're done.'

'I'd love it right now. C'mon down and meet the herds.'

She wasn't crazy about that idea. 'Do you know where Zig is? He has it in for me.'

'Yeah, Dad said you had a problem. He's not here now. I'll keep an eye out. He'll listen to me.'

'Okay!' She made herself sound hearty, hoping his authority would override the dog's bloodlust, and climbed down onto the grass and toward the fence, keeping watch on all sides, hoping her paranoia wasn't too obvious. One of the Pyrenees ambled over to investigate; she thought it was the smaller of the two. At least those dogs were calm and well behaved.

Not surprisingly, Jim had grown. He was taller than his father, about Teresa's height, though he still had the mop of brown hair and sprinkling of freckles that made him look as boyish at twenty-five as he had at ten. Two years younger than

Teresa, a year older than the twins, he'd shared her brothers' fascination with animals, and had mostly been their playmate growing up.

'Welcome to Kansas.' He took the beer she offered over the fence and pointed to the gate around the corner of the pen, opposite the chicken coop. 'Do you want to come in?'

'I'm . . . a little cautious around animals. At first, anyway.' She backed up a step as the goats gathered to investigate the newcomer, bleating and pushing at the fence, their slit-pupiled eyes looking weirdly devilish. 'Or I don't know, I don't dislike them, I just . . .'

'Just haven't encountered too many goats, sheep and donkeys in Phoenix?'

Teresa laughed. His nose still turned up, enough to be cute, not enough to seem swinish. He was still adorable, all Peter Pan boyishness and energy. 'Not too many.'

'How're you getting on here?' He took a brief pull from the beer. 'Big change from what you're used to.'

'It's an adjustment. But I wanted to help.' She decided to take a risk. 'Even if I'm not that popular around here.'

Jim's face clouded. 'Yeah, it's hard on everyone. My dad and your mom don't see the situation the same way. Grandma was doing great before she fell, so it's hard to see why she couldn't do great again after she recovers. It's not like she's a frail ninety-year-old.'

'Mom's a worrier. And she's right that it's better to move her before the dementia gets worse.'

He was looking at her strangely. 'Dementia? Helen? She doesn't have dementia, just the surgery confusion.'

Teresa shifted uncomfortably. Not surprisingly, he was taking his father's tack. 'And if she fell once, she could fall again, maybe worse the next time.'

'She fell because one of the goats jumped onto the crate she was standing on and knocked her onto a trough. That could happen to anyone.' His voice was calm and matter-of-fact. 'My dad broke his ankle last year jumping off a ladder onto uneven ground. I cracked some ribs when I got between a scared horse and a wall. Farm life can be dangerous.'

Teresa was incredulous. Mom had been so clear about what happened. What crap had James been telling his son? 'Actually, she lost her balance in the kitchen.'

'Uh . . .' He took another sip of his beer, then turned his attention to the animals. 'You heard that from your mom, I guess, huh?'

Teresa stiffened at the implication. 'Maybe that's what Helen told her. And I didn't know post-surgery dementia was a thing. Maybe Mom didn't either.'

Jim nodded slowly. 'So, I was there when Dad explained the temporary confusion thing to her over the phone, slowly and clearly, just like the doctor explained it to us. She didn't want to hear it.'

Teresa felt the ground shift. 'Maybe she didn't believe him.'

'Dad doesn't . . .' Jim blew out a breath, then raised the bottle toward his lips, but stopped before drinking. 'I think that's where I bow out of this topic, cousin. You're here and I'm glad to see you. I don't want us to be part of this fight.'

Teresa made herself relax, shoulders, diaphragm, abdomen, ashamed of rising to the bait and embarrassed he'd been the sensible one first. 'Sorry, Jim. I promised myself I'd do my job and let the rest roll off me. You're right. Mom and Uncle James can figure it out.'

'I'll drink to that.' He did take a sip that time, still looking out at the herd. 'How are you and Cheddar getting along?'

'Not bad, actually. I think he likes me.'

'Course he does. You're his cousin too.' He turned back toward her, all freckles and fun again. 'Has he whistled tunes for you yet?'

'Don't think so.'

'You'd know. Try whistling to him. He'll do it back if he's in the mood. Quite the virtuoso. You know the escape story?'

'No. Or at least I don't remember.'

'Helen was determined not to clip his wings, because he wouldn't be able to fly as far or as well. So one day the door gets left open by mistake, and zoom, he's through it and gone. They can't find him anywhere. Helen gets desperate and calls the police to report him missing.

'Two days later, she hears from the police. Someone down the street had called in and said, "You're going to think I'm crazy, but there's a bird outside my window whistling the Ode to Joy from Beethoven's Ninth Symphony."'

Teresa cracked up. 'I thought I remembered he could do that, but it seemed so unlikely I assumed I'd dreamed it.'

'After that, Helen agreed to have his wings minimally clipped to keep him safe. You probably noticed he can only fly short distances, and only downward.'

She hadn't noticed, but would pay attention now. 'He's good company.'

'And here's another miracle coming toward us with her pals. Cleopatra, the sexiest goat you'll ever see.' He pointed to the goat – goatess? – in the middle of a second pack coming to investigate. 'Check her out.'

Teresa checked. Cleopatra was ambling toward them, hips swaying, taking slow, dainty steps that nearly crossed over one another, like a model slinking down the runway. She had a beautifully shaped face, wide forehead with narrow slanting eyes, and long, long lashes.

Teresa let out a whistle. 'You are right, that is the sexiest goat I've ever seen.'

'Right? She's really sweet too. Hey there, girl.' The goat stopped and leaned against his thigh as he petted her flank. Teresa didn't know, but it sure looked like goat affection to her. Trust anyway. 'You want to come in and meet her?'

The goat crowd jostled and bleated, noses pushing through the wire toward Teresa.

'No . . . thanks. Not yet. She's gorgeous, though. After a few more days I'll be braver.'

Maybe.

'No rush.' He took another swig of beer. 'So how d'you like being all alone in the middle of nowhere? Must be kinda strange if you're used to the city and not into animals.'

'It's been okay.' She wouldn't mention the tears and misery. 'I only got here yesterday. Not much time to get lonely.'

'So Chloe – my girlfriend – and I are meeting friends tonight to go dancing. You wanna come with us?'

Predictably, her *no* reaction kicked in. No, she was tired. No, she was shy of strangers, No, she wasn't much of a dancer. No, she wasn't really that into the club scene. But as in Phoenix, she refused to be that wet-blanket person.

No fear.

'Sure!' Teresa nodded enthusiastically, stomach tightening with the familiar dread of the unfamiliar. She wouldn't know anyone. She'd feel too tall and too clumsy on the dance floor. The music would be too loud. Everyone would be drunk, and she'd have to keep pace in order to relax. 'That sounds great. Thanks.'

'We'll pick you up around nine. That okay?'

More nodding, more stress, while she mentally went through the clothes she'd packed. 'What's the vibe?'

'Totally casual. It's a seventies bar, supposedly. People wear bell-bottoms, gold chains, et cetera. but it really doesn't matter what you wear. All ages go. It's really fun. At midnight they play "Car Wash" and spray the crowd. Bubbles and all. Crazy.'

'That's . . . Oh!' She pointed urgently to a donkey making a beeline for Jim. 'Incoming.'

He turned nonchalantly. 'Heya, Smoke.'

Teresa watched him stroke the coarse gray fur and felt something like envy. She'd never had a pet, always been vaguely creeped out at the idea of an animal loose around the house where it could jump out and startle her at any moment. Moot point since Mom didn't want either the extra work or the expense. 'They trust you.'

'These guys are really gentle. Once they get used to seeing you around, they'll trust you too. I don't have superpowers.'

'Yeah, but you grew up with them.' He looked so peaceful standing between goat and donkey, both obviously crazy about him. It gave Teresa a funny feeling, sort of a wistful sadness.

'Donkeys are naturally protective. That's why Helen put them in with the sheep and goats. They'll kick the crap out of anything that bothers the herd. The Pyrenees, too – you've met Pearl and Tusk. They're guard dogs, Zig is a herder. He and Cleopatra are the only animals named for their behavior rather than their color. Zig stands for Zigzag, but border collies traditionally have one-syllable names. Easier to yell commands.'

'No kidding.' Teresa watched the donkey's huge eyes go soft with bliss as Jim stroked his fur. It didn't *look* dangerous.

'By the way, Dad wanted me to tell you, while you're here feel free to eat from the garden. There's not tons there yet. Lettuce and greens, peas and radishes. They'll go to waste if you don't use them.'

'Oh. Okay.' Teresa had never pulled anything out of a garden in her life, but she wasn't about to admit that to Nature Boy. 'You don't want them?'

'We have our own garden, a community plot. Dad has one at his house.'

'Right.' Of course. Gardens galore.

'I'll get your eggs. We keep them in a bowl outside the coop, take as many as you want.'

Teresa was appalled. 'Not in the refrigerator?'

'They come out coated with a substance that keeps them safe from . . . Okay, well to be blunt, a chicken's poop and eggs come from the same place, so—'

'I'm good.' Teresa held up her hand. 'Don't need to hear more.'

'Got it.' His grin wobbled as Smoke nudged him, a reminder that the petting had stopped. 'If you wash eggs, they need refrigerating. But they'll keep for a couple of weeks without. Oh, and if mosquitoes bother you, Dad gave Grandma a repelling machine for Christmas. It should be by the back door, with the instructions.'

'Okay.' While he spoke, Teresa stood taking in her surroundings, the older sheep and goats grazing, little groups of baby goats – kids – racing and jumping around, climbing onto whatever they could find, only to jump off again. The lambs seemed more timid, sticking close to their mothers. The sounds were constant, a mom–baby duet of maas, baas and bleats. In the paddock beyond, cows and calves made long shadows in the setting sun. To her left, chickens in various vivid colors and sizes pecked and scratched around the coop. Behind her, in separate paddocks, the mule and bulls stood planted and powerful.

'This place is really special, isn't it?' Jim had been watching her. 'Helen made it what it is. A one-woman tour de force.'

Teresa wrinkled her nose. 'Grandpa Kevin started the farm.'

'Yeah, no, that was different. He had a modern industrial farm here, corn and soybeans, pesticides, chemical fertilizers, genetically modified seeds, the whole bit. When our little place couldn't compete with larger farms, Grandma Helen begged him to change to greener methods. She'd gone to a lecture where they preached the gospel of healthy soil and sustainability, and really got into the concept. Grandpa Kevin was too stubborn to listen, even while the place was hemorrhaging cash. After he died and Grandma sold most of the land, she insisted it go to an organic farmer, even though she had much higher offers.

'Then she had to get rid of the corn, replenish the exhausted dirt and plant native prairie grasses for grazing. So much hard work, but she was determined. Or a little obsessed, as Dad puts it. He and Kevinjay worked really hard right alongside her, and they turned the place around.'

'Mom too.' Teresa was stung by the omission. Cheryl had developed her distaste for farm life by being up to her eyeballs in it from the moment she could walk.

'Cheryl was gone by then. Married and outta here.' He cleared his throat. 'But I don't think she ever cared for that kind of work.'

Teresa couldn't disagree with that. She could disagree about the farm, however, which Mom said had thrived under Grandpa Kevin's care, but she had to admit it was unsettling how sure Jim seemed of his facts. Maybe the farm had gone downhill after Cheryl left Kansas and Kevin hadn't wanted to admit as much to his beloved daughter?

She was starting to see how decisively the family had been split into Kevin and Helen camps, and that the ugliness she and Jim both wanted to avoid was a wide and muddy spot in the path between them, one it would be hard always to step around. According to Mom, Uncle James resented his older sister because she'd been able to escape farm life through marriage at eighteen, and he'd been stuck here. Totally unfair to Mom. So farm life wasn't for her, to each his own. And nothing about her leaving meant James had to stay.

Jim glanced at his phone. 'I'd better go. I have some work to get done before the fun starts. Thanks for the beer. We'll see you at nine?'

'You will.' She waved, backing toward the house, saw his focus shift before she heard the dog behind her. Teresa whirled around to see Zig heading straight . . . past her and up to the fence, tail a blur of wagging, following Jim's progress toward the gate, giving an excited bark when he emerged through it.

'I forgot about this guy.' Jim took the dog by his collar. 'Okay if I introduce you?'

Teresa reluctantly retraced her steps. 'Don't let him loose.'

'Not a chance. Here, put your hand down and let him smell you.'

'He won't bite?'

'I promise.'

Teresa put her hand down. The dog sniffed her fingers, tail wagging. 'Okay? Better now? No more jumping?'

'Try petting him.'

She swallowed, determined not to show her anxiety, and laid a hand on the dog's head, jerking it back when he abruptly changed its angle.

'Try again. Move slowly. He won't bite. His ears are up, tail wagging. He's just checking you out.'

She tried again. More sniffing, slower tail-wagging, then he looked pleadingly up at Jim.

Teresa snorted. 'I hear what he's saying. "Can I stop being nice to the weird lady now?"'

Jim laughed. 'It's progress. Sorry he was behaving strangely before. He knows you now. That should help.'

Should.

'Thanks. See you tonight.' She considered walking backwards all the way up to the house, but decided that might look as if she was keeping an eye on Jim instead of Zig, so she summoned her courage and turned around, expecting at every step doggy paws planted in the middle of her back.

Safely inside, she all but collapsed. Between poor sleep and a long day of complicated discussions and discoveries, plus dread over having to socialize that night with complete strangers in a venue that would make conversation nearly impossible, Teresa just wanted to go to bed and stay there.

Without the cat.

She did go to bed, but only for a nap, limiting it to half an hour so she wouldn't be groggy, then woke with an unpleasant jolt of adrenaline. *Why* had she agreed to go out tonight? The evening would be such a strain.

Back in the living room, remembering her promise, she let Cheddar out of his cage and brought him to the basement, where the trunk remained tantalizingly open. She picked up the second lidded carton, its corner catching on black cloth underneath, which moved to reveal in the trunk's main body a riot of iridescent colored beads swirling across black velvet.

Wow.

She put down the carton in favor of this new excitement, which turned out to be a dress, sleeveless, intricately beaded, looking every inch vintage flapper, which it undoubtedly was, with kick pleats and gauzy black fabric knotted at intervals at the hem's edge. Too early for Helen's generation. Not the kind of dress Teresa associated with her grandmother's conservative Midwestern parents. Had Helen bought it in Paris? From a vintage shop maybe? Where had she worn it? More to the point, for whom? If it was hidden in this trunk, undoubtedly not for Kevin.

Giving in to temptation, Teresa took off her clothes and carefully slipped into the dress. On a woman of normal height, the hem would reach mid calf. It hit Teresa just above the knee. She ran upstairs to Helen's room, where she remembered a full-length mirror on the back of the closet door.

The dress was fantastic. Transformative. It skimmed over her skinny, tubular body and hung elegantly, her figure made for the style, where modern clingy formalwear demanded curves and cleavage. It shimmered when she moved, flouncing saucily at the hem. The look needed only pointy-toed strappy shoes and a beaded headband stuck with black ostrich feathers to be complete. Had Helen felt the same way inside it? Sexy and available?

Teresa's grin faded; she went back downstairs and put the dress aside, carefully folded. She wasn't the kind of woman who wore dresses like that. It would probably sell for a bunch to some one-percent woman with plenty of places to wear it.

Back in her own clothes, wistful for the glimpse of the woman in the mirror, Teresa returned to her work on the trunk. The second tray, like the first, was full of paper mementos – letters, travel brochures, ticket stubs, city maps, all from wonderful faraway places: Istanbul, Morocco, Tahiti, Costa Rica, Japan.

She stared queasily at the riot of printed color. If Kevin refused to travel, these must be evidence of Helen's annual affairs – vacations with 'friends', Mom said she'd called them – carefully preserved right here in Grandpa Kevin's house, under his nose.

Teresa continued leafing through the tray, using the tips of her fingers as if the paper was contaminated. Mom's stories of hearing Grandpa Kevin weeping alone had cut deep.

How would Helen meet all these jet-setting men in a farming community in Lawrence? Did she advertise? *Lonely Kansas farmer's wife seeks sugar daddy for exotic travel adventures*? Did she have her own money for the trips and pick up guys once she was there?

God forbid she'd used money Kevin earned from the farm. That would be really low.

Teresa bit her lip, disturbed to remember Jim's insistence that there hadn't been much money, certainly not enough for overseas travel. Whether or not he was right about the profitability of the farm, something didn't add up.

At the bottom of the compartment, she found a sleeve of pictures from a drugstore developer and opened it reluctantly, bracing for photographic proof of her grandmother's betrayal. If Helen had died first, either Kevin or her kids would have found these easily. Was that what she'd wanted? It was hard to fathom such carelessness.

All the photos contained some configuration of three adults in various cheerful, friendly poses in various gorgeous locations. The tall blond woman from the Paris pictures, Lilianne. Helen herself. And a very handsome dark-haired man.

Teresa shuffled through the keepsake brochures and ticket stubs, hoping for clues, but found only the occasional scribbled address or phone number. She looked through the pictures again, turning each over. Finally she found one with a scrawl on the back: *L & G Tahiti 1993*.

L & G, Lilianne and Gilles? But . . . Helen said they'd gotten married. So she *did* go on vacations with friends? Married friends she'd known from Paris? That wasn't cheating. Where did the affairs fit in?

Unless Lilianne and Gilles were complicit and there was another man on these trips? Maybe the person behind the camera, which would explain who took all the photos and why he never appeared in any. At least Helen hadn't been thoughtless enough to keep incriminating evidence.

Teresa arranged the pictures and papers back in the box and closed the lid, sick and uneasy. She'd done practically nothing today but stumble over conflicting facts and viewpoints, the result of misunderstanding and miscommunication and maybe false assumptions. But on whose part? And why?

A glance at her phone – she'd been down here a while – showed it was time to get ready for the upcoming social disaster. She moved to close the lid of the trunk for dust protection and noticed under the cloth covering the flapper dress more black velvet. A large bag, with a gold cord drawstring and something bundled inside.

She absolutely had to peek.

The drawstring cord took a while to untie, but once unknotted, it loosened smoothly. Teresa pulled back the soft fabric and gasped, reaching eagerly.

A stunning doll with sad eyes, round cheeks and chin and a sweet mouth, dressed in a fantastic emerald gown and a faux-fur cape closed with a costume jeweled brooch. Around its neck, more rhinestones, and more still in the tiara on its dark head of realistic curling hair. The doll was about two feet tall, and heavy. An exquisite work of art that made the collection in the closet Teresa had loved for so many years look cheap and tourist-tacky.

Teresa cradled the doll, looking down into the child-like face so at odds with the fancy outfit, and felt unexpectedly moved, even more unexpectedly possessive. The doll seemed in good shape, hair a little crooked, seam unraveling on the hem of her gown, one leg a little wobbly, but otherwise perfect. Why was this beauty lying in a trunk, hidden in a musty bag instead of on display with the others? What had she meant to Helen that earned her this time in dark imprisonment?

Back at the trunk, Teresa uncovered another dress, this one demure blue cotton with a full ruffled skirt, puff sleeves, brightly embroidered bodice and a sweetheart neckline, about as different stylistically from the flapper gown as champagne to sarsaparilla.

Who was Helen? Farmer's wife? Parisian seductress? Sinner or saint?

More mystery, more confusion. Teresa had come to Kansas prepared to do the difficult job of organizing and making decisions about the contents of this house while navigating her mother's pain, her uncle's disapproval and her grandmother's reluctance.

But the myriad contradictions had both unsettled her and piqued her curiosity. Now, in the short time she had left here, she also wanted to get to the truth.

ಎ Chapter 7 ೨

Teresa sat out on Helen's deck, miracle mosquito repellent deployed, nursing a mug of coffee and a mild hangover, watching clouds flow and evolve across the sky, layers moving at different speeds, colors ranging from muted gray to pristine white to threatening charcoal. Here and there bits of blue sky promised a sunnier day to come.

The coffee was hot and delicious. The hangover sucked. Last night at Funky Town, she'd done exactly what she'd predicted. Jim, his girlfriend Chloe and two other couples had been nothing but welcoming, but the friends were clearly a years-old unit, and it was impossible not to feel like an outsider. Socially awkward, overstimulated by the noise and crowds, dorky on the dance floor, Teresa had coped the way she did clubbing in Phoenix with her friends, downing drinks to cover her nerves and grinning maniacally to show how much fun she was having. Chloe was a pixie ball of energy with a pierced nose, pink hair, tattoos on her wrists and dance moves that made Teresa feel like a telephone pole. In fact, a drunk guy had wandered over to her and asked how the weather was up there, an exasperating line that every tall person in the world wanted stricken from the universe. Drunk and fraying, Teresa had shouted, 'Shh, my tarantula is asleep in my pocket,' which, as hoped, startled him into scuttling off.

Jim et al. had been having such a good time, they'd stayed until closing, which meant at midnight they were all still on the dance floor when the song 'Car Wash' came on and the crowd was sprayed with soapy water, which made all the girls in the place scream and the guys open their mighty jaws for a 'wooooooh' that nearly broke Teresa's eardrums.

Somehow she'd missed the gene that would have enabled her to love this type of evening, also a favorite of her Phoenix crowd, which made her feel even more like an uncool misfit.

She'd gotten out of bed late after a fitful sleep from too much alcohol and the usual coyote concert, plus cat-in-her-bed. She was losing the fear that Monarch would rip her throat out in the dark of night, but it still half panicked her to find a furry body next to her every time she woke up. Shortly after noon already, and she'd been sitting for a couple of hours watching the ranch do its ranch thing. That had been her day. Oh, and brooding. Her expertise.

The number of contradictions was unnerving. Did Helen have long-term dementia or didn't she? Did she lose balance in the house or get knocked down by a goat in the yard? Did she agree to move to a retirement facility or didn't she? *Should* she move to that facility or shouldn't she? And that didn't even touch on the sordid issues from her past.

Finally Teresa told herself she couldn't figure it out sitting there, and to stop trying. So instead she watched the donkeys peacefully grazing on the prairie grasses, goats and sheep milling around them, tails and ears flicking, and groups of kids occasionally overcome by a need to dash somewhere else, racing and leaping like demented imps. All amid the antiphonal duets of moms and offspring.

As time passed, the watching became a type of meditation, the movements of the animals hypnotic in their simplicity.

Cows, bulls and mule grazed with delicate deliberateness, standing contemplatively, lying down to enjoy a rest. Calves occasionally wandered too far and moms would bellow for them to rejoin the herd. In jerky, strutting contrast, the vividly colored chickens were constantly busy, scratching and pecking, occasionally chasing each other away from coveted patches of ground.

All of them could just be. No grandmothers to worry about, sibling rivalry to get stuck between, no cartons to unpack, no mysteries to grapple with. As much as she still wasn't crazy about the idea of getting physically close to any of them, Teresa could glimpse the attraction of being able to tune into their simple, natural energy every day.

Nearer, also intriguing but less interesting to gaze at, the vegetable garden. Now that her coffee had done its work perking her up, and breakfast toast had calmed her stomach, with psycho dog off somewhere she couldn't see and the Pyrenees – Pearl and Tusk, Jim had called them – hanging with the cattle, Teresa decided to investigate, maybe find something she could have for lunch. This would be a first for her, getting food from anywhere but a supermarket or occasional farmer's market.

On her feet, she went inside for a basket she'd noticed in a kitchen closet, and – keeping a careful eye out for Zig – made her way toward the garden. The plants were arranged in neat rows, lines blurred here and there by weeds that should probably be pulled. There must be garden tools somewhere.

She opened the wire fencing and stepped inside.

Problem.

Teresa had never harvested anything in her life. The Paradise Valley house she'd grown up in, back when Dad still felt like being her father, had a flawless, chemically maintained, mechanically watered lawn in which a garden would have been out-of-place chaos. Mom's yard in Coronado was rocks. Some of Teresa's friends' parents had raised bed or container gardens in Phoenix, but when the girls got together for play dates, their focus had not been on vegetables.

Nearest to her, tall tangled plants with dangling pods. Peas! That one she knew. At least harvesting those was straightforward – pinch the pods carefully off the vine. She figured that out after her first yank nearly uprooted the entire plant. In a matter of minutes she had a nice pile in the basket, and felt like a true daughter of the earth.

The greens gave her pause. She recognized chard and lettuce, maybe arugula? Did she cut the leaves she wanted or pull out the whole plant? Her trusty phone was happy to give instruction. She cut stalks of chard and thinned the lettuces so they could grow larger, terrified she was doing it wrong – the plants left looked lonely and bedraggled. There were other things growing she didn't recognize that also looked to need thinning. A tug on one unearthed a bright pinky-red rounded root.

Radishes! Check it out! Teresa laughed. Pop, out they came, red and gorgeous from thick brown dirt. A minor miracle.

She ate out on the deck, plowing through a ho-hum ham sandwich, then eating her Teresa-harvested salad the way she ate French fries at the Stand burger joint in Phoenix. Maybe her body was starved of vitamin whatever-was-in-salad, but she'd swear it was close to the best vegetable experience of her life, and that was after three months dating food purist Joe.

Another cup of coffee, consumed leisurely on the deck, and she was reborn. The clouds had reorganized enough to let the sun peek through in random patches of yellow scattered across the dark green landscape.

Impulsively she stood again and went down the steps, a record second time venturing out of her comfort zone, this time to approach the donkey-goat-sheep pen. She wanted to watch the animals from closer up, including Cleopatra, the sexiest goat alive. How funny even to think of a goat as sexy, and how enviable to be her, blissfully unaware that she evoked such thoughts. Teresa would love to have no idea of her own ranking on the attractiveness scale. She could put on Helen's beaded dress and parade around anywhere she liked.

As they had yesterday, the sheep ignored her, but a group of goats and kids came over to investigate, their strange horizontal pupils taking her in, muzzles pushing against the fence, unselfconsciously sexy Cleopatra among them.

One of the donkeys – Smoke? Ash? – ambled up to the fence. Teresa recoiled as he put his nose over to investigate. 'Hi. Please don't eat me.'

He stood quietly looking at her, soft eyes veiled by thick lashes. Teresa didn't know what else to do, so she looked back at him. He kept looking. She did too. And it all seemed pretty unthreatening, so Teresa put out a trembly finger and touched the top of his head, half expecting him to jump and scream at the contact. Which was what she'd have done if he'd tried to touch her.

His fur was coarser than she expected, but not unpleasant. He didn't rear up and snap off her finger with his big teeth. So she touched him again, letting three fingers, then her whole hand linger on the small tuft of hair that grew between his ears like a funky mohawk, arm tensed to pull back if he reacted badly.

He didn't, in fact he seemed pleased, so she did it again, even stepping closer to continue stroking down his neck, all she could reach over the fence. He – she decided he was Smoke – went completely still, a paralytic trance that reminded Teresa of how she'd do the same when Mom or a girlfriend brushed her hair, or a boyfriend stroked her, not wanting even the faintest twitch of a muscle to break the sensuous spell.

She kept petting him, feeling bolder and more relaxed, and frankly pumped by her own courage. The donkey's trust in her, a total stranger, was exhilarating and oddly moving.

Then he turned his head, and Teresa turned hers, and there was psycho dog, skulking toward them, head down, tail going side to side, more lashing than wagging.

'Go. Away.' Teresa was no longer brave, or in love with nature and its bounty. She wanted to be safely in the house behind a wall of locked glass. Glancing desperately around, she zeroed in on a nearby stick and moved slowly toward it, keeping watch on her nemesis, who followed her every move.

Closer . . . closer . . . With a desperate lunge, she grabbed the stick. Ha! Armed!

Which didn't make the slightest difference to Zig. He still approached, now with an extra gleam in his small bright eyes.

'No.' She lifted the stick. Immediately the dog tensed, dropped low, coiled energy waiting.

D'oh! Dog + stick = fetch. Perfect!

She threw the stick as far from the house as she could, which, her being a non-jock weenie, wasn't very far, but far enough. Both of them took off like a shot, dog for stick, non-jock weenie for the house. Just as she was about to hurl herself inside, she heard a sharp whistle. 'Here, Zig.'

Teresa turned, body halfway to safety. Zig was bounding toward a stranger – stranger to Teresa, obviously not to the dog – which meant her urgent need to be inside disappeared.

She closed the door slowly behind her, taking in details of the newcomer's appearance. He wore jeans and boots and a mustard-colored shirt over an orange tee. Not tall, under six feet, and a few extra pounds on him. Boyish face, short straw-colored hair with a cowlick in back that stuck straight up.

'Teresa?'

She nodded.

'Danny Pierson. Friend of Jim's going way back. Thought I'd stop by, check on the animals and meet you. I'm around pretty often, so I'm familiar with the place.'

'Oh. Okay.' She waited on the deck, unsure if he'd want to get his job done and go, or if he'd want to chat.

He chose social, climbing up onto the deck to shake hands. 'Nice to meet you.'

'Same.' He had a pleasant face with almond-brown eyes, unusual with blond hair. His gaze was direct, body relaxed. 'Jim and I met at KU, both wanting to be large animal veterinarians. He went straight to grad school in Manhattan, I took a couple of years off, now in my fourth year.'

'You can study to be a large animal vet in Manhattan?'

'Sorry, Manhattan, Kansas. About an hour from here. Kansas State College of Veterinary Medicine.'

'Oh.' She wasn't sure how to follow up on that one. He seemed very easy in himself, standing on Helen's deck, while she was suffering from an attack of what-to-say-next.

'How are you liking Kansas? You're from Phoenix, right?'

'Yeah. I like it a lot. I mean, I've only been here a few days, but it's pretty. Very green. There's not much green where I come from. You know, desert.' She saved herself at the last second from laughing, having said nothing funny, or coherent for that matter.

'I don't think I could handle that. I need to be around growing things, the cycles of seasons. Big animals. It's in my blood, I guess.' He patted his chest. 'What do you do in Phoenix?'

She hated being asked. People never knew how to respond. 'I do fundraising for a community college.'

'Ah.' He nodded a few times, silence growing along with Teresa's stress.

'Pays the bills.' A nervous laugh she didn't stop in time.

Danny gestured toward the house. 'How's the job here going?'

'Not bad. I'm playing hooky so far today.'

'You went out with Jim last night, huh?'

Teresa nodded, feeling defensive that he'd make that connection without knowing her, then telling herself she shouldn't be defensive because the connection was right on the mark. 'But also it's all been a little intense. Family . . . stuff.'

'Sure. Sure.' He reached down to pet Zig, who was standing by his side, the perfect docile animal. 'You been able to see anything of the area yet?'

'Not really. The hospital. Supermarket. That's about it so far. I only got here Sunday.' Two days ago. It felt like much longer.

'You should check out Baker Wetlands, one of the most beautiful places in Kansas. Today's a perfect day for it, too.' He glanced at his watch. 'In fact, if you want, I can take you this afternoon. I have the day off from work. I should be studying, but it's clearing up and I'm in the mood to play hooky too.'

Huh? Teresa opened her mouth to say no, but couldn't think of a single polite excuse. She'd as much as admitted she was free, and 'sorry, I don't know you at all' was too hard to say without being rude.

'Well. That would be . . .'

'. . . weird. Sorry. Mouth goes on ahead of brain sometimes.' He looked embarrassed. 'You just met me and I'm trying to barge in on your afternoon.'

'Oh no, it's okay. It was nice of you to offer.'

'Yeah, so . . .' He made a quick circle with his hand. 'I'm going to walk around and check on things, want to come along?'

That she couldn't refuse without looking obnoxious, and as long as he was there, she figured she'd be safe from beast attack. Besides, after a few days observing the animals, they all seemed pretty placid, and, except for the dogs and chickens, safely behind fences. 'Sure.'

They stepped off the porch together, Zig walking calmly by Danny's side. Soon after, Pearl and Tusk spotted them and came over to investigate, their big gentle tails wagging.

They inspected the chicken coop, which Teresa noticed needed the latch moved or replaced – the coop must have settled and it was off-kilter, then checked in on the mule and bulls in the adjoining lots. They looked over the goats, sheep and donkeys, making sure they all seemed healthy and had enough water, then headed toward the cattle pastures.

'So what did you think of Funky Town last night?'

'Oh. Yeah.' How honest could she be? 'It was . . . funky.'

He gave her a sidelong look. 'Really.'

Too honest? She didn't want to lie.

'It was sweet of Jim to include me. His friends were great. Pretty crazy place.' They reached the fence penning the cattle. 'You know about how at midnight they play "Car Wash" and—'

'Spray everyone, yeah. Clubbing isn't my thing. Too crowded, too noisy.' He stood by the fence, eyes roaming over the cattle. Teresa found herself curious about what he was noticing, since all she saw was cows. 'I'd rather stay home with a book or watch a movie.'

Her too. 'Yeah, it was . . . I don't know, it was a fun time with nice people.'

He turned, eyebrows raised. 'But . . . ?'

She grinned, liking him already. '*But* dance clubs aren't my favorite way to spend time either.'

'So why go?'

She dutifully recited the mantra Mom had raised her with. 'Because if I wimp out on everything except what makes me comfortable, I'll miss out.'

'On being uncomfortable?'

That got her smiling again. Something about him, maybe his cherubic face or his no-bullshit air, kept his challenge from being too personal. 'Well, yes, but if I give in to shyness every time, I'd be cheating myself out of new experiences.'

His face cleared. 'Oh, so you haven't been clubbing before.'

'No, I have. A lot, actually, in Phoenix, with my friends.' She laughed nervously, waiting for him to pounce on the logic flaw.

Instead, he nodded. 'Ah, okay, now I understand.'

'You do?'

'Sure. You're a masochist. But that's fine. Everyone has a right to do what makes them happy.'

Teresa cracked up. She was definitely liking him. 'I know, it sounds like it makes no sense. And maybe it doesn't. But I love my friends, and that's what they like to do, so I go.'

'What is your favorite evening?'

'I guess the classic introvert stuff. Small groups, quiet bars, movies. Or . . .' She paused, interrupted by Katie's voice telling her the last thing she should admit to a guy was the extent of her nerd brain.

Danny lifted an imaginary microphone to his mouth. 'We're here on this lovely Kansas ranch for this week's episode of *Geek Confession*, waiting to hear from Te-*re*-saaaaa. Teresa, what gets your geek on?'

She leaned toward his fake mike. 'Board games and jigsaw puzzles, Danny.'

'Excellent! Bowling?'

'Totally fun.'

'Checking out the library?'

'Best *e*-ver.' Or used to be . . .

'Video games?'

'Mmm, no.'

'Ohhhhh, sorry, you did not win the grand prize.'

Teresa threw up her hands in mock disappointment. 'Why, are you a gamer?'

'Used to be. Too busy since I got into grad school. I'm working for a vet this summer here in Lawrence. Mostly sweeping floors. But learning what I can.' He moved farther along the fence and pointed to the next pasture over, empty now. 'See there? That's where I delivered my first calf, last year, about this time. Helen picked up that there was something not normal about the mom and called Jim. He was sick, so I came. Going into my third year, no clinicals yet, had only read about what to do.'

'Why didn't she call a vet? I mean, a fully licensed one?'

Danny shrugged. 'She was sure I could do whatever was needed. A lot of times nothing can be done, which is really hard. Helen tries to let nature take its course as much as possible. Though I've seen her when things go wrong, it gets to her. Even if the situation was hopeless start to finish, if an animal dies under her care, she feels she's let it down. Ironic since she raises most of her animals for food, so death is part of it.'

Ironic since Helen didn't seem to treat humans all that well, or care what her actions did to them.

'What was the problem?' Teresa wanted to get off the subject of Team Helen.

'This is normal birth position . . .' Danny put his head down and stretched his arms forward, like a superhero in flight, then crooked one arm behind him. 'This little guy had one leg back.'

'What did you do?' She was more curious than she thought she'd be, imagining a calf tucked up like that inside a cow.

'I brought the other leg forward.'

She wasn't sure she understood. 'How?'

'With my arm.' He stretched his out again. 'All the way in.'

Teresa turned to stare at him. 'In.'

'Yeah, it's the only way to figure out what's going wrong. I was able to get the leg forward, and the mom did the rest.' Danny pointed at a group of cows not far from where they stood. 'He's right there, third from the left. I named him Lucky, because if he'd been breech, I might not have been able to save him. Those are tough.'

'Wow.' She was trying to put out of her mind the idea of what he'd had to do.

'I was terrified, totally inexperienced.' He was watching Lucky with pride. 'But Helen insisted I could do it. She has a way of putting faith in people that brings out their best.'

'Really.' That was definitely not what Teresa had heard. But maybe Helen had been kinder to people outside her own family. 'Well, I'm glad it worked out.'

Danny shook his head. 'I have to be the smoothest dude on the planet. We just met and I'm talking about sticking my arm inside a cow.'

Teresa burst out laughing. She was comfortable with Danny, like he was another cousin. 'It was interesting. In a . . . horrifying way.'

'I know, I know. I talk about this stuff so much, I forget how it sounds to normal people. Anyway, now we've checked on the animals and can—'

'That's it? That's all you do? Even in the morning and evening checks?' Teresa had assumed the visits were about complicated feeding schedules and medicines and . . . whatever she couldn't do.

'Mornings you let the chickens out of the coop and gather eggs, evenings they know to go in, you just latch the door behind them. Everyone else is okay in summertime. Animals know how to live. They have good food out here, water, protectors, what do they need us for?'

'Obviously I have no idea.'

'The only thing you need is an eye for unusual behavior, and you get that from being around them enough. Anyone who cares can do it.'

They walked back toward the house, dogs trailing, sun out in earnest now, clouds dissipating into fluffy masses.

'I'm still going to visit the wetlands from here. You want to come?'

Teresa checked in with herself and found that aside from her normal inclination to say no, she really was curious. Danny seemed like a nice guy, and one day wasn't going to throw her off schedule. She didn't really have a schedule. Her only deadline was getting back to her unsatisfying job in Phoenix. Out in this green space, standing in breezy sunshine, even thinking about the air-conditioned cubicle made her feel claustrophobic.

'Sure, I'll go.'

'Is that "Sure, I'll go" because it's awkward to say no, or because you really do want to come?' He asked casually, as if it were all the same to him if she went or not, which made her feel even more comfortable.

'I'm sure I want to go.'

'Good.' His smile was sudden and sunshiny, a treat in his so-far serious face. 'It'll be nice to have company. Seeing beauty on your own feels incomplete. The emotions get trapped in your chest with nowhere to go. Like a belch.'

Teresa laughed again, taken aback by his openness. Guys she hung out with didn't talk about beauty and emotion. Belches, sure. 'I know what you mean.'

'Yeah? So what kind of beauty makes you bloat up?'

'Hmm.' Danny was exactly what Teresa needed this afternoon after a morning spent wallowing in angst. 'Music mostly. Neko Case's "Vengeance is Sleeping" and "Calling Cards", Joni

Mitchell – pretty much any song on the *Blue* album, but mostly "Case of You" and the title song.'

'All right. We'll see if we can get as good as "Vengeance is Sleeping" in the Kansas swamps.'

They drove out to the wetlands mostly in silence, radio blaring. Teresa made some initial attempts at get-to-know-you chatter, feeling as she always did, irrationally, that if silence hung, she was responsible for filling it. But after a while Danny's body language – the slight head-bob when a song he liked came on the radio, the grins he'd toss her across the cab of his pickup – made it clear he was having a fine ride, and the silence didn't seem awkward after that.

'Almost there.'

Teresa looked around dubiously. Flat farmland, same as they'd been driving through for the past ten minutes. The most beautiful spot in Kansas? Maybe not saying much.

A short time later, Danny turned at the Baker Wetlands sign, and pulled into the lot by the park's discovery center. They emerged into improved weather, with only patchy clouds providing occasional shade. The breeze would keep the air light and the insects from investigating too closely. 'There are a few different trails. Do you want to look at the map to choose or do you trust me?'

'You choose. I'm along for the ride.'

They ignored the discovery center and set out on a trail that soon put visions of flat cornfields to rest. The landscape was lush and colorful – greens, yellows, blues and purples, enchanting to look at and listen to. Between the thick patches of meadow and reeds, glimpses of water, sometimes ducks or geese, and the constant chatter and darting-about of birds and butterflies, many of which Danny was able to identify, either by sight or song.

'You must come here a lot.'

'My parents were determined we grow up with a firm grounding in what they considered the correct side of environmental protection. Their theory was that the more you knew about nature, the harder it would be to want to dominate or destroy it.'

'Makes sense.'

'Plus, Mom is originally from Massachusetts, and I think the whole agriculture landscape here drove her a little crazy. This is a great escape.'

'It's beautiful. Unexpectedly. I never thought of myself as a nature-lover. In Phoenix I'm all about the city. My job, our apartment, stores, restaurants . . .'

'And dance clubs.'

'Yeah, those.' She inhaled the humid air that seemed so alive to lungs used to the desiccated version in Phoenix, and found herself feeling confessional. 'I was a really shy kid. Everything made me anxious. Mom pushed me to get out and do things, no matter how terrifying they seemed. She was worried I'd end up with too small a life. I'll always be grateful for that. It made me braver.'

Danny nodded, looking wary. 'My parents pushed me to try everything too, but only once or twice. If I hated it after that, then okay, maybe it wasn't my thing.'

Teresa stopped at a section of boardwalk, gazing out at the water, scattered with white-blooming lily pads. She thought about how often she went to bars and clubs in Phoenix with her roommates, other friends from college or on dates. Had she ever truly enjoyed herself beyond the adrenaline rush and a somewhat desperate intention to live life to its fullest?

If she were being honest, living life to its fullest mostly exhausted her.

'Mom grew up here, back when it was Grandpa Kevin's farm.

181

She didn't like the life, and Grandma Helen didn't let her out much.' It occurred to Teresa for the first time that Cheryl had left Kansas at eighteen. Teresa hadn't been out much by that age either. 'I think Mom wanted to make sure I had the city experiences she missed out on.'

'That's cool.'

She wrinkled her nose. 'I'm making her sound like one of those parents who force their kids to have the childhood they wanted.'

'Was she?'

'No, no, no, not at *all*. She encouraged me in my own interests too.' By the time Teresa was halfway through the last sentence, she realized her mistake, and that he was going to ask . . .

'What are those?'

It was Teresa's dad who'd encouraged her interests, in baseball, in carpentry, in building model cars and setting up miniature trains and the villages they served. All of those hobbies had disappeared when he did. Mom had decreed that the kids could each pick one activity, because that was all she could afford, and while all three kids clamored for baseball, Mom agreed for the boys and signed Teresa up for ballet, to try to combat her lack of grace.

She felt her face flame. In college, she'd studied hard, gotten good grades, done some theater – backstage, in props. Since graduation she'd spent weekends gossiping, shopping and going out with her roommates.

'I guess I've . . . lost some of them.' She heard the catch in her voice and tried to pass it off as a cough waiting to happen.

'Or maybe you haven't found what you're into yet. Sometimes it takes people a while. My aunt Barbara is a writer, but she didn't start until she was thirty-five. Dad took up tennis at fifty.'

Teresa turned toward him, touched by his rescue attempt. 'You're a nice person, Danny.'

'I grew up with four sisters.' His gaze shifted past her, eyes widening. 'Heron!'

A large grayish-blue bird with an enormous wingspan, long neck doubled back over itself, glided slowly over the water and landed on wader's legs across the pond. As they watched, it took a few awkward steps, then froze, holding itself absolutely motionless, until Teresa finally leaned in toward Danny to whisper, 'Are we scaring it?'

'It's waiting for a fish to make one false move . . .'

A few seconds later, the long, sharp beak stabbed into the water, so quickly Teresa could barely take in that the bird had moved before it was shaking its head to clear away plant material snagged along with the fish. Tipping its head up, it swallowed dinner whole.

'See?' Danny whispered.

'See what, the fish?'

'No. You just need patience, and what you want will come to you.'

'Thank you, Swami Danny.'

'You're welcome.'

They wandered on a bit farther, Teresa sweating in the unaccustomed humidity, greedily absorbing every detail of the surrounding lushness that to her desert eyes seemed crushed together in such abundance it was a wonder any of it could survive. Grasses, bushes, trees, insects, flowers, birds, on and on to an unimpeded horizon. Rich marshy earth and flowery green smells, with the occasional faint tang of vegetal rot. And water! Water as if there was so much it couldn't resist showing itself off every chance it could, in channels, puddles and ponds, clouds reflecting in it, blurred by the occasional breeze.

She'd need to go on more hikes back in Phoenix, to surround herself with nature. It was beautiful there too, though very different. She and Dad used to go fairly often when she was a kid. Mom wasn't into anything strenuous. Teresa couldn't imagine her roommates wanting to go either. Her brothers?

Maybe she needed some new friends. 'I'd come here all the time if I lived here.'

'I'm glad I introduced you. It's an awesome place to watch sunsets. Sunrises too. All that color reflected in the water and on the foliage.'

'Sunrises and I do not get along, but I'll definitely come back some evening.' She found herself imagining how fun it would be to watch a sunset with this man, maybe drinking a glass of something . . . maybe not drinking.

They continued on, parallel to the Wakarusa River, stopping here and there to notice and comment – Danny thought he saw an otter, but Teresa missed it – and then, as they approached the trail's end and the discovery center again loomed in the distance, Teresa realized she had a chance to get unbiased and, from what she'd intuited about Danny, honest information. 'I want to ask you something about Helen. If you don't mind.'

'I don't mind. What about her?'

She watched a yellow butterfly flying a seemingly random pattern over by some tall grasses, lighting, moving on, lighting, moving on, testing until it found where it wanted to land. 'Were you around when she fell?'

'I wasn't with her, no.'

'How did you find out it had happened?'

'I got a call from Jim that she was in the hospital because she'd been knocked over by one of the goats. James had been after her to keep her phone with her at all times. I think he threatened to superglue it to her hand. So she called him that she needed help, that it hurt too much to walk. He came right over and called an ambulance. There was a lot of joking about her arriving at the hospital with goat poop squashed in her hair. She was in terrible pain, but refused to go in until she'd combed it out. That's all I know.' He gave her a curious look. 'Didn't anyone tell you?'

'It's complicated.' She took a deep breath and decided to trust him. 'Mom told me she'd fallen in the house.'

'Hmm. Maybe Helen told her that so she wouldn't worry.'

'I don't think there's any way to stop my mom worrying.'

'Then that's probably why. Farm life can be dangerous. Tripping over your feet indoors sounds less dramatic.'

Teresa nodded. 'One more question?'

'Sure.'

'What do you think of Helen? As a person?'

'One of the best I know. Smart. Funny. Honest. Patient. Accepting. Hard-working, loyal.'

Teresa wanted to roll her eyes. Team Helen again. 'Negatives?'

He didn't hesitate. 'Stubborn. Sure she's right, though often she is. Can be blunt to a fault. Works hard for other people and neglects herself. And I've always had the feeling . . . How do I put this? That she's content, but not really happy, if that makes sense.'

'Thanks, yes.'

Danny turned to her. The afternoon light in his hair brought out blonder highlights, emphasizing the contrast with the rich brown of his eyes, causing Teresa an unexpected shock of attraction. 'One thing is for sure. I would trust any of them – Helen, Jim or James – with my life.'

She nodded, ill at ease again. There was no doubting that Team Helen had fiercely loyal members. 'Thanks.'

'I hope that helps.' He touched her shoulder when she nodded. 'I've had a great time, Teresa, thanks for playing hooky with me.'

'You need to get back?' She was disappointed.

He made a face. 'Books are calling.'

They drove to the ranch in companionable silence that hardly bothered her at all, a definite first, especially for someone she'd just met. At the house, she hopped down from his truck. 'Thanks for bringing me. It's been really fun.'

'Sure.' He grinned. 'Next time Jim invites you to go dancing and you need an excuse, tell him we have a date to sit and read the dictionary.'

Teresa laughed. 'I would actually enjoy that.'

'I would too.' He put the truck in reverse and she closed the door, feeling a tingle of excitement that he'd mentioned seeing her again, and about a thousand percent better than she had that morning. Hangover gone, nice new friend, and a little more solid perspective on her grandmother's fall. She believed Helen had fallen because of a goat, and that she'd thought it would worry her daughter too much, so she'd invented a tamer story for Cheryl.

'Good news.' Teresa let Cheddar out of his cage, feeling guilty for making him stay in so long. 'Looks like my family isn't as big a mess as I worried it was.'

Cheddar thought this was great news, and celebrated with chirps and bobs that were becoming seriously endearing. Teresa fed him some lettuce and watched him peck and shred it, until the pull to get something more constructive done interfered.

A couple of hours later, she came back up from the basement, having knocked off the last of the boring boxes in the storage closet. The evening light was spectacular, gentling from the harder yellow of midday. She got Cheddar re-caged with some fresh seeds and took a can of grapefruit-flavored sparkling water out onto the deck, where she sat watching the animals do their animal thing, idly thinking that the goat kids might like another little box or stool to jump on and leap off, and maybe she should make them one.

She took another sip, rearranging her legs, letting out a long breath, surprised after such a short time to find herself feeling peaceful in the same setting that had made her feel isolated and vulnerable on arrival.

Had she ever felt this relaxed in Phoenix? Maybe reading in bed at night, but even that could feel busy if the book was complicated or exciting. There was always big stimulation going on: roommate conversations to be had, traffic noises, social interactions, scheduled evenings. Life went by at a much faster pace. Teresa had always imagined herself thriving on the adrenaline and the stimulation, one hundred percent a city girl. Now she wondered if she was just stressed all the time. Though all this peace might get seriously boring after the novelty wore off.

In the relative silence, she heard a truck coming up the driveway. Jim or James, come to do the evening check – Danny must not have told them he'd showed up earlier. After seeing what checking on the animals entailed, Teresa might volunteer to take over. Not that she'd know what to do if one of the animals was in distress, but if it was just a question of looking around and closing the coop behind the chickens, she could certainly do that.

James came around the side of the house, whistling an unidentifiable tune. Zig ran to greet him. Pearl and Tusk joined them.

'Hi, Uncle James.' She surprised herself, and him, by coming down off the deck without a thought and without a weapon. The posse advanced, James no longer whistling, Pearl and Tusk ambling along with their slow, powerful gait, Zig bouncing, edgy and energized. Teresa tensed, but reminded herself that he only messed with her when they were alone.

Devious animal.

'Hey, Niece Teresa.' James stopped several feet away. 'Just came from the hospital. Mom says hello.'

'Oh, thank you.' She heard herself speaking with a touch of frost. Helen's disrespect for Cheryl's attempts to help still rankled. 'How is she?'

'Tired. A little discouraged. She wants out of there so badly. How's the work going here?'

Teresa kept her shoulders from hunching. Innocent question, asked casually. If only there wasn't a boatload of baggage dragging it down.

'I have a handle on the basement boxes. Mostly old documents, but I did find some fun stuff from Grandma Helen's year in Paris. Postcards, photos, souvenirs and a doll. A big one.' She spread her hands apart to show the size.

'Oh yeah. I forgot Mom went abroad that year after college. I remember some stories, but Dad got crabby when she mentioned the trip. He hadn't wanted her to go.'

'Oh.' After reading Grandpa Kevin's letters, Teresa wasn't surprised. 'I also found a fancy beaded dress, from the nineteen twenties I think. It's gorgeous.'

'Cool.' He seemed more pleasant today, less guarded. 'Mom lived a pretty spare life, though. Not likely to be many more hidden treasures.'

'Oh, speaking of . . .' She was glad he'd reminded her. 'Mom was asking about a liquor cabinet? Portable. With crystal decanters and glasses inside, does that sound familiar? I haven't been able to find it.'

The way his face darkened while she was speaking told Teresa she'd stepped in it again.

'That was from Dad's family. She gave it back when he died.'

'Oh.'

'Disappointed?' There was a distinct edge to his voice that annoyed her.

'Why would I be disappointed?'

'Sorry.' He pressed ink-stained fingers to his forehead. 'Tough day. I'm being an asshole. Mom gave it away. She didn't want anything to do with alcohol in the house.'

Teresa nodded sympathetically, understanding now. 'After she went sober.'

James looked at her sharply. 'After . . . *she* went sober?'

Stepped in it again. Deeper this time. No idea why. 'She didn't stop?'

'There was nothing *to* stop.' Zig whimpered at the change in volume; James bent to reassure him. 'Dad was the problem drinker. Mom barely touched it.'

Teresa could only stare. 'No.'

'My father was an alcoholic.' He spoke quietly, but with bitterness. 'A mean drunk. Abusive. He drank himself to death.'

Teresa went cold, feeling as if he were trying to tell her that black was actually white. 'But . . .'

She knew better than to go on. *Mom said* . . . He'd be off, and Teresa would again be trapped between he-said and she-said.

'My sister told you *Mom* was the drunk?' James swore, taking off and replacing his Kansas City ball cap. 'Okay, I'm going to say this bluntly, because you deserve to hear it. Your mom sees the past the way she wishes it was. That's probably what she's been telling you.'

'What . . .' Teresa couldn't believe he'd stoop that low. 'Are you saying she *lied*?'

James sighed, his eyes dulled and weary. 'Your mother has serious issues, maybe even believes what she's saying to some extent. But that doesn't make any of it true.'

'That is complete—'

'You might as well know all of it. Since she was a girl, Cheryl's always acted as if life owed her better than she got. She had Dad wrapped around her finger, then did the same with your father until he wised up and ran.'

Teresa gasped. 'That is *not* true. My father cheated on her and dropped us like trash.'

'He did not drop you kids. Cheryl kept him away.'

'*What?*' She was sick with outrage. 'No! That's a total lie.'

'She told your dad not to contact you, that you and your brothers were so angry you didn't want to see or hear from him again. She threatened legal action, a custody battle, a restraining order.'

'*No.*' Teresa was panting with fury. She wanted to punch her uncle in the face, ram him in the gut. Anything to stop his poisonous attack. 'He left us cold, all of us. How can you make up such bullshit?'

'It's not bullshit.' James's face was stony. 'Richard asked me to intervene, but it wasn't my place. Finally Helen gave in and shared your email addresses with—'

'Oh, come on, that is the stupidest soap-opera bullshit ever.' She sounded completely undone, could barely see through the fear and rage. 'You're trying to get back at Mom because she left and you got stuck here.'

He looked at her as if she were speaking gibberish. 'I love it here, Teresa. I've always loved it. Kansas is my home. I'm angry at my sister because of what she's done to you and your brothers and your father and too many others.'

'What, sacrificed and worked her ass off to raise and support three of us *by herself*?'

He lowered his head, jaw clenched. 'Fair enough. Let's start with a simple one. My father's death certificate should be among

Mom's papers somewhere. Find it and look up cause of death. See it in print. You don't have to believe me.'

'Good, because I don't.' Teresa stalked back up to the deck and closed the sliding door hard behind her, breath coming too fast, shocked and shaky. She couldn't remember ever losing her temper like that, yelling without filter or fear, barely aware of what she was saying.

But she couldn't believe the depths to which James would stoop to get back at Cheryl for ... whatever she did. Or to get back at his father for ... whatever Grandpa Kevin did. Or maybe he was a bitter jerk trying to cause trouble because of ... something. Obviously he'd taken Jim in as well. And Danny. Or maybe this was all coming from Helen, because she was mad at ... someone. As for Dad ...

Yes, there had been emails, begging her to give him a chance to explain what had happened, to agree to meet him for coffee, lunch, anything. She hadn't. Didn't even finish reading before she deleted the notes. Because of the pain he'd caused them all.

Teresa sank into a chair at the dining table, and made herself breathe slowly for a long time until she'd calmed down.

None of this made sense.

Your mother is like her father, like Kevin. Both of them worried only about themselves.

One thing is for sure. I would trust any of them – Helen, Jim or James – with my life.

My father's death certificate should be among Mom's papers somewhere ... You don't have to believe me.

Teresa got up and walked the length of the hall to Helen's room, went inside and over to the small desk in the corner.

Forgive me, Mom.

She jerked open the right-hand drawers, one after another. Office supplies, pads of paper. Scarves. Purses.

Left-hand drawers – the top one looked like a mess of to-be-filed.

Next drawer, a double with folders and files. Teresa scanned the tabs. Alphabetical. A-B-C-D-E-F-G-H-I-J-Kevin.

His will was on top. She scrabbled through its pages and lifted it away. Next in the file, there. A single page.

Certificate of Death, Kansas State Department of Health and Environment. Vital Statistics. Kevin Foster. Male, September 25, 1996. Douglas County . . .

Teresa swallowed hard, and skipped to the bottom of the page, *Cause of Death.*

Immediate cause: Hepatic encephalopathy

Due to, or as a consequence of: Cirrhosis of liver

Due to, or as a consequence of: Chronic alcoholism

She sank to the floor with the folder open, reading and rereading, telling herself James had changed the death certificate, telling herself this was some other Kevin Foster, telling herself anything that might possibly explain this except the obvious, until her brain finally, slowly, reluctantly let go of beautiful, kind denial, and accepted the truth of his death, which came with an even uglier truth.

Mom had lied. Best possible case, a lie of omission about her father's drinking, out of her protective love for him. But a lie. And if that was a lie, one she'd maintained throughout Teresa's life, what else on the she-said side might also be untrue? Helen's drinking? Her affairs? Her abuse? Her dementia?

Mom wasn't a monster. Monsters were easily identifiable as such. Big teeth, hairy all over, fangs, warts, claws, bad smell, etc.

But. Mom. Had. Lied.

Teresa closed the folder with shaking hands, aware that her quest to uncover the truth about Helen's life had just been massively complicated by a need to uncover the truth about her own.

✺ Chapter 8 ✺

It was a beautiful day like this one that set this love on fire, with everything to lose.

Long wandering dream of an ephemeral hour, an hour of birds, perfume and sun, of forgetting everything.

Marceline Desbordes-Valmore, 'Jour d'Orient'

Dear Helen,

I haven't heard from you in several days. I'm still writing to you every day like we promised. Maybe it was a naïve promise, easier to say than do, but it's frustrating not knowing where you are, what you're doing, if you're still thinking about me, if you're even safe. Okay if every day was too much for you, but your parents say they haven't heard from you either, since last week. I was embarrassed having to ask them and admitting you're not in touch with me either. What's going on? You're starting not to sound like you in your letters. Formal, and I don't know, academic.

It's just me, Helen. I don't need the SAT words and brainy concepts. Tell me how you are. Tell me something mundane and funny. Tell me how much you miss me. That's what I want to hear. Not some dead person's ideas about church-building or the anti-American attitudes of those snotty French.

There's so much to do to get our farm ready for planting in the spring. I need you with me. For one thing, I never learned to cook and can't make anything worth eating. I'm going out a lot, making a lot of burgers here at home. It's a bachelor's existence at a time when I thought I'd be with the love of my life, and that makes it extra lonely.

Thanksgiving will be so hard without you. I'll be with my family, my kin, as Granny calls us. You'll be badly missed by everyone. They loved having you with us last year. I bet over there they don't have turkey and gravy like Mom can make. Do they even know what cranberries are? Now that's a feast, one I can't wait to share with you next year as husband and wife. I want a short engagement, short as possible, summer wedding. My June bride!

Only you can make this empty house feel like a home. I ache for you every day. I want to hold you and love you and keep you with me for the rest of my life.

All my love every minute of every day,
Kevin

Thursday, November 27, 1975

'Today something special.' Natalie opened the closet in her room and pointed up to the shelf, too high for her diminutive figure. 'My mother's jewelry box. Can you reach? In the back there, behind my handbags. Maman got it for her tenth birthday.'

Helen stood on tiptoe and thrust her hand between a pair of leather purses, one burgundy, one black, until it encountered a box, which she gently pulled toward her and down from the shelf. Unsurprisingly in this house, the jewel case was nothing like the floral pink plastic one Helen had had at ten, with a tiny ballerina figure that turned *en pointe* to a music-box tune when she opened the lid.

This was made from dark, nearly black wood – ebony? – with lighter-colored wood accents and three tiny drawers with half-circle pulls of gold metal fashioned to look like laurel wreaths. Helen held it up admiringly. 'What a gorgeous piece. It looks like a little dresser.'

'That's exactly what it is.' Natalie brushed her small hand lovingly across its top. 'In those days, cabinetmakers would make miniatures to give potential clients a taste of their skill, and to provide current clients with a model of what they planned to build, in case changes were wanted. Someone somewhere owns this dresser full-size. I don't know how my grandparents found this piece for Maman, but I've always loved it.'

'Do you wear her jewelry?' Helen thought she knew the answer by the way the box had been pushed so far back in her closet.

'No.' Sadness crossed Natalie's face. 'I associate it with her, and I associate her with loss and pain.'

'I'm sorry.'

'Thank you. But! It's time these things were dealt with. You can set the box there.' She pointed toward the finely carved rosewood writing desk in the corner of her room and brought a second chair over so she and Helen could sit side by side. 'She's been gone so long, and I was so young, but she's still vivid to me.'

'It must have been awful.'

'*Oui*. So.' Natalie took off her navy sweater and draped it over the back of her chair, smoothing the back of her skirt as she sat. 'Let's see what we have.'

She lifted the curving top of the mini dresser, revealing a thin white marble slab on which knelt the gold figure of a woman holding a tiny tilted umbrella. Around the edge of the umbrella were small hooks on which dangled four spectacular rings – gold and platinum, diamonds, rubies and emeralds. The dresser drawers revealed brooches, gold pocket watches, jeweled hat pins, bracelets and necklaces. It was hard to take in the splendor.

'My gosh!' Did your mother wear jewelry like this every day?'

She must have sounded like an Indiana cornstalk, because Natalie laughed. 'I don't remember. Maman came from money, so she was used to it. But my father did well too.'

Helen drew out a necklace, delicate platinum filigree supporting one large diamond surrounded by several smaller ones. 'What will you do with them?'

'Well, this is the question. They are meant to be worn, and they're not being worn. Yet I hate to sell them because they were my mother's.' Natalie unhooked a gold ring topped with a row of square-cut diamonds and turned it to watch the sparkle. 'How ephemeral and artificial this idea of something's worth. You young people with your mood rings and braided rope bracelets, you have power over these old pieces. If you never value the artistry, they become worthless. Rocks and metal, better left in the earth. I see this ring's beauty and find that a shame. Then I look again and see the wealth, privilege and power it represents and has represented for so many centuries, and I think you young people are onto something. What does one do? It's a big question.'

She slid the ring onto her middle finger, where it hung loosely. 'I could give it to someone in the street, throw it in the trash, hide it in a crack in the baseboards for someone to stumble over years from now – what does it matter? It has no intrinsic value. It does nothing but exist.'

Helen shook her head vehemently, replacing the necklace. 'Looking at it that way, the *Mona Lisa* is only paint and canvas and does nothing but exist, so why not throw that away too?'

'Ah, good question.' Natalie smiled proudly at her student. 'I would say because *Mona Lisa* is shared with everyone, and everyone can be part of her in their imaginations, create their own stories about her and what she represents. These jewels can only be admired and envied.'

'True.' Helen picked up an emerald brooch, the rich green stone enhanced by diamonds set among gold leaves. 'But you won't throw anything away.'

'No, I won't.' Natalie slid the ring off her finger and hung it back on its tiny hook. 'I'm getting philosophical in my old age, questioning everything, like your least favorite philosopher, Descartes. When I try to be practical and get rid of things, some instinct stops me. Am I being sensible? Or is it in my greedy aristocratic blood to hold onto emblems of privilege and power?'

'I think your instinct is saying something important. The value isn't the point. If you inherited a cracked pitcher from the family farm that your mother bought with her last cent, it would be worth as much to you as these. It's not your fault the sentimental things in your life are expensive.' Helen laid the brooch back in its drawer. 'Think of all this as a cracked pitcher and keep it.'

'*Ah, ma petite philosophe!*' Natalie laughed and hugged her. 'You are very wise. And different, I think, than when you came two months ago.'

'Different?' Helen was intrigued. She certainly felt different, but she hadn't realized it was noticeable. 'You mean fatter from the cheese and pastry?'

'*Mais non.* You have a lovely figure. But you have more . . .

élan, more spirit. You are more self-assured, more confident in your person and more confident expressing your ideas.'

'Thank you.' Helen was surprised by Natalie's perceptiveness, and yet she did feel more fully fledged, certainly more independent. Exactly what she'd hoped would happen by getting away from family and . . . well, not getting *away* from Kevin, but delaying becoming part of him. She'd marry him now knowing better who she was, which would make her a better wife.

And there *he* came into her head, as he'd been doing since she met him that day in the flower shop a couple of months ago. The girls and Gilles had spent a lot of time together when Gilles wasn't on an assignment. He'd even invented a rhythmic ring of the doorbell so whoever was home could buzz him up without having to ask who was there. Helen always made sure other people were invited on their outings, but it hadn't stopped the two of them getting closer, finding more and more in common in their tastes and ideas and outlooks. More than she and Kevin shared, at least on an intellectual level.

But shared intellect wasn't the most important thing in a relationship. She and Kevin were good in other ways, on other levels. They came from the same culture and similar families with similar values – Kevin's more conservative, but not by much. They liked the same comedy, music, movies, sports and games. He was there whenever she needed anything, and gave generously of his time and emotions. She hoped she did the same for him. They were good together. Really good.

Helen picked up a pocket watch and examined its exquisite details, the engravings on the cover – loops and scrolls and a flat polished circle in whose center initials had been carved in such ornate script she couldn't make them out.

She was having to force her thoughts away from Gilles more and more often. But she was determined to enjoy her crush for what it was: a product of this exotic and exciting escape from real life, and an outgrowth of her new feelings of freedom in it. Period. That afternoon they were meeting his friend Anneke at the Père Lachaise cemetery. Helen had invited Connie and Lilianne as well, but Lilianne was busy at work and Connie had her cooking class – it was sauce week, sacred to the French, and not one to miss.

The rest of the morning was spent on the astounding array of valuables. Helen tried and failed to imagine what it would be like to buy such precious items without considering anything but what she felt like owning. Given her solid middle-class upbringing, it seemed wasteful self-indulgence. But if she'd grown up surrounded by people dripping jewels, it could become as easy as buying soap.

After she and Natalie had oohed and aahed their way through all the drawers, and after Natalie had still not been able to make any decisions, her distinguished white-haired cook, Lucas, announced that lunch was ready. Natalie led the way to the dining room, her defeated expression brightening as she reached the closed double doors, usually wide open. 'I have a surprise for you. That is, Lucas and I have a surprise. Today is your American Thanksgiving. It's not easy to find turkey and cranberries in Paris, but we managed.' She flung open the dining room doors to reveal the astonishing sight of roast turkey and trimmings. '*Bon appétit*!'

'Oh my goodness!' Helen clapped her hands to her cheeks. She'd remembered the holiday that morning, pictured her family gathering without her, and Kevin, with his family, missing her. She'd felt faint wistfulness, then moved on to the rest of her day. By now the celebration felt as far away in her thoughts as it was in miles. 'Thank you. I am so touched you thought of this. What a nice thing to do.'

They sat down and helped themselves, Lucas carving the servings of turkey. The meal was predictably delicious, turkey moist and tender under more of a sauce than a gravy, chestnut and currant stuffing, tiny and intensely flavorful French green beans, *haricots verts*, glistening with butter and garlic, rich mashed potatoes, and canned cranberry sauce from what Natalie called 'my American store', where expats could buy products they craved, like Oreos and peanut butter. To end the meal, a pecan tart instead of pumpkin, because Lucas had refused to serve a vegetable for dessert. *C'est affreux!*

After lunch, bolstered by coffee to combat the glass and a half of excellent Beaujolais she'd had with the meal, Helen floated off – figuratively; she was weighed down by too much food to float – to meet Gilles, fizzy with anticipation for the afternoon ahead, hoping he wouldn't be called away to cover some news event, which had happened more than once when the roommates included him in their plans. The day was glorious after several that had been chilly and gray with rain or drizzle, and it was delightful to catch the Métro at La Muette, change at République, then exit at Gambetta without having to refer to a map. Like a native! Though she couldn't be much of a native full of turkey and cranberry.

Gilles was waiting at the nearby cemetery entrance with Anneke, ubiquitous camera hanging from a strap over his shoulder. Helen grinned broadly, quickening her steps for the kiss-kiss ritual she'd become mostly accustomed to; first with Anneke, to avoid appearing too eager, and then Gilles. She hadn't seen him in a week. He'd been summoned to Spain to cover the death of Generalissimo Franco. Not for the first time, Helen was glad they weren't alone. The lunch wine put her in danger of betraying her puppy love. He was so ridiculously handsome and tall, gentle and intelligent, funny and . . .

Shh.

Anneke was a big-boned blond Dutchwoman with blue eyes and a wide grin, studying for her master's in medieval history at the Sorbonne. She and Gilles had met while he was covering the visit of the UAE president to Paris earlier that year, and he'd nearly run her over with his motorbike rushing film back to the Agence-France office before deadline.

'*Allons-y*!' Anneke waved her map and led the way into the graveyard between massive stone pillars against whose bulk lay the open iron entrance gates. 'We start with your list: Proust, Apollinaire, Balzac, Molière, Beaumarchais. And a few surprises along the way.'

Gilles gestured to her to precede them on the path. 'We trust you.'

Anneke strode on at a brisk pace that left Gilles and Helen side by side, trying to keep up.

'Today is your American holiday. Happy Thanksgiving.'

'Thank you.' Helen beamed over at him. 'Natalie made a full feast for me.'

'Ah! You will have to make that for us one day.'

'I'd love to.' She liked that it was second nature to include Gilles in the roommates' doings, often with the addition of whatever peripheral friends were free, and whomever Connie was dating that month, or week, or day. Currently she was into Jean-Gilbert, a thin, hunched poet with a thinner mustache, black clothes, constant cigarette and always-tortured expression. Tie a sweater around his shoulders, slap a beret on him and he'd be the perfect cliché.

'Did you miss being with your family and your . . . Kevin?'

'Not as much as I expected.' The truth came out without thinking. She didn't dare look at him, in case he read more into her glance than he should. 'But I thought of them. Tell me all about Spain.'

'Have you been?'

'No. I'd love to someday.' She'd found herself now and then fantasizing about future travels, searching for ways she might be able to escape, even knowing it was unlikely she and Kevin would have the money, or that she could be spared from the farm or from Kevin.

They followed Anneke's brisk pace, talking comfortably. Gilles told her about people he'd interviewed after Franco's death, the extremes of opinion about the dictator. He described the immense crowd that packed itself together to see the body of this cruel, destructive man sent to its grave, supporters waving hundreds of white handkerchiefs, chanting his name. They discussed people being drawn to those who pretended to have all the answers in an increasingly complicated world, those who reduced issues to black and white, love and hate, us and them. They wondered why their followers didn't notice the bluster and ego, which led to whether man could live without an authority figure, and whether that need was the impetus for the rise of religion.

In short, they had the kind of provocative, challenging and complex discussion that Helen couldn't have with Kevin. Kevin liked to pronounce things. He listened to her, he respected her, but he wanted the last word. He was often right, there was no doubting his intelligence, but in this type of situation, where both she and Gilles were feeling their way through questions for which there were no pat answers, Kevin would need to find and announce one, then be counted correct. Typically male, very understandable, though in Helen's family her mother played this role more often than Dad.

She'd need to spend time with people like Gilles in Kansas – except not male and available and so temptingly attractive. It was unfair to expect Kevin to be everything to her, and in spite of his declaration that she was everything to him, she knew he must have needs she couldn't fill either. They'd both need their other friends. That was normal for any couple.

Thinking about it made her feel a little panicky, so she concentrated instead on what was around her. Père Lachaise had been opened by Napoleon in the early nineteenth century after the existing cemeteries in Paris ran out of room. While graveyards in the US tended to be spacious and orderly, this one was spectacularly cluttered with graves. Most were not simple markers like those Helen was used to, but larger, more ostentatious structures. Some were tiny stone chapels a person could squeeze into for prayer or to pay respects, others were monuments, mausoleums or great horizontal stone slabs, looking like above-ground coffins, decorated with sculptures or carvings or statues of the dead. Pots of colorful flowers and other offerings adorned those most remembered, loved or admired. The high cemetery walls muted traffic noise, and sun dappled the cobblestone roads through trees whose leaves shimmied in the breeze. The perfect setting for a long, contemplative wander.

Today, however, Helen and Gilles were forced to keep up with Anneke's energetic pace. Not quite the way Helen would have liked to visit, but efficient.

Proust, under a polished black granite slab, check. Move on.

Apollinaire, a weathered granite pillar over his stone, on which was a heart-shaped inscription: *Mon coeur pareil à une flamme renversée.*

'My heart is like an upside-down flame.' Gilles formed a heart with his fingers, then turned it over. 'From the other side, like a candle.'

Check. Move on.

Balzac, a vertical monument under an enormous bronze-gone-green bust of the writer and poet. Check. Move on.

Helen was starting to feel a little desperate. She wanted to stop, to look, to *feel* the person buried, think of all he'd accomplished.

'Now we see Victor Noir.' Anneke rushed off down one of the cobble streets.

'Victor who?' Helen found herself asking Anneke's vapor trail.

Gilles shrugged, looking amused. 'We can come back together one day and take more time.'

'I'd like that.' She turned to follow their guiding whirlwind, marveling at how Gilles so often put voice to her inner thoughts. He'd be hard to leave in February. Hard, but necessary. There was no point falling any deeper into infatuation. Gilles was not going to be her life.

They caught up with Anneke in front of their next assignment: a man lying on his back, another bronze-turned-green statue with two notable exceptions where the reddish-brown shine of the original metal had been preserved: on Victor Noir's lips, and on his very prominent . . .

Helen gasped and started blushing. 'What on earth?'

'The sculptor, Jules Dalou, gave him an erection,' Anneke said matter-of-factly. 'We don't know why, but it's very impressive.'

Gilles aimed his camera. 'So people have been . . . polishing?'

'It is believed that if a woman puts a flower in his hat, which is there lying next to him, and then kisses him and rubs his . . . bump? What do you say in English?'

Helen struggled not to giggle, annoyed at her prudery. Kevin would also be embarrassed. Her parents would cease to exist. 'Bulge.'

'Yes, bulge . . . they will have many children, or good sex, or find a husband.' Anneke bent down to give Victor's shiny spot an affectionate rub, a gesture Gilles captured on film. 'You want to try, Helen?'

Helen hesitated, face burning, aware of Gilles's eyes on her, all her Midwestern bits shrieking no. At the same time, the Paris bits that had lately been gaining a stronger voice started demanding to know what harm could possibly come of it.

'Sure.' She heard herself agreeing, felt her body moving forward, then cold metal under her fingers and . . .

Nothing horrible happened. Not a thing. Her initial hesitation seemed absurd.

'There you go!' Anneke was triumphant. 'Lots of children and a husband who gives you good sex.'

Helen caught Gilles's mischievous grin and laughed, at her silly reluctance and in celebration of her victory – though there was still enough prude in her to be relieved he hadn't photographed her fondling some dead guy's privates.

Anneke clapped her hands. 'Let us keep on.'

They left poor eternally unsatisfied Victor and marched onward, Helen taking in as much as she could as they passed, though it wasn't long before Anneke stopped in front of a black iron fence protecting an enormous white stone sarcophagus supported on four vast white stone legs.

Helen squinted at the plaque. *L. B. Poquelin* . . .

'Oh my gosh. It's Molière.' She clasped her hands to her chest, heart fluttering with adrenaline and excitement.

Gilles stopped close behind her, hand on his camera, not lifting it, staring with her for a long, awed moment. 'It's unreal.'

Helen couldn't take her eyes off the magnificent tomb. This was even more mind-boggling than seeing her personal poet, Marceline Desbordes-Valmore, at the Montmartre cemetery, and that had been quite moving. She'd read many works of the authors they'd seen, but Molière was in a different class, the Shakespeare of France. 'Have you been here, Gilles? Seen him before?'

'No, believe it or not.' He stepped forward, put his hands on the fence. 'Typical, not knowing my own city.'

'It's hard to take in that we're close to his actual body.' Helen stepped to the side of the sarcophagus, where Molière, the stage name he used to avoid shaming his family with his life as an actor, was spelled out in iron letters bolted into the stone. 'And hard to comprehend that he was just a man. People passed him in the street, fell in love with him or hated him, argued with him, made him pay bills. He got colds, he got cranky, he got mosquito bites and indigestion . . .'

'Mortal,' Gilles said. 'None of us thinks of him that way. We're used to his literary genius, to thinking of him as a giant, a force of civilization. I feel more awed by his brilliance here, confronted with his physical remains, than when I'm reading his plays or seeing them on stage.'

'I know what you mean.' Helen came back to stand next to Gilles at the fence. 'His works have taken on a life of their own, apart from the man who wrote them. Here we're forced to bring the two back together.'

They gazed longer in companionable silence, broken by Anneke clearing her throat. 'We should get to Beaumarchais.'

Gilles lifted his camera and aimed it at the tomb. 'Why so much hurry, Anneke?'

'I'm going to meet . . . a friend. I was going to see him later and have the afternoon with you, but he had a change.' She looked stricken.

So did Helen. She and Gilles would be alone together for the first time since he'd driven her home on his motorbike two months earlier.

'You go have fun, Anneke. We can find the graves.' Gilles held out his hand. 'Leave us the map. We'll find them.'

'Are you sure?' Anneke's face began to turn red. 'It would be nice to change my clothes before I see him. I live so close.'

'*Bien sûr, bien sûr, ne t'inquiète pas*, Anneke. Don't worry. Go have fun. We'll do fine.'

Helen wasn't so sure. It was entirely too lovely and romantic a spot to be left alone with Mr. Temptation. She'd need to keep Kevin firmly in mind.

'I know!' Anneke's face brightened. 'I'll leave by the main gate. There's Chopin on the way, and another odd grave to see. Then you can go back to Beaumarchais if you want.'

Helen and Gilles followed her energetic pace to Chopin. Behind a thick mass of floral tributes stood his monument, the familiar profile carved in stone under a statue of Euterpe – the muse of music, according to Anneke – whose head bent in sorrowful weeping.

'Ah, Chopin. His music makes me cry as well.' Gilles gave Helen a sheepish glance. 'I think American men don't cry, yes? They're all John Wayne.'

Helen laughed, touching the petals of a rose bouquet tied to the fence. 'Some truth to that. I love Chopin's piano music especially, though if he heard me playing it, he'd shove me off the bench.'

'Me too,' Anneke said. 'It's frustrating when the music in your head won't come out your fingers.'

'I played clarinet.' Gilles mimed playing. 'I wanted to be Benny Goodman. My parents bought me a camera to stop me, I think. I was very bad at the clarinet.'

'And very good with the camera.' Helen smiled at him.

He smiled back, acknowledging the compliment. Anneke had wandered off, and Helen stood enjoying the masculine beauty of his features, his dark tumble of hair and the warmth of the feeling between them, trying to keep it in perspective.

Not particularly successfully.

'Stay there. Like that.' He pointed his lens at her. 'No, no, smile like you were.'

She imagined his face behind the camera, pretended the metal contraption wasn't there, and that she was looking into his eyes. This time he clicked, clicked again and put the camera down. 'Beautiful, Helen.'

'Thank you.' Helen pretended to look for Anneke, trying to cope with unwelcome emotions of vulnerability, and always this simmering attraction she couldn't seem to suppress.

'Come. Look.' Anneke was beckoning them toward another grave, a slab on which reclined the weathered-green statue of a full-sized man holding a disembodied female head.

Helen approached warily. 'Who is *that*?'

'Meet Fernand Arbelot.' Anneke stepped back so they could see better. Fernand's shoulders rested on a stone support, enabling him to look directly into the woman's eyes. A tear had been sculpted to flow down her cheek. 'Like Victor, this man is now famous only for his tomb, designed so he could look on the face of his wife for all eternity.'

'It *sounds* romantic.' Helen stared dubiously. 'But the more you look, the more it seems . . . I don't know.'

'Disturbing.' Gilles was scowling. 'Why isn't *he* crying? And where is the rest of her?'

'Ugh.' Helen folded her arms. 'It's like he cut her head off.'

Anneke wrinkled her nose. 'There are stories that he murdered her then took his own life.'

'That makes it even uglier.' Gilles knelt to take a picture. 'As if he holds her to keep an eye on her.'

'For all eternity.' Helen shuddered.

'Rumors, rumors only. And now I really must go. So fun to show you these.' Anneke rushed toward them for the kiss-kiss *au revoir*, grinning shyly at their good wishes for her date, then rushed off.

Helen smiled after her, feeling awkwardly alone with Gilles. The afternoon would need recalibrating. 'Someone's excited.'

'If I'd known, I would have told her not to come.'

'She got us this far.'

'She did.' He turned abruptly from Arbelot and his wife's head. 'I don't want to see this one anymore. Men who want to own their women. It's disgusting.'

His voice was surprisingly vehement, his normally straight posture hunched. Helen waited, not wanting to pry.

'I have a cousin like this. I don't know where it comes from. Some demon need to control his wife, always wanting to know where she is, who she's with, what she's doing. When she comes to visit alone, he calls every day, sometimes twice, always suspicious. His wife . . . I don't know why she puts up with this treatment, or why she doesn't . . . Well, you don't need to hear my family trouble.'

'I don't mind.' Except his description had reminded Helen uneasily of Kevin's recent letters, and she was ashamed to have made the connection. Kevin had good reason to be upset.

'It's nothing I can change. I don't want it to spoil our beautiful day here.' Gilles turned the map around and back and around again, until it was upside down. '*Alors*. This will be easy.'

Helen laughed. 'It's so beautiful here, even if we get lost it's not a hardship.'

'True.' He scanned the map. 'Beaumarchais . . . that way? That way? This way. Yes, this way.'

They started that way. '*Oh merde! Non.*'

Retraced and tried another route. '*Oui, oui . . . non.*'

They never found him. Or maybe didn't recognize his grave. Or stopped caring. But they paid tribute to him anyway, his playwriting and his comic genius, chatting about whether he'd written *The Barber of Seville* or *The Marriage of Figaro* first, and which one they liked better. They both voted for *Marriage of Figaro*, and then, because of the Mozart opera of that name, discovered Gilles was a big symphony fan but lukewarm on opera, and that Helen wasn't wild about either but willing to try again.

'Now.' Gilles stopped at an intersection and put the map away. 'If it's okay, we will go this way, for a grave I want us to see together.'

'Of course it's okay.' Helen was intrigued. She was enjoying his company more and more. Dangerous, but only if she let it become so.

It took them a while to find their way, but she was in no hurry. Without a crowd of friends around, interrupting and teasing, they were able to talk freely. Gilles had grown up in a wealthy suburb of Paris, relieved when his younger brother showed a passion for the telecommunications business their grandfather had started, and Gilles could escape into the city with his love of books and photography. He'd studied at the Sorbonne, then stayed in Paris, though he'd always wanted to explore the US and thought he could envision himself in New York someday. If stranded on an island, he could cheerfully live on bread, cheese, wild raspberries and chocolate.

Helen told him about Zionsville, her parents and her brothers, her early love of France and her lonely feelings being the only academic of the Kenyons. She told him about the family hardware stores and the house her grandfather built, and that she couldn't live without peanut butter, peaches, fresh corn and cheeseburgers.

'*Et voilà*. Here we are. The one I want to show you. To talk a little.' They stood before an enormous gothic chapel-like structure, with columns supporting a multi-spired roof protecting a sculpted couple lying close together on an enormous stone block.

Helen stood, reverent but also, for reasons she didn't understand, afraid. 'Who's here?'

'Héloïse and Abelard.' He put a hand on her upper back and left it there, making her stiffen against twin desires, to lean into him and to step away. 'Lovers who were kept apart.'

'Oh.' Helen's heart started pumping.

'Do you know the story?'

'No.' She didn't want to hear it.

'Abelard was an educated man who taught in the cloisters at Notre-Dame in the twelfth century. Héloïse was much younger, also very educated, fluent in many languages.' Gilles took his hand away, leaving a chill. 'She was one of his pupils. They fell in love and she became . . . how do you say *enceinte*?'

'Pregnant.'

'Pregnant. Her uncle was one of the clergy at the cathedral. He found out about the affair and sent his men to castrate Abelard.'

Helen gasped. 'Good God, how barbaric. What happened?'

'They were separated. Abelard became a monk. Héloïse went into a convent. In spite of how deeply they loved, they never saw each other again.' His voice was low and husky. 'But they wrote letters back and forth for the rest of Abelard's life. Beautiful, powerful love letters, some of which survived all these centuries. Here they are finally able to be together.'

Helen closed her eyes, undone, and not only by the plight of the tragic couple and its parallel to their own. Gilles's empathy, his capacity for emotion, his ability to express it . . . so like hers.

A tear slid down her cheek, a live, liquid version of the stone carving on Arbelot's wife's detached face.

Gilles touched her shoulder. 'It's hard not to feel that story.'

'No kidding.' She wanted him to keep thinking that was all she was grieving.

'During the last century, at the height of romanticism, young people would come to this tomb to cry over loves they'd lost. Or loves they couldn't have.' He touched her wet cheek. 'Maybe that tradition hasn't died.'

Helen stepped away from him. 'No.'

'No what?' He laughed, eyes crinkling, lifting his arms in a shrug. 'I haven't asked you anything.'

'You're right.' She wiped away tears with her hand. 'But no anyway.'

'I'm falling in love with you, Helen.' His voice broke, but his eyes were steady.

Lightning, from her chest down to the base of her spine. 'Oh gosh. But no. No, you—'

'You're here three more months. I can't anymore pretend I'm only your friend.' He looked over at the tomb, took in a breath. 'I need to know how you feel.'

'Gilles, I *can't* have feelings for you. Kevin is—'

'Kevin, I know. But you are changing. I've watched you change here.' He stepped closer, eyes warm and earnest. 'Kevin has not changed back at home, I can tell you this. So maybe you go back to him in February and find out you don't fit him anymore. And then you and I never find out what this is *entre nous*. I think it's something special. Maybe I'm right, maybe not right. But I want to know. I don't want to have to send you letters for the rest of my life and never see you again. I want you with me, in my life, my lover for the months we have left. If then you decide to go back to Kevin, that is your choice.'

Helen felt herself shaking, head to foot. 'I can't do that to him.'

'Then do it for you. I am asking.'

A young couple came up and stood beside them, murmuring over the tomb.

Gilles took Helen's hand and pulled her away, along the road they'd come down. Or maybe a different one; she had a feeling neither of them knew or cared.

'You can take time, Helen. Take a few days and think. Okay?'

She should say no. Right now. Stomp out the ember before it blazed. And yet . . . it wouldn't be fair to Gilles, or to herself, or to Kevin, if she kept trying to pretend that cracks weren't developing in her certainty over her future. 'Okay.'

'Good.' He squeezed her hand and let it go. 'I can wait a few more days, but then I will . . . what is *éclater*?'

'Burst.' Helen laughed, a little hysterically. 'If you do, I know a great cemetery.'

'Yes. Thanks.' He grinned at her, then came to a stop and held up the map. 'Do we care anymore where we are?'

'No.' She pointed right. 'That way.'

They wandered in silence, on this path then that one, no idea if they'd find an exit or were walking in a circle. After a few steps, Gilles took her hand again, and Helen let it lie in his, torn apart by internal conflict while paradoxically enjoying the peace of walking with this man, no longer needing to pretend that he meant nothing to her, not having to fill the silence with her usual nervous chatter. They understood each other and what this might mean, could mean.

Shouldn't mean.

Around another corner, she grabbed Gilles's arm with her free hand. 'Sarah!'

An enormous stone monument with low arches and a sloping roof. On it in large letters, deeply etched, filled with shining gold: *Sarah Bernhardt 1844–1923.*

'There she is.' Helen was laughing, breathless. 'Oh my gosh, what a perfect surprise.'

When he didn't react, she turned to him, lit with excitement, to find him standing close. Not laughing. The look in his eyes nearly undid her.

Then he was kissing her, sure and firm, his mouth warm, grasping her shoulders to bring her closer, then sliding his arms around her. A torrent of desire nearly overcame her, a dark, sensual passion of a kind she hadn't known existed, one she could easily disappear into if she let herself be overcome.

Following that came creeping fear that what she had with Kevin was only a shadow of what love could be.

Chapter 9

It's a book of angels when one is loved
If one of the two changes, the book is closed!
  Marceline Desbordes-Valmore, 'L'adieu tout bas'

Helen let herself into the apartment on rue Pierre Nicole, flushed and shaky, split in half by wrenching guilt and by thrills that wouldn't stop chasing around her body.

Lilianne was at the kitchen table, poring over the kinds of financial reports she was always poring over, none of which held the slightest interest for Helen.

'Hi.' She put on a bright smile, intending to walk briskly to her room, close the door and collapse.

'Hey.' Lilianne stood and put out a hand as Helen tried to pass. 'What happened? What's going on?'

'I'm fine, I just . . .' Sobs burst out of her in a humiliating rush. Lilianne put her arms around her hesitantly, as if she weren't quite sure how. Helen relaxed against her and bawled out her confusion and grief.

'You're okay. You're okay.' Lilianne patted her with awkward gentleness that undid Helen further.

Finally she was able to control herself and raised her forehead from Lilianne's now-soggy shoulder. Lilianne gave her a sympathetic smile. 'I'll get you a tissue.' She moved over to the

215

counter and returned with a box. 'C'mon. Into the living room. We'll talk this out with Sarah.'

'Thanks.' Helen took a stuttering breath. 'I'm sorry.'

'Why? You're upset. You cried. That's how humans work.' She led Helen into the living room and stopped in front of Sarah, installed regally on a side table. The doll had essentially become their fourth roommate. Connie had been known to drape her in scarves when it was chilly, and even Lilianne showed a playful side and bought her an elegant feather hat from a doll store, which they'd periodically swap out with her 'diamond' tiara. Helen, not to be outdone, bought the most delicate wool she could find and was knitting her a nightdress. On Connie's birthday in early November, Sarah had helped blow out the candles and had been so much silly fun joining in the party games that they declared her necessary for all their birthdays from then on. 'Sarah, darling, we have a crisis and need to talk it out if that's okay with you.'

Helen let out a soggy sigh. 'I saw Sarah today at Père Lachaise. She has a lovely resting spot.'

'No kidding!' Lilianne looked delighted. 'Hear that, Sarah? You're settled in style in death as in life. Now come sit, Helen. There's nothing good friends and a horrible orange couch can't make better.'

'Thank you. I'm a disaster.'

'Shh, you are not.' Lilianne sat with her. 'I assume this has something to do with Gilles. That's what Sarah thinks.'

Helen nodded, tears starting again.

'Either he declared his love for you and you're freaked out, or you declared yours and he rejected you. How close am I?'

Helen forced back more tears and blew her nose. 'The first.'

'Did you see this coming? Connie and I did.'

'I thought I could control it. Or that we could control it and just be friends.' She hiccuped. 'So stupid.'

'Not stupid at all.' Lilianne gave Helen's knee a few quick pats. 'Where did you leave it?'

'He didn't pressure me. He said I should take a few days to think about what I want to do.'

'Very gentlemanly. I'm a big fan of Gilles's.'

Helen buried her face in her hands. 'I can't do this to Kevin.'

'What you can't do to Kevin is marry him when you're in love with someone else.'

'I can't be in love with Gilles. I barely know him! I don't have *time* to get to know him. I can't upend my life because of some hormonal rush.'

Lilianne pulled Helen's hands down and gave her a mother-knows-best look. 'You don't seem like the type that falls for every hot guy who smiles at you.'

Helen shook her head. 'I'm not. I'm generally not. But things are different here.'

'Not that different. Repressed parts of you might pop out but you can't change fundamentally.'

'I hate this.'

Lilianne pushed Helen's hair back from her face. 'Life sucks sometimes. If it's any consolation, I don't get the slightest bad vibe from Gilles. I haven't met Kevin, but . . . I can't imagine the you I know now living that life with him.'

From the kitchen came the unmistakable sound of Connie wrenching open the door and slamming it closed. 'I'm home, did you miss me?'

'No,' Lilianne called.

'Of course you did. Hello, darlings, how is Sarah today? Did she . . .' Connie appeared around the corner and gasped. 'Oh no. What's wrong?'

'It's happened. Gilles declared.'

'Took him long enough.' Connie came into the room, bringing with her a powerful wave of perfume.

'Good God, Connie.' Lilianne waved her hand in front of her face. 'What have you done to yourself?'

'Ambush at La Samaritaine, cosmetics department.' Connie sniffed her wrists rapturously. 'Ladies came at me from all directions. Lancôme, Chanel, Guerlain, Dior. You name it, I'm wearing it. So we're having a powwow? Do we need wine? I think we do. Sarah certainly does. She drank like a fish at my birthday party.'

'Not me,' Helen said glumly. 'I'd probably jump in the Seine.'

Connie unwrapped a jingling tie-dyed scarf from around her neck. 'Two men in love with you, you poor, poor thing,'

Lilianne glared at her. 'A little sympathy?'

'You know I'm teasing. We need wine. I need wine. I do my best advising when I have a glass in front of me. Or two.'

'You drink too much,' Lilianne said drily.

'You notice too much.' Connie went over to the cabinet and popped the cork out of an open bottle, poured herself a healthy slug. 'So where were we when I barged in?'

'Confused,' Helen said.

'I was trying to point out that Gilles is everything any woman could ever want. But Helen seems to think being nearly engaged to Kevin means she owes him something.'

Connie pretended to choke on a sip. 'How strange.'

'I also told her—' The phone rang in the hall. Lilianne jumped to her feet. 'Probably for me. I've been waiting for a call. I might have to go to Cairo next week.'

Connie and Helen exchanged glances as she rushed from the room.

'Maybe we should come with you,' Connie called. 'Sarah can watch the place.'

'*Allo? Oui, c'est moi.*' Receiver to her ear, Lilianne picked up the base and moved it to the length of its cord, out of their hearing.

Helen looked questioningly at Connie. 'Cairo?! Would I be way off if I guessed CIA?'

'Who knows. I don't think so, but with Lilianne, anything is possible. Such a mystery woman.' Connie plunked her jingling perfumed self down on the overstuffed brown chair across the room.

'And is she . . . ?' Helen shifted, curiosity temporarily overcoming her misery. 'I mean, I never see her dating.'

'No. She doesn't date.'

'So does she . . . ?' Helen paused, desperately hoping Connie would jump in and rescue her. Connie sat sipping her wine, smiling blandly. 'Does she like women?'

'Sure. I like women too. Don't you?'

Helen huffed in frustration. 'No, I mean . . . You *know* what I mean.'

The bland dimpled smile got blander. 'No idea.'

'Connie . . .' Helen glared. 'You're going to make me say it, aren't you?'

Connie burst out with her trademark evil laugh. 'Yes, I am. I want to hear you say the word "lesbian" with that terrified Midwestern look on your face, and then realize it isn't going to bite, maim or kill you, and neither is anyone who is one.'

'Fine. Is Lilianne a lesbian?'

'No. She is not a lesbian. She loves women the way I love women. Deeply, but not sexually. Unless I was drunk enough.'

Helen blinked.

'That's the look! That's the one!' Connie pointed, then jumped up and walked over to Sarah, straightened and stroked her fur cape. 'I was kidding. You're safe here, I promise. From both of us.'

'I knew that.' Helen fished a tissue out of her pants pocket and blew her nose. 'I was just wondering.'

'Naturally. So now that I've had my wine and consulted with Ms Bernhardt, do you want my advice?'

'No.'

Connie tilted her head, pouting. 'Aw, c'mon, man.'

'I already know what it is. "Get all the sex you can while you can get it, because love is free for everyone, and if you want to love both Kevin and Gilles, that's even better. In fact, why not invite the French navy over while you're—"'

'*No*, not that. As a woman, you'll always be able to get the sex you want. All you have to do is say okay to whoever's around, because that's how men are. What I was going to say is that you need to trust your gut. Stop thinking about what you should or shouldn't do, stop thinking about what other people expect of you, stop worrying about pleasing other people, and listen to your insides.'

Helen sighed. Almost the advice she'd given Natalie that morning. 'My insides are a garbled mess.'

'Ask them the right questions. Ask whether you love Kevin because you and he are in the same groove, or because you've always been together and it's too scary to change. Ask whether you love Gilles because he's hunky and here, or because you match and belong. Then listen. Even if your gut doesn't use clear words, it will tell you in other ways. You'll feel sick if you choose the wrong way. Leaden, miserable, trapped . . .'

'I hope you're right.'

'Of course I'm right.' Connie stepped back to the cabinet and topped off her wine. 'Just don't be hard on yourself, sweetie. People grow and evolve. If you're digging Gilles, it doesn't mean you never loved Kevin. Stop worrying so much and go with it.

See Gilles while you're here. By the time you need to go home, you'll have your answer.'

'I can't see Gilles while I'm dating Kevin.'

'Ah, but here's where I go against your Midwestern grain. Yes, you can. This is your life, the only one you get until you turn to stinky rot in the ground. You owe it to Gilles to know how you feel, you owe it to Kevin to know for sure, and mostly you owe it to yourself.' She gulped down more wine and brandished the glass in a dashing pose. 'Have I made my point or should I go on, because I could do this all day.'

'I get it.' Helen had listened, she'd heard, but her heart wasn't convinced that cheating was ever the right answer. And yet she couldn't be honest with Kevin. To have him sit home and wait, knowing she was dating someone else for the next several months, would be horrifically cruel. Her heart was already melting into a tender mess at the thought of hurting him that badly. Which proved she still had those deep feelings for him. Hurting Gilles? She was pretty sure he could handle it.

Calmer now, though still unsure, she let Connie pour her a glass of wine and went with her into the kitchen to prepare a simple supper of reheated roast chicken and warm mustardy potato salad for the three of them, joined soon by Lilianne, who, it turned out, would indeed have to go to Cairo the next week.

Somehow Helen got through dinner, managing to act normally, then excused herself early and went into her room, where she got out an aerogramme. At the very least she could write to poor Kevin. He deserved more than her cowardly silence. Especially now.

Before she started, she took a long moment to clear Gilles and his kisses out of her head, to concentrate on the man who'd been so important to her for so much of her adult life. It was only fair. Gilles had been around often in the past two months. Kevin deserved equal time. She focused on his smile, his laugh, his protectiveness; the way he dropped everything her junior year and drove her to Indiana the day Dad went into the hospital for emergency heart surgery; the way he quietly took care of everything her distraught family was too exhausted to handle. The way he asked her to the prom on his knees, arms full of daisies, wearing a jacket and tie, a boater hat and Bermuda shorts with sneakers; the time he and three friends serenaded her on her birthday with a barbershop version of 'Love Me and the World Is Mine'. The time he brought her broth and saltine crackers when she was miserable with stomach flu, sat by her bed and read to her. The first time they made love, serious and sweet, with such a feeling of inevitability, a quiet certainty that they fit together, body and soul.

Then she put her pen to the paper, hoping the right words would come to her as she wrote.

Dear Kevin,
Happy Thanksgiving! I had turkey and trimmings for lunch today with Natalie. It was so sweet of her to think of me. I'm thinking of you now, probably sitting with your family as I write, enjoying the afternoon feast.

I'm sorry I haven't written as often as you want, but it's hard to communicate from such a distance all the experiences I'm having, which must seem so far away and foreign to you. I keep thinking I can catch up, but then by evening I'm exhausted and unable to give you the attention you deserve. Connie and Lilianne are full of energy, Connie in particular, and we go out all the nights we can afford to, or have friends over to the apartment here.

My days are full of joyful new experiences. I'm learning

so much, and feel as if my world is expanding, and as if I'm expanding with it. It's exciting being here, Kevin. I feel I'm growing and changing.

Helen put down her pen. She wanted to describe the visit to the graveyard today, the profound moments she'd had standing beside the mortal remains of some of history's greats. She wanted to share with him the image of Fernand Arbelot holding his wife's head, of the stone tear carved on her face and the unease the image bred.

But it was impossible to bring up the visit, one she'd already shared so deeply and effortlessly with Gilles, not only because it was the scene of her betrayal, but also because she'd be feeding Kevin another experience he wouldn't understand or appreciate. He wouldn't find it at all awe-inspiring that Molière's body was in his grave – where else would it be? And he would find a husband's need to gaze on his wife for all eternity nothing but romantic – like writing daily letters.

Determinedly, she reached back to her memory of that last evening on his farm, surrounded by clear clean air and by friends, that deep love of and connection to the place, to the house, to the earth and to the man. The feelings washed over her again, all safety and sweetness, calm and certainty, easily called up. The simple beauty of hard work providing for the world's food chain, not lofty, not intellectual, but real, substantial, important and lasting. From that view, Gilles could become a gaudy jewel, a frivolous temptation, a symbol of what Kevin lacked, maybe, but hardly vital enough to negate what she and Kevin had.

If only she knew which view to choose, which steps were the right ones to take next.

I'm so pleased that you are working on getting the farm in shape. I can't wait to see the equipment you bought, and I look forward to being part of it and helping the land thrive for our children and grandchildren.

I won't say that I'll try to write more often, because I can't promise that. But I hope you will also try to understand what life is like for me here, and appreciate it for its differences.

I love you, and will be back soon to all we've planned together, but only after I've lived here to the fullest possible.

Helen

She folded and addressed the letter, then held it, unsealed, uneasy with what she'd written. Like Natalie and her mother's jewelry, Helen had decided only that she couldn't decide. She owed Kevin more than that.

Out in the hall, the phone rang. Seconds later, a tap on the door, then Connie's worried face appeared around it.

'Brace yourself. It's Kevin.'

'Oh my gosh.' Helen pushed back her chair so quickly it nearly tipped over. Had something happened? Phone calls were so expensive. Was her family okay? His?

She rushed into the hall. 'Kevin. Has something happened? Is everyone all right?'

He chuckled, his deep voice comfortingly familiar. 'Can't a guy call his future wife to say Happy Thanksgiving?'

'Oh my gosh. Of course you can. Happy Thanksgiving, Kevin.' She was giddy at the sound of his voice, his familiar Midwestern twang. He'd have no idea how important it was that she'd heard from him that day. 'Are you with your family?'

'Just about to start eating. I couldn't wait to hear your voice. You haven't been writing.'

'I know, I know, I'm sorry.' She frowned. He sounded strange just then, gravelly and harsh. 'Actually, though, I just finished a letter this second.'

'Oh sure. I just bet. We said *every day*, Helen.'

His slurred words shocked her more than his anger, which she knew how to soothe. Was he drunk? At his *family's* place? That wasn't like him. She'd seen him drunk and mean before, but only a few times, in college, and the temper was never directed at her. After they'd started dating seriously, he'd stopped over-indulging. 'I explained all that. I've been so busy. This is such a magical place to—'

'Oh, and we're just a bunch of duds here in the US, is that it?'

Helen's smile and eagerness vanished, replaced by sick dread. Why had he done this to himself? Because of her? 'That's a pretty big leap of logic, Kevin. I can have fun here and still love my country.'

'You're right. I'm sorry. I miss you so much, baby. It's like daily agony not knowing what you're doing or who you're with.'

She closed her eyes, guilt tearing at her. 'I'm enjoying myself, making good friends.'

'What did you do today?'

She had to sit down. 'I . . . went to a graveyard. Père Lachaise. It's one of the most—'

'Oh, fantastic. Hanging out with dead French people.' He laughed coarsely. 'Probably just as snooty as the live ones.'

Helen kept quiet for a long moment. This was the last thing she needed from him right now, with Gilles in danger of entering her heart. 'Actually, it *was* fantastic. We saw the graves of Chopin and Molière and—'

'*We?* Who'd you go with?' He made the innocent question into an accusation, startling Helen into thinking of Gilles's controlling cousin.

She bent her head, a burn of adrenaline and fear in her chest. She'd never lied to Kevin about anything. She wasn't going to start now. 'Our friend Gilles, and *his* friend Anneke.'

'Jill? That's a guy's name? Buncha fairies over there.'

'You're being a jerk, Kevin.'

'I'm being smart, *Helen*. Something's going on, something's not right with you, something you're not telling me, and I don't like it.'

Helen swallowed, barely able to breathe. He was right. He was absolutely right. She was responsible for his agony, and for him turning to alcohol to cope. She owed him the truth.

But not when he was like this.

'I want you home, Helen. *Now*.' He spoke with an ominous intensity that chilled her. She'd never asked him about his tour in Vietnam – he'd made it clear he would never talk about it. But this was the first time she could imagine how he might have operated over there.

'I think we need to wait and discuss this when you're sober.'

The vicious obscenity and abrupt hang-up were so unexpected, Helen sat for a good thirty seconds repeating his name into the phone, unable to believe what had just happened.

He'd call back. It was a mistake. The line was cut or . . .

Connie and her wine appeared in the living room doorway. She'd obviously been listening. 'You okay?'

Helen stood to put down the receiver. 'He was drunk. He hung up on me.'

'What happened? Did you tell him about Gilles?'

'No. No. Not when he was like that.' She turned to Connie, trying to focus. 'He practically ordered me to come home. It's like he knew what happened today.'

Connie shrugged. 'Maybe he does on some cosmic level. What did you tell him?'

'That I wouldn't discuss it until he was sober. Then he swore at me and hung up.'

She grinned. 'Attagirl. Don't let the bully win.'

'He's not a bully,' Helen shot back. 'He was feeling insecure. He hates being in situations where he's not in control.'

'How romantic.'

'He doesn't control *me*, or even try.' She gestured around her. 'He let me come here.'

'*Let* you?' Connie gestured with her glass. 'Like you're a pet he allowed out to play and now decided he wants back in because you're having too much fun?'

'That's not how it is.'

She lifted an eyebrow. 'Okay, but Helen, understanding the reasons behind his shitty behavior does not make it forgivable. I don't understand why you would want to be with someone who'd treat you that way. Ever.'

Another echo of Gilles's words in the graveyard.

Deeply shaken, Helen went back into her room, picked up Kevin's last letter and scanned it, seeing his insecurity in every line, his need, his fear, his insistence that she fix it all for him.

It was the weight of that insistence that she'd been resisting by not writing, the weight of that need and his loneliness. He was right that something was different, and it had little and everything to do with Gilles. Helen was changing. She could imagine someone matching her more perfectly than Kevin. Whether or not that was Gilles was beside the point.

Only you can make this empty house feel like a home. I ache for you every day. I want to hold you and love you and keep you with me for the rest of my life.

Helen sank down on the bed, staring blankly at the page, searching her memories again to find the Kevin she knew, the Kevin she loved. The only image that came to mind was of

Fernand Arbelot's strong stone hands gripping the head of his weeping wife.

She spent a mostly sleepless night, tossing and turning, tormented by what she desperately wanted and desperately feared at the same time.

In the morning, exhausted and spent, but full of determination, she pulled out another aerogramme and her pen, angry at herself for not having the courage to do this before.

Dear Kevin,

You are right. I have changed, my feelings have changed, and I should have owned up to it instead of ignoring them and you until you hit boiling point. I apologize. That was immature and unfair of me.

I have things I need to figure out about the relationship I want. It sounded on the phone as if you do too. We both deserve good things and the right people to complete us. Maybe we will end up together as we planned. I'm not betting against us yet. But one thing is clear, we are not able to handle this relationship long-distance. You are feeling neglected, and I am feeling bombarded.

I think it's best we take a break until I'm back in the States in February. Then we can see where we are. Please respect this decision.

All my love,

Helen

Before she could change her mind for the forty-seventh time, she got dressed, took the clanky elevator down to the apartment mailbox and slid the letter in.

✒ Chapter 10 ✒

Morning light peeked through the blinds, confirming that it was useless for Teresa to pretend she might get back to sleep. Monarch, a by now familiar – though still not welcome – lump in the bed, made cranky protesting noises when she pulled off her covers.

'Yeah? You want a grumpy contest? I'd win.' She pushed herself out of bed, and the matted mess of hair out of her eyes, where it promptly fell back. It was going to be one of those days. Yesterday had been one of those days too.

Teresa had spent most of the last thirty-six-plus hours trying to get her mind around the fact that her mother had lied. Not a little lie. A honker. And if Mom had lied about the family's abusive alcoholic, and if James had been telling the truth about her seeing the past the way she wished it had been, what else had she lied about?

Possibly everything.

What did you do when the bedrock of your family – of your life – turned out to be landslide mud? If you were Teresa, you acted hyper-chatty on the phone with her, and the rest of the time sat miserably brooding, accomplishing only what was necessary to avoid death, your own and those in your care.

Eventually, that way to live would not work anymore. Maybe today she'd be able to do something else. Like shower, and put on fresh clothes.

That was such an inspired, if Herculean, task that Teresa dragged herself into the bathroom and got clean.

It helped a little. At least she no longer felt sticky and stinky, and her hair wasn't such a frizzy mop, though she didn't bother with the endless routine of stroking it perfectly straight.

Makeup wouldn't hurt either.

She put on makeup.

Better.

While Cheddar cracked and crunched his morning pellets and seeds, Teresa ate a bowl of Cheerios and a blueberry yogurt, then took her coffee out onto the back deck. Skies were gray and threatening, but a brisk breeze kept away mosquitoes, so she didn't have to make the supreme effort to find and deploy the repeller.

As she sat preparing to dive into another brooding session, it occurred to her that she might actually make some headway into this problem by sharing it with someone who was part of it.

Feeling stupid for not having thought of her brothers sooner, she dialed Ike, older by two minutes and the one she felt closer to, though the twins were so inseparable it was hard to feel like anything but an intruder around them.

'Treece! Whatcha doing? Animals eat you yet?'

'Ha-ha. I'm kind of freaked out. You got some time?'

'Shoot, not much. What's up?'

She wasn't even sure how to begin. Connecting with someone who knew Mom as well as she did had been pure instinct. 'So . . . did you ever wonder about Mom?'

He snorted. 'All the time. What in particular?'

'Like whether she . . . tells us the truth?'

Her brother groaned. 'Oh boy.'

'Yeah, so it's been really weird here, Ike. Like everyone

230

outside our family has lived a different version than the one she told us. At first I thought they were gaslighting me. Then two days ago I found proof that Grandpa *Kevin* was the alcoholic. He drank himself to death. I saw the death certificate.'

'Holy shit. That's intense.' He didn't sound as surprised as she expected.

'I don't know what to think.' She was near tears.

'Ah, Treece. Okay, so Mike and I talked about this a bunch when we were younger. Mom is kind of a case. It's like nothing that happens is ever her fault, you know? She's always the victim, of everyone around her. Her boss, her friends, her mother, her husband . . .'

Teresa had to close her eyes and breathe to quell a surge of nausea. 'You never talked about this with me.'

'Well it's not like we knew what we were talking about. Plus you and Mom have always been close, and it wasn't like she was torturing us. We love her, you know? She's our mom. All we decided was that when she got going, we'd joke her out of it when we could.'

Teresa opened her eyes to watch the roiling sky. 'What else do you think she lied about?'

'I don't know. I really don't. Mike and I kinda checked out of all the drama. Maybe not the best way to cope, but hey. We're guys.'

Teresa laughed unwillingly. 'I believed her.'

'I know, Treece. We did too, for a long time. It's depressing. Like we don't know, is she just neurotic or certifiable? Does it matter? We decided it didn't.'

It was hard to imagine something so painful not mattering. 'What do we do now?'

'I don't think we have to do anything. We're definitely not equipped to fix her, she's not a danger to anyone or herself, so . . . that's Mom, and we live our lives. I know it sounds flip, but we couldn't figure out any other way to deal.'

Teresa got up and wandered down toward the animals, her misery slightly lessened when the goats crowded forward to greet her through the fence, sexy Cleopatra at the fore. Humans weren't her favorite species at the moment. 'Did you ever wonder about Dad? I mean, the things she told us about him?'

Ike coughed awkwardly. 'Yeah, so . . . we're actually in touch with him. Past few years.'

'*What?*' The pain slammed back.

'Remember, we told you he'd written to us again, after gradu- ation. You were kind of outraged we'd even consider responding, but we were curious. And so we've been emailing, talking on the phone, having lunch sometimes. We seem to have this rule that none of us will talk about the past. We just tell him how we're doing, and he tells us how he's doing. It's pretty chill. He seems like a nice enough guy. He was really unhappy married to Mom. Handled it badly, then she did the rest.'

Teresa started to cry, not a sweet, tear-trickling kind, but the kind that felt like her throat was in a vice. Her mouth opened to gasp for air, but no air went in or out for what seemed like eternity, until finally breath rushed into the vacuum she'd cre- ated and the world's ugliest sob emerged.

'Oh man, Teresa. I'm so sorry. God, you must feel . . . betrayed or something. It wasn't like that. It was just for us. *Shit*, my ride's here. Hang on.'

She hung on, using every ounce of her strength to force the grief wave under control.

'You still there?'

'Yes. I'm here. I'm okay, Ike. You go ahead.' She sounded as if she were slowly being deprived of oxygen. It was her best effort. 'Thanks for telling me.'

'Seriously, Treece, I don't have to go, I can—'

'No, no. Go. I need time to think.'

'Oh Christ. Is there someone you can call? I hate that I did this to you. I'll get Mike to—'

'No.' She held up a stop hand, as if he could see her. 'You didn't do this to me. I'm okay. I just need to process. I'll be fine.'

'You sure?'

'Yes, I'm sure.' She snorted. '*I* don't lie to you.'

'I'm grateful for that.' He chuckled drily. 'Take care. I'll call you as soon as I can.'

Teresa stared robotically at the donkey that had come up to the fence to be adored.

'Smoke.' She put her hand to the coarse fur. 'I'm a mess.'

He seemed very concerned.

'A huge one. My mom. And then Dad . . . my dad . . .' Another wave hit, doubling her over. She squatted down and let the grief have its way, hand planted on the ground, not caring how hideous her sounds were, glancing to make sure she wasn't panicking the animals, but they seemed indifferent. Apparently, to them she was just exhibiting another strange human behavior.

When the sobs finally released her, she steadied herself, letting her breath slow, tears and snot dripping onto the ground. Then she lifted her head.

To find Zig standing next to her.

Teresa shrieked and fell back on her butt. Immediately he was on her and . . . started licking her wet face.

Ick!

'Stop!' She rolled away from him, giggling helplessly, then got to her feet and dragged a tissue out of her pocket to scrub her cheeks, sniffling and gulping. 'That was disgusting.'

Zig looked up at her, tail wagging, not seeming to feel the least bit guilty.

'*And* you scared me to death. Next time . . .'

Her head jerked up. Danny had appeared around the side of the house, carrying a small foil-covered plate.

Oh no! She had ugly-crying face. With dog spit. Even so, she couldn't think of anyone she'd rather see just then.

'Hey, Teresa, you're up early. I was going to leave these on the deck.' His grin faltered. 'Uh-oh. Is this a bad time?'

'Yes. But please stay anyway.'

He handed her the plate. 'I brought you cookies. Oatmeal chocolate chip. I made a batch yesterday and had extras.'

Her stomach fluttered. Even she knew there was no such thing as extra chocolate chip cookies. 'That's sweet of you, Danny, thanks.'

'Looks like you and Zig are doing okay?'

Teresa pointed to her cheek. 'Extreme licking. He must have a saline deficit.'

'Trying to cheer you up.'

'There must be better ways. Canine vaudeville or something.'

'You okay?' The gentle concern in Danny's eyes made her heart skip a beat. 'I mean, it's none of my business, but if you need to bitch or whatever, I'm okay listening.'

Her eyes filled with tears. 'Got about a year?'

He shrugged. 'I have whatever time you need.'

'God, you're a nice person.' She sniffed and wiped her eyes. 'Do you take pills to get that way or is it natural?'

He smiled. 'See how I do. If you really bore me, I'll get up and leave.'

'Deal.' They climbed back onto the deck. 'Need any coffee? Or will it keep you awake while I'm talking?'

'I'd love some, thanks.'

She went into the house and poured him a cup, plus more for herself, thinking she'd never felt this comfortable around a guy

234

she'd known such a short time. Maybe it was the circumstances here? The farm? Her precarious emotional state? Or that they hadn't met on a date. That he hadn't come on to her. That he wasn't a forbidden co-worker, or a potentially dangerous stranger, or one of her friends' new boyfriends trying too hard to get along. He was just . . . Danny.

'Here you go.' She handed him his coffee and sat next to him. He offered her a cookie, which she took to be polite since her stomach was not in the mood for food. Until she bit into it. 'Omigod, these are delicious.'

'Mom's recipe. We call them crack cookies.'

'I can see why.' She finished it, wishing they could sit here drinking coffee and eating cookies until all her problems went away.

'So you're having a shitty morning.'

'I'm having a shitty life.'

'Wait, wait.' He fidgeted in the chair, adjusted his pant legs. 'If it's your whole life, I need to get more comfortable.'

Teresa let out a goofy post-cry giggle. She really liked this guy. Not only was he willing to listen to her weird and sad tale, he was trying to cheer her up, using a method she liked much better than Zig's.

Keeping details and emotions to a minimum, she told him the basics, watching the story take hold of him. His face fell, jaw tightened; he shook his head at the worst moments.

'Damn, Teresa. That is quite the shitshow. What do you think you'll do? What's the plan?'

'Crawl in a hole and rot?'

'Sure, sure, always a good option.' He rolled his eyes good-naturedly. 'Or . . . ?'

Her mind scrambled and came up blank. In an unwelcome epiphany, she realized this was where she generally failed. She wasn't a girl of action. She reacted. Pleased. Fell into things. The job in Phoenix that a college counselor steered her toward. Relationships with whatever guy showed interest. Dancing and drinking because friends enjoyed it. Anything and everything her mother told her to do . . .

Making a choice of her own, based on her own needs and desires, especially one that might put her in conflict with someone else? Yeah, no.

But having wallowed in this disaster for two days, and with Danny looking at her expectantly, she was ashamed. If she could force herself to go to nightclubs, force herself to date men other people would admire, force herself to please everybody else, she could certainly force herself to do something about this mess.

She sat up a little straighter, focusing this time on the problem, on the players in it, on what she knew and didn't know, and the next step became ridiculously obvious.

'I think I need to talk to Helen.'

Teresa walked apprehensively into Helen's room, carrying a peace-offering vase of peonies from the front of the house and the doll from the trunk in a paper shopping bag. Her grand-mother was sitting up in bed, graying bob clean and brushed, cheeks a healthy pink. She was reading *Circe* by Madeline Miller, a title Teresa had heard people talking about at work.

'Oh! Teresa.' Her grandmother closed the book with a wide smile. 'How lovely. I worried when you didn't come back. And with peonies! From the ranch?'

'I thought you'd like a bit of home around here.' Teresa set the vase on a wall shelf opposite Helen's bed, relieved her grand-mother was willing to put the unpleasantness of their last visit behind her. 'What do you think of the book?'

'Fabulous. Greek mythology was one of my favorite parts

of grade school. Oh, don't those look wonderful.' Helen gazed rapturously at the pink and white blossoms, while Teresa made a mental note to buy *Circe*. 'I'm so homesick. You are sweet to have thought of bringing me some. I was terribly afraid I scared you away at your last visit.'

'Only a little.' Teresa smiled apologetically. 'I've been through some . . . stuff lately.'

'Stuff.' Helen said the word as if it tasted bad.

'I was wondering . . . If you have time, I'd love to talk about it.' Teresa wrinkled her nose ruefully. 'My *stuff*, that is.'

Helen put the book on the table by her bed and indicated the two chairs in the room. 'Why don't you and your stuff have a seat.'

'Thanks.' Teresa sat, feeling as if she'd entered an interrogation room without any idea what her line of questioning would be. She rubbed her palms back and forth on her jeans. 'I don't know how to approach this tactfully.'

'Then don't. Tact is for diplomats. I'm family.'

'Yes.' Teresa took in a long breath. 'Is my mother . . . has she always had a problem with the truth?'

'Ah.' Helen's expression clouded. 'This is the big stuff. Do you want the short or long answer?'

'Short, please.'

'Yes.'

Teresa swallowed hard. She'd been expecting it, but it still hurt. 'Have you been diagnosed with dementia, other than post-surgery?'

'Good heavens.' Helen's voice had lowered, grown husky. 'No. Thank goodness. Some friends aren't as lucky.'

'What did you tell my mother about how you broke your hip?'

Her eyebrows rose. 'The truth. That a goat knocked me over.'

'Did my father . . .' Teresa had to stop to fight the emotion, 'ever ask you to intervene with Mom so he could try to be part of my life again? Mine and my brothers'? Did you give him our email addresses?'

Helen's expression grew sadder. 'Yes.'

Teresa made an involuntary sound of grief.

'I'm sorry.' Helen held out her hand. Teresa went over and took it, looking into the clear blue of her grandmother's eyes behind the enlarging lenses. 'I deeply regret not getting involved further. But at the time, taking his side against my daughter felt impossible. I always hoped, though, that you and your dad would find a way back to each other. You two were close.'

Teresa looked down at their clasped hands. 'My brothers are in touch with him. I found out yesterday.'

Helen gave her fingers a squeeze. 'Well then, you see. It's not too late. Short of death, it isn't ever too late.'

'I suppose not.' Teresa forced herself to move on. Dwelling on her father was too emotional to sustain for long. 'One more question?'

'Only if you sit next to me.' Helen let go of her hand and patted the mattress. 'We should be closer for this kind of talk.'

Teresa sat at her grandmother's side, still struggling to free herself from the mire of her mother's stories.

Lies. Her mother's lies.

'I found . . .' She didn't know how to get around this next one. She had no right to ask outright if Grandma Helen had cheated on her husband. 'Vacation photos. Places like Tahiti and Rome and Costa Rica. Of you and Lilianne and Gilles.'

'Oh yes, they were both quite wealthy and very generous. We traveled together once a year for several years. Marvelous trips. They live in Connecticut, or did then. I'd fly to JFK and we'd take off together on these fantastic adventures around the world. As much as I loved farm life and Kansas and Kevin, it was thrilling to get away.' Helen let her head drop back on the pillow, delighted expression fading. 'It upset your grandfather terribly, though. He wanted to be everything to me, wanted our *farm* to be everything to me, or at least to be enough.

'I really did try. For years. But life was going by so quickly, and I couldn't bear to spend all of it in one place. Especially after Kevin began to change into someone I barely recognized. I needed those trips to survive.' She shrugged. 'That sounds melodramatic, but I'm not exaggerating how it felt.'

Teresa let out breath she didn't realize she'd been holding. She no longer had any reason to disrespect or keep her distance from her grandmother. The last – she hoped – of Cheryl's lies had been exposed. The vacations had simply been a way for Helen to escape her unhappy marriage.

'One more thing. Not a question, show and tell.' Teresa got up from the bed and brought Sarah back in her velvet bag. 'I hope I'm not tiring you.'

'This is important, Teresa.' Helen pushed herself higher up on the bed. 'I won't shatter from being tired.'

Teresa brought Sarah out into the light of the hospital. 'Who is this?'

'Oh!' Helen broke out a smile and clapped her hands. 'Sarah! Sarah Bernhardt. What fun that you two have met.'

'Where did you get her?'

'From the woman who invited me to Paris that first time, in 1975, Natalie Laurent, my French professor at the University of Kansas. She got Sarah from her stepmother, Jeanette, an English actress who married Natalie's widowed father. All of us had such fun with her, me, Lilianne, dear Connie and Gilles. She was our constant companion.'

She took Sarah into her arms, stroking the doll's hair, touching the bulbed chin and cheeks. 'I forgot how heavy she is. And I forgot her hair was on crooked like that. Funny how memory works. Or doesn't. I haven't been down to the basement to visit her in so long. That trunk contained part of my life I had to put away for a while. It seems it's been long enough that I can revisit it now.'

Teresa looked down at her hands, fidgeting in her lap. 'Have they said when you can leave the hospital?'

'Next week! James is still looking for a candidate to be with me in the house. I'll need help until I'm fully recovered.'

Teresa lifted her head. An idea had popped into it, one she barely dared acknowledge. She'd need to call the college and see what vacation time she had coming, and whether they could spare her for longer. There were no important mailings going out in the near future, and managing the database could be done remotely. The rest of her job a decently intelligent monkey could do. Or so it felt many days.

Helen smoothed Sarah's crumpled emerald gown, stroked the fur of her cape, straightened her rhinestone circlet. 'What a lot of memories this young lady brings back. And what a travesty to keep such beauty and spirit hidden. She should be loved, not stored away.' She looked up suddenly, eyes alight. 'Would *you* like her?'

'Oh.' Teresa put a hand to her chest. 'I couldn't take her from you.'

'Why not? I'm older than Natalie was when she gave her to me. Sarah belongs around youth.'

Teresa struggled between politeness and honesty. She loved the doll, had been drawn to her immediately. But Sarah had obviously meant so much to her grandmother . . .

'You see,' Helen stood Sarah on her lap, facing Teresa, 'her power is to inspire elegance and adventure, and to provide companionship during the best and worst times, a wonderful listening ear for one's joys and troubles. She did that for all of us. But for me now she can only bring up tired old memories.'

'They don't sound tired to me. They sound exotic and wonderful.'

'They were back then. Lilianne and Gilles and I had such a special and unusual friendship.' Helen stroked Sarah's hair, clearly far away. 'I miss them terribly.'

'Why don't you invite them to visit? I'd love to meet them.'

'Oh.' Helen pursed her lips. 'We haven't been in touch for many years. It was all very complicated at the end.'

Teresa waited. Helen didn't elaborate – clearly a no-trespass zone. But her wistful expression pushed Teresa on. 'Wouldn't you want to know if either of them was in a hospital?'

'Oh yes, I would.' Helen looked surprised. 'Yes.'

'They could provide moral support. Or maybe they could stay with you after I have to leave.'

'That would be lovely. But it's been too long. They might not even want to see me.' Helen handed Sarah back to Teresa and lay back again, looking vulnerable and sad. 'After all these years, it's probably not a good idea to stir up the past.'

'Oh really?' Teresa gave her a look. 'So I shouldn't reach out to my father?'

A faint smile crossed Helen's lips. 'Clever girl. That's different.'

'How?' She knew she was dangerously close to being a pain in the butt, but for some reason this mattered to her, and she felt in her bones it mattered to Helen, too.

'Because your break with your father was based on lies. Ours was necessary, at least at the time. By now it's best to leave it alone.' Helen patted Teresa's hand. 'I'm getting tired, dear girl. I'm going to ask you to let me rest.'

'Yes, I'm sorry.' Teresa stood, feeling guilty for pushing. 'This must have been exhausting.'

'No, no, as I said, our talk was very important, one I've long hoped for.' Helen touched Teresa's face, her voice breaking. 'I'm getting my granddaughter back. That's worth whatever it takes.'

Teresa leaned down and kissed her grandmother's cheek, deeply sad for how she'd been led to misjudge Helen, and for the lost years between them. As if she were thinking the same, Helen wrapped Teresa in a long embrace that had both of them sniffling.

'Come back soon.' Helen released her, eyes wet, but a warm smile on her face. 'Can't get enough of you.'

Teresa grinned. 'We'll see if you can or not.'

'Say hello to my animals for me.'

'I will.' She stepped away from Helen's bedside as reluctantly as she'd approached. 'We're getting to be friends a little, but they miss you.'

'I'm glad for both.' Helen pushed the controls that lowered her and closed her eyes. 'We'll make a farm girl out of you yet, Teresa. Make sure to find Sarah a place of honor, both in my house and then in yours. You really must have her. It would make an old woman very happy to know she has a good home.'

'Thank you.' Teresa cradled the doll, her heart full, then gently put her back in the velvet bag. 'I'll take good care of her.'

No answer. Her grandmother's breathing deepened. Teresa slipped out of the room, closing the door after her. In spite of the difficult conversation and the complicated relationships she'd have to sort out, she felt much lighter, charged up and determined. There were brand-new things she needed to do. One, find a doll repair shop that would get Sarah freshened up like new as a surprise for Helen's homecoming. She could do that right away, call from the hospital parking lot and take Sarah over if they could accommodate her. Two, call South Mountain Community College and find out how much more time away she could take without getting fired. Three, getting trickier, and possibly meddlesome, Teresa felt in her bones that Helen wanted and needed Lilianne and Gilles back in her life but was too stubborn to admit it. And in the same vein of repairing breaches, Teresa owed it to her father to contact him, and at least hear his side.

There was one more thing she needed to do, but she wouldn't add it to this list. Just the idea made her stomach want to empty itself onto the polished hospital floor. At some point she'd have to gear up for a talk with her mother and confront her with what Teresa had learned. Ideally Mom would break down, apologize, explain, and become a completely different person on the spot.

Teresa sighed and pressed the button for the elevator.

Hallucinations aside, she'd at least have to let her know that Teresa was planning to do the exact opposite of everything Mom had sent her here to accomplish.

๑ Chapter 11 ๑

Ah! I should have died, sleeping peacefully
In this charming mistake where I was your loved one
Must I wake up from this confusing dream
To think of it always, yet believe in it no longer?
　　　　　Marceline Desbordes-Valmore, 'Élégie'

Do Not Open Until December 24
Dear Helen,

I've respected your wishes that I not contact you, but I couldn't let the Christmas season go by without telling you I'm thinking about you every day and miss you deeply. I'm hoping this reaches you in time so you can have my Merry Christmas wishes with you when you fall asleep on Christmas Eve.

I also want to let you know that I haven't touched a drop of alcohol since Thanksgiving, nor will I in the future. I'm working hard on becoming someone you can trust again. It's a great comfort to me, as I hope it'll be to you, that you'll never again have to watch me turn into that beast. You said in your final letter that you felt guilty for pushing me that far. In no way should you feel responsible, Helen. You are completely blameless.

It was warm early in December this year, without more

244

than a dusting of snow on the 10th. We'll be ready to plant our first crops in only a few months! You can bet I'm excited to get in on the farming boom across this great nation. Our little plot will be part of something huge and important, to the United States and to the world.

I'm still hoping with all my heart that when you come back in February we will be planning to contribute to that effort together. On Valentine's Day I still plan to kneel at your feet and ask you to be my wife, Helen. I'll be offering you a good honest life here, one that will fit and benefit both us and our children.

God bless you and keep you safe until you return to me. I will honor your wish to remain silent until then.

All my love, as always,
Kevin

Thursday, December 25, 1975

'You want us to come back for you in a few hours?'

Helen turned with a jolt from the bewitching view of the Mediterranean to Lilianne and Connie's amused faces. The trio – quartet, really, because Sarah was with them – was spending Christmas week in the town of Hyères, in a charming cottage Natalie's father had bought for her stepmother. During lunch one day with Natalie, Helen happened to drop that she'd never seen an ocean before, which had sent Natalie into a spluttering fit of horror and outrage. In short order, the girls' plans for a quiet holiday at home had turned into a rent-free Christmas vacation on the Côte d'Azur, or what Helen knew as the Riviera. Saint-Tropez, Monte Carlo, Grace Kelly, Scott Fitzgerald, Matisse . . . and now Helen Kenyon.

Once Helen Kenyon had set eyes on the Mediterranean, the day they arrived – even though technically it was a sea, not an ocean – she'd been so captivated that she'd come every day, unable to keep away, and not only because this could be her one chance. She could sit for hours and watch the water's constantly changing mood, color and movement. Utterly mesmerizing, like fire, babies or clouds.

'I'm coming.' She inhaled one last salty lungful and turned to go back to their house, a whitewashed cottage with a red tile roof, similar to others around it, only a few blocks from the beach. It was too cold to swim, but that hadn't stopped her poking in an experimental foot or hand, amazed at the tight, slightly sticky feel on her skin after it dried.

'It's Christmas!' Connie threw out her arms, spreading her wool shawl like wings. 'We have dinner to cook. Presents to exchange! Champagne to imbibe!'

'I know, I know.' Helen hugged her sweater around her shoulders and hurried to join her friends. She was in a strange, solitary mood, missing Gilles – he was with his family somewhere in the Alps, where they traditionally celebrated – but also deeply touched by the letter she'd opened the night before from Kevin, in which he'd sounded calmer and more secure.

It made sense, she supposed. She'd be a pretty shallow person if she could toss off her love for Kevin just because he wasn't around. At the same time, her feelings for Gilles had grown at an alarming rate since that overwhelming first kiss at the cemetery. They were dating, though she hadn't been able to bring herself to make love while she still felt caught between the two men. But staying out of the bedroom had done nothing to keep her from falling further and further into what was starting to feel like an entirely new emotion, one that had her questioning if she'd really loved Kevin the way a wife should love her husband.

And yet her relationship with Gilles was still so shiny new, so untested by time or by circumstances.

On the way back to the cottage, they passed a clothing shop, which had a dress in the window that Helen had been eyeing all week. Light blue, mid calf, it hung loosely under a gathered bodice with brightly colored embroidered accents that put it in the perfect spot between dressy and casual. Add the right jewelry and shoes, and she could go out to dinner. Go barefoot with a big straw hat and she could take it to the beach.

Under her mother's influence, Helen had trained herself to admire instead of want. She didn't, nor did she ever expect to, have money to spend on whimsy or indulgences. But this dress was giving her enough trouble that she'd allowed herself to daydream. Maybe when the shop opened back up after the holiday, she'd ask what it cost.

'Helen Kenyon!'

Helen started and looked up the street. Connie had her hands to her mouth, mimicking a megaphone. 'Earth to Helen Kenyon. Come in please, Helen.'

Helen rolled her eyes good-naturedly and caught up to her friends, walking swiftly, inhaling the scent of a nearby blooming mimosa. 'Sorry.'

'You're in a faraway place today.' Lilianne nudged her with her shoulder. 'In Switzerland with a certain handsome Frenchman, I think.'

'I think too.' Connie opened the wrought-iron gate between two square stucco posts to gain entry into the front garden of the little house, where Lilianne had identified orange, fig, olive and palm trees, and plants and bushes that probably flowered in sequence all year long.

'Last night I opened a letter from Kevin. He sent it last week but asked me to wait.'

Both women turned with identical looks of alarm. Helen laughed. 'He was just saying Merry Christmas.'

'But you'd told him to go away.'

'He did go away. Very obediently. I was afraid he wouldn't.' She wasn't going to admit that she'd been very glad to get the letter and proud to hear that Kevin had been upset enough by his behavior during the Thanksgiving phone call to take charge of the situation and make sure it never happened again. Helen would feel fine writing back to him with thanks, though without encouragement. They could talk everything out in February when she went back.

Gilles had made no secret of the fact that he wanted Helen to return to the US only so she could make arrangements to come back to France permanently. Having unlimited time ahead in which to explore each other and the world was a tempting fantasy, but abandoning her country and taking such a dramatic turn away from the life she and Kevin had long ago planned would be a huge step, one Helen wasn't yet ready to take.

'Just make sure he stays away,' Lilianne said. 'Gilles is worth about a hundred of him.'

Helen smiled reassuringly, aware by now that trying to defend Kevin to these two was a useless exercise. 'You don't need to worry.'

'Good. All hands to the kitchen.' Connie directed them toward it like a traffic cop. 'Easy dinner, we'll have it ready in no time.'

'Easy for you maybe.' They were having roast pheasant, a first for Helen, but apparently often served on French Christmas tables. 'You're the chef-in-training. And Lilianne might as well be.'

'We'll find good sous-chef chores for you.' Lilianne tied on an apron decorated with sprigs of herbs. Connie was wearing one sprinkled with images of wine bottles. Helen chose olives and jugs of oil. 'First, though, we open the champagne. There really isn't much work involved. We can roast the potatoes and carrots whole with the bird.'

'What the hell did you do, Lilianne?' Connie was holding up a bottle of Taittinger champagne. 'There's about half a case of this stuff in there. It's crazy expensive.'

'Not me!' Lilianne held up her hands to mime innocence.

'Natalie's Christmas present to us. She told me where she'd hidden it in the cottage. I snuck it in the fridge this morning.' Helen had no idea how much the wine cost, but knowing Natalie, probably double what her parents spent on their biggest splurge.

'I love that woman.' Connie cradled the bottle like a baby.

A short time later, the pheasant was in the oven and they were drinking the excellent champagne – even Helen could tell it was special – and eating slices of foie gras on toasted brioche spread with a thin layer of sour cherry jam. In between bites, they struggled to open the oysters bought at a fish market the day before, giggling and swearing until they'd conquered the dozen – Lilianne did most of them, Connie managed four, and Helen got one open and swore off the job forever. She said the same after she'd tried one. Tasted okay, but . . . slime.

Dinner was a success, tender pheasant flavored with tarragon and brandy, served with a red burgundy that made Helen doubt she'd ever be able to drink any wine but expensive French, which meant she'd never drink wine again.

She started at the thought, disoriented by Kevin's sweet letter. If she chose to stay in France, she could drink as much as she wanted.

After the pheasant, Connie brought out a bakery *bûche de Noël*, the traditional French rolled cake, cut and frosted to look like a log, complete with meringue mushrooms and sugared sprigs of rosemary.

Stuffed to the gills, as Helen's mom would say, they washed up quickly and took glasses of cognac into the living room for the gift exchange, which they'd promised each other would be home-made only. Helen had knit a cream-colored scarf for Lilianne out of the same fine wool she'd used for Sarah Bernhardt's nightgown and matching cap. For Connie, she'd fashioned an outrageously colorful striped winter hat. Connie had made collage books of photos, many of which Gilles had taken, combined with her own crazy cartoonish drawings, and maps and menus from places they'd been together. Lilianne had made each of them an assort-ment of chocolate truffles with various flavorings.

'That was so lovely, thank you! But even though this will make me sound drunk and sappy, the best gifts are having you two in my life.' Helen raised her glass of cognac and took a sweet, rich sip, thinking she really needed to stop or she'd have to stay in bed the next day.

'But wait . . .' Connie reached under her chair and brought out a large flat box. 'There's more! For Helen. From the two of us.'

'What? No fair! You broke the home-made rule?'

'Yup.' Connie handed it to her. 'Deal with it.'

'You guys . . .' Helen unfastened the ribbon and gently removed the paper, then opened the box and stared in aston-ishment, first at the blue dress from the window and then at her friends. 'This is the dress I coveted! How did you know?'

'Because you stared at it with drool hanging out of your mouth every time we passed the store.'

'I did not.'

'Did too,' Lilianne said. 'Try it on. We want to see how it looks on you. You're going to be beautiful.'

Helen lifted the smooth cotton out of the box, then stood,

took off her shirt and stepped out of her pants, hamming it up when Lilianne and Connie made rude whistles of approval. She slipped the soft material over her head and drew it down into place. 'Oh my gosh. It's so pretty.'

'Oh my *gosh*! It's perfect.' Connie beamed. 'You look like a sweet lamb, and also very sexy.'

'Someone should paint you.' Lilianne was looking at her with shining eyes. 'Men are going to hang themselves in a long path behind you.'

'Oh come on.' Helen blushed violently.

'Ask Sarah.' They turned to look at her, adorable though still mournful in her new Christmas nightie and cap.

'Yup.' Connie nodded vigorously. 'She agrees. You'll kill 'em.'

'Thank you. Both. So much.' Helen embraced her friends warmly, took off the dress and laid it carefully back in the box. 'I'll get a lot of wear out of it and think of you both every time.'

Afterwards, they sang all the Christmas carols they knew the words to, which wasn't many, and chatted by candlelight until only Sarah was able to keep her eyes open.

'I'm exhausted. And drunk. And fat.' Helen yawned loudly. 'I gotta hit the sack.'

'Not so fast . . .' Connie grinned conspiratorially at Lilianne. 'There's one more thing.'

'Huh?' Helen had staggered to her feet. 'I can't stay up any longer or fit anything else in my body. There can't be more.'

'One more present for you, *ma chérie*, to take to bed with you. And no, it's not Gilles, but . . .' Lilianne reached under her chair again and retrieved a bright red envelope, which she handed to Helen. 'It's from him. Merry Christmas.'

Helen was suddenly wide awake. 'From Gilles? Sent here?'

'Yup. Luckily we got to it first.' Lilianne shook the envelope insistently toward Helen.

'It says "Merry Christmas",' Connie said. 'So we decided you had to wait until tonight and hid it from you.'

'Oh no.' Helen took the envelope in dismay. 'I didn't do anything for him.'

Connie waggled her eyebrows like Groucho Marx. 'That's not what we hoid . . .'

'You can make it up to him later.' Lilianne made shooing motions. 'Now go. Read it in private. But then tell us what it says later.'

'No, no, no.' Connie grabbed Lilianne's hands to stop her shooing. 'Read it here and tell us right now.'

Helen laughed. 'Tell you what. I'll read it in the kitchen, then come right back and tell you.'

'No, we'll go in the kitchen.' Lilianne pulled Connie after her. 'You read it here by candlelight. It's more romantic.'

'Deal.' Helen watched them leave, thinking herself about the luckiest woman in the world to have been in the Jardin du Luxembourg that day. She was even grateful for the creepy guy who'd bothered her, because it meant she'd got to meet these two fabulous women.

She lowered herself into the soft chair opposite Sarah and smoothed her hand over the red envelope, wondering what Gilles was doing right then with his family, picturing a tiny chalet somewhere in a small town, with his parents and brother gathered around a fire.

Dear Helen,

I hate that I'm not with you for Christmas. I hate any-time I'm not with you, but Christmas seems particularly important for us to share. I try to console myself picturing future Christmases together, but I know right now that is just my fantasy.

I don't think you will be surprised to hear that I am missing you terribly. I'm sure you and the girls are having a great time in Hyères, but I wonder if I could selfishly ask you to spend time with me this holiday as well?

My parents rent the same place every year, here in St Moritz, and they host a New Year's Eve party for family and friends. They are excited to meet you, and of course you know how I feel about having you with me. So, I am inviting you to spend the New Year with me and my family, and hope this will be a symbolic beginning of a new time in our lives together.

There are travel instructions enclosed, my phone number and collect call dialing instructions. Call anytime and we can talk about it. I can't wait to hear your voice.

Je t'embrasse très fort,
Gilles

'Oh wow.'

'What? What?' Connie's voice came from the kitchen. 'Did he pop the question?'

'He's not going to pop the question in a card.' Lilianne led the charge back into the room, where she and Connie stood eagerly waiting.

Helen held up the envelope, cheeks flushed from alcohol, the delicious feeling of new love, and the guilt over Kevin and how quickly she'd turned from him. 'He wants me to go to Switzerland and spend New Year's with his family.'

Connie gasped. 'Meet the parents! This is huge!'

'How do you feel about it?' Lilianne was watching with that stare that seemed to penetrate Helen's brain.

'Happy. Nervous. Terrified. Unsure.'

'Aha.' She gave a decisive nod, apparently satisfied. 'That sounds about right.'

'You'll go.' Connie folded her arms. 'I command you.'

'How am I going to get to Switzerland?'

'Train. There has to be one.' Connie looked to Lilianne for confirmation. 'We can call in the morning.'

'Probably through Lyon. It'll take hours. Do you have a number for him?'

'Duh.' Helen smacked her forehead. 'He said he sent instructions.'

'There's another sheet in there.' Connie pointed to the envelope.

'Good.' Helen pulled it out and scanned it. 'Oh gosh.'

'Durned if it ain't a double "Oh gosh" Christmas!'

Helen handed the paper to Connie, rolling her eyes. Lilianne leaned in to read over her shoulder. They both gasped.

'You'll fly from Toulon directly to Samedan Airport?' Lilianne was shaking her head and grinning. 'That's private jet stuff. Charter anyway.'

Helen felt panicked. 'Private jet?'

'He'll pick you up and take you to the hotel in St Moritz.'

'St Moritz!' Connie gave a blast of laughter. 'That's like total playground of the rich.'

'It *is*?' Helen nearly wailed in dismay. 'I was picturing a cozy Heidi cottage in the Alps. With goats.'

'He's been holding out on us.' Lilianne was obviously proud of him.

'Far. Out.' Connie was starry-eyed.

Helen was pretty sure she looked like she'd been electrocuted. 'I don't belong in a place like that.'

'Breathe.' Lilianne put a steadying hand on her shoulder. 'He's Gilles. There is nothing he could fake about that.'

'I'm not . . . I can't. I'm from Indiana, for God's sake. I've never seen an ocean or a mountain. I don't know how to ski. And I don't have clothes warm enough for snow, or enough fancy ones. He said a party . . .'

She plunked into the chair in despair.

'You brought Natalie's flapper dress for our New Year's Eve faux-ball here.' Connie knelt in front of her, peering up into her face. 'That will be perfect anywhere.'

'Gilles will be with you,' Lilianne said soothingly. 'He wouldn't invite you somewhere you'd be uncomfortable. He'll make sure you're okay. He's the best man out there.'

Helen half turned. 'You sound like you're in love with him.'

'If I had to get married, he'd do fine. I admire a lot about him.' Lilianne shrugged. 'But I don't have to get married. And I'm thrilled that you and he found each other.'

Helen let her head drop, confused by the passionless way Lilianne spoke, but not in the mood to analyze because of her current freak-out. She'd been so happy and relaxed here with such great friends. Now she'd be thrust into an uncomfortable situation where she wouldn't feel she belonged, and where she'd know only Gilles.

Exactly like she'd been thrust into Paris, a totally foreign country, where she'd only known Natalie. Look how that turned out.

She lifted her head to find Connie grinning at her. 'Why don't you call him now?'

'Now?'

'Yes. See, you pick up the phone and . . .' Connie made rotating motions with her finger, 'you dial all the numbers in the same order that he gave them to you.'

'She's right. Hearing his voice will help.' Lilianne squeezed

Helen's shoulder and removed her hand. 'Otherwise you'll lie awake all night inventing scenarios that won't happen.'

'That is definitely true.' Helen got to her feet, feeling fizzy at the idea of hearing Gilles's voice. 'You're right. I'll call.'

'Can we stand here and listen if we're really quiet?'

'No.' Lilianne marched a giggling Connie firmly back into the kitchen.

Helen dialed the number, taken aback when an unfamiliar male voice answered. '*Allo*?'

'Uh . . . *Bonsoir, monsieur. Joyeux Noël à vous. Est-ce-que je peux parler à Gilles? C'est Helen.*' Somehow she stuttered her way through, only sounding half idiotic.

'*Joyeux Noël, mademoiselle. Je vous le passe.*'

Helen waited for whoever it was – his father? His brother? The butler? – to get Gilles, absurdly smoothing her hair, as if he'd be able to see her.

'*Joyeux Noël, mon amour.*' The sound of his deep voice flowed over her, forcing out tension. Lilianne had been right. No matter how much seemed different, he was still Gilles.

'Merry Christmas. I miss you.'

'*Moi aussi*. Next Christmas is us together.'

Helen couldn't stop smiling. From the wobbly English, she'd guess he'd also been enjoying wine tonight. 'How was your day?'

'Hectic. Loud. But fun. You? How are you enjoying the French Riviera?'

'It's beautiful. I'm in love with the Mediterranean.' She filled him in on their doings and on the meal they'd just eaten, then listened to his family's Christmas traditions – their big meal and gifts had been shared on Christmas Eve, followed by midnight mass, so Christmas was mostly a day of relaxing.

'I got your card. Thank you for thinking of me.'

'When do I not think of you, *ma chérie*? You must come. I think I might die without you.'

'I think you better not.'

'*D'accord*, okay.' There was a burst of laughter in the background. 'What day will you arrive?'

'What day would you like me?'

'Tonight?'

She giggled like a teenager. 'I think any ticket you buy tonight would be ridiculously expensive.'

'No, no. No ticket. It's my father's plane. For his business. You can come any time.'

A thrill went through her. Or was it terror? Or horror? It was hard to tell. 'That's . . . How luxurious.'

'My parents have too much money. How do you say *sortir par tous les pores*?'

'Comes out of their pores.' She made a face at the image. 'You never told me that.'

He made a distinctly French sound, like a verbal shrug, *bof*. 'It's not something I like to announce right away, "Hello, I'm Gilles, my family is disgustingly wealthy." I have always felt separate. They have it, I don't think about it.'

'I see.' She did, and yet she wished she'd known about this earlier. It shouldn't make a difference. Certainly her feelings wouldn't change if she discovered he was poor. But tremendous wealth seemed threatening to her in a way poverty wasn't.

'You and I can go off, spend time on our own. The family will find that normal. I'm always disappearing, as you know. But here, well, there's only so much of this fabulous luxury I can take.'

Helen's smile reappeared. Once again, he'd performed his mind-reading trick and said the one thing she needed to hear. 'Where are you? Do your parents have a house there?' She was still hoping for the cozy Heidi cottage in the mountains.

'No, no, their tradition is to stay in the penthouse of the Carlton Hotel. The staff keep it for them every year.'

Hope died. Carlton. As in Ritz-Carlton. No Heidi. No goats. 'Okay.'

He chuckled. 'I know it sounds . . . how do you say *effrayant*?'

'Scary? Frightening? Producing a feeling of anxious dread in people from the Midwest who aren't used to astounding wealth?'

He chuckled. 'Yes, yes, that's it. But you and I will be bourgeois together and have a wonderful time. You will love my family, they are very kind. They will love you too. Do you ski?'

'No.'

'The other? *Ski de fond*? When you ski on the flat, like big walking?'

Helen hid a snort. 'Cross-country skiing. No, I don't do that either. I can ice-skate, though. *Patiner*.'

'Ah, good, yes. There is skating here on the lake, or I can teach you cross-country. This is easy transition.' Another burst of laughter in the background, then a roar of . . . approval? Disapproval? 'Tell me what day you can come, and we will arrange.'

Helen opened her mouth to relinquish the lovely safety of staying in the familiarity of this cottage with Lilianne and Connie and Sarah.

'How about the twenty-ninth? That gives me a few more days here with the girls.'

'Yes, good. I will speak to my father. May I have the number there?'

'Of course.' She read it from the center of the dial, and they said fond goodbyes.

Helen sank onto the couch. What girl wouldn't be thrilled? To be flown in a private jet from the local airport at her convenience, met at the other end and whisked off to the pent-house of the Carlton in St Moritz for an extended luxurious, all-expenses-paid stay with a man she was falling in love with? Seeing Gilles in the context of his family might help her make her impossible decision. She couldn't let Kevin keep planning a Valentine's Day proposal if she wasn't intending to accept.

But being around that much money was so foreign to her, and so unexpected, she couldn't imagine herself feeling anything but ill at ease.

The memory again surfaced of that last night in Kansas, sitting on the house's back deck overlooking hundreds of acres, theirs to nurture. Silence except for crickets chirping and the soughing breeze. Overhead, the swift, elusive shapes of swooping bats. Kevin's handsome face had been lit with pleasure, hand resting casually on Helen's thigh amid the warmth and camaraderie of long-time and new friends, laughter and gentle teasing born of years of trust. One of those rare perfect moments during which if someone had offered Helen any other experience, anywhere in the world, she would have turned them down flat.

Her feelings for Gilles were powerful and consuming. But she couldn't lose sight of what she'd felt that night at Kevin's side: not only love for him, but also peace and deep contentment among the simple, enchanting facets of the life he was offering to share.

⤳ Chapter 12 ⤳

Do you remember the young girl with the tender look, the sweet and gentle manner?

Scarcely, alas. In the spring of her life, her heart felt it had been made for you.

There were no vows, no empty promises; she was still too young to understand either

Her pure soul loved drunkenly, and she gave herself without shame or struggle

She lost her cherished idol, that sweet joy lasted less than a day

She is no longer in the spring of her life, yet she's still in her first love.

Marceline Desbordes-Valmore, 'Le premier amour'

Monday, December 29, 1975

Only when the tiny jet bumped to a landing at Samedan Airport did Helen take her white-knuckled hands off the cushiony arm rests. She was not an experienced flyer, to put it mildly – the flights in September, Kansas City to Chicago, Chicago to Paris, had been her first. Those planes had felt too heavy to be up in the sky; this one felt as if every breeze could drive it into the

260

ground. In other circumstances, she would have gotten a kick out of the luxury interior. Wooden tables, comfortable-looking leather chairs, a cream couch draped with a bright tapestry, a work desk with notebooks, stationery and typewriter, all resting on an assortment of Oriental rugs. If she'd been able to move her butt from the first-class airline seat, she would have thought it hilarious to be able to lounge around, drinking a cocktail and eating the fancy hors d'oeuvres that were offered.

But cocktails and fancy hors d'oeuvres didn't mix well with terror. It had been rainy and windy in Toulon when she boarded after lunch, and the situation hadn't improved much during the flight.

'You made it.'

She grinned sheepishly at the pretty brunette stewardess, Marie, who'd done her best to calm and serve her only passenger. 'I'm grateful.'

'You did well. Next time? Even easier.'

'Mm.' Next time, she was walking.

'You can . . .' Marie pointed to Helen's seatbelt.

'Right.' Helen unbuckled and stood to put on her coat, which Marie had whisked away as she'd settled in, and had just now whisked back.

Finally convinced that she was not going to die in a fireball, she admitted it was pretty cool to walk on and off a plane when she felt like it. No tickets, boarding passes, no waiting in line. The plane had touched down in Toulon, Marie had emerged to escort her on, and off they'd flown.

'Thank you for everything.'

Marie handed over Helen's suitcase. 'You are very welcome.'

Outside, it was cold, much colder than Paris, probably in the twenties, enough to make Helen long for her parka, left behind in Indiana.

She climbed down the stairs onto the tarmac, huddled against the biting wind. Across from her, a small building with a welcome sign. She headed for it, shivering in her light pants and sweater until she noticed someone running toward her. Gilles. Helen's heart swelled. She hurried forward, suitcase clumsily bumping against her thigh, and they collided with a breath-whooshing impact that neither of them minded. His arms came around her and he kissed her as if she'd just come back from the dead.

A girl could get used to this.

'I'm so happy you're here. I missed you, Helen.'

'I missed you too.' Not until she saw him, heard him, touched him did she realize how much.

'Come inside.' He took her case, put his arm tightly around her. 'You aren't dressed for this weather.'

'I don't have winter clothes.'

'We'll find you something. How was the flight?'

'Terrifying, but efficient.'

'Very safe plane. Or I wouldn't have allowed you on it.' He let her precede him into the blessed warmth of the tiny terminal for a brief respite before they walked out the other side, where a black car pulled up and a uniformed driver got out.

'You're joking,' Helen murmured. 'Is that a Rolls?'

'Sorry,' he murmured back. 'It's part of the hotel service.'

'Welcome, Miss Kenyon.' The driver opened the door for her.

'Um . . . my bag.' She pointed. 'Where should I—'

'I will take care of that for you.' He gestured graciously to the car's interior. 'Please.'

Helen got into the Rolls, feeling more like a girl from Indiana than ever, betting the next four days would give her many more opportunities to top even this one.

Gilles climbed in next to her and grabbed her hand. 'Thank you for giving up part of your Riviera vacation for me.'

'You're welcome. I'd never seen salt water, but I've also never seen an Alp. Or any mountain actually, except in pictures.'

Gilles shook his head. 'I'm going to have to show you many more places in the world.'

Helen leaned over for a kiss to avoid answering. Maybe he'd get to take her everywhere. It certainly sounded thrilling. A life of travel was so far from anything she'd ever imagined for herself.

'The family are skiing today. They'll be back soon. I should tell you that in the penthouse, there is one suite for my parents, a bedroom for my brother and his wife, and one for us. This is okay? We haven't talked about it.'

'Oh.' Helen had assumed – Indiana girl again – that his parents would insist on separate rooms for a visiting unmarried couple, as hers did. 'Well. That's fine.'

'You're sure?'

'I'm sure.' She gave what she hoped was a reassuring smile and pretended interest in the low snow-capped mountains around them, glowing in the fading light of an early winter sunset. She knew herself and the passion she and Gilles ignited. If they were in the same room all night ... Connie would roll her eyes at her prudie friend, but Helen considered sex a symbol of serious commitment, and had so far been unable to turn completely away from the future she'd planned with Kevin. Particularly in these surroundings, foreign in landscape, nationality and socioeconomic class, the farm in Kansas felt like a lifeline to everything familiar and comfortable.

'My parents will want you to call them by their first names, Brigitte and Alain. My brother is Stephan, his wife is Chantal. There will be other family and friends on New Year's Eve, but this is all you need for now.' Gilles squeezed her hand. 'You're worrying. My family will love you. You will love them. We will have a fabulous time. Back in Paris, you will decide you can't leave either me or France, and you'll renounce your US citizenship and bear me fourteen sons who will all take after their . . . What is so funny?'

'Not a thing.' Still grinning, she moved closer to him, promising herself to make this short trip all about Gilles and leave Kevin in Kansas. 'It sounds great.'

'Ah, there.' Gilles pointed left. 'St Moritz Lake. We're nearly to the town. There were two Olympic Games here, 1928 and 1948. Now it's just for us tourists and the poor locals we invade.'

'And drop a lot of money on.'

'That too.'

The car hugged the frozen lakeshore for a few miles, then veered around dramatic hairpin curves to climb into the courtyard of a large, beautifully lit castle-like building combining brown and cream-colored stone capped by red turrets and a green roof. The Rolls was met by an employee who greeted Gilles – and, to her surprise, Helen – by name and welcomed them into the spectacular spacious lobby, with a magnificent decorative wood ceiling, several tactfully grouped couches and chairs, and a large fireplace warming the space.

No questions, no check-in. Helen's bag was whisked away by a bowing employee, destination unknown. She smiled politely, wishing she could wrestle it back to regain some measure of control. Everyone in the lobby, coming, going, sitting, was dressed in what she assumed were the latest styles in beautiful fabrics, men in jackets and turtlenecks, women in linen or silk with tasteful jewelry, perfect skin, hair and makeup. Everyone wore an air of casual sophistication she conspicuously lacked.

Or so it felt.

'Would you like to sit here and have something to drink, or would you like to go up to the suite?' Gilles was looking at her in concern.

Helen needed to put on a more cheerful face. Coming here was the chance of a lifetime, and she should stop thinking about how she looked and more about the generosity of Gilles and his family. 'I'd love some coffee. I was too shaky on the plane to have anything.'

'Excellent.'

The coffee helped, but she still felt awkward and anxious, expecting someone to stumble over her any second and out her as an imposter. Worse, she hadn't had the chance to change money into Swiss francs, so she'd be dependent on Gilles and his family until she could get to a bank – though the coffee she just drank probably cost more than she had in her wallet.

For the first time since she'd arrived in September, Helen was achingly homesick.

'*Et voilà, elle est arrivée*!' A tall, slim woman in a belted black jacket, wearing teal eyeshadow that exactly matched the shade of her pants, had come up to their table and was leaning down to double-kiss Helen's cheeks. 'Hello, hello, Hélène, I'm Brigitte. Welcome, welcome, we are so glad you could join us.'

Helen smiled up at Gilles's mother, elegant and beautiful, with Gilles's dark eyes and hair. Her greeting seemed warm and sincere, as did that of her husband, Alain, a wiry mustachioed man with fair skin and John Lennon glasses. Both of them spoke excellent English and could not have been kinder or more natural. A minute later, they were joined by Gilles's brother, Stephan and his very pregnant wife, Chantal, who were equally as cordial and unaffected. But along with their perfectly coordinated clothes, they wore an air of ease and entitlement that kept them on a different plane from the one Helen inhabited.

After a brief chat, they agreed to meet up in an hour in Brigitte and Alain's room for an aperitif before dinner. After dinner there was to be a special concert in town, a scaled-down performance of Beethoven's Ninth Symphony in the nearby Hotel Laudinella's concert hall.

Long evening ahead after a long day of anxious worry.

'I'll take you up to the room now?' Gilles offered Helen his hand.

'Yes, thanks.'

'*Parfait*. We'll see you in an hour.' Brigitte waved them off cheerfully.

Helen waited until they were alone in the elevator to speak. 'I like your parents already.'

'I knew you would. And I knew they'd like you.'

'How can you tell?'

'That's easy. Neither of them spat on you.' He put his arm around her, enjoying her laughter. 'It's going to be fine. I promise.'

'I'll hold you to it.' She lifted her face for a kiss that ended only when the doors opened to admit an icy-faced woman done up in such stylish perfection that Helen wanted to apologize for everything she'd put on that morning. Instead she smiled tentatively – and the ice-faced woman smiled warmly back.

Well.

On the top floor, reached by inserting a brass key into the elevator controls, the door opened into the penthouse suite. One look, and any ease Helen had gained since her arrival evaporated. Poof.

The place looked like something out of an interior design magazine for royalty. Upholstered couches, carved wood tables, crystal chandeliers. Oil paintings on the walls. Fresh flower bouquets on multiple surfaces. An antique bookcase with leaded glass doors. Oriental carpets on parquet floors. A balcony with table and chairs facing a mind-bogglingly beautiful view of the lake and the sweeping vista of snow-capped mountains beyond.

In their enormous bedroom, another balcony with an equally astounding view, a gigantic bed and a marble-topped dresser, which turned out to contain Helen's clothing, neatly unpacked, her dresses hung in the large airy closet, shoes arranged in pairs on a pull-out drawer made for that purpose.

In the all-marble bathroom, more beauty products put out for their use than Helen knew existed. Heated racks for their towels. Plush slippers, thick robes, more flowers . . .

Back in their bedroom, she put her hands on her hips and surveyed the space. 'Ya know? This totally reminds me of Howard Johnson's.'

Gilles face was blank. 'Yes?'

Of course he wouldn't get the joke. 'Where my family stayed when we traveled.'

'*Ah oui*, okay.'

Still no understanding. 'It's nothing like this.'

'This is quite a place. Very comfortable, but also . . .' He made a face. 'Everything you need and too much you don't.'

Helen nodded, standing awkwardly, feeling as if the entire room consisted of the bed and all it symbolized.

'You'll get used to it, my love. For now, don't think about it. We're here and we have the next four days to be together.' He touched her face, drew her to him and kissed her, then again, kisses that heated quickly, until Helen pulled back.

'I . . . should get ready.'

'So soon?' He glanced at his watch. 'We have some time . . .'

She swallowed. 'I'd feel better getting ready now. I don't want to be late.'

'Okay, Helen.' An amused smile curved his lips. 'I'll get ready too.'

She should know better than to try to hide anything from Gilles. He understood what she'd meant: dressing now would make her feel suitably armored. He'd never insist she do anything she wasn't ready for. But they'd been dating long enough, even for a prude, let alone one who claimed to have loosened up considerably.

Helen needed to make a decision. Ideally there would be a light-bulb moment of certainty, but who knew when or if that would ever arrive?

In the bathroom, she changed into the blue dress, unable to strip in front of him. Gilles, bless him, sensed her nerves and kept up a stream of chatter though the half-open door, about the things he'd found to do in St Moritz that she might enjoy and parts of the hotel that would be fun to investigate if the weather was bad.

She was just putting on lipstick when she heard the room phone ring and Gilles striding to answer it.

'*Allo? Oui. Bien sûr.*' He tapped on the bathroom door. 'It's my mother. For you.'

Helen's eyes went wide in the mirror. She blotted her lips and came out of the bathroom, took the proffered receiver from Gilles, nearly dropping it. 'Hello . . . Brigitte.'

It was really hard not to call her Madame Aubert.

'*Bonsoir*, Hélène. I'm calling to see if you would like to come over to our room and have a chat before the others arrive, to get to know each other a little. If you're dressed . . .'

'Yes, I am.' She lifted her brows at Gilles, who was watching curiously. 'I'll be right over. If I can find you.'

Brigitte laughed, a warm, happy sound. 'We're straight across the living room.'

'See you soon.' Helen hung up and turned. 'Your mother wants to talk.'

'Really.' He looked wary. 'About . . . ?'

She shrugged, trying to look casual when she felt anything but. 'She wants to get to know me.'

'Good.' He nodded with forced heartiness. 'That's good. She's easy to talk to. You'll enjoy her. And by the way, you look beautiful, Helen. I love that dress.'

'It was a Christmas gift from Connie and Lilianne.' She laid her hand on his cheek. 'Thank you for the compliment. I love this dress too, but I feel like a hayseed here.'

His brows lowered as he drew her close, hands warm through the soft cotton. 'Hayseed?'

'A bumpkin. A hick.' She tried not to laugh at his confusion. 'Someone from out in the country, who ain't got no class.'

'Ah. This I know. The John Wayne talking.'

Helen giggled. 'Yes, the John Wayne talking.'

'Ah, Hélène, you belong here as much as I do, which is absolutely and not at all. But we'll make the best of it and enjoy each other anyway. It's only a few days.' He bent to kiss her, noticed the lipstick and sighed heavily. 'That's coming off later. Have fun. And don't worry. She's not scary.'

Helen nodded, smiled bravely and walked out of their room and across the endless living room with its huge fireplace, and a dining room and office she hadn't noticed, one on either side of another balcony. Straight ahead, the closed door of Monsieur and Madame Aubert's bedroom.

She took a deep breath and knocked.

'*Entrez, Hélène!*'

Their room was even larger and more opulent than the one she'd just left. Heavy drapes, oil paintings and a four-poster king-sized bed. In addition, a sitting area facing the mountain view, with chairs and a table on which sat a sweating silver champagne bucket. Brigitte wore a welcoming smile and a royal-blue floor-length flared gown with long sleeves, accessorized with a twisted gold chain and gold hoop earrings. On her feet, matching blue evening slippers. A study in class and simplicity.

'What a lovely dress.' Brigitte came over to kiss Helen's cheeks. 'You look so beautiful. You *are* so beautiful. Such poise and charm. No wonder Gilles is smitten.'

'Thank you.' Poise and charm? Helen felt nervous and tongue-tied, all arms and legs that had nowhere comfortable to rest.

'Would you like a glass of champagne? I know we'll have plenty for the New Year, but I say life is short, drink as much as you can.'

'Thank you, I'd love some.' The Auberts probably drank champagne like her family drank milk. Not that she was complaining.

'Have a seat, Hélène, be comfortable. I will open it.' Brigitte twisted off the bottle's wire cage and eased out the cork with a gentle pop that allowed vapor to escape but no wine. She poured into the flutes, then sat opposite. 'Now. Here is to love and to new friends.'

'Thank you.' Helen clinked glasses and took a sip of the remarkable champagne, deep and complex, like some of the older whites she'd had at Natalie's lunch table. Did people of such wealth ever get sick of having the best of everything all the time?

'I wanted to talk, just us two, since holiday time gets complicated and more friends are coming in soon.'

Helen stopped herself from saying *thank you* a third time, smiling and nodding instead, feeling gangly and dull next to this vivacious woman.

'Gilles tells me you are from a small city in the Midwest, yes? I too came from a small town, in Provence, called Lapalud. Hardly anything there. My father was a farmer. We grew peaches. Very provincial.'

'Growing up on a peach farm in Provence sounds romantic to me.'

'Yes, yes, the exotic is what you don't know. To me, the American Midwest has quite a cachet.'

Helen managed not to snort. She'd love to hear what her parents would say to Zionsville being labeled a town with cachet.

'So this . . .' Brigitte made a sweep of the room with her arm, 'might be a new world for you?'

'Very new.'

'For me it was too. This was my husband's world, not mine. It took me a long, long time to feel comfortable. You must not worry.'

Unless Helen decided to stay in France, she wouldn't have a long, long time to get comfortable. Either Gilles hadn't told his mother enough, or he'd told her too much. 'How did you meet Alain?'

'In college in Avignon. I thought he was a terrible snob. He was everything my parents warned me about. City slicker? Is that what you say?'

Helen shoved back her laughter. Another person convinced the US was synonymous with John Wayne movies. 'That's what some people say.'

'I avoided him as long as I could.' Brigitte put out her hand, keeping imaginary Alain from approaching.

'And then?'

She grinned, blushing enough to render her careful makeup unnecessary. 'I couldn't anymore. He sets his mind on things and that's it until he gets what he wants. My son Stephan is happy following paths already laid down. But Gilles is like his father. He knew he wanted photography a day after we gave him his first camera. And I'm afraid now that he wants you.'

Helen blinked. *Afraid?*

Brigitte sipped her champagne calmly. 'He has had girlfriends

271

in his life, of course, he is very charming and good-looking and *gentille* – kind. But you are something different.'

By now Helen was desperate for Brigitte to get to the point. 'Different how? Good or bad?'

'A little of both, maybe. He has told me the situation with the boy in the US.'

Helen stiffened. Gilles had told his mother too much. 'It's . . . complicated.'

'Yes, this is what I worry about.' Brigitte put her glass down and clasped her hands, waiting for Helen to speak in her defense at this trial that was not after all about her crime of being from the wrong side of the tracks.

'Gilles was . . . unexpected. It's all happened so quickly.'

'This is what he says.' Brigitte sighed. 'I'm terribly afraid you will break his heart. So I wanted to talk to you in case . . . well, a mother worries.'

Helen gritted her teeth in a smile. 'In case I was toying with him.'

'Yes. But now, having met you . . .' Brigitte picked up her glass again. 'I don't sense you are the type to play with men.'

'No.' Helen pressed her lips together, struggling to find the polite line between reassuring Brigitte and telling her that none of this was her business.

'Now tell me, what do you think about this crazy hotel?' Brigitte leaned back in her chair, signaling, Helen hoped, the end of the interview portion of their meeting. 'My parents are appalled at the expense. But Alain's family always came here, so now we come here. It's a wonderful place to ski, anyway.'

Helen lifted her chin toward the window view, wanting to avoid commenting on the Carlton experience. 'The mountains are amazing. So sharp, so desolate and beautiful. Indiana is pretty flat, and my family never traveled outside the state, so to me it's all exciting.'

'We Europeans forget how big the US is. For us it's always a few hours by train to the mountains or the sea.' Brigitte seemed about to go on, but sat tapping a finger on the stem of her flute. Then another quick inhale. 'What is he like, this American boy? I hope it's okay that I'm asking.'

Not really. Helen gulped champagne to stall, battling resentment at the intrusion into her privacy.

'Kevin is ... not a complicated person.' The words came quickly, and she felt shame at reducing such a good man to that phrase, at the same time recognizing it as truth. 'Like Gilles, he knows what he wants and goes after it. He wants to be a farmer in Kansas, one of the states in the Midwest.'

'Yes, we all know Kansas. From *The Wizard of Oz*.' Brigitte stood abruptly and moved to the window. 'So this is his dream. And what else. Travel? Music? Arts?'

Helen shifted uncomfortably. Brigitte seemed more interested in scoping out her son's competition than getting to know her. 'Kevin is a homebody – that is, he is happiest at home. He likes country and western music and plays a little trumpet . . .'

She didn't know how to continue. How much to say. By the satisfied look on Brigitte's face, she could tell she wasn't convincing the mother of such a talented, energetic and intelligent man that Kevin was any threat.

'Ah, okay, I see. This one is safe.'

Helen felt a spike of outrage that flagged then wilted.

'Yes.' She could barely get her voice to sound. 'I suppose he is.'

'I'm sorry. I'm saying too much. I understand the appeal of life on a farm. I grew up on one. It can be a beautiful way to live. If it fits you.'

Helen forced herself to meet Brigitte's shrewd gaze as pleasantly as possible. 'True.'

'*Alors*, I will stop . . . how do you say? Cooking you? No, no, grilling.' Brigitte laughed. 'Sorry, my English is a little tired.'

Helen lunged at the chance to change the subject. 'You and Alain speak it beautifully. Where did you learn?'

'I spent a semester abroad, in London. A wonderful experience, but the winter nearly killed me. Worse than Paris. I was cold all the time.' Brigitte shivered dramatically. 'Now. People will be gathering soon, and there is another reason I asked you here. Gilles tells me you are lacking warm clothes and dresses, yes?'

Helen was afraid Brigitte would call up the hotel and open a credit line in her name. 'I was planning to be on the Riviera for the holiday. This was a surprise invitation.'

'I insisted. I wanted to meet you.' Brigitte beckoned. 'Come. Bring your glass if you care to.'

The walk-in closet was as big as Helen's Paris bedroom, filled, for a ten-day vacation, with more clothes than Helen owned.

'Hmm.' Brigitte eyed her head to toe. 'You are a little taller than I am, and probably more Chantal's style since she is closer in age, but she is wearing pregnancy clothes these days. We'll see what we can do.'

'You must be excited to have your first grandchild.'

'*Ah oui*! I can't wait. To hold a baby again . . . *Mon Dieu*, I loved the whole early mother experience. Which is good, because Alain had to travel so much for business. Now Stephan the same, so Chantal will have to be alone with her little one a lot of the time. Gilles, too, you know, always being called away, *boom* . . .' She looked speculatively at Helen, then reached for a simple linen sheath in a soft rose color. 'This, I think?'

'Oh, it's beautiful.' Helen was already worried she'd spill something. 'You won't need it?'

'No, no, I always pack too much. Alain teases me that we need another room just for my clothes.' Brigitte shrugged. 'Seems easier to bring too much than to have to plan ahead for what I'll need every day.'

'Yes.' As if Helen had ever had that problem.

'And this?' *This* was a teal print in silk with a deep V neckline, a full skirt and cap sleeves.

'It's wonderful.' She accepted the dress, running her hands over the supple material. 'Thank you so much for doing this. I have a dress for New Year's Eve, so these two will be fine.'

'Yes? And here.' Brigitte pulled a white parka off the rack. 'You will need warmer things for outside. I brought an extra ski coat.'

Which still had the Dior tags on it. Helen thanked her again and added it to the pile, wondering about the transition from Brigitte's humble beginnings to her life as a shopping maven, thinking of the vast array of Natalie's mother's jewels. The only stone Helen had ever counted on owning was whatever Kevin could afford as her engagement ring. The only dresses she craved were enough for daily wear, church, and a fancy night out once in a while.

Had Brigitte and women like her grown up craving more than they had, or did access to unlimited wealth change them?

If Helen stayed in France with Gilles, she might find out someday. The thought made her uneasy. 'The clothes are beautiful, Brigitte. Thank you so much for thinking of me.'

'I'd love to take credit, but it was Gilles who thought of you.' Brigitte cupped Helen's cheek and looked intently into her eyes. 'His heart belongs to you. It is a very precious heart. Please take care of it.'

'I . . . will.' Helen felt more like a phony at that moment than she had for the past several hours in this playhouse of the

275

rich. She couldn't promise that. Not yet. To leave her country behind, to smash Kevin's heart, to change the life ahead of her so completely, to disappoint her parents and devastate Kevin's family . . . she had to be absolutely sure.

Dinner with Gilles's family was a delicious and delightful affair, cooked by staff in the penthouse kitchen and served in the dining room by candlelight. A light puréed zucchini and pea soup was followed by a succulent braised breast of veal with abundant herbs, tomatoes and pearl onions. Salad followed, then a sublime apple strudel served with cinnamon whipped cream. Conversation flowed – Helen warmly included – mostly in French, with occasional bursts of English, which all but Chantal spoke fluently. In-jokes were explained, stories of Gilles's childhood offered, hilariously inappropriate suggestions about what to name the coming baby proliferated, all amid affectionate teasing and obvious love.

Helen kept her smile on, laughed at the funny, tsk-tsked at the sad, answered questions and asked some of her own, still shaken by the talk with Brigitte. The number of people's emotions held hostage by her decision had grown, and the pressure was becoming intense.

After dinner, the party went downstairs, where a pair of drivers waited to whisk them off to the concert. By that time, Helen was tipsy and exhausted, not in the mood for a long classical piece that would go over her head, not in the mood to make more conversation with more people she didn't know well. She wanted to crawl back upstairs and bury herself under the covers. Even better, she wanted to be back in the little cottage with Lilianne, Connie and Sarah. Or back in her own bed at home in Zionsville, with no more pressure than making sure she got up on time to scoop ice cream at Henkel's.

Hotel Laudinella was a five-minute drive to the other side of the lake. The large, attractively lit white building blended with the snowy trees and mountains around it, and the waning moon wasn't bright enough to blot out a sky crammed with stars. Warm in her borrowed parka, Helen wanted to linger in the vast space, take in the icy air and watch it float out of her lungs in a frosty mist. She wanted to count the stars, make snow angels and warm her cold lips on Gilles's.

But she traipsed dutifully into the elevator up to the concert hall, already about three quarters full, with more beautiful people arriving by the minute. The family found seats scattered through the hall – Helen and Gilles grabbed two near the middle so they could be on their own.

The chorus and orchestra were already on stage, the instruments making the pleasant cacophony familiar from concerts Helen saw on the KU campus – her roommate Stefanie played violin. Around them a similar cacophony of people chattering, greeting one another from near and far distances, seeing and being seen. At five past the hour, the concertmaster entered to tune the orchestra and the audience settled. The conductor and four soloists swept in to warm applause, the conductor lifted his baton, and the piece began.

And went on. And on. As she had in college, Helen tried hard to pay attention, but though there were some tuneful bits she managed to follow and enjoy, most of it seemed like a lot of occasionally stormy dithering. Eventually she gave up and thought about whatever she could think of that had nothing to do with Gilles or Kevin or what she'd do about either. She examined the players and singers, wondering about their lives, where they lived and what kind of people they were offstage. She enjoyed the tapping sandaled foot of one of the cellists and the way the bald trumpeter's face and head turned bright red when the piece got loud.

After each movement, she allowed herself to stretch a little, aware that Gilles sat in rapt stillness throughout. If only she had his ears for this experience, mostly wasted on her.

Finally the voices entered, soloists and chorus, sweetly blending around a tune she knew, and she found herself not only paying attention, but enthralled.

The sound grew and evolved, the familiar melody weaving around only to disappear and appear again, richer and more beautiful, until the force of the entire chorus joined to blast it into the crowd, bounce it off the ceiling and walls, embracing them all, a bear hug of aural beauty and color.

Helen's breath grew shallow. She felt as if she'd been lifted into an alternate plane of existence where everything about her and her life became mundane compared to such power and magnificence. When the piece ended, she leapt to her feet with the rest of the audience, clapping until her palms burned, eyes shining, wanting the feeling to go on and on, because coming back to reality would be such a let-down.

She turned to look at Gilles at the same moment he turned to her. His face was an exact reflection of her excitement. And she realized with a shock that sent adrenaline through her and stilled her hands that the rest of her life with Gilles would be full of such new-to-her transcendent moments, engaging, challenging and enriching her until death did them part. And that if she'd done as she'd wanted to and stayed on the Riviera, done what she'd wanted to and skipped tonight's concert, she would have missed not only the music but the joy of sharing its emotions with a loved one who also felt them.

How smug Helen had felt after high school planning her escape from Zionsville and the small, predictable life attached to

Kenyon Hardware. *She* was going to college. *She* longed to travel the world. But she could picture the rest of her life with Kevin as if she'd already lived it. Year after year in the same place, living the same cycle of growth and decay, no new experiences, no surprises, nothing she wouldn't already be equipped to handle.

Brigitte was right. Kevin was safe.

Back in the penthouse at the Carlton, pretending fatigue she wasn't feeling, Helen opted out of the late-night glasses of brandy, thanked Brigitte and Alain for a lovely evening, did the kiss-kiss all around and nearly dragged Gilles into their bedroom.

He didn't seem to mind.

Door closed, she pressed herself against his tall, warm body, wrapping her arms around his shoulders. Their kisses grew more and more passionate. Helen didn't resist, but moved them toward the bed.

'Are you sure?' Gilles whispered.

She smiled up into his beautiful dark eyes, no doubts anymore. 'I'm sure.'

On the bed, in his arms, clothes shed, Helen's nerves about first-time fumbles, about only having been with one man before, faded into the naturalness of her and Gilles together. Not that the sex was perfect, more that neither of them was trying to make it perfect, but exploring and learning each other, and therefore imperfections were part of the experience.

They laughed at their adjustments, Helen answering shyly about what she needed and liked, emboldened to ask him the same. He didn't appoint himself in charge of their lovemaking; the pleasure was something they discovered together, and the passion was deeper and more intense as a result. When Helen climaxed, she did so with her whole heart, pulling Gilles closer, saying his name without realizing until she heard her own voice.

They lay together listening to their breathing slow. Then Gilles lifted his head and looked down at her, their gazes connecting as if they were entering each other's souls.

'I love you, Helen.'

'I love you too.' She traced the strong line of his jaw, feeling peaceful, content and utterly sure what she wanted and needed. 'After I go home in February, I'm coming back, Gilles. To France. To Paris. To you.'

৩ **Chapter 13** ৩

Teresa opened her eyes to find early daylight peeking into the bedroom. Somehow, with all she had on her mind, she'd slept, though it had taken her a while to get there. The coyotes had only wakened her once; she'd managed not to panic too much, and eventually drifted off again. Even Monarch had only annoyed her a couple of times with his intractable form occupying the place her body needed to stretch into.

Today began a messy and complicated day of recalibrating and reconsidering, reaching out and mending breaches. Lying here between soft sheets, it was easy to contemplate how her life might change. But once she slid from the bed's protection, the reckoning would begin, and the promises she'd made to herself the previous day at the hospital would kick her onto a road already in motion.

Zero incentive to get up. Ever.

In spite of her apprehension, yesterday's determination hadn't entirely left her, so she sat up and swung her legs over the edge of the bed onto that moving road, which led her into the bathroom for a shower and half-hearted blow-dry, then into the kitchen for one of the earliest breakfasts Teresa had eaten happily. She'd discovered that fresh eggs from free-range chickens were delicious, shells thicker, yolks a vivid orange.

It was a restless, cloudy day, humid and buffety. She took

her coffee out onto the deck to watch what she'd decided to call Ranch TV. Even after almost a week here, there was always something new to absorb. It had occurred to her late last night that if she could stay here longer than the supposed-to-be-in-Vegas two weeks to be with Helen while she recovered, and if it then turned out her dementia-free grandmother wouldn't need to move to the retirement home, Teresa would no longer need to go full tilt clearing out the house. Something Helen said had stuck with her – that she should find Sarah a place of honor, first in this house, then in Teresa's own. It would be fun to make her a fancy wooden chair, maybe upholstered with fabric to complement her green dress. Sarah would have the proper setting, and Teresa could make use of Kevin's workshop while she was here and see if the skills Dad taught her younger self had stuck.

A truck rattled up the driveway; its door slammed. She turned toward the corner of the house to see which animal-checker would appear today, hoping it was Danny. They'd gone to lunch the day before, after Danny bore up so well during Teresa's tale of woe, and had stayed at the café talking for nearly two hours. She really . . .

Well anyway.

'Hi, Jim.' Teresa went down the deck stairs, glad to see him in spite of his non-Dannyness. 'Mind if I come along on the rounds today? I'm thinking I can start taking over.'

His freckled boy-face stretched into a grin. 'That would be great.'

She appreciated that he didn't comment further. *Has our Teresa gotten over her silly spooks? Good girl!*

They started by the goat pen, where as usual the goats massed curiously, kids leaping and jostling, and the sheep and lambs ignored them.

Teresa checked the animals over. 'They look fine to me.'

'Me too.'

They continued the rounds at the chicken coop. Teresa made a mental note to buy a new latch when she was getting wood for Sarah's chair – and hadn't she thought about building platforms for the goats to play on and jump off? She watched carefully as Jim checked each nest for eggs – she was going to have to start eating daily omelets to catch up. Then, escorted by Pearl and Tusk, she and Jim strolled past the happily grazing mule and bulls.

'You were a topic of discussion last night at dinner.'

'Uh-oh.' Teresa wasn't sure she wanted to hear this.

'Danny and I ate at my parents' house. Mom had a theory about Zig. She's almost your height, same build, same hair length. She and Zig have great wrestling matches every time she comes over. She wondered if at first he thought you were her.'

'Wow.' Teresa nodded slowly. 'I like that. Even if it's not true, I'm going to believe it. Thank your mom for me. It makes his attacks less personal.'

'Yeah, he's not the type to hold grudges.' They strolled over toward the cows. 'See anything there?'

Teresa scanned the area and noticed a calf on the other side of a partial fence, bleating his pitiful isolation when all he had to do was walk out the way he went in. 'That guy can't figure out the way back to Mom.'

'You're a natural.'

She rolled her eyes. 'What do you do in that case?'

'Mostly wait. Mom will respond soon. The calf will eventually figure out how it got there and go to her. It won't starve. Good teaching moment.'

As they watched, a cow detached herself from the herd and lumbered mooing over to the little one, nosing it through the fence. Jim opened the slightly wobbly gate a few feet from where they stood. 'Want to go in? They're pretty indifferent to humans.'

'Uh . . .' Teresa swallowed. 'Sure. Okay.'

They walked into the pasture, followed by the dogs. Within a few seconds, Pearl trotted around the half-length of fencing toward the calf, who skittered away from her. Immediately Pearl lowered herself nearly to the ground, instinctively making herself smaller and less threatening, and again crept forward.

'That's incredible. The dog knows not to spook it.'

'That's what Pyrenees are bred for. Watch. She's getting the little one used to her.'

The calf took spindly steps forward and touched noses with the dog, then backed nervously away. For the next several minutes Teresa and Jim watched the dog–calf dance, Pearl showing a touching display of patience and tenderness.

'Jim.' Teresa turned to face her cousin. Out of nowhere came certainty that this was the right time to bridge their gap. 'I owe you and your dad an apology. I talked to Helen yesterday, and I have a better idea of the real story and what your father grew up with. I guess my mom . . . has some issues. I didn't realize.'

'Of course not. She's your mom. And you don't owe us anything. Dad is kicking himself for coming down on you so hard. He'll apologize right back when you see him again.'

'Okay.' Teresa hunched her shoulders, hoping Uncle James wasn't coming by that evening. One emotional scene a day should be a universal limit.

'I'm really sorry, Teresa.' Jim's blue eyes were sad and earnest. 'I'm sure it sucks to lose trust in your mom like that.'

'Kinda does.'

'If it helps, a bunch of us are going out again tonight. A new bar just opened downtown. Live music and axe-throwing. You wanna come? It might help you get some rage out.'

Teresa laughed while her stomach knotted. The last thing she wanted. But he was being so sweet trying to cheer her up, giving her a chance to get out of the house, away from all the angst.

'Oh, thanks.' She stared out at Pearl gradually gaining the calf's trust, and remembered the conversation with Danny. 'You know, I had a great time the other night. It was fun meeting Chloe and your friends, and I'd love to hang out with them again sometime. But clubs and bars – not really my thing.'

'You and Danny, huh. No problem. How about dinner at our place tomorrow night instead? Danny's a great cook.'

'I would *love* that.' That was it? That easy? She was ridiculously relieved. Instead of a night of loud drunken hell – with *axes* – she got to have a small dinner party with Danny, her cousin and his girlfriend, during which actual conversation would be possible. 'I'm happy to bring something, but don't count on me for anything home-made unless you like bad food.'

'Danny'll figure it out and we'll let you know.'

'Okay, thank you.' The idea of Danny commanding the stove made her heart flutter, and she told it to chill. Danny was a nice guy who was paying her a little attention at a vulnerable and messed-up time in her life. She didn't need to invite disappointment by turning it into more inside her head.

The calf was nearly at the fence opening, mooing Mom following on the other side, until the baby realized where it was and bolted to its mother.

'So you think you can handle this tonight?'

Teresa looked at Jim blankly. Hadn't she just declined? 'Tonight?'

His generous grin brightened his face, and she saw Helen's features passed down to another generation. 'The animals.'

'Oh! Yes, I will. I'll do it. As long as I can text you with questions.'

'Absolutely. Good for you.' He patted her shoulder awkwardly. 'This is progress.'

They left the cow pen, trailed by the Pyrenees. Jim went back to his truck with a wave, and Teresa headed toward the house. She'd rather do some weeding, or see what else might need patching or fixing, but if she didn't keep momentum on the difficult tasks ahead, she'd never get started.

Near the house's back deck, another challenge blocked her path. Zig, looking wary, as Teresa undoubtedly was herself.

'Okay, Zig. We're going to work this out. I'm not Alicia. I'm Teresa, and I hate being jumped on. You need to be nice around me, like Pearl and Tusk. Do we have a deal?'

He wagged his tail. She took a step forward and put out her hand. He approached eagerly, sniffed and . . . obviously unimpressed, bounded off.

Teresa laughed. Another imagined demon slain. How many others haunting her had she created herself?

Inside, she let Cheddar out of his cage and took him to his kitchen perch, where they discussed the situation. He agreed that waiting to tackle her list would only increase the nerves. Better to get it over with.

The first item she'd already crossed off, having taken Sarah to the Doll Cradle in Kansas City after visiting Helen yesterday. The owner hadn't been there, but a young helper thought they could get her mended and cleaned up in time for Helen's homecoming.

Teresa settled in at the dining table with her laptop and pen and paper in case – well, they made her feel more prepared. She called her office and asked to speak to Human Resources. The pleasant lady informed her she had two more weeks of vacation that she could use if it was okay with her boss. Her boss growled and grumbled and finally agreed if Teresa did some work remotely, but no more than two weeks. Teresa thanked him profusely, gratefully, humbly, then ended the call and did a victory dance that freaked Cheddar out. Free! Two more weeks added to the time off for her cancelled Vegas trip meant she had three weeks ahead to get to know her grandmother better and delay her own return to reality.

Easy enough.

Unfortunately, that was the end of easy. Next item: Teresa's well-meaning but risky plan to reunite Helen with Lilianne and Gilles. A few minutes browsing the online White Pages turned up a Lilianne Maxwell in Connecticut, cross-referenced with Gilles Aubert at the same address. Who else could it be?

Teresa stared at Cheddar, who was pecking at some round wooden beads decorating his perch. She was trying to come up with what to say, how to bring up that Lilianne and Gilles's long-ago friend was recovering from a serious accident, wrestling with doubts over whether contacting them was the right thing to do. Best case, she'd be helping restore friendships her grandmother obviously missed. Worst, she'd be overstepping, innocently inserting herself into a situation she might not fully understand.

The memory of her grandmother's expression of longing pushed her into picking up her phone. Teresa was a neutral party letting Lilianne and Gilles know facts. How they reacted was up to them. If, as Helen feared, they didn't want to re-establish contact, then at least she'd never have to know. Teresa would save her from possible rejection.

The phone rang. Katie! A perfectly timed delay. What were best friends for?

'Hey, roomie, I miss you!' Teresa got up and went out onto the back deck, sat in her favorite coffee-drinking chair.

'*You* miss *me*? I'm *pining*! It's no fun around here. Addie's at Carter's house 24/7 being even more codependent than me and Ross, I'm in wedding hell, you're not here to help me plan Addie's engagement party, and I'm losing my mind. How are you?'

Teresa put her feet up on the railing, feeling like Katie was talking about a far-off country she'd once visited. 'Nothing but chocolate cake here.'

'Uh-oh. I know that voice. Tell me.'

Teresa told her.

'Geez-o-Pete, you are living a soap opera. Though I always kind of knew your mom was a mess.'

'You did?' Teresa put her feet down. 'Why didn't you tell me? Why didn't you say something?'

'I *did* try once. But you were, I don't know, not ready to hear, I guess. I mean, she was always putting you down, and you were all whipped-puppy around her. I hated it.'

Teresa sat stunned, casting back in her memory files until she found the one she wanted. Yes. Katie had tried, and no, Teresa had not been ready. In fact, she'd been bewildered, then suddenly and unreasonably pissed, and had left the room.

'You're right. You tried. Thanks.' Her voice thickened. 'So now I'm going to have to write to my father and try to figure out—'

'No, no, nobody writes, that will be impossible. Just *call* him.'

Teresa sat up, anxiety flooding her body. 'I can't do that.'

'Why not? That way it'll be as much on him as you what to say.'

'I'll die.'

'I guarantee you will not.' Katie groaned. 'God, it's Jake calling. Hang on.'

Teresa hung on, inhaling the warm air, watching the goats frolic. She didn't like Jake. He got drunk every time the group went out and tried to make a move on whoever was closest. Teresa made sure it was never her.

'Hi, I'm back, sorry. He wants to go out tonight. I had to say no, and I never do that! I told you things were tough here. When are you coming back? Next week, right?'

'Actually, I think I'm staying longer.'

'What do you mean, you think you're staying longer? I need you here. My mother and mother-in-law are battling it out over the wedding. It's supposed to be *our* day, and they're making it all about them. They're inviting so many of their own friends that we can't even have all the ones *we* want. Plus Mom wants Ross to get rid of his earring, and Cerise wants us to have *bagpipes* escorting us to the reception, and Dad is angry because everything is costing more than his and Mom's wedding like, hello, Dad, *thirty years* ago. And on top of it all, this party for Addie and Carter is going to put me over the edge.'

Teresa found it unusually hard to summon sympathy. 'You'll get through it.'

'I'm not sure I will. It would be so much easier if you were here. Oh, we all went out last night to a new club downtown, oh my God. I did so many tequila shots I had the spins in the middle of the night. You gotta get back, you're missing serious fun.'

A lamb thrust its head against its mother's belly; the ewe continued grazing as it nursed. A hawk flew overhead, sending chickens scattering with disapproving clucks. Teresa thought of the dinner tomorrow night with Danny, Jim and Chloe. She thought of how after college some quiet, studious friends Teresa had a lot in common with had asked her to share an apartment, but she'd chosen Katie and Addie, flattered to be asked, craving the glamour and energy of their lives.

How long had she been trying to be someone she wasn't?

'I'm kinda done with nightclubs.'

Katie gasped. 'What did you just say?'

This would be harder than telling Jim the same thing. 'I don't really like them, Katie. I never have. I just went because—'

'Lalala, I'm going to pretend I didn't hear that. You need to get out of Farmland and come home. I have so much to do at work, and now the caterers are wanting a deposit earlier than they said, and Ross and I are the only ones wanting a vegan option – Mom says vegetarian is plenty.'

Teresa raised her hand and let it slap back on the arm of her chair. 'Why don't you just elope if this is all so awful?'

'Hah! No way! I want the works, baby.' Katie sounded maniacal. 'The church, the dress, the crowd, the presents. It'll be so worth it. So anyway, you have to come back next week, because I'll need you to—'

'Katie . . . I am not coming back next week.'

'Wait, *seriously*? Why?'

'Among other things, I'm not ready to come back. I like it here.'

'*What*? You want to keep hanging around corn and cows? Are you stoned?'

'And I'm needed.' She liked the sound of that.

'Doing what?'

'I need to stay with my grandmother after she gets out of rehab, so she can finish recovering at home.'

'But . . .' Katie made a sound of exasperation. 'Can't she hire someone? I'm drowning here. I need you to plan Addie's engagement party. I was really counting on you, Teresa. I mean, she's your roommate too.'

Teresa cringed guiltily and started to speak . . . but the apology stuck in her throat. Zig climbed the stairs and sat beside her chair, panting over whatever energy-exerting experience he'd just had. His fur was warm against her calf.

'It's not like I'm dropping the ball, Katie. I had no idea we had to throw a party for Addie.'

'Well of *course* we have to have an engagement party for her. She threw one for Ross and me.'

'Why can't you have it later, after I get—'

'Wait, are you serious? You're not going to help?'

Teresa swallowed hard, reached down to touch Zig's fur. 'I'm sorry, I can't come back next week.'

'You *won't* come back next week.'

She huffed. 'Katie, just take her and Carter to a restaurant and—'

'What? Would *you* like that?'

'Yes! I'd love it.'

Silence. For probably the first time ever on the phone between them. 'You're being really weird, Teresa. And selfish. I have to go, I have an appointment with a possible stylist.'

'Katie, you—' The call disconnected. Teresa stared at her phone as if it had made a mistake, waiting for the crushing anxiety and guilt to set in, and to start desperately searching for a way to smooth over the argument, make it her fault, apologize, whatever it took. The usual.

There was some anxiety and guilt, yes, and sadness, but not crushing. And underneath was stubborn certainty that she hadn't said or done anything that deserved hanging up on. Under that? Annoyance. Katie was temporarily busy because she was getting married. Teresa's life had been turned inside out. Yet Katie's trauma took precedence. Had it always been like that? Would Teresa now have to reconsider her relationship with her best friend as well as her mother?

The thought tempted her to crawl back into bed and hide. Maybe she was evolving, and maybe that was good, but it felt like she was belly-crawling across a pit of gravel. Naked.

Luckily, all she had to do now was more difficult and unsettling things.

No fear.

After a few centering breaths that only made her feel lightheaded, nervous energy propelled Teresa to her feet. She dialed the Connecticut number quickly, before she chickened out, pacing back and forth on the deck with Zig's gaze following, practicing what she'd say. The ringing started. She half hoped the number would be out of service, but if it wasn't, she prayed the call would go to voicemail instead of either Lilianne or Gilles answering.

Her fondest hope was granted when a woman's voice announced with clear precision that Lilianne and Gilles were not able to come to the phone right then.

Beep.

'Hi. This is Helen Foster's granddaughter. I know you were both a big part of her life. And I thought you should know that she's fine, but in the hospital here in Lawrence, recovering from a broken hip. She'll be out soon, but will need care for a while. I'll be here for a few more weeks, but I thought . . . well, I think she'd love to hear from you. If I'm butting in or this is unwelcome, please ignore. Thanks.'

Teresa ended the call and held up her phone in silent victory. She hadn't stuttered or said anything stupid, gotten stuck on ums or ers. In fact, a success. They could disregard or act as they wanted.

She practically danced back into the house, exchanging figurative high-fives with Cheddar, and got herself a glass of water, then allowed herself another few minutes of celebration before she made herself face the next task.

Dad.

Forget *no fear*. There *was* fear. And anger and bitterness.

Good memories and hope. Dark conviction that she was betraying her mother. And did she mention fear?

She sat back down at her laptop, still on the dining table, and pulled up a new email, checking her phone for the contact information Ike had texted her.

To: Richard Clark
Subject: It's me
Dear Dad

Half an hour later, that was all she'd kept from about seventeen different versions of the email, some written by a raging wronged daughter, some by a pleading forgiving wimp, some by an information-seeking automaton.

Maybe Katie was right and Teresa should call him, make him have to work at this first contact as well.

She wasn't sure she had that in her.

Ten minutes later, she'd gotten as far as adding her father to her phone's contacts list and staring hard at his number, when the gods sent a reprieve in the form of an angry burst of rain that had her scurrying around the house closing windows. She peered through the shower – so rare in Phoenix! – marveling at the sight of the pelting drops, curious what the animals were doing. All but the cows were heading for shelter, sheep and goats jostling into the barn, chickens into the coop. A smile spread over her face at the thought of them safe and dry inside. The mule continued grazing, tail lashing occasionally. The bulls and cows stood stoically as they were pelted. Teresa went to the dining room and opened the sliding door she'd just closed, inhaling the fresh green watery smell, feeling herself calming.

No matter what happened on this call, she would be okay. No matter what happened with her mother, or Katie, or anyone else, she would have this peaceful, simple place to come back to, here in front of her right now, and forever in her mind after she left.

She put Cheddar back into his cage so he wouldn't distract her, and resolutely picked up the damn phone yet again. Heart thudding, she pressed the number to speak with her father for the first time since she was barely adolescent, trying to stay open-minded. She'd listen, attempt to keep her emotions under control.

He picked up immediately. 'Teresa!'

His voice was so full of joy, she panicked and grabbed at the first thing that occurred to her. 'How did you know this was my number?'

'Your brothers. Isaac said he'd talked to you recently.'

'Oh.'

Awkward, hellish silence, during which Teresa's mind went blank and her father seemed to be breathing funny. Wouldn't that be even more hellish, if she'd called after all these years and given him a heart attack.

'I'm so glad you called. So . . . glad.' His voice had turned quavery and lower than she remembered. And then when another odd sound came over the phone, she realized he was crying. If the sound of his voice had upended her resolution to stay unemotional, his tears destroyed it. 'What changed your mind?'

Teresa forced her puddingy brain to focus. 'Parts of my life are turning out to be different than what . . . I'd thought.' She instinctively protected her mother, though he'd probably figure out what she meant. 'I hoped maybe you could tell me your side – your story.'

'Yes. Yes, okay.' He was still choked up. 'Give me a second.'

She waited, resting her elbow on the dining table and her forehead on her hand. It was so surreal that she was about to have the why-did-you-leave-me-Daddy conversation she'd had in her head so many times when she was younger, before she'd accepted that Daddy hadn't found her and her brothers worth staying for, and had pushed the truth and shame away as far as she possibly could.

'I guess I'll go back to the start.' He cleared his throat and continued, sounding stronger. 'Your mom was so young when we got married. We were caught up in the infatuation and the excitement of eloping. I felt like Cheryl's knight in shining armor, charging in to rescue her from the prison tower of your grandparents' farm. She made me feel like I was a superhero, like I could do anything. It was pretty heady stuff for a geeky guy who wanted to be a dentist.

'But then, like in every relationship, you know, the infatuation fades. Normal, not a big deal, you just gotta work at it. Except . . . Cheryl retreated instead. From the marriage and me, and, um, from . . . our bed.'

Teresa winced. He could skip that part, really.

'I told myself it was because she was so busy with you kids. Maybe it was, but as the three of you got older, I was still cut off. Sounds like it's not a big deal, maybe, but over time, not having affection and intimacy . . . it becomes a kind of starvation. You must have noticed how unhappy we were.'

While he'd been talking, Teresa was thinking back to when he lived with them, trying to cut through the emotion to the actual details. Trying to remember her parents ever going out together or laughing together, trying to remember if she'd ever interrupted a kiss or embrace. When they started sleeping apart, she'd accepted her mother's excuse that her father snored, though she'd never heard him. 'I didn't think about it at the time, but I mean, obviously you weren't happy.'

'Neither of us was. Your mom refused counseling. I went alone, and finally admitted to myself that the marriage couldn't be saved. Then Amy and I started getting closer, and I realized what I was missing. I would change that part if I could, Teresa. But when you're starving . . .' He exhaled loudly. 'God, it's so hard to put myself in that same mind frame now. When you're starving, you lose your moral and rational perspective, and will do anything for food. I convinced myself that if I had an affair, I could get my needs met and still keep the family together. Sounds stupid, huh.'

'It was a nightmare for all of us. Mom most of all.'

'It was, and I'm to blame for that. But I couldn't have gone on that way. People act like it's noble to stay in a marriage no matter what. I say there's nothing noble about you and your spouse turning each other into the worst possible versions of yourselves just because you're still together.'

Teresa felt herself go angry and hard, listening to him talking about wanting to be the best Richard Clark he could by turning his back on his family and jumping on some new hot babe. The way he described it, Mom had practically pushed him into Amy's bed. 'You left us cold.'

'That wasn't supposed to happen.' His gentle voice thinned and rose. 'If I'd known I'd lose you . . . I wanted joint custody, and stupidly assumed Cheryl would want that too. I never dreamed she'd fight me so hard.'

Teresa closed her eyes. Even with what she'd already learned about her mother, this part felt dangerous all over again, like edging out onto a crumbling ledge. 'Why would she do that? Why would she want to deprive us of a father?'

Her dad blew out a frustrated breath. 'Your mother . . . has trouble with people opposing her. That's the nicest way I can put it. I fought at first, but the situation escalated so horribly that I decided to back down, to see if she'd relent and be reasonable. That never happened.'

Teresa jerked her head upright. 'You could have come over to see us. We would have survived seeing Mom angry. You could have come by school. You could have invited us to your place.'

'Yes.' She heard the tears in his voice. 'A stronger man would have. But I was torn apart, and exhausted by the guilt and the stress. I started to believe your mother when she said you didn't want to hear from me. I worried that continuing to try would do more damage. So I retreated into my new life. And then I sent you all those damn emails, praying you'd come around eventually. I'm sorry, Teresa. I know it wasn't enough. It sounds trite, but I mean it profoundly.'

'Thank you.' She wasn't ready to forgive him yet. Not entirely. He'd certainly found plenty of strength to start a new family. The pain he'd caused . . . Maybe Mom hadn't handled the disaster of their marriage any better, and maybe she'd been the source of some or all of the problems. But at least she stuck around for Teresa and her brothers, and raised them herself, not perfectly, but with dedication Dad hadn't quite managed.

They talked for several more minutes on less difficult topics. He asked about Teresa's life in a way that convinced her he really cared, and he responded to her stories with humor and to her accomplishments with pride and to her self-deprecation with encouragement. It took a lot for her not to compare his reaction with Mom's. Of course he was trying to get on her good side, and how easy to stroll back into her life now and play the perfect father retroactively. But his easy acceptance underlined what a judgmental and critical parent Mom had been, which made Teresa want to lie back and howl over being deprived of the chance to grow up knowing her dad.

However, what-could-have-been was a useless thing to long for, so she decided, after blowing her nose and adding the tissue to the pile at her elbow, that she'd take time to think over the conversation and the relationship and decide how much resentment she could put to rest, and how much of her father she wanted in her life after so many years without him.

They hung up promising to stay in touch. By that time Teresa had decided she didn't want to speak to anyone on the phone again for the next week. At least.

And yet, as exhausted and wrung out as she was, she also felt a combination of relief and triumph mixed with pride. *No fear* had finally been used in the service of something she really wanted instead of what she thought she was supposed to want.

Yay her.

Battling nervous energy, she spent the next hour carting loads of paper up the stairs and into her car to take to the recycling center, then tidied up the clips and folders and broke down the boxes, which she took to the garage in case they were needed. That done, she vacuumed the basement, glancing periodically at her phone to see if Lilianne had called or if Katie had texted an apology, which would be nice.

Neither.

By the time the basement was clean and the rain had finished sweeping through, Teresa felt a lot less wobbly. She drove the load to the recycling center, then found a hardware store, where she bought a new latch for the chicken coop. On the way home – she caught herself using the term and smiled – she detoured to a pet store and bought a present for Cheddar to apologize for having shoved him back in his cage during the call with her father. On a whim, she also stopped at a bookstore for a copy of *Circe*, determined to get back into the habit of reading.

She'd even allowed herself to remember some of the better times with Dad, and further admitted to herself that the family time in Paradise Valley hadn't quite been paradise. Maybe one day soon she'd be able to throw off the remaining weight of feeling that she hadn't been worth her father's time.

On her way back to the ranch, she'd recovered enough good mood to hum along to the radio, windows half down to catch the sweet summer-rain scent.

Once home, she installed the latch, which intrusion the chickens did not appreciate in spite of the fact that she was doing them a big favor. Inside, she ate a quick lunch, then settled down in the living room with a cup of coffee, her laptop and a sketchpad she'd found in the closet in her room, hoping to come up with ideas for a chair worthy of Her Royal Sarah. Cheddar was on the coffee table, entranced with his new toy, a mass of paper, blocks and netting, which he was trying his best to destroy.

By googling 'French armchair' in deference to Sarah's country of origin, Teresa found the chair she wanted. A fairly simple frame with a cushioned back and seat. Picking up the pad, she sketched out the various parts and sizes she'd need, and a list of materials, aware that the final product might not be as glamorous as the photo but certain that Sarah wouldn't care.

She was about to look for a place that would sell quality wood for furniture when her phone rang, shooting her through with adrenaline. Dad again? Mom? – Teresa couldn't face her yet. Lilianne or Gilles? Katie with a big fat apology for being Bridezilla?

It was the Doll Cradle.

'Hi. This is Matti Kirkpatrick. I wasn't here when you dropped off your doll.' She spoke quickly, nervously. 'I'm curious . . . where did you get her?'

'From my grandmother. She got it from a friend of hers in Paris, who got it from her stepmother.'

'Do you have any idea what you have here?'

Teresa stuck out a finger for Cheddar, who was squawking in annoyance, and put him on her shoulder. 'A Sarah Bernhardt doll?'

'She's an A. Marque doll. Albert Marque was the maker.' The woman was practically panting, her voice shaking. 'Those dolls are the pinnacle of . . . They are *so* rare – I can't believe I'm holding an original A. Marque!'

Teresa let out a whistle, which set Cheddar off chatting and chirping. She would certainly offer Sarah back to Helen if she was valuable, though Teresa had liked the idea of having Sarah for company, and loved her grandmother's description of the doll's power. 'I didn't realize.'

'A. Marque dolls sell in the low hundred thousands.'

Teresa froze. Hundred *thousands*? 'Are you serious?'

'Completely.' Matti gave a hysterical giggle. 'This doll is every collector's dream. Especially in good condition, as Sarah looks to be. There were only one hundred of these dolls made in 1915, each dressed differently in costumes designed and sewn by the Jeanne Margaine-Lacroix house in Paris as a promotion. Out of those hundred, only about twenty are accounted for. You have discovered another one. We are all going out of our minds here in the shop. It's like finding a Gutenberg Bible.'

Teresa was unable to take this in. It had to be a prank, or a mistake. 'Oh wow.'

'And then it gets even more unbelievable. I called a friend, who came to look. Sarah's jewels are the real deal. Necklace, brooch, tiara . . . all diamonds. The fur is also real. This is the most remarkable Marque doll I've ever heard of.' Matti gave a wobbly laugh. 'She could easily be worth half a million. Maybe more.'

❦ **Chapter 14** ❧

Listen! If the evening caused us such pain
Soon the day will reunite us
And the joy of our memories
Will again mingle with joy itself.
Marceline Desbordes-Valmore, 'L'adieu du soir'

Dear Helen,
We got your letter of January 4. Your father and I are quite giddy imagining you on the Riviera for Christmas, and then at a luxury hotel in Switzerland for the New Year celebration. It's certainly not the kind of vacation we ever managed to give you, or to have ourselves.

But we are very concerned about your relationship with this man Gilles, and that you are thinking about returning to France to live with him after your flight home in February. Neither your father nor I slept much last night for worrying.

Before you jump to conclusions, we aren't worrying that you have this attraction. Kevin was your first and only, and it's natural for your head to be easily turned at your age, especially so far away from what you know and are accustomed to.

What worries us is that you are giving the feelings more

seriousness than they deserve. You and Gilles don't know each other well enough to be making any kind of decision about the future. It's easy to be carried away in those first heady months of passion, and to imagine they signify more than they do. The feelings are so deep and strong and feel so right. But you haven't been tested as a couple. How you handle the bad times together is vital to understanding if what you have can last. I had several crushes and a few boyfriends before I met your father; it was how he supported and helped me through a difficult period in my life that told me he was The One. Being together through happy times is easy to do with anyone.

Secondly, Paris is not the place for a girl who was planning to be a farmer's wife. You're not a city girl, Helen. Remember those letters to us from college complaining about the dorms and how you felt everyone was on top of you? Multiply that by the nth degree, and then as time passes, the nth degree again.

Finally, living where you don't belong is key to unhappiness – not right away, while the shiny newness is still enticing, but eventually. All the love in the world can't change that. You might love Paris, you might love France, but you won't ever truly belong there.

This letter will no doubt make you angry. That's fine. I didn't write it thinking you'd be thrilled to hear what I had to say. It would be much easier for both of us if I patted you on the back with a hearty 'Great idea!'

I want you to pay attention to that anger. If this letter annoys you because you already know all this and have thought it through deeply and calmly, and are half laughing because I'm being patronizing and not acknowledging your ability to judge situations wisely for yourself, then fine. That is all to the good.

But if you are angry in a hot, sick way in your belly, and want to tear this up and stomp on the pieces or throw it away to make sure it never bothers you again, and how dare I interfere, and everything I say is ridiculous because you know better, then pay attention, Helen. Because that anger means that deep down, you know I'm right.

All my love always,

Mom

Saturday, January 31, 1976

'*Merci milles fois*, Alphonse.' Natalie double-kissed the tiny, musty antique book dealer who'd showed up with two helpers to haul off boxes of books dating back to the eighteenth century. '*À bientôt.*'

'*Merci à vous, madame.*' He tipped an imaginary hat and left.

Natalie closed the door behind him, hugging her arms around herself. 'Well. That's the last of it. We have finished our work.'

'Yes.' Helen put an affectionate hand on Natalie's shoulder. Hard enough coping with her own surprising grief at the job being complete. What Natalie felt, knowing the apartment she'd grown up in was ready for its next occupant . . . 'It's hard.'

'*Oui.*' Natalie sniffed loudly and tossed her head. 'But good. The place feels lighter without generations of stuff that wasn't needed or noticed. People will cherish those books we just saw out the door. Here they gathered dust. A waste!'

A priceless waste in some cases. The little bookseller would be doing very well. But Natalie had stuck firm. The value of books was in their use, not their price tag.

Helen breathed in and out, trying to shake off the blues that had settled in over the past few weeks since she'd been back from Switzerland. Paris had been chilly, damp and gloomy, day after day, and Gilles had been unusually busy. Being cut loose from this job and the deepening daily relationship with Natalie was difficult. Finding out Lilianne had been reassigned to Cairo was devastating. Knowing Connie's restlessness . . . she might soon leave as well. February loomed. In less than two weeks, Helen would go home, pack up what she owned, and come back to a new, vastly different life in Paris. Facing that had been difficult. She still hadn't been able to bring herself to call Kevin and let him know, kept putting it off, to the point where it was becoming unconscionable. Writing would be so much easier, but she owed him more than that.

Most difficult, having decided to stay with Gilles, the infinite stretch of days ahead was still empty, undefined. He insisted she didn't have to work right away, or ever, that he could support them both until she found something worthwhile. Even better, while her time wasn't reliably booked, she could come with him when he was assigned somewhere she'd like to explore.

She loved that idea, utterly romantic in its spontaneity and sense of adventure, but the practical details were harder to imagine. She wasn't cut out for sitting at home waiting for the next trip, and she hadn't yet landed on what to fill her hours with.

'So.' Natalie adjusted the peach paisley scarf casually knotted at her neck that perfectly complemented her suit. French women had that superpower. When Helen tried out a scarf, she looked as if she were being strangled. 'To celebrate this day and the lovely news that I will not lose you next month, I've asked Lucas to make us a special American lunch of hamburgers and fries, with a hot fudge sundae for dessert. The French do not understand the concept of sundaes, *tant pis*. They will have to learn one day.'

'Oh, how fun.' Helen laughed. 'After six months, who would imagine a burger, fries and hot fudge would sound exotic.'

'*Mais oui!* Hamburger and fries of course we have, but you didn't come to Paris to eat what you can get at home.'

'Definitely not.' She followed Natalie into the beautiful dining room, set as usual as if they'd be eating pheasant and truffles. Helen would miss these crazy formal lunches, and the daily chats with Natalie about anything and everything. Of course they'd still see each other, but it wouldn't be the same.

'How is Sarah?' Natalie sat and pushed in her chair.

'She's thriving.' Helen took her seat opposite. 'Very excited to be staying in her native country.'

'My father saw Ms Bernhardt perform.' Natalie smiled at Helen's gasp. 'He said her voice was mesmerizing. Of course, her style would be considered melodramatic in this age of method acting, but she was an institution. A strong woman with strong emotions, astute in business and very aware of her own worth. From the beginning she let nothing stop her, not illegitimacy, not poverty and not failure. Like your Marceline.'

'Though Marceline was orphaned, not illegitimate.'

'Ah yes. I've forgotten the story. Her father died and then . . . South America? And some tragedy there?'

'She and her mother went over to start a new life with relatives. Not long after they arrived, the family *and* her mother died of yellow fever. Marceline was only thirteen.' Helen shuddered. 'I would have given up right then and become a housemaid.'

'No, not you.' Natalie gazed at her proudly. 'Marceline found a way back to France and made a good life for herself. Exactly as you will.'

'Eventually.' Helen unfolded her linen napkin and put it into her lap, succumbing to another wave of the anxiety that had been a regular visitor since her decision to stay. Her life had always been comfortably confined to predictable channels – ironically the main reason she'd wanted so badly to take this trip. Now, thrown into open water, she'd lost the confidence she needed to choose a direction and keep swimming.

'*Mademoiselle.*' With all the seriousness of a sommelier, Lucas presented Helen with a curvy glass bottle of Coke.

'Ah!' She grinned up at him. 'My favorite vintage.'

'But of course.' He bowed and poured for both ladies. 'Only the best in this house.'

'*Merci*, Lucas.' Natalie took a sip, then made a face. 'If I pay attention, I taste only sugar and chemicals. So I don't pay attention.'

Helen's first sip took her back to the lunch counter at Elliott's Pharmacy, now McKamey's, in Zionsville, where Mom would sometimes take her and her brothers for lunch in the summer, and where Helen had been allowed to order her first Coke.

'The two women are an interesting pair.' Natalie put down the Coke and picked up her water. 'Marceline had the one romantic disaster, with the cad who seduced and left her, and then a long, happy marriage. Sarah was with many men all her life and never settled. Both were devoted to their arts, both excelled tremendously, especially for their time. Groundbreakers. I think you could do some interesting scholarship involving the two.'

Helen's heart lifted for a second, then dropped. What could she come up with that hadn't already been carefully researched by people with experience, resources and degrees much more advanced than hers?

'*Voilà, mesdames.*' Lucas swept in and deposited plates holding plump, juicy burgers on the requisite soft round buns, and a pile of the skinny crisp fries the French excelled at. Soon after, he reappeared with a silver platter offering bottles of Heinz ketchup and French's yellow mustard, and a jar of pickle relish.

'Oh, this is fantastic.' Helen reached for the ketchup. 'Thank you, Lucas.'

'*Ce n'est rien, mademoiselle.*' He inclined his head and left the room.

'So, *ma petite.*' Natalie removed the top bun from her burger. 'Have you told your American young man that you are returning to France? Your parents?'

'I told my parents I was thinking about it. Kevin . . . no, not yet.' Helen handed Natalie the ketchup, chest heavy with guilt. 'I gave myself a little time, you know, because the decision . . . because . . . I guess I'm giving myself time to get used to it. But anyway, I'll let them know February first.'

Natalie's eyebrow lifted. 'Tomorrow.'

'Yes.' Helen coughed and reached for the mustard. 'Tomorrow.'

'That won't be easy.' Natalie was piercing Helen with her keen blue eyes. 'But maybe easier than to go home and wonder "what if" for the rest of your life.'

'Much better.' Helen forced a smile. 'I'll be so glad when it's been settled.'

Natalie kept looking at her for a few beats, then switched the conversation to her own plans. She'd stay in the apartment for another six months so she could move in more pleasant weather, and so her nephew had enough time to acclimate his kids before their new school started in the fall.

They talked more about Marceline, how so much beautiful poetry came out of so much pain and sadness, and what the world might have missed if she'd had a happier life. It reminded Helen of the conversation with Lilianne and Connie that very first day she met Gilles, when she'd been so confused by the power of those first feelings, and so smitten by his charm and his brain.

'So, *ma petite*, starting over is not easy. I know what it is to leave your country. Hard times. But you have my support, you and your handsome new man. You will adjust and the new life will fit in ways you never dreamed it would.'

Helen nodded, praying that would turn out to be true. 'I'll get through it. I just need to find something of my own to do.'

'You will. Ah, Lucas, *magnifique*!'

Lucas had cleared their plates and brought out silver goblets loaded with ice cream and chocolate, whipped cream sprinkled with chopped nuts, even the requisite cherry.

Helen clapped her hands. 'You've outdone yourself.'

'*Ah, mais non.*' He waggled his finger, *non-non-non*. 'This is child's play. When I make a perfect *gâteau Opéra*, or a *marjolaine*, *then* I have outdone myself.'

Helen cringed apologetically. 'Yes, of course, so sorry.'

'*Bon appetit.*' He did his half-bow and left.

Helen and Natalie exchanged amused glances and dug in. With the first bite, that perfect combination of warm chocolate and creamy vanilla, Helen found herself transported back to the land of the free with a wrenching and unexpected burst of homesickness. Sometimes on summer nights, Mom would put out a banana-split bar for the family – sliced bananas, a half-gallon of ice cream striped vanilla, chocolate and strawberry, and sauces: her own hot fudge, which hardened to chewy thickness when it met the cold; strawberry made from local berries; and marshmallow melted with cream. Beside those basics, bowls of whipped cream, chopped walnuts and cherries. They'd eat until they got sick.

Kevin's favorite dessert.

Tears rose in her throat and she swallowed them with another mouthful, determined not to dissolve at the table.

'Have you and Gilles found a place together yet? You said you'd be looking.'

'Mm, yes.' Helen put down her spoon, glad for an opportunity to stop eating while her emotions settled. 'We'd made some appointments for this afternoon. Then he had to go to Avignon.'

'Ah, the stolen Picasso paintings.' Natalie shook her head. 'Unimaginable. Will you go alone?'

'Yes.' Helen picked up her spoon again and plunged it into the sundae. She dreaded the afternoon meetings, was heartsick when Gilles had been called away . . . again. When those summonses came, he would stand abruptly, no reluctance or apology, the taut, concentrated look on his face indicating he was already somewhere else. It could happen anytime, anywhere. Gilles would always be preparing to leave.

'Many changes ahead for you. When does Lilianne go to Egypt?'

Helen swallowed a creamy bite, hardly tasting a thing. It still seemed impossible their tight trio would be breaking up. Just when she needed friends most. 'Next week.'

'Oh my. And what are Connie's plans? Any hope of her staying a while longer?'

'I doubt it.' Helen sighed miserably. 'Knowing her, she'll wake up one morning and say, "Oh, Taipei" or someplace, and be gone that afternoon.'

'She's a delight. They both are.' Natalie's expression softened. 'This is the end of an era for you.'

Helen glared at her. 'Are you trying to make me cry?'

'No, *ma petite*.' Natalie brought up her napkin and dabbed her lip with a corner. 'I'm trying, obviously very clumsily, to be your parent figure here, and make sure you have a clear idea of what you are getting into, one not muddled by love.'

Helen ate one more cold spoonful to allow herself time to formulate an answer. 'I think I do. I mean, I know I do. It will be hard until I feel settled, but I'll get through it.'

'You and Marceline and Sarah! Through the hardship to greatness.' Natalie gazed at her fondly. 'My dear. You are so much more grown up than the child I invited to come help me here. Paris has been good for you. I pray it will continue to be so.'

'Yes.' Helen forced back tears again. 'I do too.'

Instead of being an exciting, romantic search for a place to live together, apartment-hunting in Paris that afternoon was a nightmare. Helen had set out with high hopes and nervous excitement, and come back to rue Pierre Nicole exhausted and humiliated. All the anti-American sentiment she'd heard or read about but mostly been spared, apart from the occasional cranky shopkeeper, came out today. One look at her in her yellow raincoat and rubber boots, water dripping off her hood, and out would come *C'est loué, mademoiselle.* Already rented. She'd never encountered people who knew how to be so polite and so rude at the same time. One man didn't bother with the politeness: *I don't rent to foreigners. Paris is for the French.* Her explanation that her boyfriend was French didn't fly. *Really? Where is he?*

Women apparently weren't able to transact business. Or at least women like Helen. Lilianne would probably have the guy on his knees begging for mercy.

The afternoon only emphasized the feeling she hadn't had since her arrival in September, but that had dogged her since deciding to stay. She didn't belong here. *Étranger.* Foreigner. The

French used the same word for 'strange'. Fine to be a tourist, they were used to throngs of them gawking at the astounding beauty of the city. But it seemed if you let on that you'd like to view Paris through native eyes, the welcome doors clanged shut. *Non! Jamais!*

As for the apartments themselves, Helen knew what she liked, but she had little instinct for what Gilles would prefer. He'd be paying most of the rent, since her income was yet to be determined, aside from the pittance she earned at Fleurs du Coeur. So did he want the large, elegant three-bedroom with the fireplace and remodeled kitchen, or the quaint creaky garret she fell for? Wherever they ended up, it would be Helen spending time alone there while Gilles was on assignment. Should her opinion therefore carry more weight? Was it a bad sign that she didn't have a better idea of what he would want? They'd talked about finding a place only in abstract terms, mostly excited about their new life, the travel possibilities and the freedom to be together without the looming end-date. There was still so much to learn: moods, patterns, habits . . .

Now she was dragging her drippy self up the street, boots clunking at every step, toward the apartment she shared with the girls, while a tiny-hipped Parisienne click-click-clicked effortlessly ahead of her under a cheerful umbrella in a tight skirt and spiky heels Helen wouldn't be able to stand in.

'Hey, you sexy American! Wait up!'

Helen turned with a weary grin. The voice was unmistakable.

Connie dashed across rue Pierre Nicole, all flowing bright fabric, jingling bells and dimples, narrowly missing being hit by a swerving taxi. The driver opened his window to shout at her.

'Yeah, yeah, your *mère* wears army boots, buddy.' She rolled her eyes. 'Hey, roomie! You look like you've been through the wars. What's shakin'?'

'Grim day.' Helen told her briefly about the failed apartment-hunting, grateful to have a friendly ear. 'I should have told them their mothers wear army boots as well.'

'Yeah, not my best comeback. I need to work on it.' Connie linked arms with her. 'It's a grim day weather-wise too. What do you say we hit up a café for a glass of whatever?'

'That would be great.' Helen couldn't think of anything she'd rather do. Seeing Gilles right now would only make her more anxious and upset. Once she made the calls to Kevin and her parents the next day, cementing her decision, everything would get easier.

She hoped.

They found a free table inside a café on Boulevard Port-Royal and ordered a carafe of the house red and a plate of country pâté served with sour gherkins, mustard and fresh bread.

'*À ta santé.*' Connie clinked with Helen's glass. 'I'm glad we have time to talk. You've been a little off lately. What's going down?'

Helen sighed. It was bad if other people had noticed. 'I'm feeling a little nervous about being here. I mean, how it's going to be. Big difference between a fantasy vacation and a permanent stay.'

'Nothing's permanent.' Connie jingled away the idea. 'You don't like it here, you go somewhere else. Gilles would follow you anywhere. I can tell by how he looks at you. I bet he'd even go Stateside if you wanted him to. Don't look at it like being stuck here forever. It's an experiment. All of life is an experiment. A big beautiful endless experiment until you kick the bucket.'

'True.' Helen watched Connie help herself to pâté, not sure her friend's solutions worked for her. She was about commitment. She wanted a permanent home, a stable environment in which to raise children.

'I think the bigger question . . .' Connie spread pâté on a slice of baguette, 'is are you feeling trapped for some other reason?'

'What do you mean?'

'Like maybe this move isn't really what you want?'

Panic settled into Helen's belly; she tried not to think about her mother's letter. 'I do want it. I want Gilles.'

'And this life comes with him.'

'Yes.' She took a gulp of wine, horrified at the tears and doubts. 'I know it's what I want. It's just the transition part I'm afraid of.'

Connie cocked her head, listening but skeptical.

'The thing is . . .' Helen had to swallow hard, 'back in the US, my life was set. I was going to help Kevin grow a business, to be an equal partner in the hard work. He'd be home every day to help raise our kids. Here . . .'

Connie nodded sympathetically. 'Gilles is gone at a moment's notice, sometimes for days, maybe longer, maybe in some other country.'

'Yes.' Helen looked up at her. 'How do you do it? Make so many changes?'

'Because I'm the opposite of you, my sweet.' Connie squeezed Helen's wrist. 'You crave stability and belonging, and I'm deathly afraid of both.'

'Why?'

'If I settle someplace, there are no more surprises.' She shrugged her jingling rainbow shawl into a better position. 'I am where I am doing the same things every day, and then I die. Thud.'

'But then no chance of growing a deeper relationship with a place, and richer, more rewarding relationships with people who love you and whom you love.' Helen heard herself with horror. The whole reason she'd decided to stay in Paris was to avoid the sameness Connie just described.

'Well, I don't know, it's funny. Leaving here, having our trio break up, this is the first time I've found it hard to move on. First time I've really felt that if we kept on being a threesome – foursome, sorry, Sarah – in our ghastly little apartment, I would not be the one to leave. That's new. So maybe as I'm getting older, I'm also getting boring, and soon . . .' Connie shoved another bread–pâté combo into her mouth and kissed the tips of her fingers toward Helen, 'I'll be you!'

'Oh, thanks very much.' Helen sent her an affectionate grin. 'Natalie was asking me where you'll go next, by the way.'

'I've been thinking Greece. Maybe Crete, where my grand-parents were from.' Connie drained her wine glass and poured herself more. 'Dig that: she who avoids putting down roots is planning to look for hers.'

'Good for you.' Helen's voice cracked; she looked down to keep from bawling outright. 'I'll miss you terribly.'

'Aw, sweetie. Same here.' Connie's eyes filled up. 'It'll be brutal. But! We'll stay in touch, and I'll keep popping up in your and Lilianne's lives when it's least expected and most incon-venient. Plus Lilianne has all that cash, she can pay for us to vacation together every year. Somewhere tropical with umbrella drinks and foxy servers. Just the three of us.'

'I'll drink to that.' Helen raised her glass, feeling hollowed out and defeated.

'Seriously, you will do great here.' Connie blew her nose on the café-supplied napkin. 'Picasso and Gertrude Stein and Hemingway must have had some tough times, but they loved it and made lives here. I mean, wow, there's such a vibe to being the foreigner in Paris who makes good, you know? You're fol-lowing in great footsteps.'

'Amen.' Helen attacked her wine, hoping the alcohol would

lighten her mood. Hadn't she just been thinking about her lack of greatness?

'So when do you see Mr Perfect again?'

'Tomorrow. He's staying overnight in Avignon. The stolen Picassos.'

'Yes, it was on the radio.' Connie fanned herself. '*Such* a glamor job he has. What do you think you'll do? You could teach English to little Frenchies.'

'I could. But then I'd be tied down to the calendar. Gilles wants me to be able to travel with him.'

Connie's eyebrows went up. 'Gilles wants?'

'Oh, I want that too.' Helen nodded too hard, remembering when he'd taken her on an assignment to see the first launch of the superspeed jet, the Concorde, a couple of weeks earlier, how thrilling the prospect had been, and how once there she'd felt useless, jostled around, always in someone's way, an extra body nobody needed.

Connie looked at her speculatively. 'You need to try the test.'

'What test?'

'Close your eyes and think about both sides of your big issue. Pros and cons. Don't judge, just think about each part, experience both in your mind. I guarantee you'll have your answer. One will call to you more strongly. Your subconscious is a smart little booger. It knows what it wants better than you do.'

'Is that from some guru you studied with in India?'

Connie laughed so loudly people turned. 'No, no, my sweet. It's from my Greek grandmother, Lydia Pappas.'

They chatted for another half-hour, until the wine was gone – Connie had most of it – then, linking arms again, they headed home and into the clanking elevator, Helen thinking wistfully of that first trip up, when she'd been so hopeful that friendships with these women would make Paris feel more like home. They had. And if they had, then Gilles and his friends could do the same for her again.

She didn't understand why she wasn't convinced.

Connie got ready for her date – Helen had lost track of who it was with these days – and kissed her goodbye, leaving strict instructions to trust her grandmother's wisdom.

Helen heated the previous night's *pistou* for dinner, a Provençal soup of vegetables, beans and pasta in a plain broth, into which one stirred an elixir of tomato paste, basil, garlic and cheese, which made it a fantastically flavorful meal. She ate in the kitchen, feeling loneliness creeping into her bones spoonful by spoonful, trying not to think ahead to the many nights like this while Gilles was away.

After dinner, she picked up a book he had recommended, *The History of Photography* by Beaumont Newhall, but her thoughts kept spinning to the calls she'd have to make the next day, to the apartment she'd failed to find, to the flight back home and her parents' inevitable anger and disappointment, until Helen was so overwhelmed, she snapped the book shut and got to her feet.

She couldn't do this anymore. It was artificial and cowardly to have waited for some arbitrary date to make the calls. She'd made her choice. Kevin deserved to know. Gilles deserved to know she was serious. And Helen deserved the peace that would come with the matter being settled. She didn't need to meditate, she needed to move forward.

Over to the phone in determined strides, she picked it up, scrabbled for the piece of paper with Kevin's number on it and dialed, praying he was home. Praying she could do this in the gentlest way possible.

Ring.

Her heart was hammering. She dragged the hall chair closer, sat and tried to breathe, managing only stuttering attempts.

Ring.

'Hello.' His deep voice undid her. So familiar, that way of answering. Not a question, hello? But a greeting. Hello.

'Hello, Kevin.'

'Helen! Oh my Lord, Helen. It's so good to hear your voice. Sweetheart. Hello. Hi.' He gave a goofy laugh. 'I've missed you so much. I have so much to tell you, about the farm, about our plans. It's been hell not being able to share all this with you.'

'It's been . . . a long time.' She sounded like a machine.

'I was just in our room. I was just . . .' He gave that nervous laugh again. 'I actually haven't been sleeping in there. I was saving it . . . Sorry, sweetheart. I'm completely scrambled hearing your voice. It's been terrible without you, Helen. Terrible.'

'I'm so sorry, Kevin.' She spoke in a trembling whisper. This was agony.

'No, no. Listen, it's fine. It's been good. Really good. I've done a lot of thinking, a lot of work. I've been sober two months now. I've paid a lot of attention to . . . Well, I've been working with someone. Anyway, I'm feeling like a different person, and I want to apologize again for that last call, and for ways in which I was . . . rigid maybe, before that. And selfish.'

'Oh Kevin. You . . .' She laughed stupidly. 'You were great.'

'I'm better now. Happier. Stronger. And I have to tell you, our room looks fantastic. I got a bedspread, blue, I know you like blue. And curtains with bluebirds on them, bluebirds of happiness. And a rag rug, the kind your mom has in her room, that you said you liked. It's a beautiful room. Our windows look out onto the barn and the fields beyond. They're snowy now, but come summer the earth – our earth – will be six feet high with corn. I've also cleared land for a vegetable garden. Oh, and I bumped into John and Lacey the other day. They can't wait to see you. And I'm talking way too much, sorry. I've been so lonely for you, and it all poured out. Your turn. Sweetheart, I'm so glad you called.'

Helen bent over, arm across her stomach, eyes screwed shut. While he'd been talking, her world had tilted. It was as if a tractor beam had pulled her into the house in Kansas – their house – as if she'd been ripped out of the city around her, the last five months dissolving like so much cotton-candy fluff.

The life he had for her to share was real. It was solid and certain. Helen belonged in it. For the last month she'd been trying to force herself to accept a different life in a different place. All the resulting depression and anxiety had finally revealed themselves as they really were, as Natalie had said, as Connie's grandmother had said, as Helen's mother had said – her instinct telling her that she was making a terrible mistake.

She was finally listening.

The knots in her stomach untangled in a flood of relief. She might love Gilles – she *did* love Gilles. She would always and forever love him, and leaving him would tear out part of her heart that she would never get back.

But France was not her country, and being pulled around as the wife of a photojournalist while trying to cobble together some kind of identity here – that was for a more dynamic and audacious woman, the Marcelines and Sarahs of the world.

Helen was meant to be a true partner in building something important and lasting, raising children in one place, eating dinner every night around the same table, hearing about their days, laughing together, teaching them about hard work and family and God and country. She was meant to be a farmer's wife.

She was meant to be Kevin's wife.

Gilles's life encompassed the entire world and its people – their fears, foibles and fights. Kevin's life encompassed five hundred acres of rich Kansas soil and Helen.

Love and longing overtook her. For Kevin, for their future, for the good old USA. She straightened, whole, powerful and certain. Paris was the flapper dress she'd worn New Year's Eve at the Carlton Hotel in St Moritz, waltzing amid bowls of caviar and champagne fountains, glittery and fun, delicious to dress up in and pretend. But the dress and that life belonged to someone else. Helen belonged in plain blue cotton, working at her husband's side in a Kansas cornfield.

'I love you.' She couldn't get the words out fast enough. 'I can't wait to come home.'

Joy and relief exploded over the transatlantic line, and she realized how terrified Kevin had been for all these weeks of their silence, and how brave and respectful not to use that fear to pressure her. She vowed that for the rest of her life, she'd never tell him how close she'd come to leaving him.

They ended the call not long after, having spoken to each other more freely than she ever remembered, Helen more confident and open, Kevin more receptive to both. Mom had been right. *How you handle the bad times together is vital to understanding if what you have can last.*

She hung up the phone and had all of five seconds to enjoy the release of the terrible pressure she'd been under, and the renewed glow over her future with Kevin.

Because on the sixth came the distinctive rhythmic summons of the apartment buzzer telling her that Gilles was back from Avignon, standing outside on rue Pierre Nicole, asking to come up.

✺ Chapter 15 ✺

You don't answer me, you turn your eyes away. Alas!
You try in vain to hide your grief.
    Give me the courage to leave you. Listen to reason.
Leave. Let go of my hand!
    Marceline Desbordes-Valmore, 'L'adieu du soir'

Gilles. For several seconds, Helen stood frozen in the hall next to the phone, staring at the apartment intercom on the wall. She'd told Kevin she was coming home to him, and now here was Gilles, back from Avignon, maybe even having come straight from the train station, anxious to see her, to hear about her day of apartment-hunting for the two of them, a place to start their forever-after.

She wasn't sure she had the strength to face him.

The buzzer again, his special rhythm, bzz-bzzzzzz-bzz-bzz.

Helen pressed the button to unlock the door. There was no point drawing out the anguish for either of them.

She walked toward the kitchen, numb to the pain she was about to inflict, not only on Gilles, and listened to the elevator, remembering that first day standing here with Lilianne and Connie, holding her red rose, smothering giggles, waiting for him to appear. Something in her panicking, pounding heart must have known even then what this man would come to mean to her.

It seemed a lifetime ago.

She opened the door to his tall, grinning, beloved form, to the enormous bouquet of red roses held in his arms.

Immediately his grin dropped. The roses next, onto the kitchen table. He took hold of Helen's shoulders. 'What is it? What's happened?'

She had no idea what to say, how even to begin to prepare him for this news, how to describe the path of her thoughts and the emotions that had led her – led them – to this dreadful impasse.

'I love you, Gilles. But I can't stay here. I don't belong in your life or in your country. I'm so sorry.' The blurted words were clumsy and melodramatic, everything she hadn't wanted them to be.

'What are you ... ?' His worry gave way to incredulity. '*What?*'

'I'm going to stay in the US. I'm sorry. I have thought about it and thought about it, and I just can't . . .' She gestured helplessly. 'It's not that I don't love you, I do love you, immensely. But I can't live in your life. There's no place for me.'

'Of course there is a place. With me. We ... What makes you think this?'

'I am not a Parisienne, Gilles. I'm a girl from Indiana.' Her voice broke. 'A farmer's wife.'

'A farmer's wife? You? This is crazy talk.' His eyes narrowed. 'You're not thinking of going back to Kevin, are you? You can't be going back to him, Helen.'

Her response was her silence, her misery, the sob that came to her throat.

'No, this cannot be what you want.' He was examining her minutely, looking for cracks he could get into. 'You don't belong with that ... corn farmer. For God's sakes, Helen. You are wasted on him. I thought you knew that, I thought being here all these months . . . that you'd come to realize that.'

Helen closed her eyes against the pain. She was wounding him, and his first thought was for her.

'Helen, *mon amour*.' His eyes were wide, pleading. 'You need to give this time. I know it's a big move, I know there is a lot that will change, and that there will be hard parts, but I promise you that we will be okay. Together.'

She wished with all her heart that she could believe him. 'I just told Kevin I'm coming back.'

Gilles let go of her arms as if they'd become too hot to hold. He backed up, nostrils flaring with breaths too big and anguished to contain. 'This is a mistake, Helen. For both of us. You must understand that.'

'I'm sorry.' Such pathetic, empty-sounding words. She could think of no others.

'Helen . . .' He pressed his lips shut. Stood for several seconds with his chin lifted, staring at the ceiling, swallowing – tears, rage, she didn't know, maybe both. 'Okay.'

That she didn't expect. 'Okay?'

'Yes, okay.' His face twisted. 'Would you rather I begged? Would you like me to get down on my knees and beg you not to go? Would that satisfy you?'

'No, Gilles. Of course not.'

'You've absolutely decided. No second chance.'

Helen held his gaze, tears streaming. 'I love you, Gilles. But yes. I've decided. I belong in my own country. On a farm.'

He made an inarticulate sound.

'I'm sorry. I'm so sorry.'

'Don't be sorry.' He opened the door. 'If Kevin and a piece of Kansas are what you want, then you deserve them both.'

The door closed behind him. Helen stood in the empty

kitchen with the flimsy table and chairs, the tiny refrigerator, the stove and so many memories, listening to the elevator noises in reverse, taking him away from her.

Panic hit. She took a step forward to call him back. Impossible that it was over between them. Impossible that it would end like this, so quickly, with so little said.

She laid her hand against the closed door, head bowed. What more was there to say? She loved him, but she'd made her choice. Better to end it now, spare them the slow death of everything that had been so wonderful and hopeful between them.

Five floors below, the elevator doors opened, closed. Footsteps growing fainter. The distant metal clank of the building service door closing.

He was gone.

She stood in the kitchen for who knew how long, waiting for the next thing that would happen, unable to anticipate or decide what that might be, certain she would never be completely happy again. Meeting Gilles had split her life in two, neither half quite enough. So she stayed motionless, as if she could delay the rest of her life without him.

Maybe she could stand there forever.

Improbably, a giggle erupted as she imagined her hair growing to the ground, toenails emerging through her shoes to take root in the linoleum. She'd be a modern-day Daphne, the naiad of Greek mythology pursued by Apollo, who'd turned into a laurel tree rather than submit to him.

In the middle of that thought came the tears. An agony of tears. Tears that dropped her to her knees, convulsed her throat, contorted her face. Tears that went on and on, until she couldn't cry anymore. A blessed minute or two of peace, then another wave of pressure and the release again, salt water spotting the floor, crying so ugly and loud that until Lilianne came through the door, Helen had no idea she was on her way up.

A gasp, the thud of a bag hitting the floor. Lilianne knelt and gathered Helen to her, rocking her until Helen was able to get herself under control.

'You told him,' Lilianne whispered. 'Yes?'

Helen closed her eyes. Yes. But not the 'him' Lilianne thought.

'Of course it hurts. But you're doing the right thing. The strong thing, choosing love over habit, challenging yourself, following your heart.'

Helen pushed out of her arms and got to her feet, looking down into Lilianne's astonished face. 'I chose Kevin.'

The astonishment turned to disbelief. Lilianne stood, the two women identically blond, nearly equal height. 'You're joking.'

'It's what I want. What I've always wanted.'

'Okay, no. No.' Lilianne took her arm and pulled her into the living room. 'We're going to Sarah on this one. You still have time to change your mind while Gilles is in Avignon. Let's—'

'Gilles just left here. I told him.'

'Sit.' Lilianne pushed Helen down onto the orange couch. 'It's not too late, but you have to fix this.'

'No.' Helen's annoyance, or rather the strength it gave her, was her saving grace. 'I just did the fixing. Staying here would have been wrong.'

'You chose out of fear. You chose because the next few months will be scary and disorienting, and you turned chicken.'

The annoyance hardened. 'I don't belong here, not in Paris, not in Gilles's world, and definitely not as a wife waiting alone for her husband to be home long enough to say hello. I belong in Kansas with—'

'Bullshit. On a farm? Picking corn and soybeans on land so flat you can see the whole state end to end? My God, Helen, the life Gilles is offering you. Intellect, wealth, world travel, and a husband who would never, under any circumstances, become drunk and abusive.'

Helen clenched her teeth. Connie must have blabbed. 'Kevin doesn't drink anymore. He's grown up a lot. He's—'

'Bullshit again. You're throwing away your life on some bloody stupid hick when you could have a real man like Gilles!'

Something snapped inside Helen. 'He's free for you now, Lilianne, so why don't you go after him like you've always wanted to?'

'Oh, how sweet. Thank you.'

Helen forced herself to breathe. 'Sorry, that was low.'

'Certainly was.' Lilianne sat next to her, laid a comforting hand on Helen's upper arm. 'Gilles loves you in a mature, real way, which I know, without ever having met Kevin, that he can never match. In Kansas you might be content for a while, but never truly happy. That life offers you only eventual stagnation.'

'Whereas here it would be one thrill after another sitting around feeling like excess baggage, waiting for Gilles to get called away so I can go with him somewhere I also don't belong and sit around feeling like excess baggage until he has time to see me? What's happy about raising kids with a dad who's gone all the time? What's happy about being treated always and forever as a foreigner? What's—'

Lilianne put a shushing finger toward Helen's lips. 'Listen to you. You've decided everything about your life here without even trying it out to see if you're right or not. Take a year, take two, take five. You haven't given Paris or Gilles a chance. Kevin will be there if it doesn't work out; if not *your* Kevin, then a whole host of other corn-and-soy-fed Kevins throughout the Midwest.'

Another flash of rage. Helen looked Lilianne straight in the eye. 'I know who I am and I know what I want.'

'Ha.' Lilianne radiated disgust. 'I doubt that very much.'

'Screw you.'

'Not interested.' She leaned forward until she was an inch from Helen's face, icy and intimidating. 'You're a fool if you do this. In Paris you were just beginning to find your potential. And look . . . it scared you.'

'My *potential*?' Helen escaped the couch and Lilianne's scrutiny, hard pressure in her chest, tears threatening that her pride refused to allow. 'Who made you the authority on Helen Kenyon?'

'I'm not wrong. Look at you fighting back.' Lilianne gestured calmly, as if she were admiring Helen's outfit instead of dissecting her personality. 'When you showed up here in September, you were Kevin's little mouse. That's the tragedy of all of this, Helen. If you can stop being afraid and defensive long enough to pay attention, you'll see what I mean.'

Helen turned her back to the relentless accusations, shaking with fury. 'I'm going to pack. I'll stay with Natalie until I leave. If Kevin calls, tell him that's where I am.'

'If Kevin calls, the only thing I'll tell him is to go to hell.'

'I wish you'd join him.' She ran into her bedroom and slammed the door like a child having a tantrum, pulled her suitcases out from under the bed and started throwing things into them, heaving breaths that seemed to pull in no oxygen. She'd call Natalie first, then the airline, to see if she could change her ticket, go home sooner, on standby if she had to. Having made her decision, there was no reason to linger.

While she was packing, she heard Lilianne leave the apartment and was relieved. Much easier – and yes, more cowardly – to sneak out without having to confront her again. Helen would call Connie to make sure they could say goodbye before she left. She doubted her friendship with Lilianne would survive this disagreement. Fine by her.

Room packed up in a manic, miserable rush, she went into the bathroom and cleared out her stuff. There was nothing she'd bother taking home from the kitchen. In the living room . . .

Sarah.

Helen stood next to the doll, tears flowing again. Dear Sarah. She'd become so much more than a toy; she was a friend, part of the gang, the fourth roommate, who'd shared so much of the joy and laughter over the past months, there for celebrations, mourning and advice. What had started as silly fun had become so much more.

She touched the rounded cheeks and chin, staring to memorize Sarah's features, her fur, the jeweled circlet in her hair, the sparkling necklace and brooch, the elegant emerald gown and matching evening slippers peeking out from under its hem.

Then she turned away, picked up her suitcases and left the apartment without her.

> *He came too close to my soul, and his soul dazzled my eyes, I was blinded by this double flame, yet I saw too much when I saw the sky again.*
>
> *I was too naïve to save myself. I stay alive to forget him.*
>
> Marceline Desbordes-Valmore, 'Jour d'Orient'

Friday, June 19, 1981

Helen put down a scuffed plastic plate on the dining table in front of Cheryl's booster chair, and another on Kevin Jr's highchair tray. With a tender smile, at her and Kevin's places, head and foot of the table they'd bought together, she set plates from their wedding set. Five years ago today they'd been married in a beautiful ceremony at Helen's family's church in Zionsville, followed by a reception in the Kenyons' backyard for roughly fifty family members and guests. Helen's mom had served baked ham and biscuits, salad and cake, and Helen's dad had popped bottles of Asti Spumante that made it very easy for Helen, with her French-honed taste for champagne, to skip alcohol and make it look as if she were supporting her sober husband.

The day had gone off without a hitch, the June weather had been perfect, and Helen managed to be much happier than she thought she could be so soon after leaving France. She'd never heard from Gilles after that awful scene in the apartment kitchen. Shortly before she and Kevin were married, on an after-dinner walk in a park near her parents' house, Kevin had asked if there'd been someone else in Paris. The half-expected question had stopped Helen short. She'd turned to him and nodded, wanting him to know the truth, praying he wouldn't ask for details. He had flinched, but thanked Helen for her honesty, said he understood why she'd been tempted after how he'd behaved. She'd nearly melted with love and relief for his understanding and acceptance.

That moment witnessing his courage, his no doubt hard-won forgiveness and his new-found humility had finalized Helen's emotional separation from her time in Paris, though it was nearly a year before she could think of Gilles without pain. Neither she nor Kevin had mentioned the subject again.

The years that followed were filled with happiness. She and Kevin had been exactly the loving, respectful team of equals she'd hoped for, working harder than she'd ever thought possible, morning to night, to nurture this farm they adored, and the children they adored even more. For the most part, France receded to a lovely memory tinged with sadness.

Helen had kept in regular touch with Natalie Laurent, who

was happily ensconced in what she described as an 'adorable Natalie-sized apartment in the Trocadéro with a view of the Seine'. From Connie, Helen had had only one scrawled wish-you-were-here postcard from a vacation in Mallorca. From Lilianne, there had been two terse but devastating letters, mailed from Connecticut, where she'd returned to live after completing her assignment in Cairo.

The first, a little over a year after Helen's return from France, contained the announcement of Lilianne and Gilles's engagement, 'for practical reasons', and a wedding invitation, along with a stiff acknowledgment that the news would most likely be a shock.

She was correct. As were Helen's emotions. She'd stood frozen next to the mailbox, paper trembling in her hand, stunned by the depth of her reaction, fighting a fierce battle with tears and razor-sharp cramping in the back of her throat. She could not face Kevin over supper that night with eyes swollen from grief over another man.

When she'd finally gained control, she'd walked past the house down to the chicken coop, where she'd shredded the letter and invitation into tiny bits and mixed them among the cedar shavings for the birds to poop on. Not her most mature moment, but 'practical reasons' her ass. Lilianne had been in love with Gilles for years, had probably been scheming to get him the second Helen left the country.

The following days had been a test of her ability to function normally while in deep pain, a payback taste of what Gilles must have suffered knowing Helen was marrying Kevin. When had he fallen for Lilianne? How long after Helen left? Did he now think of Helen as a sweet crush he used to have? The thought was pure torture.

The second letter arrived a year later. Cheryl had been a

stubborn, sturdy one-year-old at the time, and Helen and Kevin were eagerly trying for another child. The farm had been thriving, not as profitable as Kevin had hoped, but doing a good deal better than it was now. Their marriage was solid. The life Helen had chosen was a good one. She'd told herself she had no regrets and had moved on.

This letter, gentler in tone though crueler in impact, brought the gutting news that Connie had died in an accident on Crete, and that Lilianne and Gilles had adopted an infant daughter. Helen's grief over her dear friend's loss had been intense and unrelenting, impossible to hide, not that there was any reason to. She still found it nearly unbearable to think of the world deprived of such a cheerful, colorful spirit, searching for beauty and spreading love wherever she went. For the first time Helen had regretted letting Sarah go. The doll would have kept part of Connie alive and with her.

In a secondary blow, the intimate picture of Lilianne and Gilles as proud parents to a new baby had reopened the door Helen thought she'd finally closed on her feelings for Gilles, forcing her to lean all her weight toward slamming the damn thing shut once again and double-devoting herself to her beloved, hard-working husband. Kevin didn't deserve any less than all of her.

'I don't want that fork.' Cheryl had climbed up onto her booster and was scowling at her plate setting. 'I want the *pink* one.'

'The pink one is in the dishwasher, baby girl.'

'I'm not a baby. Kevin Junior is the baby.' She pointed to his playpen, which Helen had set up in the open area between the kitchen and dining room, where most of the time he'd play contentedly with whatever toy or book she gave him. A huge relief after Cheryl, who'd screamed within seconds anytime she wasn't the center of attention.

'He's a toddler, hon. Nearly two years old.'

Cheryl shook her head, pigtails flapping. 'He's a baby. Daddy says so.'

'Does he?' Helen found it easier not to argue. Cheryl had been devoted to her father since she recognized him. By now, Helen had adjusted to her child's strong preference, but it still stung sometimes. She hoped it would change as Cheryl matured. 'If you want the pink fork, you can get it out and wash it yourself. Would you like to do that?'

'No. I don't want to.' That was too easy. Cheryl hated anything that sounded like a chore. 'What are we having for dinner?'

'You and Kevin Junior are having polka-dot macaroni and cheese and green beans.'

Cheryl's eyebrows, thick for a little girl, drew down in suspicion. 'What are you and Daddy having?'

'Steak and potato.'

Instant outrage. 'I want that!'

'You don't like either steak or potatoes. Come help me get Daddy's present, to surprise him.'

'Ooh! Presents!' Her rather dull eyes brightened. 'Do I get one?'

'Not today.'

Instant pout. 'Why *not*?'

Helen stayed calm as she'd learned to, or risk setting Cheryl off. 'Not your birthday.'

'Was it 'spensive? My friend Maeve says the best presents are 'spensive.'

'She's wrong. The best presents are given and received with love.'

Cheryl wrinkled her turned-up nose. '*That's* not a good present. Anyone can get that from their mommy or daddy.'

'Let's go, peachlet.' Helen led the four-year-old down into the basement, where she'd hidden the blue sweater she'd started knitting the summer before she left for France. Six years to finish a sweater! They'd been so involved setting up the farm, then she'd gotten pregnant with Cheryl and had put the sweater aside in favor of knitting for the coming baby. After Cheryl arrived, their already busy lives had become a lot busier. 'Here it is.'

'Ooh, a *big* present!' Cheryl carried the box upstairs by herself, refusing help even though she kept losing her grip on the large package, leaving Helen counting to ten – then twenty – for patience while her daughter struggled up the stairs, one slow step after another.

By the time they reached the top, Kevin Jr was at the side of the playpen whining to be let out, water was boiling for the macaroni, and the potatoes were nearly ready.

As she did every night, Helen juggled this and that, glancing at the clock once in a while, hoping Kevin wasn't going to be late. Dinner at 6 p.m., that was his preference, and she'd done pretty well keeping to it over the years. But if he was going to shower after another hot day in the fields, he was cutting it pretty close.

At 5.45, steaks ready to go in the pan, Kevin came in the front door, hiding something behind his back. Cheryl ran to him, hugging his thighs, begging to be picked up, which she kept doing no matter how often Helen reminded her that big girls didn't need to be held.

'Hello, sweetheart.' Helen leaned in next to Cheryl's head for a lingering kiss, noting the scent of the peppermint gum he'd been chewing regularly for the past few months. Worry, probably, over the farm finances. Corn prices down, interest rates above nineteen percent, and Kevin had gone way into debt to get the farm started, convinced the boom would last forever. 'Dinner's almost ready.'

'Great, I'm starved.' He sidled down the hall, keeping his back to the wall. 'I'll shower fast.'

'Why are you walking funny, Daddy?'

He beamed at her. 'Because I'm a crab, and crabs go sideways. Come be a crab with me?'

Ten minutes later, six on the dot, with Cheryl having crab-walked off with her dad, Helen had dinner on the table. She lit candles in the silver candlesticks Kevin's parents had given them, picked up Kevin Jr from his playpen prison and called the rest of the family to the table.

Kevin appeared first, wholesome and handsome in clean jeans and the white shirt she'd ironed for him, his hair wet and neatly combed. Behind him showed Cheryl's pink bobby socks and white tennis shoes. 'Here we are.'

'Not crabs anymore?'

'Nope.' Kevin grinned broadly. 'Ready, little girl?'

'Ready, Daddy!'

'Ta-da!' He moved aside to reveal their daughter holding up a bottle-shaped package.

'Guess what it is?' Cheryl could barely contain her excitement. 'Champagne!'

'Sham-*pame*!' Kevin Jr echoed.

'Ooh, how wonderful!' Helen winked at Kevin. 'Let's see, is it . . . lemonade champagne? Or . . . ginger ale champagne? Or . . . Seven Up champagne?'

Cheryl was shaking her head. 'No, Mommy. Champagne! From France! For your anniversary! Daddy bought it!'

'Daddy boddit.' Kevin Jr started bucking in Helen's arms. 'Boddit, boddit, sham-*pame*!'

Helen met Kevin's eyes. They hadn't had alcohol in the house since she'd been back. If friends wanted to drink, they brought their own and left with any extra. 'Really?'

'Sure.' Kevin looked too casual. 'It's a special day. I can have one glass. I'll be fine.'

Helen looked down at the bottle. 'I don't know . . .'

'Mom, it's your *present*!' Cheryl was appalled.

'C'mere, I'll open it. Wanna help, punkin?' Kevin led Cheryl into the kitchen.

'Hungwy, hungwy, Mommy, I'm hungwy!' Kevin Jr was finally out of his considerable patience.

'I know, sweet pea.' Helen put him into his high chair and served him mac and cheese dotted with sliced hot dogs and a helping of green beans – he was the only person in the family besides her who loved vegetables. Kevin and Cheryl would live on cheese pizza and burgers if she let them.

An explosive *pop* in the kitchen, a gleeful shriek from Cheryl and strangled shout from Kevin before they both dissolved into giggles.

Helen smiled, loving the sound of her family's laughter. What harm could one glass do on a special occasion? Things had been financially rough on the farm for a while now; why not celebrate tonight? Five wonderful years, their first big milestone, made even more precious after their marriage had come so close to not happening. No Cheryl, no Kevin Jr. None of the glorious nights sitting out on the back deck hand in hand, exhausted from the day's work, happy, healthy kids tucked in to sleep, gazing out at the thriving crops and the fruitful kitchen garden, talking over the days, the weeks, the months of the life they'd built together.

Helen shoved down her misgivings and served up the rest of dinner.

Over the course of the meal, her contented glow dimmed. Kevin's first glass was followed by another half, and then another half after that. She caught his eye with a look; he toasted her with a devilish grin she couldn't help returning.

Maybe she was worrying too much. He'd been so careful for so long, and was having such a good time, her hard-working husband. Maybe he deserved this tonight. For that matter, Helen hadn't gotten a good buzz on since she'd left France. It would be fun to be relaxed and silly together again, throw their concerns out the window for one night and celebrate the success of their marriage. They might regret it tomorrow, but ... why not?

Just this once.

She toasted him back with love in her eyes, and held out her glass for more.

ꙮ Chapter 16 ꙮ

Saturday night, Teresa had a blast with Jim, Chloe and Danny at their apartment not far from the University of Kansas. Danny and Jim had first rented the place as juniors. When they graduated, Chloe took over with a roommate who conveniently left at the end of each school year in time for Jim, and then Danny, to move from their doctorate program in Manhattan back to Lawrence for summer jobs and internships. Now Jim and Chloe shared the place full-time, with Danny their summer resident.

For dinner Danny had made chicken souvlaki served in pita bread, with tomatoes, parsley and a gorgeously garlicky yoghurt sauce that Teresa couldn't stop eating. For dessert he'd made a lemon pudding cake garnished with local ripe strawberries. Conversation, amidst all the gorging, was natural and wide-ranging, from goofy fun to stories of their youth, to sharing the tough stuff they'd been through in their first few decades. Chloe had lost her dad young. Danny's youngest sister struggled with addiction. Jim and Teresa were coping with Cheryl's reluctant relationship with the truth. Without excessive drinking fueling the openness, it was startlingly personal sharing, and felt totally safe.

After the meal, Jim and Chloe insisted on doing the dishes, and shooed Teresa and Danny out onto the balcony. Matchmaking?

Teresa hoped it worked. A crush was definitely settling in for a stay. And now she had three more weeks to enjoy it.

The two of them sat on small metal chairs crowded around a tiny table. The sun had set, and daylight was beginning to fade. Teresa would have to get back to the farm when it got dark, but there was at least some time now for a private chat.

'Your dinner was so delicious.'

'Glad you liked it. Pretty simple stuff.'

'Uh . . .' She snorted. 'Not when you're consistently defeated by boiled rice.'

Danny laughed. 'My mom's a good cook. She taught me young. I did a lot of it around the house growing up. Good practice . . .'

Something in his face made her curious. 'You did a lot of it because you had to or wanted to?'

'Sorta both.' He shrugged, overly nonchalant. 'My sister's mental health battles started pretty young. She took a lot of Mom and Dad's time and energy. Pretty typical for special needs.'

'And so . . . you became the kid who didn't need anything?' She found herself protective of little Danny. 'The one they could always depend on?'

'I don't know about that. I raised my share of hell. But yeah, I was always aware of the burden they carried, so I made really sure . . .' he sent her a mischievous look, 'that I never got caught.'

Teresa burst into giggles, loving the way Danny made her laugh no matter how serious the subject. 'Good for you. My mom had so much to deal with. She was a single parent, and my twin brothers were hell on wheels – emergency room visits, principal's office visits, a policeman once. So I did everything I could to be the perfect child.'

'Wow.' He looked impressed. 'I've never met anyone perfect before.'

'Aw, you know, I don't brag about it too much. It can kinda make people resentful.'

'Sure, sure.' Their exchanged smiles lingered. A group of students passed below them, laughing and talking loudly. Teresa had gotten so used to the silence at the ranch that for a disorienting, indignant second she wanted to shush them.

'I guess it's too much to ask that life be totally smooth.' She drew a horizontal line through the air. 'But I feel like I wasted a lot of time wishing mine was different.'

'Same. It's hard to keep from wanting more than you have.'

'Then let's mix it up.' Teresa leaned forward, elbows on the table. 'What do you want that you *can* have? A big thing. A life thing.'

'So . . . not peanut M&Ms?'

'Sorry.'

'Hmm.' Danny folded his arms across his chest and stared up at the dimming sky. 'Probably to set up a practice around here, with Jim, that focuses on preventative care instead of constant medicating after illness sets in. Better living conditions, better feed, better exercise, all the stuff humans should be doing.'

'I bet you'll do it.'

'That's the plan.' He turned toward her. 'What about you?'

Teresa furrowed her brow. 'This is kind of a work in progress for me. Right now, I'm focusing mostly on what I don't want.'

'Which is . . .'

'I don't want to continue living the way I was.'

'That counts. What would you change?'

'Oof, I don't really know yet.' She was flattered that he seemed so genuinely interested. 'That's the in-progress part.'

'Gotcha.' His thigh touched hers under the table; he jerked

it away as if she'd burned him. 'What do you want that you absolutely *can't* have?'

For him to move his thigh back. 'A superpower.'

Danny grinned his surprise. 'Which one?'

'I want to be able to turn people into animals.'

He blinked.

'I'm reading a novel about Circe, the Greek goddess/enchantress. I think some people would contribute a lot more to the planet if they were a nice bird or rabbit. I could also pad out endangered species, bring back a few extinct ones . . .'

'Hey, that would be great.' He nodded enthusiastically. 'You could start your own ranch.'

'I could. Though being turned into an animal wouldn't always be punishment. Yesterday I was watching the goats, and thinking damn, not one of them ever had to cope with a lying mother or a father who deserted them.'

'Actually,' Danny cleared his throat pointedly, 'they all had to deal with a father who deserted them.'

'Oh. Right.' Teresa wrinkled her nose, wishing it weren't getting so dark so fast. 'What would your superpower be?'

'That's easy. I'd like to be able to fly.'

'Where would you go?'

'Probably I'd go . . .' he stroked his chin thoughtfully, 'up.'

Teresa laughed so loudly people passing below looked up to see where the sound came from. 'Up is good. Have you ever hang-glided or hung-glid or whatever you say?'

'Nah. Don't trust 'em. I'd need feathers.' He pointed to the sky. 'First star.'

Ugh. Teresa would have to get back to the ranch. She was loving being out here. 'I should go soon. It's getting dark.'

'Sure.' He stood up and moved his chair so she could get by. 'I'll walk you to your car.'

'Thanks.' Teresa stood too, disappointed. Yes, she had to leave, but . . . well, he could have objected, or they could have done that thing where she kept saying she had to leave but didn't, while he continued talking to keep her there longer. 'By the way, thanks for saving me from having to go axe-throwing yesterday.'

Danny's eyebrows shot up. 'How did I do that?'

'You confronted me with how I kept going out to places that weren't my thing. And so then Jim suggested this evening instead.'

'Cool.' He gestured her inside. 'I've definitely enjoyed it. Even without axes.'

Teresa said goodbye and thanks to Jim and Chloe, then she and Danny went downstairs and out again into the night, sweet-smelling in spite of its relatively urban location.

'I'm parked over there.' She pointed down the street, feeling nervous. She'd hung out with Danny a few times, but for whatever reason, this felt more like the end of a date.

They stopped by her car. Teresa checked out her sneakers, for the first time finding it hard to look at him, and not because he was wearing a green T-shirt under red and navy checked flannel. She loved that he owned his inner geek; she needed to work on owning hers, too.

'Thanks again. I had so much fun tonight. It was good hanging out with you, Danny.'

'I had a great time with you too.' He waited while she opened her car door. 'You go back to Phoenix . . . in a week?'

'No!' She couldn't believe she'd forgotten to tell him. 'I'm staying longer. Three more weeks now. I asked for more time off to be with Helen when she gets out of rehab. *Then* I have to go back.'

'Oh. I see.' He spoke evenly. Disappointed or indifferent? Teresa wished she knew.

She stood smiling at him, wanting to stroke down his cowlick and watch it spring up again, while Danny stood unsmiling at her, his almond-colored eyes nearly black in the dim light, and she thought maybe there was some chemistry happening, because she got that buzzy, liquid feeling of anticipation. But just when she was about to lean in with a big ol' pucker, Danny shoved his hands into his pockets and stepped back.

'Okay, well. Drive safely.'

Ah.

Teresa got into the car and waved cheerfully, embarrassed that she'd misread the moment. On the way home she brooded for a while, and then, in a new move for her, decided she had too many more complicated and painful things to brood over. A fling would have been great, but having a friend like Danny for the short time she'd be here was not a problem.

At home she checked on the animals, loving the soft coolness of the evening, the cricket sounds – hadn't those freaked her out her first night? She still felt uneasy being so isolated, but more and more the animals felt like company, and the fierceness of the Pyrenees felt like protection.

She really should spend the next three weeks thinking more deeply about the rest of her life and what she wanted from it. In Phoenix she'd been spinning in place, as if she were waiting . . . for what? Someone else to sweep in and make her life happen?

Didn't work like that. It was all up to her.

As the remaining light gave in to darkness, Teresa went inside to work on Sarah's chair. She'd done more errands that morning, bought a small piece of mahogany at a cool store called East Side Woodshop, and supplies to fix a wobbly fence post she'd discovered over by the cows. It was great to feel useful, and in charge of a place that had surprised her by becoming so important in a very short time.

Teresa bent over the mahogany board, examining the grain, looking for the best area to place the chair pattern pieces, hoping to arrange them neatly enough not to waste wood, ideally leaving enough for the mistakes she was bound to make on first tries. At a craft store, she'd examined possible materials for upholstery, and decided it would be smarter to bring Sarah with her to avoid clashing shades with her dress. The wood would keep her busy for a while.

She still couldn't quite believe Sarah was such a rare find. While she'd still been struggling with shock on the phone call with Matti, the shop owner had gone on about the work she could and wouldn't do. She'd clean the doll, iron her clothes, sew up the loose hem and fix her leg, but she didn't dare try to straighten the crooked hair for fear of damaging the wig or the doll. She promised to make Sarah a priority, wanting her out of the shop as soon as possible because of the liability. She also recommended Teresa contact an insurer.

For ten minutes after she'd gotten off the call, Teresa had sat staring at the living room wall, trying to absorb what she'd just learned. Of course she'd give Sarah back to Helen, who must have no idea what her little friend was worth. But for a stolen moment Teresa had allowed herself to fantasize. What would she do with that money? Pay off the horrible student loans, start building up a nest egg, use some for a down payment on a house of her own.

Mom would go completely out of her mind when she heard.

A warning bell had sounded immediately. Teresa had been delighted to accept the doll as a gift, loving her grandmother's descriptions of Sarah as mentor, guardian angel, inspiration and friend, and was looking forward to spending time in Grandpa Kevin's shop to make her a chair of honor. But once Teresa found out what Sarah was worth, she started seeing only cash?

Sarah was worth a lot more than that, especially to Helen, and someday probably to her granddaughter as well. Teresa did not want to turn into her mother.

She straightened abruptly from her examination of the wood. In fact, she didn't want Mom to know about Sarah's value, not while Cheryl was on an increasingly high-pressure crusade to get what she could out of Grandma Helen's house.

Teresa had felt justified not telling her she'd been in touch with Dad, because the news would only hurt her. Not telling her about Sarah . . . Teresa couldn't justify that deception so easily.

She put her hands to her temples. Look at her, obsessing over two sensible secrets kept from a woman who had repeatedly lied about deeply important issues affecting Teresa's life. Was this how it was going to be with Mom from now on? Little cracks accumulating one by one in their relationship until it threatened to collapse? She couldn't bear the thought. Yet she also couldn't keep on this course of pretending everything was normal. That wasn't fair to either of them. Teresa would have to confront her mother about her lies. At least some of them.

Ick.

In a fit of determined courage, she pulled out her phone. She wouldn't be hostile, she'd just . . .

She didn't know what she'd do.

'Hi, sweet sugar. I missed you today. How's life at the stinky farm?'

'Hi, Mom. I'm doing fine.' Teresa squeezed her eyes shut. The force of what she wanted to say pressed irresistibly hard against an immovable object. She loved her mother. That other person, that liar, that monster – that wasn't this person who called her 'sugar', who wanted to know how she was doing, who missed her and always wanted to chat, any time, any day, working or not. This person who'd raised her, loved her, fed and clothed her, fought back her brothers' teasing, pushed Teresa to be the best she could be. 'How's Phoenix?'

'Lonely. Hot.' Mom chatted on, about the jerks at work who'd been riding her, about how she was dying to retire but didn't have enough cash saved, that if things had been different, she'd be vacationing in the South Seas with a mai tai in her hand and cabana boys attending to her every need.

Teresa bowed her head, phone pressed to her ear, one hand on the rich mahogany. How often had she listened to her mother with empathy, taken on her pain and tried to find ways to help? Now she couldn't listen without noticing what Mike and Ike had seen, that it was always the world against Mom.

'So tell me more about what's going on. Your grandmother okay? James treating you well?'

'Yes.' She pressed her lips together, aware that if she said anything positive about either one, her mother would start tearing them down. And it struck her that she'd kept dozens upon dozens of secrets from her mother throughout her life, by censoring herself, making sure she didn't say anything that would set Mom off, coddling and curating their conversations at the expense of honest sharing. And wasn't that another form of lying? 'They're doing great.'

'Well, you are brave to put up with all that. Luckily you'll be home in another week! Can't wait to have you back.'

Teresa couldn't say anything. Not that she wasn't coming back next week. Not that she couldn't wait to be back with her mother. And certainly not that she was brave. Maybe the conversation with Danny had been the catalyst. Maybe the truth had been inside her for a while and only just now made it into her consciousness. She didn't know.

But it had just come to her in a certain rush that she didn't want to go back. She'd only been here one week, but she'd fallen hopelessly in love with the ranch and the routines and the Kansas countryside, and this other branch of her family, and she didn't want to go back to living in Phoenix, dealing with friends she had little in common with, a job she was indifferent to and a mother who fed on her soul.

Ever.

'Hello? Hello? Where'd you go?'

She roused herself to answer. 'Sorry, Mom. You disappeared for a while. Good to talk to you. I'm beat. Long day. I better hit the hay, as we say here on the farm.'

Her mother snorted. 'Yee-haw. You get your beauty rest, sugar. I'll talk to you soon.'

'Sure. Bye.' Teresa ended the call and stared blankly at Grandpa Kevin's work table.

She was tired, that was the truth. In no shape to make a major decision. She wanted her next move to be the right one, not an easy jump from discomfort to comfort. Here, she'd be loved and supported by family, in a place where she felt peaceful. But would she be making a smart choice or running away from problems and complicated relationships that deserved more than abandonment? Which had Dad done by leaving? Grandma Helen had talked about making decisions based on instinct instead of fear. How was Teresa to know which was which?

The questions couldn't be answered tonight. She was too tired, too overwhelmed, too confused by currents pulling her in too many directions, tumbling and dizzying her. She turned out the lights and went back upstairs, settled Cheddar for the night, let Monarch in, locked up and got ready for bed, sure she wouldn't sleep, wishing for Danny or Jim or her brothers, someone who could ground her.

At least she had *Circe* for inspiration, a story about a woman of considerable power, exiled from her family, who also had to make hard choices. And turn men into pigs.

As she was about to silence her phone for the night, a text came in, one that stopped her in surprise. *Goodnight, Teresa. Sleep well.*

Not Danny, not her brothers, but exactly what she needed. She nestled under the covers, less alone, less burdened. Such a simple gesture, one that pulled her out of the storms in her head and brought her back to the musical sounds and sweet smells of a Kansas summer night.

Thank you, Dad.

Teresa woke, as usual, to Monarch curled against her back. She lay blinking for a few minutes before it hit her what was strange. She'd slept through the night. No angst, and even more remarkable, no coyotes. Either that or the unthinkable had happened and she hadn't heard them. That didn't seem possible. The noise was crazy loud.

She turned over and petted Monarch absently. The cat gave a *mrowph* of indignation at being disturbed, then curled into a C of bliss, head upside down, exposing his throat, which vibrated in a purr. Teresa shook her head. 'One day I will have a bed to myself again, and I will not miss you at all.'

Monarch stretched luxuriously and sat up, looking at Teresa with withering contempt. How stupid could this human be to think for a second she'd prefer to sleep without feline company?

'Yeah, you wait.' She pushed off the covers and sat up, remembering in quick succession that letting out the chickens, gathering the eggs and checking on the other animals was her responsibility, and that the previous evening she'd seemed to want to move here permanently.

Testing . . . testing . . .

She still did.

She'd have to find another job – health insurance and her still daunting student loans wouldn't pay for themselves. But if she did move, Teresa would be here for Helen as long as her grandmother needed her. She'd have her family and could make friends wherever she found work – the university must always be hiring – or through Jim and Danny and Chloe.

That was the easy part. Harder would be losing any chance of retaining a close relationship with her mother, and constant worry about Mom being lonely and depressed without her daughter around. Balancing that was her new awareness that being around Mom might not have the optimal effect on Teresa's personal evolution. To put it delicately.

Luckily, she still had three weeks in which to decide.

She washed up, not bothering to blow-dry her hair, and went down the hall, whistling to Cheddar, who chirped his cheerful good morning back. Maybe other people could get him to whistle in response, but he seemed to prefer bird words around her. She got him breakfast and stayed for a brief conversation while he started eating. Then she let Monarch out and checked on the animals, throwing off more and more of the previous night's misery as she greeted them. She batted her eyes at Cleopatra, mooed at the cows and tossed a stick – way too many times – for the inexhaustible Zig. Through it all she tried to picture herself doing this every day. Would she tire of it? Would it be too much for her in howling snow or dangerous storms? There was no way to find out without trying. But increasingly the idea excited and energized her.

Back inside, she got herself a bowl of yogurt with banana and berries and some wheat toast, wondering how hard it would be to learn to make bread. Maybe Helen knew and could teach her. And she wanted to take another stab at knitting. Plus she had about a thousand questions about caring for the animals.

She took her breakfast outside, leaving Cheddar with his new toy, promising herself to check in on him regularly. The day was warm and humid, which made her hair shorter by about a third from when she straightened it, curls coming to life in the moist air. She was surprised by how much she liked the tousled look, the way it framed her face, the bouncy fun of tossing it one way and the other when she moved her head. Sorry, Mom, ugly frizzies suited her.

The goats bleated and jumped, the lambs called and their mothers responded. Zig ran up to say hello, ran off again, ran back a few minutes later and settled on the deck at her feet. Teresa finished breakfast and, coffee in hand, got down to business thinking about the day ahead.

First off she should weed the vegetable garden, then take a stab at fixing the fence, work on Sarah's chair and see about designing a play structure for the goats. She couldn't help grinning, relishing the idea of the day ahead the way she never even began to in Phoenix. How could she have spent so many years of her life half asleep? Here, she'd be able to . . .

She froze. Zig raised his head with a jerk to see what was bothering her.

Her fantasy had just crumbled. It would work out fine to stay while Helen needed her, but thinking long-term about this place was a pipe dream. When Helen died, or if someday she declined enough to have to move to a retirement home, her three kids would want the money from a sale. Even if Teresa could bring herself to sell Sarah, there wouldn't be enough to buy them all out.

Her disappointment was fierce, but brief. The important lesson out of all this was what she'd admitted to Danny last night on the balcony. She wouldn't be satisfied going back to the same existence. She could stay in Phoenix with different roommates and a different job, to be close to her mom and brothers, or she could move to Lawrence to be closer to her extended family and stay on the farm until it was sold, or . . . really she could go anywhere.

Except 'anywhere' was too much choice for her. Phoenix or Lawrence were enough.

For the rest of the morning, she worked on the farm, though with less energy and joy since realizing forever-after wouldn't happen. She weeded the garden, then looked up on YouTube how to fix the wobbly fence post with the materials she'd bought. Incredibly, after a few tries, a lot of sweat and several swear words, she managed to stabilize the post in a way that was nearly unnoticeable and rock solid.

After a quick refresh shower, she drove to the hospital, windows down, singing at top volume to Adele's 'Set Fire to the Rain'.

In room 417, Teresa found her grandmother up and fully dressed, looking radiant. 'Wow, Grandma, you look fantastic.' She gave her a hug, warmly returned by Helen's strong arms.

'This morning they told me I'll be able to go home Wednesday.'

Teresa cheered. 'I'm so pleased. We'll have a party for you.' At which she'd present her grandmother with a refurbished Sarah, along with the amazing news of her pedigree.

Helen nodded, beaming, looking years younger. 'I'm ready. The person James is thinking of hiring may be able to start after you leave.'

'Actually, if it's okay, the person James is hiring will be me, except free of charge.'

'You!' Helen turned so fast she nearly pitched over. Teresa grabbed her waist to steady her.

'Is that a bad or good reaction?'

'Oh Teresa.' Tears came into her grandmother's eyes, which she blinked repeatedly to keep them away. 'It's the best news I've had in years.'

'I got two extra weeks off from my job. So I'm now here for three more.'

'Oh.' Helen's elation dimmed. 'Only three weeks?'

'It's all I can do without being fired.' Which didn't seem like a bad thing, except – references.

'Yes, of course, of course.' Helen waved away concern. 'I'm being selfish. Don't mind me.'

Teresa hunched her shoulders, then pushed them down. 'To be honest, I'm liking life here better than in Phoenix. So far anyway.'

'Really?' The blue eyes got rounder. 'So you might stay permanently? Or at least you'd be open to it?'

Teresa took in a long breath, not ready to commit. 'I'm thinking about it. But it's a huge decision.'

'Well.' Helen was beaming. 'No pressure, of course. We'll see how it goes. But this accident has made me feel my age for the first time. Your mother was probably right that I shouldn't be running the place alone. So maybe this busted hip will turn out to be a good thing, or at least a wake-up call.'

'Could be.' Teresa would like to think Mom did have Grandma's best interests at heart, at least some of the time.

'Not still so afraid of the animals?'

'Not as. And I've taken on a few repairs. I hope that's okay. Dad taught me to be pretty handy.'

'Of course, of course. Treat the place as if it's yours. And thank you. It probably needs sharper eyes and younger hands than mine. Come, let's walk.' Helen pointed toward the door. 'I've graduated to crutches, thank goodness. I hated that walker.

Useful, practical, but it made me feel like an old woman. Can you get them for me, dear?'

Teresa brought the crutches and helped her grandmother fit them under her arms. 'That feel okay?'

'Perfect.' Helen took a few jerky steps toward the door. 'Your mother called earlier today. I gather you haven't told her yet that you're staying longer. She was still expecting you back next week.'

'I haven't.' Teresa followed her into the hall, good mood threatened by anxiety. 'I've been . . . busy.'

'I understand.'

'Busy putting it off.'

Helen giggled and leaned in so she and Teresa bumped shoulders. 'If I may . . . I've found over the years that the best way to deal with your mother is not to argue or confront her, and never to contradict her directly. There lies the way to hell's fury.'

'Then how do you disagree with her?'

'Same as in any difficult conversation with someone you're close to. Be cheerful. Be loving. Say what you feel, and be ready to compromise unless you are absolutely sure her position would do harm, then stand your ground like a bull. A gentle one. Honestly, staying calm is the hardest part.'

Teresa sighed. 'I'll try. All my life so far, I've coped by agreeing with everything she says.'

'You were working from a power imbalance. But you're older now. Maybe this separation will help you gain some perspective.' Helen moved aside for a young woman in a wheelchair, then resumed her slow, jerky pace. Step, swing, step, swing. 'I've been thinking on what you said about Lilianne and Gilles. It's funny how we tell ourselves something is X or Y, and put it away in the X or Y box. Sometimes those Xs and Ys need

351

taking out and dusting off for another look. Like Sarah, and the pictures from the trunk.'

Teresa couldn't help a secret victory grin, thinking of her call to Connecticut. She'd played that one right, thank goodness. 'Have you taken Gilles and Lilianne out for another look?'

'I have. I'm going to tell you a difficult story now, one I glossed over before. But if we're going to get to know each other again . . . I think you should know.' They reached the end of the shiny hall and turned the corner onto another. Helen cleared her throat nervously. 'Not long after your father left, your mother found out what I was doing on those vacations with Lilianne and Gilles, even back when Kevin was alive. In her hands, what had been discreet and beautiful became an ugly and terribly hurtful weapon.'

Teresa recoiled, feeling as if she'd been sent back to Start when she was just about to finish the game. Mom had not lied about the affairs. Helen had been meeting that other man, the one taking the pictures Teresa found in the trunk. She felt sick with dismay. Cheating was not beautiful, even if it was discreet. In fact, there was no end to its ugliness. 'How did Mom find out?'

'When your father left, I flew to Phoenix to support her. Lilianne and Gilles flew out to support me. I was devastated, both for my daughter and at the thought of you and your brothers without Richard to protect you from her . . . dysfunction.

'While we were there, your mom must have overheard something that confirmed what she'd suspected. It shattered her. She accused me of robbing Kevin of his pride, and essentially causing his death.' Helen stopped walking, looking distraught. 'I suppose in a way she was right. What I did was unforgivable. It was also, during some rather miserable and desperate times, a way to make my life tolerable without breaking up our family or abandoning my husband to his demon.'

Teresa suppressed a groan. She'd just heard this rationalization from her father. A devil's bargain if she'd ever heard one.

'Of course, like all cheaters, I never expected to be caught.' Helen took another step forward with the crutches, swung her leg to catch up.

'Of course not.'

'I hurt a lot of people. Kevin certainly.' Her voice wobbled. 'Kevin especially. Though I believe what hurt him most wasn't what I was doing on those vacations, which he must have suspected, but that he knew why I had to take them, which made him furious. Not at me, at himself. But he didn't know how to separate the two.'

Teresa thought of the picture Mom had painted so often, of Grandpa Kevin sobbing on the floor. This was a slightly different view of that agony, which doubled some of the blame back on his drinking. Fairly or not?

'Your mother cutting me out of your lives was devastating, but I understood her anger. Her devotion to her father was absolute. My sad attempt to atone for my sins, useless in retrospect, was to cut those friends out of *my* life, a vow I've held to all this time, I suppose in the vain hope that my daughter would relent and become family again. So now you know my darkest secret. Or rather my only dark secret. There are no others.'

Teresa took a few steps on the polished linoleum, not knowing what to say. She was still protective of her mother, having lived through what the news of Helen's cheating did to Cheryl so soon after she'd learned of her own husband's betrayal. Now, having contacted Lilianne and Gilles, Teresa might unwittingly have put Helen on track to reconnecting with the fourth member of their annual trips, the mystery lover behind the camera.

Mom would be shattered all over again.

Teresa didn't know what to think, who to blame, how to feel. Though it was on her right now to break the loaded silence.

'Well . . .' She floundered through sentences in her mind. 'It sounds like a complicated time for everyone.'

Helen burst out laughing. 'Oh Teresa, you are a gem. The perfect tactful and evasive comment. Well done. Except I'd rather you cut the tact and tell me how you really feel.'

Teresa counted the squares on the floor, tried to step into the exact center of each one. 'It was hard to hear. I was with Mom when she found out about Dad cheating. She was a wreck. We were all wrecks.'

'Yes. I'm sure.' Helen seemed to be waiting for more. 'Go on.'

'She didn't tell us at the time about you. Mostly her rage was heaped on my father. Not until we were older did we start hearing Grandma Helen stories. Some I've now found out weren't true. She told us you were the alcoholic.'

'Oh my Lord. How terribly sad.' Helen's voice thickened. 'She so adored her father. I suppose she couldn't face thinking any less of him.'

'But I guess Mom was right about your . . . vacations.'

'Yes. She was.'

They covered five more floor tiles in silence.

'My brothers and I missed coming to the ranch to visit. Mom said we couldn't afford it, because of Dad leaving, and we accepted that. But I guess she was also angry.' Teresa looked up from counting squares. 'Thank you for telling me. I'm sure it was hard to do.'

'Awful.' Helen wobbled back on her crutches, vulnerable for a startled second, then rallied. 'But if you shrink from tackling the hard stuff, it just keeps buzzing around you like a horsefly, waiting for a chance to land and bite.'

They walked to the next corner, turned onto the next shiny hall.

'Why did you clear out Mom's room?'

'Cheryl asked me to. She wanted everything personal out of my home and sent back to Phoenix. I suppose I deserved that, too. I have a room for my sons in which their childhoods are intact, and a hotel room for a daughter I no longer have. I keep the door closed and imagine her in there the way it used to be. Barbie's Dreamhouse and her dress-up trunk, model horses and posters of the Partridge Family and the Osmonds. Jacks all over the floor – oh, those hurt to step on – pads of drawing paper and markers . . . she was a total slob. Isn't that funny? I'd love to see that room a cluttered mess again.'

'So . . . you miss her?'

When Helen didn't answer, Teresa glanced over to find her brows down, mouth bunched. 'I don't know if miss is the right word. I grieve the woman I hoped she'd become. I love her as she is, because she's my daughter. I wish we had a better relationship, but I have mostly made peace with who she is and the fact that we don't.'

Teresa nodded, then jumped when her phone rang. She pulled it out, hoping for Danny or Ike or Katie, or anyone but . . .

'It's Mom.' She started to put the phone back in her purse.

'Want to talk to her together?'

She almost grabbed at the offer. It would be hard for Mom to gaslight her if Helen was standing right there. And yet if they talked alone, Teresa could start some of the conversations she and her mother needed to have. Before Mom became a horsefly.

No fear.

'I think it's better if I talk to her alone.'

'Good for you. Go ahead and pick up. We're almost back at my room. I'm fine on my own.'

'I'll call her outside.' She texted: *Hey, Mom. I'm with Grandma. I'll call you in about ten minutes*. 'I need to tell her I'm staying with you for a couple of extra weeks. And tell her you don't have dementia and don't need to move. And then hold the phone out so I don't go deaf from the shrieking.'

Helen looked anxious. 'Yes, it might be loud. But seeing her more clearly is an important step. You'll figure out the rest from there. You are stronger than you know.'

'Thanks, Grandma.'

When they reached Helen's door, Teresa stopped, expecting her to go back into her room. Instead, Helen took one wiry arm off the crutch and crushed her granddaughter to her in an embrace that left them both misty.

'I'll see you soon.' Teresa waited to make sure Helen was safely back in bed before she walked back to the hospital entrance a mass of conflicting emotions – what else was new? Out in the parking lot, she debated whether to return to the ranch and have the conversation in comfortable surroundings or just get it over with.

Getting it over with would be quicker.

Before her nerve failed, she dialed her mother, leaning against the car, keeping Helen's advice in mind, every nerve buzzing, every muscle rigid, wishing Danny was around to make her laugh.

'Hi, Mom. I have lots of good news.' She sounded way too chipper.

'Well, that's good to hear.' Her mother spoke loudly, background noise breaking through occasionally, sounding as if she were in the middle of a crowd.

'Are you at work?'

'Oh, no. No. They gave me the afternoon off. Let's have it, Teresa. The good news. I could use some.'

'Okay. For one thing . . .' Teresa had to swallow to ease the dryness in her mouth, 'Grandma Helen doesn't have dementia. What you were hearing was temporary, after the surgery. Isn't that fabulous?'

'What do you mean, she doesn't have dementia? She was talking nonsense. I heard it.'

'Yes, I did too. It's a reaction to the anesthesia and the stress of surgery. She said you spoke to her today? You must have noticed she's completely lucid now.'

Long pause. 'I . . . don't know what to say. With me she's been totally nutty. For a long time now.'

'Hmm.' Teresa hugged her free arm around herself, fighting off nausea. 'That's weird. James and Jim haven't noticed a decline either.'

'They hear what they want to hear.'

'Maybe. Anyway, it's good news. And the second thing is that they're releasing her on Wednesday. So I'm—'

'Oh shit. That's sooner than I thought. I don't think her apartment will be available for another—'

'No, it's fine. I . . .' Teresa cleared her throat, 'I got a couple more weeks off work, so I can stay with her when she comes back to the ranch.'

Silence except for her mother's breathing. Teresa's stomach roiled.

'Isn't that great, Mom?' She sounded like Cheddar. *Chirp chirp chirp.*

'No, it's not great. She should not go home. I told you this, Teresa, it will make it much harder for her to move to the new place later.'

'Yes, you're right. The thing is, I'm not sure she needs to move yet. Maybe not for years. Don't you think? If she doesn't have dementia, her health is good and someone is with her at the

357

ranch to help . . .' She waited, car hot against her back, insides in a thousand knots.

'What the heck is going on with you, Teresa Maria? Haven't you and I been through this? The move is for your grandmother's sake.'

By now Teresa was sickeningly sure that it wasn't. 'Being in her own house will—'

'It's my father's house.'

Deep breath. 'Okay, being at your *father's* house will be best for her. I know you want her to be hap—'

'No. Just no. This is all set up, Teresa. I've already contacted a realtor to look at the house and the acreage. We need to move forward. Home and land values are in a good place now. Who knows where the economy is headed? Waiting might cost us. A huge percentage of old people who break their hips die within a year.'

'Mom.' Wringing every drop of patience from her nearly empty tank. 'Don't you think this should be more about your mother's happiness than money?'

Mistake. Huge mistake. She knew it as soon as she said the words.

'Oh, isn't that noble.' Her mother was snarling, a tone Teresa had only heard her use at Dad. 'St Teresa with the bitch mom who dares to do what should be done. You're there a week and I'm tossed out like garbage, is that right? Let me ask you, when has my mother ever concerned herself with *my* happiness? All those years of drinking and abuse and affairs? You tell me when she thought about me. And speaking of the importance of a mother's happiness, why are you more worried about *her* happiness than mine?'

For the first time, with one of Mom's rages directed at her, Teresa could imagine how her father had felt. *Yes, Grandma, staying calm was the hard part.* 'I hear you. I just don't think she needs to move.'

'Oh, you don't think. Never mind that her doctor recommended it to me.'

'He did?' Teresa pushed herself off the car, then slumped back onto it. 'No he didn't, Mom. He said she could go home Wednesday.'

'I suppose *she* told you that. So you're on *her* side now. Jesus, Teresa. My husband betrayed me. My mother betrayed my dad and me. My boys barely speak to me. You were all I had left. Now you're leaving me too? For a liar and a cheat?'

Teresa closed her eyes. How had she not understood the depth of her mother's issues? How many excuses, at what expense to herself, had she made for this woman, over and over and over? The only person Mom had left? Teresa was the only one weak and enabling enough to keep hanging on.

'I'm sorry you feel that way, Mom. I have to go now.' She ended the call with a jab of her thumb, wanting to enjoy the feeling of not having given in, of standing her ground and setting a boundary instead of collapsing into her usual fawning apologies.

But as she was in the car driving back to the ranch, all she could think about was the pain her mother had suffered, losing her dad, losing her husband and her fancy life, descending into financial hardship and drudgery. Now, thanks to Teresa, everything Mom had put into motion to improve her life was crumbling.

Worst of all was the insidious certainty that every interaction between them from now on would be an unwinnable and exhausting battle.

✐ Chapter 17 ✐

Teresa crept out of the chicken coop holding a broom and a bucket of diluted vinegar, dirty, sweating and reeking. On the back deck sat Helen, sipping an iced tea. 'Finished?'

Teresa peeled off her rubber gloves and swiped at a lock of frizz that had escaped her baseball cap. 'I dare you to find a speck of dirt in that coop.'

'Brava,' her grandmother applauded. 'You realize what this means . . .'

'That I stink of chicken poo?'

'That you passed the test.'

'What test?' Teresa coiled the hose and brought it back over to the garden.

'Rancher Teresa test. I'll tell you more after you clean yourself up.'

'What, you don't like me filthy?' She retrieved the scrubbing brush and the bucket and climbed the steps, grinning. Helen had been back home for a week and a half, graduating during that time from crutches to a cane, which she now used only on uneven ground. She was on her last week of outpatient therapy, and Teresa knew more than she'd ever imagined about caring for someone after hip surgery.

And had enjoyed every minute.

'I love you filthy. But not near me.' Helen held her nose

delicately. 'Just be glad that horrible job only has to be done a couple times a year.'

'I'm just glad you get to do it next time.'

'Hmm.' Her grandmother smiled and sipped her tea. 'I think my chicken coop scrubbing days are over.'

'I bet you can still scrub with the best of 'em.' Teresa went inside, dumped and rinsed the bucket, then showered and changed, thinking she'd probably feel every muscle the next day. She'd discovered over this last week or so that she absolutely loved working with her body and hands every day, and that she absolutely loved her grandmother.

More than that, having been around Helen for this time, being encouraged and praised and treated like her opinion and thoughts were important, she'd begun to realize how toxic life with her mother had always been. It was hard to imagine how Teresa could salvage that relationship, but she was determined to try. Mom had been giving her the silent treatment since their disagreement. She'd always used that punishment on the rest of the family when Dad, Mike or Ike went up against her, but this was a painful first for Teresa. At any time before this trip, she would undoubtedly have bent over backwards to appease her mother. Yet even though the lack of contact gnawed at her, Mom's silence gave her room to breathe. There were still a lot of things she had to work out.

Back in the kitchen, clean and refreshed, she poured herself some tea and joined her grandmother. The day was hot, but the shaded porch and the breeze made it comfortable sitting.

'All right, what test did I pass?' She dragged her chair back and put her feet up on the railing. 'No longer chicken around chickens?'

'Not only that.' Her grandmother leaned forward, looking

serious. 'You've taken wonderful care of the ranch, Teresa, and if I'm not mistaken, you've enjoyed it.'

'It's been so satisfying. I didn't expect that. The first night I was here, I nearly turned around and went home.'

Helen's eyebrows rose over the rims of her glasses. 'What made you stay?'

'I wanted to prove Mom wrong. She expected me to fail. I suppose I did too, on some level.'

'Oh dear. I'm sorry.' Helen made a pained face. 'I'm very glad you decided to stay, and glad you don't regret it. Being in the hospital gave me a lot of time to think – after they put my brain back in, that is.'

Teresa chortled. 'That was quite a line.'

'Scared you, didn't I?'

'A lot.' She tilted her chin, smiling affectionately at her grand-mother. 'What did I know? Hospitals make mistakes.'

Helen's turn to grin. She looked so much younger and stronger since getting out of the hospital, though she still became occasionally confused, and tired easily. 'Being injured brought home that I'm in my seventies and mortal. Which made me think about what I want for the rest of my life, however long that turns out to be.'

'I'm betting decades.'

'If I'm in good health, I'll take as many as I can.' She bent down to pet Zig, who'd jumped up to lie at her feet. 'Hello, Ziggedy doo-dah. As much as I love my home, I've been going through the motions for a while, living here and doing what I do without really paying attention to the years passing.'

Teresa raised her hand. 'Guilty of that since graduating college.'

'It's an easy trap to fall into when life is good enough. And despite all the messes, life here has definitely been good enough.

But there's more out there, and I'd like to be free to leave when the urge takes me, to enjoy a larger world again.'

Teresa's mood slipped into dread. Mom's dream was about to come true. Helen had decided to sell.

'So I've come to a decision that will not be popular with everyone, but too bad, because it's my place.'

'Yes.' She reached miserably for her tea, unable to sit still and take what was coming.

'If you'd like to own it, I'll change my will and leave the ranch to you.'

Teresa's eyes shot wide; the tea wobbled in her hand, and she had to set it down. '*What?*'

Helen smirked. 'Is that "What?" as in "I didn't hear you"? Or as in "I can't believe what I'm hearing"?'

'I definitely can't believe what I'm hearing.'

'Fair enough.' She straightened from stroking Zig and rested her arms on the chair, hands clasped. Zig lowered his head, looking abandoned. 'If you agree, I'd like you to stay on permanently, to keep learning how to run the place, so if I want to pick up and go somewhere, you'll be here. When I kick off, you'll own it outright. And you really should close your mouth or something will fly into it.'

Teresa snapped it shut. 'I don't know what to say. Thank you. I mean, this is amazing. I have dreamed of how to . . . but then I don't really feel ready to commit to that kind of . . . What is so funny?'

'You certainly *don't* know what to say.' Helen gave her shoulder a playful shove. 'Of course it's too much to expect you to decide right now. I've been thinking this through for some time, and you didn't see it coming. Take all the time you need.'

Excitement started small in Teresa's chest, then began to warm, growing larger and larger until . . .

'Mom would have a fit.'

'Yes, she would.' Helen watched her soberly. 'You would have to deal with that.'

Teresa hunched her shoulders. 'Ick.'

'Before you remembered your mother, before you started to think rationally, what was your reaction?'

Teresa knew this one: the same pumped-up feeling she'd had during the Lean Cuisine dinner with Mom at the idea of coming to Kansas to clear out Grandma Helen's house. 'Joy. Excitement. Kind of a weird power trip.'

'Aha.' Helen clapped her hands. 'That's your real desire, the one you follow. The rest is fear and insecurity. Pay no attention.'

'What if it's legitimate fear and insecurity?'

'You work to overcome them. It would make me very happy to have the ranch stay in the family. It would have made your Grandpa Kevin happy. James would feel the same, and Kevinjay doesn't care. *But . . .*' she pointed emphatically, 'you are under no obligation to live your life for anyone's happiness but your own. Not mine, not your uncles', and definitely not your mother's. It will feel selfish at first, but it will spare everybody a world of pain. You most of all.'

Teresa turned her head, taking in the land in a slow sweep, imagining herself living here through all the seasons. Imagining not having to go back and sit at her desk in her cubicle and work annual circles for something connected to her only by paycheck.

So tempting. But she wasn't the risk-taking type, and this one would be huge.

'I started from scratch here,' Helen said. 'By the time I took it over, the kind of farm Kevin made had nothing to do with what I wanted to create. You'll be stepping into a process already in motion. And I've been watching you for the past week or so. You have a natural touch, a natural affinity. For repairs, for the animals, now that they no longer frighten you, even for cleaning chicken poop.'

Teresa rolled her eyes, remembering Danny's story about delivering the breech calf, how inexperienced and terrified he'd been, and how Helen had made him feel he could do anything. 'Thank you. For your faith in me.'

'You haven't encountered enough faith in you.' Helen shook her head. 'I remember trying to teach you knitting, and before you could even begin to grasp what it was about, your mother shut you down. Said you were bad at it, and it was no use.'

'I *was* bad at it.'

Helen put a hand on her arm. 'Everyone is bad at the beginning, Teresa. You were no different. It made my heart cry to see how you believed her so readily. There is no way I'd offer you this place if I had any doubts that you could handle it.'

'Thank you, Grandma. And thank you for the offer, and for your trust in me.' Teresa gave a goofy half-laugh, still not quite believing this was happening. 'I will definitely think about it.'

'Good.' Helen squeezed her arm and let go. A loud honk sounded from the front of the house, accompanied by the hum of a very large motor. 'What the heck is that?

Teresa stood up. The honking sounded again. 'Sounds like a bus trying to get our attention.'

Helen rose slowly but with returning ease, and grabbed for her cane. 'I don't know anyone who owns a bus.'

They went through the house to the front, where Teresa opened the door. Pulling up outside was an enormous silver motor home with huge side mirrors that looked like bug antennas.

'Must be at the wrong house.' Helen stepped out next to her. Zig was already investigating, Pearl and Tusk close behind.

The RV motor cut. The door opened, and from the driver's side stepped a tall woman with expertly cut gray hair, wearing large sunglasses and a stylish outfit of white capris and an electric-blue belted tunic. On her feet, strappy sandals and a silver ankle bracelet. 'Hello, Helen. And . . . Teresa? Am I right?'

Helen gasped and started toward her. 'Lilianne! Good Lord, I can't believe it. We were just . . . Oh my dear friend, I am so happy to see you!'

As the women embraced, and Teresa stood with her mouth hanging open for the second time that afternoon, a tall, equally sophisticated-looking man with a shock of gray hair and dark eyes came around from the passenger side of the monstrous vehicle.

Gilles. Had to be. They were actually here, and Helen was happy to see them. Maybe Teresa had done something good, even if it meant Helen might find her old lover, if he was still alive out there and single. Maybe that wouldn't be so bad. After all, Kevin had been gone for nearly thirty years, and Teresa's mom . . . maybe didn't have to know?

Ick.

'Look behind you, Helen.' Lilianne stepped back; Helen turned. Instantly her joyous expression sobered, her mouth opened in an *oh* of wonder and she staggered on her cane. Gilles reached her in long strides, steadied her with one hand on her shoulder, then laid the other on her cheek. Helen grasped his wrist and gazed up at him with such a naked expression of love that Teresa's eyes jerked behind Helen to Lilianne, who was . . .

Smiling. But . . . she couldn't see Helen's face.

This did not feel right.

Lilianne opened the door to the silver monster and climbed in, disappearing from view.

Gilles bent down until his forehead touched Helen's and they stood there, bodies nearly touching, tears coursing down Helen's cheeks, Gilles's lips moving. Then Helen lifted her face for a kiss that was *definitely* not one between friends.

366

Teresa froze. What the *hell*?

'Champagne!' Lilianne emerged triumphantly from the RV, bottle in hand. Gilles and Helen turned, stepping discreetly apart. 'Cold, even. There's plenty more. We have tons to celebrate.'

'Teresa.' Helen was walking toward her, Gilles's arm supporting her. 'Meet Gilles.'

And . . . Lilianne? She's here too, Helen!

'Uh. Hi, Gilles.' Teresa stuck out her hand woodenly. 'Thanks for coming.'

He shook solemnly, but his eyes were dancing, perhaps in amusement at her formality or looking forward to more making-out behind his wife's back. 'Thank you for inviting us.'

Helen did a double-take. '*Teresa* invited you?'

Teresa nodded, and then they were all looking at her, so instead of saying *I made a terrible mistake*, she said, 'I did not expect the RV.'

Lilianne burst into musical laughter. '*No one* expects this RV. We rented it from an obscenely rich neighbor of ours. It's a ridiculous piece of equipment, but very comfortable. We would have been here sooner, but we were abroad when you called, and then we just had to surprise you.'

'You'll never guess what's in the middle.' Gilles pointed to the belly of the beast. His voice was deep, his accent faintly French.

'A spa?' Helen guessed. 'A zoo? Wall Street?'

'Watch this.' Lilianne pressed a button on her key fob. A door swung open on the side of the vehicle, revealing . . . '*Et voilà*. A Mercedes sports car. Came with the bus.'

Helen scowled. 'That is disgusting.'

Teresa was also scowling, but because she was thinking of all those pictures in the trunk of the three friends smiling from expensive places around the world. Where was the rich hottie playboy who meant nothing to Helen but a brief chance to escape Kevin's alcohol-fueled decline and cruelty? Had she been having the affair with *Gilles*? What the hell was 'discreet' and 'beautiful' about boinking your best friend's husband under her nose?

She wanted to throw up. What had she done?

'We'll show you around inside her later.' Lilianne shook her head. 'Completely over the top.'

'It'll remind you of the hotel at St Moritz.' Gilles quirked an eyebrow at Helen, who blushed. 'One of my favorite places.'

Ick!

Teresa wanted to get into her rental car and drive back to Phoenix, so she could pretend this whole two weeks hadn't happened. Except her roommate and mother weren't speaking to her, which would make it a tough pretense.

Lilianne slung her arm over Helen's shoulder and they started toward the house. 'It is *so* good to see you. We have much to discuss. How's the hip?'

'Coming along. Not bad.' Helen pressed her cheek against her friend's. 'I can't believe you're both here. Teresa, you are a miracle.'

Teresa wasn't so sure.

'How long can you stay?' Helen directed her question to Gilles.

'As long as it takes to convince you to come back to Connecticut with us.'

Helen's brows lifted, but Teresa saw the excitement in her eyes and had to close hers. She could forgive her grandmother for cheating on Kevin with that mystery man, but Helen had betrayed a close friend. Worse, they both looked dying to start in all over again. Maybe Mom hadn't gotten all the facts straight, but she might have come close to the truth.

How many people had Teresa trusted who were turning out to be unworthy? Was Danny a polygamist? Did James and Jim belong to a devil-worshiping cult that sacrificed virgins? How could she retain any faith in her instincts after this?

As soon as the front door opened and they started filing in, Cheddar let out a volley of chatter and screeches of greeting.

'Oh, the bird!' Gilles headed into the living room. 'What was his name?'

'Cheddar.' Helen limped to stand next to him, looking happier than Teresa had ever seen her. 'Remember what you taught him, Gilles?'

'No, no.' Gilles held up a finger. 'I didn't teach him. I was whistling and he caught on.'

'Try, Gilles.' Lilianne peered in from the doorway. Teresa stayed in the foyer, wanting to run away. Anywhere. She felt complicit just by existing in the same space.

Gilles bent his tall frame. Cheddar cocked his head. The handsome Frenchman began to whistle the Ode to Joy from Beethoven's Ninth Symphony. Rich-toned musical whistling. Helen's smile turned into a nostalgic grin. She grasped his arm.

'*Et bien*. Now your turn, Cheddar.'

Cheddar opened his beak and whistled something unrecognizable. The friends laughed, causing the bird to whistle harder, shuffling back and forth on his perch, bobbing along to his own tune.

Gilles tried again, the beautiful tune emerging clearly into the silent room.

This time, out of Cheddar's beak, right from the brain of Beethoven, the theme emerged with startling clarity. While Lilianne remained entranced, Gilles and Helen exchanged goopy smiles.

Teresa turned away. This was too much.

Cheddar having been admired, the trio toured the rest of the house, drinking in the views from the large windows.

'Sarah!' Lilianne's eyes went wide as the group came into the dining room and she spotted the regal doll in her corner. 'Oh, how lovely to see her. She looks amazing.'

'She's had work done. Teresa sent her to a doll salon.' Helen picked Sarah up out of her chair as if she were handling a glass bubble and handed her to Lilianne. The shop had done a remarkable job. Her hair and clothes were no longer dusty and flattened. Her dress had been hemmed, and her fur cape – Russian sable, apparently – cleaned and brushed. The newly polished jewels sparkled in the light coming in through the sliding door. 'Isn't she perfect?'

She *was* perfect. Too perfect. Teresa had spent the last week terrified something would happen to her. Even Helen had said the doll didn't feel like the same companion anymore.

'Where did you find the chair?' Gilles picked it up admiringly. Teresa had kept the design simple to show off the rich grain of the wood, and stained it dark to set off Sarah's vividness. For the seat and back, as planned, she'd found a green brocade that complemented the emerald hue of Sarah's dress. 'It looks made for her.'

'It was.' Helen beamed at her granddaughter. 'By Teresa.'

'Really!' Gilles turned to her. 'You should do this professionally.'

'Thank you.' Teresa was proud of the chair. But she didn't want this man giving her compliments.

'Teresa, that's a great idea.' Helen looked thrilled. 'You can custom-make chairs for doll-owners. Not just chairs. All sorts of furniture. Advertise on the web. I bet the place that fixed Sarah up would refer people to you.'

'It's so lovely to see her again.' Lilianne stroked the doll's impossibly soft cape. 'We'll have to toast her tonight.'

'But there's even more astonishing news,' Helen said. 'The woman at the shop nearly had a fit when she saw our Sarah. Tell them, Teresa.'

Teresa reluctantly faced Lilianne and Gilles and told the story, including new information from Matti at the Doll's Cradle, who'd traced Sarah back to her first owner. Thomas Haynes, a wealthy widowed Englishman, had bought her in Paris in 1915 as a Christmas gift for his daughter, Penelope, who'd passed her on to a girl in her service, Jeanette Alcott, who became an actress and Natalie Laurent's stepmother. 'They say she could be worth half a million dollars.'

'Good Lord.' Lilianne turned to Helen in horror. 'We dragged her all over the place. Remember at Connie's birthday? We played pin the corsage on Sarah! And Connie waltzed her around the room, drunk out of her mind. She could have dropped her. Then there was my birthday, when we took her on that picnic in the Bois de Boulogne and it started raining. We could have ruined her.'

'I stuffed her in a trunk!' Helen said.

'We had *no* clue.' Lilianne gazed at Sarah.

'You two brought her back to me on my birthday.' Helen reached to touch them both. 'And for a long time I'd take her out each year on that day and think of you. She and I would have a quiet celebration in the basement. I think I baked us a cupcake one year when the kids were busy and Kevin forgot.'

'Ah, Helen.' Gilles kissed her temple. 'No more lonely birthdays.'

'No! We're not letting you do that again,' Lilianne said. 'No offense to Sarah.'

'She's Teresa's now.' Helen beamed at her granddaughter. 'I thought it was time to pass her along. Sarah should be around youth and spirit.'

'Lovely.' Gilles didn't take his eyes off Helen. 'I hope you enjoy her.'

'I hope you *dare* enjoy her!' Lilianne contemplated Sarah's wistful face. 'It is funny how different the money makes her. It shouldn't, but it does.'

'Come, let's go outside.' Helen moved toward the back door. 'I want to show you the animals.'

Gilles was already at her side.

'You two go on. I'll stay here.' Lilianne set the doll gently back in her chair.

No no no no no. Teresa moved toward the couple, already at the door. They must absolutely not be alone.

An iron hand gripped her arm. She stopped and looked back questioningly at Lilianne.

'Let them go,' Lilianne said quietly. 'They've been apart too long.'

Teresa stared, completely at a loss. 'But . . . he's your husband.'

Lilianne laughed, making her delicate silver earrings swing. 'Helen and Gilles and I have been friends for a long, long time. I love them both and they both love me.'

Oh no. No no no. Not a threesome.

Teresa was going to hurl.

'But while the three of us are good friends, those two truly belong to each other. I've always known that.' Lilianne's voice wobbled until she forced it back to firmness. 'The rest is up to Helen to tell you or not.'

'Okay.' That sounded a little better – at least given the choices.

'Now I'm going to lecture you and you're going to have to listen and pretend you agree with me. But after that, when you stop wanting to kick me, I want you to really think about what I've said. So sit.' She let go of Teresa's arm and pointed to one of the dining chairs. Teresa sat, wanting desperately to put her hands over her ears and sing, like her brothers used to do when she was yelling at them for whatever prank they'd pulled on her.

Lilianne leaned both hands on the table, naturally assuming a power position – CEO about to scold the useless employee. 'We all have to make choices. Some easy, some hard, some impossible. Helen chose Kevin over Gilles years and years ago. That did and did not turn out well, as you probably know.'

Teresa gripped her hands together in her lap. 'Yes.'

'Eventually she decided that stealing a week or so of happiness out of every fifty-two was preferable to exploding her family, especially if it meant custody battles and Kevin getting the kids in his condition.'

Teresa stiffened. Third time she'd heard those words this month. Dad, Helen . . . She was starting to hate them.

'So what I want to say to you . . .' Lilianne leaned closer, her voice steely, 'is that you have a choice too. Not to decide if what they did was good or bad, because that's done. But whether you really want to judge them, and whether losing Helen is worth that judgment.'

'Oh, I see.' Teresa knew exactly what Lilianne was saying. 'That was your choice, wasn't it? You married him, and then you had to—'

'Nope.' Lilianne smiled tightly. 'Different situation. Not your business.'

'Okay.'

'Good.' She relaxed her stance, transitioning back from interrogating superior to gracious guest with practiced smoothness. She'd make a good FBI agent. 'So! You're here visiting Helen? Taking care of her while she recovers? Taking care of the farm?'

If Teresa had wanted out of the small talk before, that feeling was double now. 'Yes.'

'Good for you. We intend to kidnap her and bring her back to Connecticut to celebrate her birthday in a couple of weeks.'

'Oh.' Teresa just wanted to be alone to think. 'That will be nice. Look, I need to go . . . meet someone.'

Lilianne smiled, sympathetically this time. 'Little shell shock?'

'Uh-huh.'

'Go. I'll cover for you. Got a name I can use?'

Teresa looked at her blankly. 'A name . . .'

'Someone you might realistically be going to meet? Or someone you'd want a private conversation with outside of our hearing range? Best friend? Parent? Favorite pet?'

Teresa got up, nodding, and headed for the door. Not Katie. Not Mom. Even if they were on speaking terms, both women would just tell her what to do, how to feel. But there was someone who'd listen carefully and help her think through her options without ultimatums or judgment.

'Danny.'

'Here you go.' Danny handed Teresa a double scoop of strawberry ice cream in a waffle cone. He'd answered her text immediately and suggested meeting at an ice cream store on Massachusetts Street in the Lawrence Cultural District. 'I can't believe no one's sent you here yet. Sylas and Maddy's is about as good as ice cream gets.'

He paid for their cones and they crossed the street to South Park and found an unoccupied bench in the shade with a view of a domed gazebo and flower gardens in full bloom.

'This is gorgeous. Thanks for coming to meet me.'

'Sure.' He sat next to her. Teresa snuck a peek at him. He was wearing a tan World of Warcraft shirt and brown cargo shorts, his cheeks flushed, blond hair tousled. To her eyes he looked even more delicious than her ice cream. 'What are friends for?'

Friends. Right. 'You didn't have to work today?'

'I worked this morning. Got the afternoon off. Jim and I are driving to Kansas City to see a Royals game.' He turned toward her on the bench. 'Want to come?'

'I better not, thanks.' She took a bite of her ice cream, tasting of summery ripe strawberries. 'Oh my God, that's good. Want to taste?'

He nodded and tried it, then offered her his butter pecan, rich and full of fresh, crunchy nuts.

They both said 'Mmm' at the same time.

Danny should not be any part of the reason she'd choose to stay in Lawrence. Because ... friends. But being around him today made that a difficult resolution to keep.

'So what's going on?' He spoke casually, but she knew her attempted cheer wasn't fooling him.

'Crazy stuff.' She filled him in as they ate their cones, starting with the arrival of Lilianne and Gilles, keeping details to a minimum, not wanting to tarnish Helen in his eyes. 'I guess the three of them did a lot of traveling together while Kevin was alive. Apparently he wasn't thrilled about it.'

'Yeah, I think I know this story. Jim told me.'

A relief. She wouldn't have to balance on eggshells. 'A bit of a shock. I mean, Mom told me about it, sort of, but I guess when it became obvious she wasn't telling the real story about a lot of things, I sorta hoped. And then Helen told me that she ... hadn't been faithful, so I imagined some hot foreign guy she'd hook up with once a year for some fun, and then done. But true love? I feel for Grandpa Kevin, I can't help it. And I've seen Mom's pain. It sucked. So I know they've worked out this

375

weird incestuous thing and it's not my business, but I wish . . .
I don't even know what I wish.'

'That Helen was perfect?'

'Yes!' She gestured with her cone. 'And my dad. Is that so
much to ask?'

'Sounds totally reasonable to me.' Danny nodded sympathetically. 'You know, it helps me to separate out my sister's addictive
behaviors and concentrate on who she is.'

'That works?'

'Sometimes.' He hunched his shoulders, blew out a breath.

'I'm sorry.' She wanted to hug him, but would probably get
ice cream all over his shirt. 'Why can't everyone be simple and
delightful? Like us?'

He nodded with exaggerated gravitas. 'I ask myself that every
day. We need more strawberry and more butter pecan, and
fewer flavors like monster peanut butter marshmallow mud,
or whatever.'

She snorted. 'It helps talking about it, thank you. Keeps it
smaller or something.'

'Good.' Danny flashed his sunshiny grin. 'That kind of thing
is never as black and white as it should be.'

'Exactly. There should be good and evil, and big red and
white signs that show who's what.' She mopped up a strawberry drip with her tongue, thinking about Lilianne's speech,
but probably not the way Lilianne wanted her to. *You have a
choice.* 'The thing is, I don't want to have to deal with this. I
don't want to have to choose whether Helen is right or wrong.
Whether my mom is right or wrong. Or Dad for that matter.
I'm not St Peter.'

'So don't choose. Go right on feeling both at once.'

Teresa started to laugh, then saw he was serious. And so she
thought about it some more, while she licked the last of the

mounded strawberry deep into the cone so each bite to the end would have both cone and ice cream. Very important ritual.

'That makes sense. I think you might have cured me, Danny.'

'I take no credit.' He crunched the last of his cone and wiped his fingers. 'I went to see someone over the mess with my sister's addictions. The therapist handed me that concept on a silver platter: "It's okay to have exactly opposite feelings about the same thing." Total relief.'

'Total.' Teresa bit off cone and ice cream, giddy over her new coping mechanism, imagining herself telling Lilianne where she could shove her lecture. 'I owe you.'

'Nah.'

'I do.' She crunched off another bite. 'I owe you the solution to your next major life problem.'

'Cool.'

She sent him a sidelong grin, which he returned, and then they were having another one of those chemical moments that should involve kissing. Or she thought so anyway. He made no move or sign that he agreed.

Friends. Sigh.

'Was that it?' He glanced at his watch. 'Our session isn't quite over.'

Teresa forced a smile. She'd have to rein in her crush or she could be on this roller coaster for a long time. 'Yes. Another hugely important choice came up this morning.'

'Oh good. Because really, you can't have enough torture in one day.'

'Worse, this one I can't have both ways.' She finished her cone and crumpled up the paper. 'Helen invited me to stay on the ranch with her. Permanently.'

Danny stiffened. His face turned stony.

Teresa hadn't expected him to jump up and down with joy,

though she wouldn't have minded. But this was definitely an ego-pricker. 'Uh . . . is that bad news? I thought it was kind of cool.'

'No. Sorry. No.' He looked like he'd been stuck with something barbed. 'Go on.'

'Well . . . I mean it's a big decision.' She felt herself turning red. Apparently she'd used up her time a while back. 'I mean whether I move here or not.'

'I imagine.' He sounded like he couldn't wait to get away from the conversation. 'So . . . are you considering it?'

'Yes, I am. Strongly. Surprisingly strongly. In fact, I think I might do it, if I can work up the nerve. I guess when I told you, I thought you might feel . . . I don't know. Never mind.' She stood briskly and brushed her hands together, though they weren't sticky. 'Anyway, I should probably get back to the – *mmph*.'

Danny had leapt up, spun her toward him and was kissing her. Kissing Danny was really, really good, like everything else about Danny, except maybe his wardrobe.

Then he stopped, leaving her breathless, and peered anxiously at her.

'Danny!' She laughed. 'What the hell?'

His face fell. 'Sorry, I was . . . I mean, I should have – *mmph*.'

She really, *really* liked kissing Danny. But eventually she stopped so she could grin goopily into his face, and he could grin back. 'I've wanted you to do that for a long time.'

'I wanted to do it for a long time. But not if you were leaving in a week. Or even three.' He tangled his fingers in the unruly curls she'd grown to love. 'You're not, are you?'

Teresa spoke without thinking. 'No. I'm not.'

And there it was, like the other times when she heard herself announcing a big decision without consciously deciding, then found she wasn't planning to qualify or take it back.

Maybe this was real too.

She and Danny spent the next half-hour together, until Danny absolutely *had* to go to meet Jim.

Teresa floated over to her car and climbed into its hot interior, rolled all the windows down and started back to the ranch, where she planned not to choose one side or the other on Helen's love triangle, to love her mother but not like much of what she did, and to choose to stay on the ranch forever.

A red light stopped her car, and a thought yanked her down from cloud nine.

Thud.

She would have to tell Mom she was staying in Kansas, and that Helen was going to leave her the ranch. How could she justify inheriting such a fantastic property and new life if it meant her deeply flawed but long-suffering mother would rot out the rest of her years in that tiny home she hated so much?

The light turned green. Teresa drove miserably on, imagining how hurt her mother would be. Judas Iscariot, Benedict Arnold, Julius and Ethel Rosenberg and now Teresa Clark. Her own daughter, taking away something she'd been counting on to relieve her financial worries for the past fifteen years.

How could Teresa ever compensate her mother for the loss of what she saw as her birthright? Her family property? Her father's life's work? She had no money, owned nothing that came close to the kind of cash that—

Oh my God.

The answer was so obvious she was ashamed she hadn't thought of it sooner. The perfect solution, one that would satisfy her mother and enable her to fulfill her dream, and allow Teresa to stay at the ranch guilt-free for as long as she wanted.

A solution that also made her want to pull over to the side of the road and empty her stomach of its strawberry cone.

She had something more than valuable enough to compensate her mother for the property loss.

She had Sarah.

Dinner that night with Gilles, Lilianne and Helen was fun and celebratory, but exhausting. Teresa couldn't help feeling queasy every time Gilles and Helen touched or kissed, but she did her best to hide the reaction, and by the end of the delicious dinner – Lilianne had made a fantastic pasta dish with greens from the garden, lemon, olives and feta cheese that Teresa would have to remember to copy – she'd made herself focus on the fact that Kevin was long gone and Lilianne obviously had no problem with the relationship. It therefore wasn't hurting anyone, and was clearly making Helen's world complete. There was no room anywhere in the picture for Teresa's judgment.

The talk was mostly reminiscences, of the months in Paris, of the later trips that had stopped when Teresa's mom found out about them and connected the dots. Looking at Gilles and Helen now, Teresa was able to see past her mother's pain and imagine the pain that separation had caused them as well. With Kevin gone, the continued estrangement between the friends had been Helen's attempt to assuage her own guilt and pacify her daughter's outrage. Maybe there had been other reasons as well that were no longer valid.

Teresa did not need to know them.

After dinner, Lilianne insisted – trying to go up against her was like trying to knock over a cement wall with a French fry – that she and Gilles do the cleanup, and sent Helen and Teresa out onto the deck to watch the sunset.

Full and getting drowsy, Helen had agreed. Full and not in the mood to be alone with the free-love couple, Teresa had also agreed.

Outside, the heat had settled, though the humidity was still fairly high. Teresa turned on the mosquito repeller and sank into her chair with relief. Another complicated day.

'You all right, Teresa dear?'

She turned to find her grandmother watching her anxiously. 'Yes, fine.'

'You don't seem fine.'

Teresa grinned, filled with love for this remarkable woman who had fought for what she wanted, failed and succeeded, but come through solid and unscathed. 'You can read me that well?'

Helen shrugged. 'You're my granddaughter.'

'I'm . . . I didn't realize that . . . you and Gilles . . .'

Helen looked astonished. 'Oh my word. I was sure I told you.'

'Sort of. Not specifically. I knew there had been someone, but . . . You traveled with Lilianne and Gilles. They're married. So I thought there was another guy along.'

'Good Lord.' Helen pressed a hand to her chest, then gave a snort of laughter that swelled into a fit of giggles. 'Oh dear. What you must have thought of me when they arrived.'

Teresa caught the humor from her grandmother. So much easier just to laugh. 'Way too out there for me.'

'No, no.' Helen wiped at the corner of one eye. 'Their marriage is good for both of them, but it's not based on . . . what you and I would want.'

'Convenience?'

'More than that. They love each other, just not . . . romantically. Not sexually.'

'Oh.' Lilianne must be gay. That would make sense.

'I fell in love with Gilles in Paris. Deeply in love. He asked me to stay there with him, and I was tempted. So tempted.' Helen shook her head wistfully. 'But back then, no matter what I did, I couldn't see myself in that life. It sounds like such a strange thing to believe, because of course I had never tried it, how would I know? But I felt so sure. And I did love Kevin. For a long time I did love him. Looking back now, however, I think the decision to leave Paris came less from instinct than my fear of the unknown.'

Teresa held herself still in the silence, practically not breathing, in case the slightest noise or movement stopped her grandmother from speaking.

'So.' Helen lightly slapped her thighs. 'I want to make sure when you're thinking about staying that you can see yourself in this life, even if there's fear. Maybe especially if there's fear. More important than the pro and con lists your brain makes. At least I think so.'

Teresa looked out at the darkening shapes of the animals and trees, listened to the restless quiet murmurs of the Kansas night. And knew she was sure. 'I don't know how it happened, but I can't see myself anywhere else. Even though, yes, it is super scary to think of such a complete change from what I've always known.'

A slow smile spread over Helen's face. 'I could not be happier, my dear. Come help me up for a hug, I'm too pooped to stand on my own. The champagne didn't help.'

Teresa hauled her grandmother up and wrapped her arms around her, deeply happy. Her mom would be furious, but appeased by the gift of Sarah. Teresa had Danny to look forward to, to see where that went. She had family all around, family she trusted and also looked forward to getting to know better.

'I will tell James, is that all right?' Helen asked. 'And Kevinjay?'

'Yes. Of course. They should know.'

'They will be very pleased. And your mother . . .' She waited, glasses glinting in the light coming through the dining room door.

Teresa knew what she was asking. But she had a different answer from the one Helen was expecting.

'I still have my flight back to Phoenix a week from Monday. I'll need to make arrangements to move. I can tell her in person.'

'Good for you.' Helen hugged her again. 'That will be hard. But I'm so proud of you.'

Teresa nodded, then pulled back. She couldn't go through with her plan without telling her grandmother. 'Since Mom isn't inheriting the land here, I thought . . . that I would give her Sarah. To sell.'

Helen took a few moments to process that. 'Sarah is yours, you may do what you want with her. But I will say this. It isn't possible to do enough to satisfy your mother.'

Teresa stiffened. That wasn't fair. Except for the good years with Dad, when had Mom ever had enough? Why wouldn't Helen take that into account?

'I'm not saying don't do it.' Helen put a warm hand on her shoulder. 'It's an incredibly sweet gesture, Teresa. Just . . . well, I said it already. So go ahead. If it will ease your conscience, so much the better.'

'That's part of it, yes.' Teresa tipped her head to make an affectionate trap for Helen's hand between her shoulder and cheek. 'Are you going to Connecticut with Gilles and Lilianne?'

'I'd like to. For a few weeks. Will you mind?'

'No.' She lifted her head. 'I seem to be doing pretty well here, and I have lots of backup if I need it.'

'Hey, you two.' Lilianne stepped out onto the porch. 'I'm turning in. Long day. What time do you get up in the morning?'

'Early . . . usually.' Helen smiled seductively at Gilles, who'd followed Lilianne onto the deck. He smiled intimately back.

Ick. Teresa was really happy for her grandmother, but didn't care to think about what would be happening in Helen's room tonight. 'I'll see you all in the morning.'

Big cheerful wave, thank-yous for dinner and cleanup, another hug for Helen, and Teresa was outta there.

In her room, a text from Danny.

Best ice cream ever. Sleep well.

She patted her chest in a comical swoon and texted him back. *Best ever. See you soon?*

Not soon enough!

Teresa sent him a heart. She really liked this guy. And felt like a fool for spending so much time with men she had to change to be with, hide the traits she didn't think they'd like, put on others she thought she should have.

Chapter 1, paragraph 1 of *What Not to Do to Find the Perfect Mate*.

Across the hall, she heard laughter, then a very grumpy yowl from Monarch at her door. Teresa grinned and let him in. 'Been supplanted?'

He gave the quick cranky syllable that showed his disdain. *Mruh.*

She cleaned up in the bathroom, then climbed into bed with the orange tabby. 'I didn't miss you after Helen came back. Not a bit. But it's not terrible to see you again.'

Mruh. He settled down next to her, taking up way too much room, as usual.

Teresa lay for a while thinking about the day, about the crazy pace at which her past and future had revealed themselves, and how she was learning to cope with it all. How people and their actions were much more complicated than what Mom had always taught her. As Danny put it, it was sometimes possible to love someone and hate their behavior.

She rolled over and grabbed her phone.

I'll be in Phoenix week after next. Maybe we can have lunch? Drinks? Dinner?

The reply came in immediately.

Yes! Yes! Yes!

She grinned as she typed her reply. *Sleep well, Dad.*

∽ Chapter 18 ∾

Don't write – I am sad and want to extinguish my soul
The beautiful summers without you are like nights with
*   no flame*
I have closed the arms that can no longer reach you
To knock on my heart is to knock on a tomb
Don't write!

Don't write – let's learn only to die by ourselves
Ask only of God, or yourself, if I loved you
From the depths of your silence, listening for your love
*   for me*
Is like hearing heaven without being there
Don't write!

Don't write – I am afraid of you, afraid of my memory
It has kept your voice, which calls me so often
Don't show fresh water to someone who can't drink
A sweet letter is such a vivid portrait.
Don't write!

Marceline Desbordes-Valmore, 'Les séparés'

Tuesday, July 9, 1991

'Where's Daddy? Why is he late?' James was clearly distressed. He was the sweetest of Helen's children, the most empathetic, and at ten, still her baby. The past decade had been hardest on him. Kevin Jr – they called him Kevinjay now – had increasingly withdrawn to his room, to his records and his books. Cheryl had taken to dressing inappropriately, mouthing off at her mother and ignoring curfew. But James was the sensitive child, the one who saw his father with wide troubled eyes that begged someone somewhere to *do* something, anything, when there was nothing to be done. It was always hardest when those eyes were turned on Helen.

'I guess he's gotten himself busy.' She handed James five plates. 'Here. Set the table. He'll be home soon.'

'But it's your *birthday*.' His face was taut with outrage. 'He was supposed to be home *early* today.'

'He'll be here. Help set the table, please?' She sounded happier than she felt, her usual mode these days. For so long feeling cheerful was a more or less normal part of her existence. Now the only good times were after Kevin had left for the day, after the kids were in school, when Helen could pretend to herself that life was still good on this beautiful farm, that there was still hope that her husband would hit the bottom of what seemed a bottomless pit, and stop for good.

She understood that it wasn't his fault. She understood that whatever made him crave alcohol was nothing he could control, that some people did fall so deeply under its spell that they could never get out. She empathized, she sympathized, she loved him and rooted for him, and cared for him deeply.

But it was hard to stop asking herself whether she deserved

387

this, whether their children deserved this, whether their friends and families deserved the eventual punishment of watching their beloved son, brother, father and husband destroy himself.

At least she'd stopped beating herself up over the champagne she'd allowed for their fifth anniversary. His drinking had already resumed by then. The late returns home, the peppermint gum, the morning fatigue and weight gain were all clues she'd ignored because she didn't want to see them.

That bottle he'd brought home was less a celebration of their love than a defiant message that booze was coming out of the closet and into their lives, an unwelcome new member of the family that every one of them – Kevin included – wanted out.

Some days were better than others. Some days still gave her hope. Some days he'd feel more guilt and shame than craving, and swear off the stuff for a sweet interval of optimism that never lasted. Summers were the hardest, with kids underfoot all day, too young to get regular jobs out of the house, their parents not prosperous enough to send them to summer camp. Library programs, zoo programs, park programs, games and playdates – Helen did what she could. Cheryl was old enough to work, but flatly refused, and as always, her adored daddy backed her up. He spoiled that girl rotten.

The front door burst open.

'I'm home.' Fourteen-year-old Cheryl's voice could be heard standing next to a 747. 'Linda's mom made us stay late and pick up. Sorry.'

She wasn't sorry, didn't even try to sound sorry. Probably hadn't even been at Linda's. Helen dealt with her the same way she did with her husband, having given up hoping she could change either one. 'You still want to frost the cake?'

Cheryl's overly made-up face twisted in annoyance. 'Oh shit, I forgot.'

'Language.'

Big eyeroll. '*Excuse me*, I forgot.'

'Thank you.' Sometimes Helen felt as if her body was a lead case, sealing in a thousand furious demons. Showing anger or frustration to Cheryl was like taunting a cobra. Which was why she chose to ignore that her daughter looked like a tramp, with wild moussed hair, a skimpy top and denim cutoffs short enough to leave little to the imagination.

But Mom, everyone dresses like this!

James went over to the silver drawer and got out forks, knives and spoons, mumbling under his breath, the only way he'd confront his sister. *You do Mom's cake every year. It's your job.*

Helen put the salad on the table.

'Where's Daddy?'

'Late.' James pushed a spoon into perfect placement on the table. 'Again.'

'He'll be here soon.' Helen was ready to get down on her knees and pray that he would be.

'Dinner almost ready?' Kevinjay came down the hall. 'Something smells good.'

'Thanks, sweetie. Can you put a couple of hot pads on the table for me? And Cheryl, will you please get the cake plate from the basement?'

'I'm going to change. I'll do it later.' Cheryl headed for her room.

Helen took a deep breath for patience, and made herself check on her birthday dinner. She'd never made risotto before, but had seen the recipe in a magazine at the supermarket and splurged on the fancy rice. The aroma was heavenly – mushrooms, peas, Parmesan and thyme – but the dish was starting to congeal in the pot and lose its lustrous appeal.

Come on, Kevin.

She checked on the cooling platter of baked chicken legs she'd made earlier, trying to relax her stomach muscles. Maybe he was buying her flowers? A present? Anything but having one more drink before he got home, so he wouldn't drink in front of the kids. And then one more, and then one more . . .

As if they couldn't tell, from the smell and the slurring and the slack-jawed expression. That man wasn't their father – resentful, quick to temper and blame. That man Helen didn't care for much at all. But increasingly over years, in a sickening bait and switch, that man was the person she'd chosen to marry.

Today Helen turned thirty-nine, the official end of her youth, and it was very hard to look toward middle age and see anything but more decay and more struggles.

She took a few quick steps toward the sliding doors in the dining room, needing air, needing escape, then pulled back, feeling James's eyes on her. It wasn't like her to be so pessimistic. Plenty of good things could and would happen. Kevin could succeed at quitting. He might finally take her suggestions that they give up on the corn and soy – impossible to compete with the huge industrial farms – and diversify, maybe think about using organic methods to improve the soil, toxic and exhausted by overfertilizing and pesticide use. So far he'd been stubbornly set against any change except more chemicals and more suspiciously modified seeds.

Some days Helen wanted to run into the middle of the fields and scream until she couldn't anymore.

Many days.

Loud music with hoarse screeching vocals erupted from Cheryl's room. Kevinjay, of the sensitive hearing and opposite musical taste, banged on her door and yelled at her to turn it down. Cheryl yelled back. Kevinjay stomped down the hall and slammed the door of the room he shared with James.

Helen got the frosting out the refrigerator and sent James to the basement for the cake plate. The two of them made quick, silent work of smearing fluffy chocolate over the layers. James added rainbow sprinkles and pushed in four candles.

'Done.' Helen let him lick the spatulas, then put them in the sink and took off her apron. 'Let's eat. Your dad will get here when he gets here. Kevinjay? Cheryl? Dinner time.'

She and James sat at the empty table. Kevinjay shuffled down the hall and pounded on Cheryl's door. 'Dinner, psycho!'

Cheryl's door remained shut.

James glanced anxiously at his mother.

'Never mind. Pass your plate, Kevinjay.' Helen served him chicken and some of the tepid clumping risotto, smiling determinedly. 'Help yourself to salad.'

'This looks great, Mom. Happy birthday.'

'Thanks, Kev.' She served James, then herself, grabbed the boys' hands and bowed her head. 'Thank you, Lord, for . . .'

The front door burst open again, with only slightly less force than when Cheryl had been behind it. 'I'm home.'

'. . . this food and this farm. For . . .'

'Daddy!' Cheryl's door opened.

'. . . our family's health and happiness. Amen.'

Helen opened her eyes to see Cheryl embracing her father, wearing pink shorts only slightly longer than the denim ones and a tight pink top with too many buttons undone.

'Hey, precious.' Her hug had thrown him off balance; he staggered, recovered and kissed the top of her head. 'Sorry I'm late. Hydraulic hose on the tractor sprang a leak and I had to go to town to have a new one made. Takes all kinds of time, but it's gotta be done.'

Helen nodded at the lies, hot with anger and apprehension. 'Have a seat and pass your plate. We've started already.'

'Sure, sure.' He weaved over to his seat at the head of the table. 'Crazy busy there, too, at the shop. Then I bumped into Frankie. You know how he talks. Jesus. You can't get him to stop.'

'Here you go.' Helen passed his dinner to James, who relayed it to his father. 'Plate, Cheryl?'

'What's this?' Kevin leaned down and sniffed at the rice. 'Pile of paste?'

'It's an Italian dish called risotto.'

'What's wrong with plain rice?'

'There's nothing wrong with plain rice.' She passed her daughter a plate of food. 'Cheryl, here you go.'

'Thanks.' Cheryl peered suspiciously at the risotto. 'Looks like baby barf.'

'Well, it won't taste like it.' Helen spoke in a clipped monotone that made Kevin peer at her from heavy-lidded eyes. She couldn't stand the way he looked when he drank. Like he was stupid and sloppy. Such a fine man.

'Did you know that Chinese workers used rice in the mortar for the Great Wall of China?' Kevinjay looked around the table, pushing his wire-framed glasses up his nose. 'I read that somewhere, can't remember. Or maybe Mr McRae told us in class.'

'No way.' James was delighted.

'Yes way,' Kevinjay countered. 'Sticky rice soup, kind of a porridge really, mixed with slaked lime, to—'

'Told you it was paste.' Kevin snorted, tried a bite and made a face. '"Risotto" must be Italian for "gummy".'

Cheryl giggled. 'Totally. Gummy paste. Try to build something with that!' Quick glance at her father to see if he found her joke funny.

'Glad you like it.' Helen loaded more onto her fork. 'It was a lot of work.'

'On her *birthday*,' James said. 'In case you *forgot*, Dad.'

Helen sighed. This always ended badly.

Kevin's head jerked up; he fixed James with a stare. 'I don't care for that tone, James.'

'Did you buy her a present?'

'None of your damn business.'

'No, you didn't. Because you forgot. Like you forgot my—'

'James.' Helen put a hand on his skinny arm, feeling it shaking. 'That's enough.'

'No, no. Let him go on. Let's all hear what Mama's boy James has to say about his father's shortcomings.'

James snorted. 'How long do you have?'

Helen gasped. Only ten. She wouldn't survive his adolescence. He might not either. 'Kevin, leave the boy alone. He's a child. It's your job to—'

Kevin's hand hit the table so hard the plates and glasses jumped. So did his family.

Cheryl looked over at her father, then back at Helen. 'Stop making him angry, Mom. You ruin everything. All the time.'

The doorbell rang.

Helen threw her napkin on the table. Anything to get away from this mess. 'I'll get it.'

'I bet it's a delivery guy.' Cheryl sneered at James. 'Mom's present from Daddy. I bet it is.'

Helen crossed the foyer, opened the door, stood uncomprehending for two seconds, then stepped back, unable to process what she was seeing.

Lilianne and Gilles. On her doorstep. In Kansas.

She had no idea how to react, what to say, what to feel. The parting with each of them in Paris had been so angry, so bitter. Her reaction to the news of their marriage and parenthood had been the same. They were supposed to be gone, barred from her life and from her thoughts. Now . . . they were *here*.

'Happy birthday, Helen.' Gilles held out a stunning bouquet of mixed blue and white flowers.

Helen didn't take them, couldn't move. She had to turn away from his gaze, her numbness shattered by the eruption of feelings she'd been so sure were successfully buried.

How ludicrously easy it was to fool oneself.

'We should have told you we were coming, but we wanted to surprise you for your birthday. We're only here for tonight, a stopover en route from LA home to Connecticut.' Lilianne peeked past Helen into the house. 'Are you in the middle of dinner?'

'Who're these people?' Kevin came to stand beside her, staring curiously up at Gilles, who was still holding the flowers.

'Hello, Kevin.' Lilianne extended her hand. She was, as always, impeccably dressed in a teal-striped shirtdress with matching belt, bag, sandals and earrings. 'I'm Lilianne Maxwell. I spent several months in Paris with Helen back at the dawn of time. And this is my husband . . .'

'Gilles Aubert.' Gilles nodded to Kevin, taking him in with keen dark eyes. He looked older – all of them did, of course – but something else had changed too. 'We're barging in on your family, unforgivably, but we couldn't miss Helen's birthday for another year.'

'Lilianne.' Kevin nodded slowly. 'Right. Helen has told me about you. And . . . Jill, was it?'

'Gilles.' Gilles pronounced it carefully.

'Right.' Kevin stepped back, having to grab at the door for support. 'Well, c'mon in. Any friends of Helen are friends of mine. Did you just come from France?'

'Oh no.' Lilianne stepped into the house and looked over the three kids, who were staring at the elegant couple as if they'd never seen strangers before. 'We live in Connecticut.'

'Then where've you been the past fifteen years?'

Lilianne gave him a tight none-of-your-business smile. 'Busy.'

Kevin wouldn't like that answer, or her chilly delivery. In fact, he wouldn't like Lilianne at all. She was too in control, too observant, and worst of all, she'd have no use for him.

'Oh?' He gave her a look. 'Too busy for your good friend?'

'So you have three kids.' Gilles pushed the flowers into Helen's hands and smiled at her, then over at the table, first time Helen had seen that smile in so many years that it hurt. 'Hello, three kids. I'm Gilles, and this is Lilianne. We're old friends of your mother's from when she lived in Paris.'

'You lived in *Paris*?' Cheryl opened her mouth wide. 'How come you never told us that, Mom?'

'I guess I thought I had.' Helen put the bouquet in the middle of the table, touched that they remembered her fondness for blue, happy to have something to do besides standing there gawking.

Gilles was here. Gilles and Lilianne, friendly, cheerful. Here. It was still impossible.

'This is Cheryl.' Kevin laid a hand on her shoulder. 'She's fourteen and into drama of all kinds. That's Kevin Junior, we call him Kevinjay. He's twelve and the brains of the family. That's James. He's a squirt.'

James's face fell.

'James is ten. He's a big help around the farm. I wouldn't be surprised if he takes it over someday.' Helen dried her hands, wet from moisture on the flowers, by wiping them on her overalls, wishing she'd given in to her earlier temptation to dress up.

'I will never be a farmer,' Cheryl announced. 'I'm made for bigger and better things.'

'Oh, listen to you.' Kevin mussed her hair, knowing how much she hated it.

'*Daaaaad!*' She raked her fingers furiously through the stiff teased strands. 'I *told* you not to—'

'Would either of you like some coffee?' Helen still didn't know which way to look. She felt as if she'd been plunged into a surrealist movie.

'Let them eat cake!' Kevin flung out his arms, nearly knocking over his glass.

'We brought champagne.' Lilianne took out a bottle from the bag she was carrying and proffered it to Helen. 'Because it's not a birthday without it.'

Helen's smile slipped. She shook her head infinitesimally. Lilianne's expression changed.

'Champagne!' Kevin lunged over and swiped the bottle out of her hands. 'I'll open it. Helen, bring out the cake. Get our visitors chairs. It's a celebration.'

Helen's shoulders slumped. More booze in Kevin. Lilianne and Gilles spectators to the dysfunction of her life. *Happy birthday, Helen.*

Lilianne stepped closer. 'A problem?'

Helen nodded.

'God, I didn't know.' Her blue eyes were full of sympathy. She too had changed, but only to become more beautiful. Next to her, Helen felt every one of her years.

'I'll go.' Gilles strode into the kitchen. 'Can I help, Kevin?'

'Nah, I've got this.'

Lilianne touched Helen's arm. 'Sorry to barge in. I was afraid you wouldn't let us come if we asked. Selfish of me.'

'Ah no, Kevin.' Gilles's patient voice from the kitchen. 'Not like that. The cork will explode out and you'll waste the wine.'

'Oh really.' Acid dripped from Kevin's tone. 'Well since you seem to know all about it, go right ahead. I'm just a stupid American.'

Helen felt herself shrink. Lilianne squeezed her forearm. 'I'm so sorry. You must feel so alone in this house with . . . that.'

'You hold the bottle like this, and then . . .' A soft pop. 'No spills.'

'I guess you *French* people really know your stuff.'

Helen blinked away tears. Life was easier when you barreled through each day without stopping to think. Having her friends here made her situation impossible to ignore. 'I'm okay. Really.'

'Good.' Lilianne released her, looking doubtful. 'Because if someone's ass needs kicking, I'm your woman.'

Helen gave a wan smile, torn between wanting to hug Lilianne and wanting to push her away. Wanting to go into the kitchen and tell Gilles she'd never stopped loving him, and probably never would, and wanting to prove to both of them that she'd made the right choice coming back to Kansas fifteen years ago.

Fifteen years. How time could pass when you weren't paying attention.

Cake slices were doled out, a modest amount of champagne poured into four glasses by Gilles. They sat in the living room and toasted Helen, who pretended to be delighted they were all there together, her kids, her drunk husband, her former lover whose heart she'd smashed, and an old friend with whom she'd parted bitterly.

While they ate, Cheryl snuggled up to Kevin on the couch, occasionally begging for sips of his champagne and bragging that cakes looked a lot better when she decorated them. Kevinjay sat solemnly shoveling in his dessert, ignoring the rest of the room. James refused cake, complaining of a bellyache, and sat peering at Lilianne and Gilles as if they were members of another species.

Meanwhile, Kevin held forth on the art and science of crop farming as if he knew his guests had come all this way specifically to learn from him, slurring, cracking farmer jokes no one understood, emptying his glass as if he were drinking water.

Helen ate as much of her cake as her unsettled mood and

stomach would allow. After working so hard to shelter friends and family from Kevin's problem, she was mortified to have the very last people she'd ever want to know here for the full show. She sat imagining Lilianne and Gilles's house, the lack of dust on hardwood floors and furniture, rugs and expensive art, bookcases lined with leather-bound tomes, elegant dinner parties with chef-worthy meals and carefully matched extravagant wines, pool in the backyard, tennis every weekend, summers on Cape Cod or Nantucket. A daughter with sophisticated taste and perfect manners.

And the travel. Everywhere they wanted to go on a moment's notice, no thought to budget, animals taken care of by a pet sitter, plants watered by a hired service. How they must pity her. That was the worst part.

'How about more of that champagne?' Cake finished, Kevin extricated himself from Cheryl and attempted, unsuccessfully on the first try, to get up.

'I'll get it.' Gilles stood with his usual grace and went into the kitchen, leaving Kevin frowning after him.

'Hey. Jill. Didn't I just say I'd get it?'

'No, you didn't actually.' Lilianne smiled sweetly.

'Sit back down, Daddy.' Cheryl patted the cushion next to her. 'Let him do it.'

Gilles returned with the bottle. 'Here we go.'

Kevin sat, grumbling, while Gilles refilled Helen's glass. She inhaled his familiar scent, one that took her back to places she had no business thinking of with her husband in the same room.

'So, Jill,' Kevin said. 'What's your line of work?'

'Art photography.' Gilles brushed an affectionate hand across Helen's shoulder and moved on to pour for his wife. 'And portraits.'

'He has a studio in Fairfield, with a gallery.' Lilianne beamed proudly. 'Very successful.'

'That's wonderful.' Helen tried to be happy for him and found she was, though surprised at the new career. 'What made you give up photojournalism?'

'I needed a change.' He gave her a rueful smile and poured a smaller glass for Kevin. 'And boy did I get one. From traveling the world's hotspots to shooting weddings in country-club Connecticut.'

'Oh, that's not fair,' Lilianne said. 'You have art photographs in museums and galleries around the country.'

'Congratulations.' Helen couldn't imagine Gilles content with such a passive form of the craft he lived for. Had he given up photojournalism for Lilianne? The thought grated too much to contemplate. 'You are so talented, I'm glad you stuck with it.'

He shrugged. 'It's who I am. I can't stop.'

'I suppose not.' She searched his face. His eyes were still dark and deep, still made her fizzy, but he seemed . . . somehow less than himself.

There were so many other questions she wanted to ask both of them, but not in front of her husband and children, and the conflict made it hard to know how to say anything. She'd wanted these two people out of her life for so many years. Now that they were here, so familiar and so dear, the reasons seemed to be slipping away, replaced with memories of the good times and the friendship. And memories of how she'd felt in Paris, so much more than she was now.

Perhaps to Gilles, she too seemed less than herself.

Kevin pushed himself off the couch, making it on the first try. 'I'm gonna get a glass of ginger ale.'

Helen closed her eyes wearily. They didn't have any ginger ale.

'Helen.' Lilianne jumped up. 'Come outside with us. I want to see your farm and give you your birthday present.'

399

'Ooh, a present. Is it from France? Can I come?' Cheryl put her plate on the coffee table, ready to go. 'I want to see it too.'

'Not right now.' Lilianne gave her an icy smile. 'This is just for us old friends.'

'Whadya mean?' Kevin stood glowering over his glass of 'ginger ale', stomach pushing out the front of his polo shirt in a way that would have horrified him as a younger man. Helen's heart ached. 'You're leaving your own birthday party, Helen? Leaving us?'

'If that's okay.' Gilles smiled and took Helen's arm. 'We'll borrow her for a quick stroll and bring her right back.'

Cheryl leaned in to stage-whisper to her father. 'Oh my God. That is so rude.'

'I bet you'll get over it.' Lilianne propelled them toward the door. 'It's a special case.'

'Helen.' The tone made Helen turn back. Kevin stood like a confused thundercloud, not sure whether to storm, or on whom. If only his bleary eyes would clear. If only he'd stop ingesting the poison that had turned her from adoring wife to long-suffering companion. Useless to hope anymore. She knew better. The only way to survive with the least damage possible was to concentrate on her own happiness and that of her children. She couldn't change this. She couldn't change him.

'Kevin?' She lifted her chin, daring to show defiance with her friends flanking her.

His features relaxed. 'You go on. Have fun. I'll be here, we'll all be here, when you get back.'

'Thanks.' She gave him a grateful smile and stepped out of the house, feeling as if she were escaping from a courtroom trial.

The air was cooling from the heat of the day, crickets chirping out territorial claims, barn swallows and dragonflies competing for insects. Helen waited until they were a few steps away from the house before she spoke. 'I'm glad you came, but I'm sorry you had to see that.'

'I'm sorry you have to live that.' Gilles touched the small of her back.

'I'm sorry we haven't been in touch to support you,' Lilianne said.

'What a sorry bunch,' Gilles said.

Helen laughed. 'Your English is really good, Gilles.'

'Practice.'

Cocoa and Truffle, Helen and Kevin's two chocolate Labs, came sniffing around, tails wagging. Gilles bent to greet them. Lilianne stepped back, which of course meant both dogs immediately wanted to be her best friend.

'It's my fault we haven't been in touch.' Helen ordered the dogs to her side; they obeyed impressively. If only she'd done that well with Cheryl. 'I thought it would make things easier.'

'It *was* easier, for a while.' Lilianne moved to the other side of Gilles, away from the animals. 'I hope that's over.'

'Me too.' Helen said the words automatically, then had to examine them to see if they were really true.

They were.

The trio reached the side of the house and stopped, facing down toward the garden, the chicken coop and the fields beyond, lush green in the late July sun.

'This is ours.' Helen swept her hand across the landscape. 'Five hundred acres of corn and soy, plus a horse, dogs, cats and chickens, and a vegetable garden. I'll show you around if you'd like to walk a little.'

'Tell you what. These shoes are not made for cornfields. And as much as I'd love to go back inside and tell Kevin he doesn't deserve you . . .'

'No, that's not fair.' She turned to her friend. 'Alcoholism is a disease. If he had cancer you wouldn't tell him that.'

Lilianne narrowed her eyes, lips pouted. 'Maybe.'

Gilles snorted. 'Lilianne believes everything can be under control if you just try hard enough.'

'I know, I know.' Lilianne cupped Helen's cheek. 'I'm sorry. But it's hard to watch.'

'For me too.'

'Yes, that's what I meant, and why it's hard for us.' She leaned in and hugged Helen tightly, then stepped back, her eyes moist. 'I'll go to the car and get your present ready. You two walk for however long you need to, and then come find me.'

Helen opened her mouth and closed it, no idea how to react. As long as they needed to?

'Thanks, Lilianne,' Gilles said. 'We have a lot to talk about.'

'We do?' She wasn't sure if she should have skipped the champagne or had more.

'See ya soon.' Lilianne gave a wave and started back toward the driveway, Cocoa and Truffle following until Helen summoned them back.

'We sprang this on you,' Gilles said. 'We've had plenty of time to plan the surprise.'

'That is true.' Helen led him down the hill, trying not to think about other times they'd been alone, how impossible it seemed that they were alone here, at her and Kevin's home in Kansas. And how wistful she felt for those months of effortless conversation between them, overwhelmed and tongue-tied beside him now. 'I want to know how you are, Gilles. Happy, I hope?'

Gilles laughed mirthlessly. 'I was about to ask you the same. I'm thinking maybe not as happy as you thought you'd be?'

'For a long time I was. Life here was good at first. We had this farm to build together, and we were a good team. The kids were blessings, that hasn't changed. Cheryl is going through a phase right now – actually, she's been going through a phase her whole life. But Kevinjay is a delight. Very smart and thoughtful and funny. He thinks deeply, very curious. He reminds me of you sometimes.'

'Me?' Gilles looked at her quizzically. 'He should remind you of *you*. You're exactly like that.'

Helen shrugged, not willing to admit she'd long ago stopped thinking about herself that way. 'James is a sweet, sweet kid. He suffers most, I think, wanting his dad's approval and attention. I can be a lot of things to those kids, but I can't be a father.'

They passed the garden, Helen's domain, along with the house, kids and chickens. The lettuces were bolting, peas fading, but the tomato, bean and cucumber plants were gunning to take over the entire farm. 'So. This is my life. I have good friends, I knit, I read, I feel part of a community here. Not the best, not the worst. Like most people's lives.'

'Yes.' He stopped and nodded to her patch of earth. 'That's a beautiful garden, by the way. You have quite the touch.'

She turned to face him. 'How did you know it's mine?'

'Because it's beautiful and extremely practical.'

She laughed, absurdly pleased to be complimented. 'Thank you.'

'Helen.' His voice dropped, thickened; his eyes held her. 'I need to know. Do you ever . . . regret?'

Her breath caught, even as she shook her head. 'There's no point.'

'That's not an answer.'

She hugged her arms around herself, looking past him toward the corn-filled horizon. 'Sometimes . . . I wonder what it would have been like. Whether we would have made it.'

'We would have made it, Helen.' He spoke fiercely, looking down on her from his height, the old light and passion she remembered restored full force. 'We never got the chance to try.'

Helen swallowed what felt like a rock in her throat. She suddenly resented him coming here and showing up her life, dangling what she could have had, what Lilianne now had.

'No, we didn't.' The words barely made it out. It was agony standing opposite this man, full of longing and rage, tenderness and frustration. He made her feel like a limb that had gone numb, after sensation started coming back, all buzzy painful prickles, nearly unbearable. She turned and kept walking. 'It's your turn. Tell me how you are.'

Gilles fell into step beside her. 'After you left, I went a little nuts. Actually, a lot nuts. The only thing I thought might help me was to be around people whose pain was worse than mine. So I begged for an assignment in Lebanon during their war, a fantastic assignment, and a cruel one.'

Helen drew in a horrified breath, not wanting to imagine any of it, desperately glad he'd survived.

'After photographing the worst of human nature, I started having trouble functioning, trouble getting places on time, trouble communicating, trouble setting up shots. Eventually I could barely get out of bed.'

'Oh my God, Gilles.' Helen turned to him, immediately feeling she should have been there to help him, then realizing that if she had been there, he wouldn't have suffered so much. 'What did you do? How did you manage?'

'There were no resources back then for non-military people with trauma, nothing to help me understand what had happened to me. I don't know if it's gotten any better now. I hope so. I went back to Paris without telling anyone, and holed up until I realized I'd spend the rest of my life that way unless I reached out.

The first people I thought of, besides you and my parents, were Lilianne and Connie.' His brows drew down. 'Did you know that Connie joined Lilianne in Cairo for the first year after Paris?'

'No. I didn't.'

'Yes, they were roommates once again. Anyway, you were gone and I didn't want to freak out my parents, so I called them. Lilianne arranged for me to go to Cairo so they could take care of me.'

Helen averted her head, embarrassed to be jealous that Lilianne had been able to nurse Gilles back to health, probably jumped at the chance. She should be grateful her friend had stepped in to ease the torment she herself had put in motion, even having done nothing but make a choice that was hers to make.

At least she understood now what was missing in him, what had been destroyed. 'What a nightmare.'

'It wasn't fun. After some time, Lilianne heard she was being sent back to the States. Connie – you know Connie – was itching to move on to Crete. Lilianne suggested I come home with her to Connecticut. To make my immigration easier, we got married.'

'So . . . are you happy? I mean with . . . Are you . . .' She couldn't ask the question, had no right to ask the question after so many years. 'So you have a daughter.'

'Yes.' His eyes crinkled into a slow smile. 'Sophie. We adopted her as an infant. We'll tell you more about that someday. I'd love you to meet her. And to answer your other question, I love Lilianne the way I loved her in Paris. As a dear friend whose tastes and lifestyle match mine well enough that I am content.'

Helen had to look away. She'd forgotten how he seemed to be able to read her mind.

No. She hadn't. She hadn't forgotten anything, only buried it to avoid the pain of remembering.

Right now she needed every ounce of her strength not to feel joy and relief. Shameful, selfish joy, because she had genuinely loved Kevin – she *did* genuinely love Kevin, and had no right to celebrate Gilles not finding that happiness with Lilianne.

'I'm glad she could help you.'

Gilles's smile widened; he stepped closer. 'There's one more thing to talk about, then we can go find your gift.'

Helen's heart started pounding. He'd saved this for last. It was the big one. She turned and started walking to the edge of the cornfield. Cocoa and Truffle followed, scattering strenuously objecting chickens.

'I – and Lilianne – miss you, very much. It was hard not having you with us to grieve when Connie died.'

Helen swallowed convulsively. 'That was awful.'

'And it was hard not having you at our wedding.'

She gave him a look. 'Are you kidding me?'

He cracked up. 'I know, I know, it's complicated. What I'm getting at is that we travel often, for a week or two or three, depending on where we want to go. I was thinking – we were thinking – that you might like to come with us, our treat, once a year or however often you could. We remembered that Kevin doesn't travel, and we thought by now enough time had gone by that we could all . . . manage it.'

Helen stopped walking again. His eyes met hers, and she felt a surge of excitement she hadn't felt in years, not just attraction, but oh my gosh, to be traveling again, immersed in other cultures, other cuisines, other languages, and all the history and art and architecture that went with them.

Impossible.

'Gilles, I don't see how I can . . .' She gestured helplessly, looking around to escape his dark gaze, trying to throw off her wanderlust in order to be sensible. 'How on earth would . . . I mean, how would this work?'

His smile faded as his expression warmed, drawing her in. 'That would be entirely up to you, Helen.'

She took a step back, trying to escape a surge of sexual adrenaline.

No. No, no, no, a thousand times no. She couldn't do that. Not to Kevin, not ever. She was not that kind of woman.

'The offer stands. We will travel until we're too old to go. Any time you'd like to come with us, you'll be welcome. We'd both love to be in Paris with you again, but there is so much more, and we want to share it with you.' He reached out and put a warm hand on her shoulder. 'Will you think about it?'

Helen glanced reflexively toward the house, backing away from his touch. Backing away from her longing for new experiences, for a wider world, for challenging discussions, for curiosity and passion that had nothing to do with corn or soybeans. Everything she'd given up when she chose Kevin and Kansas.

'We should go find Lilianne.'

'Will you think about it, Helen?'

She made him wait while she took in a breath. Then she nodded. 'I will think. Thank you, Gilles. It's a beautiful offer.'

If only . . .

They walked briskly toward the other side of the house and up the hill, dogs beside them until they bolted eagerly out of sight.

'Uh oh.' Helen broke into a run. 'They see Lilianne. Cocoa, Truffle . . .'

'Hey, you two . . . whoa!' Lilianne put out her hands to ward off dog love. 'Sorry, but I am definitely not a farm girl.'

'Certainly not dressed as one.' Gilles studied his beautiful wife with amusement. But not love. Not deep tenderness.

Lilianne glanced at Helen's face. 'Ah. You told her. Good. What do you think, Helen?'

Helen pressed her lips together, then laughed helplessly. 'Kevin would have a fit.'

'Why? Friends traveling together? He has no right to have a fit.' Lilianne opened the trunk of their navy SUV to reveal a large gift-wrapped box. 'Here's your present.'

'Oh no. It's too much.' Helen clasped her hands in front of her face. 'You were the real presents. And the flowers!'

'Not nearly enough.' Lilianne beckoned her over. 'I want you to open it while we're together alone, the three of us. I'm sorry if carving you out of your party was rude to your husband and kids.'

'No, it was . . . not much of a party.' Helen put her hand on the box, warm from being in the hot car. 'As you said so poetically, they'll get over it.'

'Good. Now open it. Before some wild animal comes out of the fields and eats us.'

Helen tore off the paper, sensing Gilles and Lilianne's excitement. She lifted the lid and gasped at the sweet, wistful face and the finery. 'Oh my gosh! Sarah!'

'Oh my *gosh*, happy birthday!'

She lifted the doll into her arms. She was heavier than remembered, and her hair seemed crooked. But she was real and she was here, bringing so many memories with her.

'Connie . . .' Helen dissolved into tears, 'should be here.'

'I know, sweetheart. I know.' Lilianne pulled Gilles in and the three embraced for a long moment, arms around each other.

'Helen!' The shout came from the front door, loud and angry. Helen would bet the champagne bottle was empty, and by the end of the night so would be whatever else he'd hidden in the house that she hadn't found yet.

Lilianne looked at her in concern. Gilles faced Kevin, hands on his hips, expression stony.

'Is he safe to be around?' he asked quietly.

'Yes, absolutely.' Helen gave Kevin a brief wave. 'He's never violent. Just angry. Mean at times. When he sobers up, he's fine again.'

Lilianne's eyes narrowed. 'How often is that?'

Helen sighed. 'I should go back. Thank you for everything. For this crazy idea of stopping over, for bringing Sarah, for inviting me on your travels and for . . . getting back in touch after I was too stubborn and afraid and—'

'Helen!'

Gilles muttered a French insult under his breath.

'That's our cue.' Lilianne kissed her cheek and embraced her lingeringly. 'We'll get going. You're in the phone book, yes? It was so good to see you again, even for this ridiculously short time.'

'Will you be back?' Helen hoped her eagerness wasn't too obvious.

'No, no, our job is to take you out of here, not add ourselves to your complicated life. Next time we see you, we'll be at JFK about to board a first-class flight to anywhere you want, okay? Think about it. Take all the time you need. Unless it's longer than a few months, then we'll have to come kidnap you.'

'Goodbye, Helen. Enjoy Sarah. She missed you.' Gilles leaned down for a French double-kiss and a whisper. 'But not as much as I have. Happy birthday, *mon amour.*'

'Helen!'

Helen flinched, but determinedly kept her back to the house, watching her friends get into their car and drive back toward the road, waving madly. Kevin would become her problem as soon as the SUV was out of sight, but right now her world was again filled with the possibility of happiness and adventure, with Lilianne, the memory of Connie, a beautiful doll named Sarah, and a man who'd offered her the world, suffered her rejection and returned to offer it again.

❧ Chapter 19 ❧

Teresa emerged from the shower in her apartment in Phoenix. She'd arrived two days earlier to round up boxes and bubble wrap and start getting ready to make the big move. The days had been a mess of packing and goodbyes, more packing and more goodbyes.

Yesterday she'd met her brothers for lunch, alternately raucous – joking about the family mess with their typical black humor – and serious, as it hit them that their sister was leaving town. She loved them, but they hadn't been close siblings, so though the goodbyes were difficult, the twins were happy for her new start, and she believed them when they promised to visit. At least that family relationship was solid.

That morning she'd finished loading the rented U-Haul trailer with help from Katie's fiancé, Ross, and a friend of his, both of whom deserved a lot more than the twelve-packs of beer they asked for, because it was brutally hot – triple-digits hot. Teresa hadn't done the heaviest lifting, but she was still dehydrated and exhausted, longing for cooling green fields and animals instead of traffic and concrete.

What a difference a month made!

She and Katie had had a tearful apologetic reunion on her return and settled into their usual chatty routine, joined by Addie for bridal this and groom that and flowers and cakes and photographers, and please God, don't let Teresa ever care that much about one day in what she hoped would be a long, interesting life. She'd nodded and giggled and had more wine than she wanted, just to keep up, feeling almost like old times, except something had changed. Teresa was pretty sure it was her. She'd learned at her mother's knee about relationships with people who put themselves first. The time in Kansas had begun to teach her how deep that lesson ran, and how much she wanted to unlearn it.

She dried herself off – moisture evaporated from her body in record time here – and dressed, readying herself for a late lunch with her father, after which she'd make sure the apartment was completely empty and drive out to have a last dinner with Mom before starting the three-day slog back to Kansas and her new life.

Tense times ahead.

She arrived at the very popular Barrio café – her favorite Phoenix spot – and found a parking place in the restaurant's lot, which boded well. Waits for a table could be long. Tuesday shouldn't be quite as bad, plus it was late for the regular weekday lunch crowd – the only break Dad could find in his day.

The restaurant was colorful and humming as usual. Her father was standing awkwardly by the bar.

'Hi, Dad.' Teresa's intention to be cool and calm collapsed. On the first syllable, she was twelve again, and went straight into his arms. He bear-hugged her nearly to suffocation, both of them tearing up, then laughing at themselves, then crying some more, because it was too big a deal to manage without tears.

When they could finally act like normal people, they were shown to a table by a smiling dark-haired waiter, and ordered margaritas right away, plus Mexican street corn, which Barrio did better than anywhere, and guacamole, made tableside, including various mix-in options to make it fully loaded and fantastic. Tempting to gorge on both, but then . . . the rest of the menu was impossible to ignore.

This she would definitely miss about Phoenix. Along with her brothers. And Mom. And maybe, once she got to know him again, her father.

He looked great. She'd remembered a skinny, spectacled man with a perpetual worried look, except when the boys were making him laugh or he was in his workshop with her. Now he'd aged, of course, brown curls thinning and sprinkled with gray. He'd put on weight that looked good on him and the frown was gone, his laugh and smile much more readily at hand. He and Teresa had both chosen turquoise shirts and long shorts, which they enjoyed making more of than the coincidence deserved.

The chatter was easy at first, lots of questions, basic information about his two kids, Teresa's step-siblings, and when they might meet, his thriving practice, his wife's new career in real estate, their house in Silverleaf, their country-club lifestyle, which he admitted sheepishly he'd fallen into because of Amy and ended up enjoying. He'd even taken up golf.

Ick.

Teresa brought him up to date about the farm and family, though he knew most of it, having kept in sporadic touch with James and Helen. And then . . . she told him she was moving. And though his face fell, he rallied genuine enthusiasm as she spoke, a visible transition from sorry for himself to happy for her.

She liked her dad. It was exactly as Danny had said, she could hate what he'd done, but still enjoy being with him, maybe love him again someday. He'd missed so much of her life that though he was intimately familiar, he also felt like a stranger she'd need to get to know.

'How will you manage financially, need any help?'

They were eating ethereal chicken mole that made Teresa want to stop after each bite and try to identify the complex flavors inhabiting her mouth. 'I'll probably need to get a part-time job. Gotta pay off those pesky student loans.'

Her father put down his fork, looking startled. 'What student loans?'

'Uh . . . the loans I took out to pay for being a student?'

He continued to stare. 'I paid for your education, sweetheart. Yours and the boys'.'

Teresa didn't know what to say to that. *No you didn't?* 'Actually . . .'

'*You* had to pay?'

She nodded.

'And your brothers?'

Another nod. The three of them had spent a goofy evening years ago making up what they'd do with the money they were using to pay back the loans if they didn't have to, and trying to imagine themselves older, having finally paid them off, feeling that much giddily richer.

'I gave your mother money for college. On top of all the alimony.'

Teresa's turn to freeze. *All what alimony?* 'Mom said you gave her next to nothing.'

His expression twisted into incredulity. 'That's not true, honey. I gave her plenty. Probably more than I should have, but . . . well, guilt. She could have lived on it without working if she was careful. And I gave her the money for your education. None of you should have had to pay a dime.'

Teresa felt as if she had stepped into a very bad dream, one of those you couldn't wake yourself out of. Her mother had been crying poverty for as long as Teresa could remember.

413

'But then . . . where is that money?' Her voice came out a thin, childish wail.

And then they were staring helplessly at each other, contemplating the horror of what they'd both realized at the exact same moment.

An hour later, Teresa was nearly at her mom's, gripping the steering wheel tightly, going as fast as traffic and stoplights and fear of speeding tickets would let her. Mom wouldn't be home from work for another hour or so, but Teresa would let herself in with the key and wait.

Her mother couldn't be that awful. She could not have taken money meant for her children. There had to be some other explanation, like that she had put it all in a trust fund, expertly managed while Teresa and the boys worked jobs through high school and college. When they turned thirty, they'd get it back with considerable interest, a nice retirement nest egg. In the meantime, they'd have learned to take care of themselves.

It could happen.

Lunch with Dad had petered out pretty quickly. Very hard to recapture the ability to chit-chat when you'd both been sucker-punched. She'd had to stop him calling Mom right then, and had to hope he wouldn't do as he threatened and call his attorney.

Neither of them had wanted dessert.

Teresa turned onto her mother's street and pulled into the driveway behind Mom's Kia.

Why wasn't she at the office?

Maybe just as well Teresa wouldn't have to wait for her. Better to get this horrible confrontation over with.

She got out of the car and strode through the bitter, metallic oven of the outdoors to ring the bell, shifting impatiently.

The door opened. Her mother's plucked brows shot up. 'Hey,

sugar! I'm so glad to see you. Come in, come in. Welcome back to civilization. What have you done to your hair?'

It took work – a lot of work – to hug her mother and stay strong and suspicious at the same time, because with Mom right there, after a longer separation than they'd had since Teresa graduated college, she wanted to cling, to feel safe, to have all this ugliness she'd discovered about this person she loved so much disappear in a cloud of fairy dust.

'Mom, why aren't you at work?'

'Oh.' Her eyes darted away. 'They gave me the afternoon off.'

'Again?' Something wasn't right here. She followed her mother inside. The television was on in the living room. Dirty dishes on the coffee table. 'They seem to do that a lot.'

'Yeah, sure.' Cheryl looked around as if she'd misplaced something. Like the truth. 'They think a lot of me. And I also work from home sometimes.'

Teresa nodded. Mom was a receptionist. She answered calls and greeted visitors. According to her, she ran the place. How could she work from home? How could her small office do without her so often?

'Can I use your bathroom?'

'You need to ask?' Her mother pointed to the door next to the kitchen. 'It hasn't moved.'

Teresa went in and closed the door, turned on the fan to make as much noise as possible. Then she made the call she dreaded. A young woman answered. As quietly but distinctly as possible, Teresa asked to speak to her own mother, then listened to the answer she'd expected.

She squeezed her eyes shut. 'Are you sure?'

Yes, ma'am, she was sure.

'Thanks.' Teresa ended the call and let her head drop back, closing her eyes. The confrontation with her mother was already going to be awful this morning, then became twice as awful after lunch with Dad. Now three times.

Cheryl Foster was a pro.

Teresa flushed the toilet and stepped out of the bathroom. Her mom had cleared the plates and was rinsing them in the sink. The TV was off.

'Well, sugar. You must be glad to be home and out of that pigsty. I bet Katie and Addie were thrilled to have you back. Need anything to eat or drink?' Cheryl glanced over when Teresa didn't answer, and her face wrinkled in concern 'Baby, what is it? What's wrong?'

'A lot. A lot is wrong, Mom.'

'Oh no. It's Helen.' She dried her hands, took Teresa's arm and pulled her into the living room, then sat next to her on the couch, looking eager. 'What has she done now?'

'I just had lunch with Dad.' Teresa waited, dreading the reaction.

Her mother's eyes shot wide. 'No. You did *not* have lunch with that monster. My God, Teresa, what were you thinking? How could you do that to me? First Helen and now—'

'Where is the money he gave you so that Mike and Ike and I could go to college?'

Cheryl looked as if Teresa had socked her. 'What? What money? That's ridiculous. He gave me almost nothing. Everything went to that new wife. Every cent I have I've had to earn myself. There was nothing left for you and your—'

'I just called your office. They say you haven't worked there in nearly ten years.'

'Well, no. No.' Her hands fluttered, landed in her lap, took off again. 'I have a new job. It pays more, and my responsibilities are much—'

'Why didn't you tell me? I thought we told each other everything.'

'I didn't want you to . . . Because I . . .'

'Where is this new job? What's the name of the company.' Teresa held up her phone. 'If I call them right now, will they confirm that you're employed there?'

Her mother shot off the couch. 'Teresa Maria Clark, you will *not* speak to me like that. How dare you imply that I would tell you *anything* but the truth.'

'I think that's exactly what you tell me. Anything but the truth.' Teresa was furious, but calm and clear like she'd never been in her life, and always wanted to be.

No fear.

'I think you've been living off Dad's alimony, and I think you took my money besides. Mine and the twins'. Where is it? Have you spent it, or do you still have it?'

For the first time in her life, Teresa saw her mother at a loss for words. The ruddy, over-made-up face paled. Her plump lower lip trembled. She sank back onto the couch.

'Oh sugar. I'm so bad with money. I always have been. It's like a sickness. It comes to me and then it's gone.'

'You spent it.'

Her eyes filled. Tears spilled over onto her cheeks. 'I'm so sorry, baby. I'm so sorry. I . . . have a problem. I do. I admit it. I just can't save. I'd think I was doing fine, there would be plenty of money in the account, and then there were bills everywhere and I had to pay them or I'd lose the house and be—'

'What did you spend it on?' Teresa felt merciless, numb. An awful combination. Like she imagined dictators felt when they ordered an execution.

'I don't know. I don't know. I mean, I like to shop. But not that much. Not really. It just seems to . . . disappear.' Cheryl buried her face in her hands and began to sob. 'I know I've been a bad mother. I know it.'

Not much to argue with there. But this wasn't the moment to say so.

'Life has been so hard on me. So many awful things. After that beautiful life with your dad, I couldn't stand the humiliation of going into work every day. People not worth a tenth of me telling me what to do. They were so condescending. I couldn't take it. So I quit. And then I couldn't bear to go back.'

Teresa gave a big sigh and put a reluctant arm around her mother, who turned and gathered her daughter in a tight embrace that smushed Teresa's cheek against her breast. 'I'm so sorry. I screwed up so badly. I screwed up my life and yours. I need therapy, I need help. Can you ever forgive me?'

Teresa closed her eyes, inhaling her mother's familiar smell, the one that had comforted her so many times, when she scraped her knees, when she failed a math test, when a boyfriend dumped her. Then she gave Mom a squeeze and disentangled, feeling the loss, thinking of how Sarah could help.

'This is why it was so important to me that Helen sell that farm.' Cheryl swiped at her tears, mascara tracking down her cheeks. 'Because I knew that at least if I had that money I could make it right. I could pay you and your brothers back and atone for my sins.'

'The thing is.' Teresa spoke slowly, no longer numb, but feeling as if she'd just woken up from the same bad dream she'd felt stuck in at lunchtime. Maybe the same bad dream she'd been stuck in most of her life. 'It's not going to be sold. Helen is going to stay there, and when she dies, she's leaving the farm to me.'

Her mother stopped crying abruptly. 'To *you*?'

'Yes.'

'Well then . . . but that's good. That's wonderful, actually.'

She sniffed and brightened. 'My brothers will have a fit, but . . . I mean, Helen can't last much longer. Then you and I can sell the place and split—'

'I'm not selling, Mom. I'm moving there. I'm going to live there.'

Not a muscle moved in her mother's body. 'This is a joke.'

Teresa shook her head slowly, giving Cheryl time to absorb the blow. 'I fell in love with Kansas, with the ranch and with Helen, Jim and James. I'm even okay with the animals, I've really gotten to like them, love some of them. I've been using Grandpa Kevin's wood shop, getting back into woodworking. I might try to do that as a part-time career, make high-end doll furniture. I even met a really great guy, Danny. We've started dating, and for the first time it feels totally right. This is the life I'm meant to live, Mom. I'm really, really happy. For the first time since Dad left.'

Her mother's mouth opened. Out came a tiny choked sound.

Teresa could tell her about Sarah now, reassure her that she'd get her money in the end, just in a different form.

But she couldn't quite get the words out. And she realized that what she wanted first was for Mom to hear what she was saying, instead of listening to what was going on in her own head. To acknowledge that this great happiness had fallen into her daughter's lap. To give Teresa the immense gift of being able to feel those contradictory emotions, sorry for her own loss but happy for Teresa's gain. And maybe even to have that happiness come out on top.

Her mother's face crumpled into rage, hands fisted at her sides.

'You stole from me. *You stole from me.*'

Teresa's head dropped. Stupid, stupid waste of time. A Sisyphean exercise, hoping time and time again that her mother

419

wasn't who she was. Rolling the same boulder up the same hill and having it crash down over and over, learning nothing in the process.

Helen had been right. Nothing would ever be enough for Cheryl Foster. Not Sarah, not the ranch, and definitely not Teresa.

This time the damn boulder would stay at the bottom of the hill, where it belonged.

Teresa got up from the couch and headed for the door, turning for an exit line as painful as it was perfect. 'I guess that makes us even.'

'Thanks for the beer. I gotta get back home to Alicia.' James drained his bottle and stood. He, Teresa and Danny had been sitting together on the back deck steps, admiring the day's handiwork. Teresa had spent the past week, since she got back from Phoenix, constructing a goat playground so the beasts would have a structure dedicated to climbing and jumping and wouldn't be tempted to knock anyone else over. The three of them had installed it that afternoon, platforms of various heights with ladders to climb up and plank bridges in between. Helen had loved it. The goats had been delirious with happiness, holding competitions to see how many of them could fit on the highest spot. Great for them, and great entertainment if you were geeky enough to be into that kind of evening.

Danny, Teresa and James apparently were.

'Thanks for your help.' Teresa smiled fondly at her uncle. They'd had a good talk, not long after she got back, clearing the tangle between them, making room for a new path together. 'Say hello to Alicia and thank her again for last night.'

'Sure will. Bye, Danny.' James stepped down from the porch and strode off with a wave.

Teresa and Helen had gone to James and Alicia's house the previous evening for a send-off dinner in honor of Helen's trip to Connecticut, begun that morning. Lilianne and Gilles had declined Alicia's invitation, saying they wanted to try a barbecue place in Kansas City. Teresa suspected they were tactfully leaving the event to family.

It had been great fun, the conversation wide-ranging and interesting, everyone contributing, no one person dominating. Alicia was as cheerful and chatty as her husband was guarded, which explained where Jim's ebullience came from. The best news – she worked as a counselor at the university. She'd be a great resource in Teresa's search for someone she could talk to about . . . everything.

That morning Teresa had said a fond hug-filled farewell to Helen, Gilles and Lilianne, who'd driven off in the luxe-mobile with plans to visit St Louis on the way, then swing south to tour Bourbon country in Kentucky before heading back up the coast to Lilianne and Gilles's house in Southport. Teresa had warmed up to both of them – yes, Lilianne would always be a little frightening, but Gilles was charming, sensitive, brilliant, funny and madly in love with her grandmother. Helen positively bloomed with joy around him, making Teresa inclined to adore him just for that.

'You know . . .' Danny gestured toward the animal pen with his beer, 'in addition to your coming success with the doll-owning crowd, I can envision a bright future for you in goat furniture.'

'Ooh. Good idea.' She gave him a sly smile. 'Let's see. I could start with a pair of buck beds.'

'And plenty you could do in the kids' room.'

Teresa wrinkled her nose. 'I can't think of any more goat puns.'

'Me neither.' He got up. 'Want another beer? Glass of water?'

421

'Water, please.'

'You got it.' He went inside, leaving a cool spot where his body had been touching hers.

Teresa was crazy about this guy. He was kind, patient, loving, funny, wise . . . She could go on. She didn't have to chase him or change to keep him around. She didn't panic when he hadn't called, never worried she'd be interrupting him or seeming needy if she called him.

In fact, she didn't worry at all. A revelation.

She stretched tired muscles in her shoulders. It had been a gorgeous day, hot, but not even close to the temperatures in Phoenix, and enough humidity that she didn't feel as if she were evaporating.

'Teresa.' Danny came back without the water, looking anxious. 'Sarah's not in her chair.'

'Ah.' Teresa smiled mysteriously. 'You discovered my big secret. Promise not to tell?'

'Oh no.' His anxiety sharpened into alarm. 'You sold her?'

'Much better than that.' She wanted to enjoy the suspense a little longer, but took pity on him. 'She's a stowaway on a gigantic RV, packed in a glass dome with so much bubble wrap and peanuts that she probably can't breathe.'

'Wow.' Danny sat down next to her. 'You decided to give back the big treasure.'

Teresa nodded, whatever wistfulness she'd felt at the loss disappearing when she thought of Helen and Lilianne celebrating another birthday with their cherished fourth roommate. 'Sarah meant so much to all of them, and played such a big part in celebrating their birthdays, I thought it would be nice if she was surprise guest of honor for Helen's in Connecticut.'

'You did a really nice thing, Teresa.' His brown gaze was admiring.

'What do I need sable and diamonds for?' Teresa gestured to the land around them. 'I have weeds, goats and chicken poo.'

'Worth their weight in rhodium.' He put his arm around her. 'How long do you think Helen will stay in Connecticut?'

'No idea. I'm sure she'll want to come back at some point. In the meantime, you have a place to stay if you need it.' She'd been thinking about this a lot. If he freaked out at the suggestion of that much intimacy, then she'd rather know now than later.

'You know, I just remembered, I do need a place to stay.' He nuzzled her cheek. 'Do we get to share a room?'

'We get to share a bed . . .'

'Mmm.' His lips found her neck, making her go shivery.

'. . . with Monarch.'

'Uhhhhh . . .' He pulled back grinning, then got to his feet. 'I just realized I was so upset to see Sarah missing I forgot your water.'

'I forgive you. And thanks.' Teresa wrapped her arms around her knees and smiled at her favorite time of day, heading for twilight, when colors deepened and became ruddy from the setting sun's rays. When the animals started bedding down, in shelters, coops or wherever they stood.

So much to learn, so much to get through emotionally, but she felt . . . not total confidence, but reasonable optimism that she could handle it. There was certainly plenty of support around, plenty of people cheering for her to succeed instead of waiting for her to fail.

She'd taken Sarah's chair over to Matti at the Doll Cradle and asked her advice. Matti had been enthusiastic, saying she had several customers who might be interested, and she knew someone who could help Teresa set up an online presence as well.

Worth a shot.

A cool breeze whispered that darkness was on its way. Crickets and fireflies would emerge, coyotes prowl. Pearl and Tusk would prepare to defend their animal charges and their territory. Teresa thought of Sarah, speeding toward St Louis, or maybe parked in a hotel lot; of Helen in the arms of the man she loved. Where would she and Gilles settle? Together or apart? Here, in Connecticut or alternating?

She imagined her father, back home from work, maybe chatting with his wife, watching TV with his kids or playing catch in the backyard.

She thought of her mother, sitting in her stuffy house, encased in her bitterness, pushing people away who reflected back any part of her. If only there was a way to hang onto the good in her and get rid of the rest.

Maybe someday they could be friends again. Maybe if Mom worked through . . .

Teresa caught herself. It would take a lot to change her thinking, to accept that she couldn't stay close to her mother and be true to herself. There were only two options, going back or moving forward.

Lilianne had been right after all. Sometimes you did have to choose.

Lilianne's story will unfold in *The Jewel of Cairo* . . .

Wednesday, March 24, 1976

Lilianne stepped out of the brilliant Egyptian sunshine, so cheering after the drizzly chill of Paris, and into the cool lobby of her apartment building in the Maadi district of Cairo. As usual after work, she headed straight to her mailbox, hoping for news from or about Gilles. After Helen had crushed his heart and spirit by fleeing France in favor of her Kansas farmer fiancé, Gilles had started talking about covering the horrifying civil war in Lebanon. Lilianne and Connie, worried he was intent on a suicide mission, had mounted a campaign to talk him out of it, and Lilianne was anxious to hear he'd changed his mind.

She unlocked her mailbox and reached in to find a letter . . .

From her mother.

Dina Maxwell generally wrote postcards: *Florida is fabulous, tennis amazing, had dinner with the Morrisons, they say hello, Marjory is getting married, love you!* If Mom had bothered to sit down and write a letter, it meant she had Something To Say, usually A Whole Lot To Say, undoubtedly Things She Thought Lilianne Needed to Hear.

The letter before this one had predicted that Lilianne going to work for her father would destroy their relationship with each other and splinter the family. The letter before that had warned that the CIA was too dangerous for women, that Lilianne would face misogyny, violence, and an empty life of travel and spying. The very first letter, meanwhile, received when Lilianne was a year out of college, had been so crushing it was still too painful to look back on. So Lilianne didn't.

The door to the building opened behind her to admit her across-the-hall neighbor, Adma Sarawi, plump, cheerful and infinitely likeable. The Maadi district was home to so many foreign service employees that it was almost like not being in Cairo at all, so it was nice to have at least one local around, especially for cultural questions Lilianne might not feel comfortable asking at the office.

'Hello, Lilianne! You're home early today.' Adma smiled broadly, adjusting the strap of a bag of groceries hanging from her shoulder. 'No dinner plans tonight?'

'No, nothing tonight.' She tried not to sound too triumphant, wondering how Adma knew she was back early.

'Ah! Then you must come have dinner with us!'

Lilianne groaned inside. Always a mistake to admit she was free. Egyptians were warm, hospitable people who treated strangers as friends, and friends as family members, a custom Lilianne was still trying to get used to. She'd been in Cairo nearly two weeks, and had been able to eat alone at only a handful of breakfasts. Tonight, to preserve her sanity, she'd refused all invitations. 'Thank you so much, Adma. I would love to, but . . . I'm happy to have an evening to myself.'

Adma looked astonished. 'No, no, you must not eat alone. This is depressing and bad for digestion. I made *kousa mahshi*, you know what this is?'

Lilianne nodded resignedly. Tender summer squash stuffed

with lamb and rice, suffused with a garlicky tomato broth. Utterly delicious. But the entrée would come with a side of Adma, her husband, and their four rambunctious children.

'Eight o'clock. We will see you.'

Lilianne forced a grateful smile and took the stairs up to her apartment, annoyed at herself for giving in, but unsure how to gracefully refuse such kindness. Another adjustment from the more familiar culture in France.

Leaving Paris had been bittersweet. During her two years there she'd cemented her reputation at Maxwell Investments as something more than the boss's daughter. Meeting Connie, Helen and Gilles had been another highlight: they were the closest trio of friends she'd ever had. Yet the timing of this assignment to Cairo had been a blessing. As her mother often said, all good things must come to an end. The friendship with Helen had been irretrievably broken, Gilles was destroyed, and Connie was restless. It was easier to leave than be left, and in spite of moments of nostalgia, Lilianne was content – and relieved – to be making a fresh and unencumbered new start.

In the spacious but impersonal apartment provided by the company, she kicked off her heels and changed out of her modest suit into a muted top and a pair of gray cotton culottes bought for the move. No mini-skirts in conservative Cairo, and shorts were out of the question, though she'd been told she could get away with them here in Maadi. Slipping the unopened letter into her pocket, she rummaged in the kitchen for cheese and crackers, and poured herself a glass of Côtes du Rhône – a gift from one of Dad's friends at the State Department – which she took out onto the balcony overlooking the dusty, tree-lined street.

Unfortunately, that was all the procrastination she could muster. After a fortifying slug of wine, she tore open the letter to find out what Mom thought her daughter Should or Should Not Be Doing.

Dear Lilianne,

By now you're settling into my city. Knowing you're there has given me pangs of homesickness I haven't felt in decades, not since I bolted out of there. I was born in Egypt to Egyptian parents, but I never fit in. The US is the country of my heart, which I knew from the moment I learned there was such a place. Meeting your father, settling here and becoming a citizen have been the best gifts of my life. I put Egypt out of my heart and raised you to be 100% American.

But of course you are half Egyptian. My parents are still living in Cairo, God willing, and my brothers, and who knows how many aunts and uncles and cousins, though I haven't spoken to any of them since I left at eighteen. You may or may not want to be in touch, but I should let you know what you'd be in for.

They are kind people, good people, but they are very Egyptian in their views, and you are very American. They will frown on your career and on your goals and opinions. They will be appalled at your intention to remain single, and will attempt to match you up with every available Egyptian man they know. They will talk nonsense about me, who I was, what I wanted, without understanding any of it. They will insist on escorting you around every square inch of their city, and feed you more food than you can possibly eat, then object when you don't finish it all.

In short, my relatives will try to swallow you into their Egyptian-ness on a daily basis for as long as you are in the country. It's a form of bullying masquerading as love.

You are their long-lost granddaughter, and even if they hate me, the Law of Egyptian Hospitality says they must hound you socially. Forget Christianity and Islam. Family is that country's highest religion, and atheists are not tolerated.

I am writing with a bitterness that has surprised me after so many years, but I am not exaggerating. Egypt is a beautiful country, rich in history and culture, and its customs and social mores serve to form remarkably close-knit communities. But for women like us, they can feel like straitjackets.

You have been warned.

Love you.

Lilianne almost laughed. First, with relief, since for once the letter wasn't critical of her or her choices. Second, at the phrase 'women like us'. She couldn't imagine two more different souls. Her mother was all about her husband's family wealth, about Connecticut summers and Florida winters, about shopping, decorating, tennis and golf. Dina Maxwell had never worked a job in her life. She'd even handed off most of the work of mothering her only child to a succession of nannies.

However . . . Lilianne threw the letter onto the table next to her and propped her feet up on the balcony railing. Mom's points were well taken. Lilianne was already struggling to find time for herself. The scenario her mother described sounded like her worst nightmare.

On the other hand, these were her grandparents, her uncles and her first cousins. If she didn't get to know them now, while she was in their city, she never would. And if she never did, then Mom's choice to deny Lilianne half of her bloodline and cultural identity – in essence half of herself – could never be undone.

She scowled, unnerved by such uncharacteristic indecision, and by the nagging fear that she'd never be able to choose confidently. Choosing confidently was what Lilianne did, and had always done, from her education and career to her friends, clothes and dinner entrées.

But unless there was a shift in either her circumstances or her attitude, or unless something unexpected happened to make the decision for her, Lilianne would be stuck.

She refused to be stuck.

The wine glass clunked onto the table. Lilianne got to her feet and strode back inside, then into her bedroom, where she fished out a fifty-piastre coin from her change purse and stood ready.

Heads she'd lie low. Tails, she'd pick up the phone.

Acknowledgments

I would like to thank my adored previous editor, Kate Byrne, and my newly adored editor, Nicola Caws, the former for pushing me to invent this trilogy, the latter for making sure the story did what it was supposed to so clearly and elegantly.

I am indebted to Bryan and Carolyn Welch, who so generously shared their Kansas ranch with my husband and me for a wonderful weekend, then continued to share their knowledge and experience after we left, fielding nosy email after nosy email with humor and patience.

Many thanks also to my neighbor, Ali Chardon, for going over my rusty French with corrections and suggestions when she had twenty million other things on her plate.

A sheepish thank you to the amazing photographer/photojournalist Jodi Hilton, with whom I spoke about her complicated and important work, and was then unable to give it more than lip service in portraying Gilles.

For the poems beginning Helen's chapters, I am grateful for the book *Selected Poems of Marceline Desbordes-Valmore*, by Anna M. Evans, though all translations from the original French in *The Paris Affair* are mine.

To my children, Jason and Isabel Sill, and my stepdaughter, Emma Stodder, many thanks for help with music and lingo so I don't sound as old and unhip as I am.

And goopy thanks to my husband, Mark Stodder, who reads everything I write with a vigilant pen and a nearby box of tissues. His sniffling means I did my job well.

Dear Reader,

The Women of Consequence trilogy was born when my then-editor suggested I write three connected books taking place both in the past and the present, involving complex family relationships, set in exotic locations. My response (besides panic) was 'I don't think that's really me.' My brain, however, having apparently no sense of 'me', went to work on the challenge. In an embarrassingly short time, I had the bare bones of *The Paris Affair* and the two books that follow.

Like Helen in *The Paris Affair*, I spent 1975–76 in Paris, though I was younger than her and lived with my family. My memory still holds fragments from that remarkable year, but most of my descriptions and reactions in the book come from older-and-wiser visits. Rue Pierre Nicole, where Helen, Lilianne and Connie roomed together, was where my parents rented an apartment every May for a good many years after we kids left home, but the apartment's layout, the uncomfortable furniture, the service entrance and clanky elevator to the top floor are from the place my family rented back in '75–'76 on Avenue Gourgaud in the 17th arrondissement.

The inspiration for the Kansas setting came from a trip my husband and I took in the fall of 2021 to visit friends who own a small ranch outside of Lawrence. The sense of peace and purpose in the lives of these dear people affected me deeply, and with their permission I blatantly plagiarized their lives. The Great Pyrenees who so patiently get to know the new calf, the sexy goat, the nightly coyote concerts, the escaped cockatiel who whistles Beethoven's Ode to Joy – even the black and white dog who 'attacked' me thinking I was someone else – all those details are true, and a writer's dream.

The fancy black velvet beaded flapper dress that Helen and Teresa try on belonged to my maternal grandmother, Flora McDonald, and now hangs in my closet. Like Natalie Laurent, I have no use for many of the special things I inherited, but I love them too much to give away.

Helen's collection of dolls in the basement room was inspired by an assortment of international dolls my widely traveled aunt gathered over the years and gave to me. I so regret getting rid of them in a fit of 'maturity' somewhere during my adolescence. Over the years I've wondered if any of those dolls were worth something, but mostly I miss them!

Book 2 in the trilogy, Lilianne's story, is partly set in Cairo, where I have visited twice and where my older brother was a journalist for many years. The priceless object in that book is an invented Fabergé egg, designed by the real-life Alma Pihl, the only female ever hired by Fabergé to work on the eggs. I also did fascinating research involving the history of Cairo's doomed royal family and the last of its princesses, for whom I created a lavish diamond necklace that goes missing along with the egg . . . around the same time Lilianne leaves Egypt. I hope you will join me for *The Jewel of Cairo*!

Cheers,
Muna

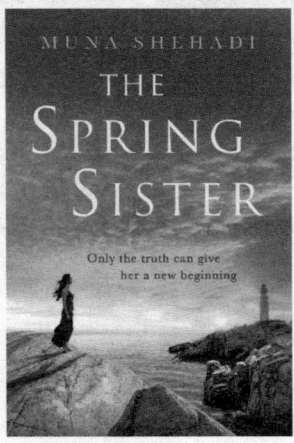

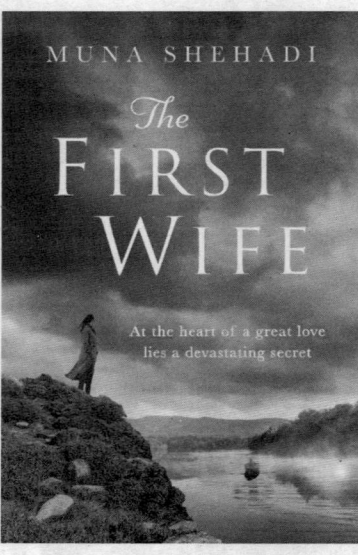